# 100 days of solitude

Daphne Kapsali

For Kaiti & Papsi

For Niko

For Joslyn

For Peter

For Eleni A

For Pia

For M

# Day 1

Today, I am alone. I woke up alone this morning. All the rooms that had recently contained sleeping people, people I had to be careful not to disturb, are empty; all the doors are open and the beds are untouched. I made coffee loudly and played music. I let the front door slam, carelessly, and no one protested. I am alone.

I will be alone for the next one hundred days. By choice.

Last May, I took my life apart in order to put it back together in a way that made more sense. I've always claimed to be a writer, and that's been both my identity, and my – rather thinly woven – safety net, but I'd done no serious writing for years. I lived in London, surrounded by amazing people and doing a job I loved, but my life was like a beautiful, serene lake: deep enough and lovely to look at, but stagnant in places, and closed in. There was nowhere to go.

So I quit my job, left my flat, stored all my stuff in my friend Mel's attic, and moved to Greece, to spend the next four months writing. The plan was to stay in my mum's spare room in Athens for May and June, then our family house in Sifnos for July and August (rent-free places, with very few expenses), and then return to London in September, having established, once and for all, whether I was actually a writer, or whether I should stop clinging to that dream and move on to something else.

Four months on, I have proven conclusively, to myself and those unfortunate enough to have been around me during this journey of self-discovery, that I am indeed a writer, through and through. It has also come to my attention that I possess all the necessary personality traits to qualify as a reclusive author, many of which are shared with arseholes, and are nothing to be proud of. I have suffered through episodes that, to me, were alarmingly reminiscent of a mental breakdown but which my poet father diagnosed as "being inspired" and entailed, among other disturbing behaviours, scribbling away manically on any available piece of paper (I learned to carry a notebook with me, wherever I go), and biting the head off anyone who as much as glanced in my direction while I was writing.

These revelations are both a huge relief and a problem because, as uncomfortable and exhausting and costly as this journey has been so far, it is also, probably, the best thing I've ever done, and I just cannot go back to the life I had before.

So I'm not going back. I'm staying. I'm staying for as long as it takes, or as long as I can, or at least until the weather gets really bad; the locals that I consulted while trying to decide just how insane this plan might be all assured me that I can comfortably make it to December, provided I invest in an electric blanket. So that's just over three and a half months; roughly one hundred days. One hundred days of solitude, and writing. One hundred days here, in Sifnos, a small and relatively remote Greek island in the West Cyclades, with a permanent population of 2,000. Plus one. And for the next one hundred days, I will attempt to live here, alone, in a summer house on the very edge of a tiny village, halfway up the island's tallest mountain. I will attempt to stay warm and sane and cheerful as the days grow shorter and darker and one by one the last of the holidaymakers return to their real lives, brave as the noises outside my window grow stranger and more frightening, and determined as this ceases to be the latest crazy scheme Daphne has adopted and becomes, simply, what I'm doing. And no one but a few loyal friends pays me any attention anymore. And I will write. Because I figure, if there's a place to be a reclusive author, it's here. And if there is a time, it's now.

And so it begins.

# Day 2

To begin with, a confession: Day 1 was technically Day 3, which means that today, Day 2, is actually Day 4. But I decided to put the technicalities aside and allow myself a couple of days of transition. Before you attribute any undeserved wisdom to this apparently sensible decision, however, let me tell you it was driven entirely by necessity: I have been alone since Friday night, and spent the weekend of my transition paralysed with fear.

I'll explain: it so happened that the last week of my original four months of writing coincided with my sister's wedding, on the 30th of August. A wedding which took place here, in Sifnos, in a field attached to our house and hastily (but successfully) converted into a suitable venue for a wedding party of fifty. That's fifty of our closest friends and relatives, all arriving to the island in the week preceding the party, and then, inevitably, departing in the days that followed.

Which meant that, in preparation for the solitude that I, ostensibly, looked forward to, I barely spent a moment by myself for close to two weeks, and that in the last week or so, I've had to say goodbye to a shocking number of people, including my grandma, my mum, my dad, my stepdad, both my brothers, both my sisters, my sister's husband, my most favourite cousin and a host of friends, old and new. This process of ceremonious and often tearful goodbyes and assurances that we'd meet again, soon, took place over several days, in an endless seesaw of emotions, and culminated in a solitary bus ride from port to home, which had all the makings of the ultimate anticlimax.

And I'm sure, as I counted out my change for the bus fare with trembling hands, as I stared out the window at the wild landscape of the island that is to be my home for

8

the next few months, that feeling of anticlimax was present, somewhere. As was relief, and excitement, and hope. But they were all drowned out by a massive tidal wave of a much more powerful emotion: the generalised anxiety that had been my constant companion throughout this week of goodbyes now gave way to a total and all-consuming terror. Which, at least, had the decency of being very specific, and vocalised itself in the following, eloquent phrase: *What the fuck are you doing?*

It wasn't a question I could answer. All I knew was that my teeth were numb with the fear, and if that isn't a sensation you've experienced, I hope you never do. It's not pleasant.

My resolve faltered; all my thoughts turned to the imagined comforts of Athens, of London, of anyplace but here. Of safety and stability and familiarity. Of teeth that feel normal in my mouth.

But I was saved by the Greek poet Cavafy and my Australian cousin Peter (a.k.a. Cousin), whom I'd just waved onto a ferry bound for Athens and then on to Sydney. Among several choice souvenirs that Cousin picked up during his week in Greece (which included a beach towel featuring a killer whale posing as a dolphin on a background of planets and palm trees, and bearing the legend GREECE) was a new translation of Cavafy. It included a poem entitled *The Satrapy* that I'd never read before. Cousin, who is in the process of forming some resolutions of his own, picked it out on the morning of his departure and showed me. 'This is a good one,' he said, 'for when I'm losing my resolve'.

It was: it is basically a warning against settle for the easy and the conventional and the obvious at the expense of our dreams, our "grand and noble acts"[i]. And with the foresight that my own resolve would be tested, frequently and in many different ways (though I didn't expect it to be as soon as that very evening), I took a photo of it on my phone so I could read it in times of emergency.

What the fuck *am* I doing? I don't know. But I'm doing it anyway. And I'm still here, despite the fear, on Day 2 or Day 4, because I don't want the comforts of Athens and London and safety and things that are easy and known. *I long for something else, ache for other things.*

*And without them, what kind of life will I live?[ii]*

# Day 3

Some days will be uneventful; day 3 was one of them. My critical self – I'll call her Antagonist, an integral part of every story – asserts that such a day doesn't even deserve an entry. We argue.

'What did you do today?' she demands.
I looked at facebook.
I did two loads of laundry.
I fed a cat sausages.
I spoke to my sister.

'And what did you achieve?'
Clean sheets.
A happy cat.

'Is that all?'
I planted radishes and lettuce in the garden.
I wrote three sentences – one of them incomplete.
I started a funding project on kickstarter.
I made a salad with leaves I picked myself.

Antagonist is not impressed. She's mean, and she feeds on my fear and my frustration. She makes a "pff" sound, and dismisses me with a flick of her wrist.
        'You might as well give up', she suggests, without even looking at me.

And I'm tempted. But then it occurs to me that if she's the Antagonist, that makes me the Protagonist, the hero of this story. And heroes become heroes by overcoming adversity, finding their way around the obstacles strewn in their path, and triumphing over the villains. And sometimes adversity takes the form of a perfectly ordinary day, in which no literary masterpieces were created, and the most heroic thing I can do is to accept that that's OK. That there will be days like this, and there'll be other days, better, worse, good and terrible, days when I will question everything, and days when I will slay the fiercest dragons and be crowned Queen of Sifnos. And each day will be worth as little or as much as the one before, and the one after.

'Hang on,' I say to Antagonist as she gets up to leave, impatient with my lack of response. 'There's more':
I swept the leaves in the yard.
I tidied up my wardrobe.
I went to the beach.
I bought tomatoes and beetroot from an organic farm.
I made a tentative agreement with the farmer to help him with planting in exchange for vegetables.
I did yoga at dusk to the sound of classical music.
I went to a dinner party and met some lovely people.
I looked at the moon.
I read my book.
I slept on fresh sheets.

Antagonist looks bored; she even gives an exaggerated, theatrical yawn to illustrate her point. She obviously has very little faith in my powers of observation.
        'Who cares', she says.
        I do. And I'm not bored. I am the hero of this story, and I don't need to slay dragons on a daily basis to prove it. And day 3 was neither a waste nor an obstacle, and I will not stumble on it. Nor will I step over it, casually, as if it meant nothing, on my way to day 4. There will be days like this. And it's OK.

# Day 4

I woke up feeling pretty rough this morning. I'd had a bad night's sleep, and even went in search of a thermometer around 5 am; my temperature was normal, but I still felt like shit. Things weren't much improved when I got up, just before 9. I took an inventory of my symptoms – swollen glands, achy head, heavy limbs and a feeling of generalised vagueness – and decided to allow myself a full day of crappiness, a day to give into it, indulge it, on the condition that I'd be fine tomorrow. (I adopted this strategy a few years ago, and it very rarely fails; except – as I learned the hard way this summer, when I fell off a wall – in the case of muscle strain: it really does take 6-8 weeks to heal, whether it suits your plans or not.)

I made myself a cup of tea (I couldn't face coffee yet), drank it while checking my email, and dragged myself over to Eleni's – my friend and neighbour, hostess of extraordinary dinner parties, and fellow solitary dweller in the Sifnos autumn. Eleni took a break from washing up the dishes from last night's dinner, made us both coffee, wrapped a shawl around my shoulders, and we sat down in her back yard. And then she asked me what I was planning to write during the next 96 days of solitude, and a really nice thing happened: as I tried to put an array of scattered, half-formed ideas into words that made sense, I began to notice a change come over me. Antagonist was mercifully absent (I suspect she's still sulking because I dared stand up to her yesterday) and I found my voice getting a little bit louder, my gestures more and more animated (I had to throw off Eleni's shawl so as not to overheat) and, for the first time in weeks, I actually felt excited about what I'm doing. What I will be doing. What I might achieve.

Because, even when the isolation isn't physical, even when you haven't given up your life to be a recluse on a Greek island, writing is a very lonely occupation. You have no colleagues, but your office space is shared with countless horrible little demons of self-doubt, and insecurity, despondency and hopelessness. And they're not very supportive at all. It's hard enough pouring your soul into something that may just come to absolutely nothing, without feeling that no one gives a shit, one way or the other. You need accountability, and sometimes all it takes is someone to show an interest, ask a question or two, acknowledge this scary, crazy thing you're doing. And it keeps the demons quiet for a little while.

I left Eleni's house knowing that I would produce no great writing today, but with renewed hope that, on another day, I might. Any day now. I just might.

So today turned out to be a good day, after all; the crappiness has been fully and pleasantly indulged, and I haven't heard a peep from my demons. I'm pretty sure they've gone off to find Antagonist, and together they are plotting how to bring about my demise. Let them. I will be ready to fight them again tomorrow when, as agreed, I will be fine.

# Day 5

I found out today that my body is an impenetrable fortress. Not in a good way: I am, apparently, completely blocked up. This according to Polyna, a permanent resident of Sifnos and practitioner of the Bowen Technique, commonly known as BowTech.

I met Polyna at Eleni's a few nights ago; they're old friends, and Eleni thought we should meet since I'll be spending the next few months on the island. So I went over and we sat in the kitchen, and chatted over a glass of wine and a smoke. And BowTech came up, which I'd never heard of before, surprisingly, since I spent two years working in a yoga centre in London, and I thought I'd come across pretty much every variation of alternative therapy there is. Polyna, who treats all her clients completely free of charge, offered me a treatment, so I could see what it was all about.

And thus Eleni and I drove up to her house this afternoon – which was a revelation in itself. Perched, all alone, at the top of a hill, Polyna's house has uninterrupted views of practically the whole of Sifnos, the sea, and the islands beyond. We were welcomed by a cat (one of several), Polyna, and her dog Coco, and ushered to the balcony which – no doubt helped by the infinity pool at its edge – felt like it literally opened up onto the ocean. It was a perfectly still, windless day, sunny but with strange, heavy clouds drifting across the sky and casting their reflections on the sea; the sort of day that, Eleni claims, you only get to experience in September. It's one of the gifts post-holidays Sifnos bestows upon those of us who stick around past the end of the summer. In any case, the overall effect – the solitary house, the stillness, the light, the clouds, the sparkling pool and the ocean – was entirely mesmerising. And made even better by the presence of two kittens lounging in the sun.

We had espresso and then Polyna led me to a room in the back for my treatment. Before she began, Polyna explained that she would apply certain moves, in sets, to different parts of my body, and then leave the room for a few moments, to give my body the time to process them and the freedom to react as it pleases. 'Don't be alarmed,' she instructed. 'Don't censor it.'

So I lay there, first on my front and then, briefly, on my back, as Polyna went in and out of the room, accompanied by Coco (who, apparently, often assists on these sessions by showing Polyna where on the client's body she needs to work). And with every move I expected something a little alarming to happen, hoped for it, even, but it never came. Certain moves felt as if they were spreading out to the wider area of the point they were applied, but my body had very little to say, and certainly nothing that might require censoring. With the last move applied to my head, Polyna told me to take my time getting up, and left the room for the final time. Coco stayed; I could hear her breathing somewhere in the vicinity of my feet.

When I stood up to leave the room, Coco lifted her head and gave me a look of concern, and then escorted me to the balcony, where I rejoined Polyna and Eleni.

'How do you feel?' Polyna asked.

'Very relaxed,' I admitted. No small feat, considering I'd spent the day in utter agitation, as a result of an earlier run-in with kickstarter. 'A bit lightheaded.'

Polyna nodded. 'You are very tense.'

'Yes.'

'In all my time as a therapist,' she said contemplatively, 'I've never come across a body that did nothing at all.'

'And that's me?'

16

'That's you. You just wouldn't let me in.'

'I'm not surprised,' I said, though actually, at the same time, I was. 'It's been a difficult summer.' And it was: the last few months have been extremely challenging, in many different ways, and I've often told people I'd put up a fence around me, to protect myself.

'A fence?' Polyna laughed. 'That's no fence; it's prison bars!'

So there you have it: I am uniquely damaged, imprisoned by my own body, and need help. But, luckily, help is at hand, in the form of Polyna, who offered (*insisted*, in fact) to give me weekly sessions for at least the next two months.

'We'll bring those bars down,' she promised. 'We need to. Especially if you want to be writing.'

I want to. That's what I'm here for.

# Day 6

My biggest fear is running out of books.

OK, I lie: my biggest fear is not being able to write. Not being able to write well. Going back to working 70 hours a week, 49 weeks a year so that I can have three weeks in the sunshine, and calling that my life. Then: the loneliness and the cold. I'm also really scared of cockroaches, but I've seen none so far, and I have bug spray.

But the thought of running out of books terrifies me. There is very little loneliness left over – not enough to send you running for the next ferry back to Athens – when you have books to read. And I came here armed with enough books to see me through the summer (and, thanks to George Eliot's *Middlemarch*, which took me a whole month to get through, I still have two left) but I hadn't planned on staying past the first week of September, and the books are running out. Just like my summer clothes are beginning to feel flimsy and inadequate. And as soon as the decision to stay was made, the fear arrived.

There are two bookstores in Sifnos; only one of them sells English books, and it will close on the 10th of October. Amazon, presumably, will deliver, but my address would look something like:
Daphne Kapsali
c/o Fotini Xenaki
Eleimonas
(just past the church, on the left, next to Mrs. Souli)
(grey gate, with a knocker in the shape of a bird)
Katavati, Sifnos
Cyclades, Greece

And I don't really like my chances. Once the books run out, that's it. Nothingness. Doom.

I am considering a Kindle, against my principles. I have resisted getting one so far, despite its obvious benefits, because I love books. Having them, holding them, stacking them up next to my bed. Flicking through them, folding the pages down to mark my spot. Their feel; their smell. But beggars truly can't be choosers. I have 94 days to get through, and principles won't do it. I have no books, but I have wifi. Bring it, amazon (address as above); I'm begging.

But in the meantime, the fear has been temporarily assuaged, thanks to a wonderful exchange scheme run by the bookstore in town. Bring in three second hand books, get one for free. So I ransacked the shelves and lugged twenty of them down into town; Eleni brought three. And then, by some miracle of literary providence, the bookstore lady received our offerings, counted them, and told us we could choose eleven (11) books in return.

'Really?' I said, before I could stop myself. 'That sounds like too much.' Knowing full well that, according to the 3:1 ratio, we were only entitled to seven.

The lady, however, shook her head. 'Eleven,' she repeated, looking bored.

Eleni and I scampered round the corner to the second hand shelves.

'But,' I said.

'Shut up,' she hissed.

And I complied.

So I've just returned home with ten brand new, second hand books, which I lugged all around town for two hours as we browsed the shops for bargains (they'll all about to close for winter) and then all the way back up the hill. And which are totally worth the pain in my shoulder.

Also, we got chocolates for free. There were only two left of the kind we wanted (candied slices of orange dipped in chocolate), and the man let us have them free of charge. And I met another kitten; we had a lovely chat. I said 'Hello, who are you, then?' and it said 'Mew!', several times.

I'm happy, and the future is bright: I have books, and the ability to talk to cats. There'll be no loneliness left over at all.

# Day 7

My strategy for perpetual good health has let me down. It appears that, despite my insistence that I am well, I have a cold. Try as I might, there's no denying the aching head, the coughing, the sneezing, and the snot coming out of my nose.

I was determined, nonetheless, to go to the beach, as it was my last chance to see Emmy, one of the friends Eleni introduced me to this week; I've only met her twice, and we've exchanged a few words, but she's lovely, and she's leaving tomorrow, and I wanted to say goodbye. So when Eleni came to pick me up this afternoon, I put on my bravest face and my hat, and followed her meekly to her car. Halfway there, I had a coughing fit.

'Oh,' Eleni said, 'you really are ill.'

'No,' I said, because I've trained myself not to use negative words, lest the universe is listening, 'not *ill*. I'm just a *different kind of healthy*.'

I can't tell you whether the look she gave me was one of amusement or pity, but she was certainly not convinced. 'We'll just have to install you in the shade,' she said. I sneezed into my hands, blew my nose, and shuffled on behind her.

I made it as far as the car park, and stopped.

'Yeah,' I said. 'I'm ill. I'm going home.' Eleni conceded that this was probably a good idea. I asked her to say goodbye to Emmy from me, and off I went, shuffling all the way back home. Where I took some leftover soup out of the fridge, poured it into a pot, and stuck it in the gas cooker to reheat.

Before I go any further with this tale, I need to share some technical details about my front door:

1) It is brand new (only just replaced in August) and cost 700 euro.
2) It has no handle on the outside. If it's shut, it can only be opened with the key.
3) If the key is on the inside of the door, it cannot be unlocked from the outside.
4) It has a tendency to slam shut, even when there is no wind.

So there I was, back in the comfort of my home, with my soup heating up on the cooker, and moments away from a nice, soothing lunch, and my bed. And then I was seized by an urge to add some fresh rosemary to the soup, so I opened the door, as you do, and stepped out and over to the rosemary bush, to pick a sprig or two.

And I heard the click. It didn't even have the decency to be a slam. Just: *click*. Such a gentle, polite little sound, with such devastating connotations. My mind instantaneously tallied up all the facts – door shut / key on inside / all windows closed / gas fire on – and produced the following output:

FUCK FUCK FIRE FUCK BREAK DOWN DOOR SEVEN HUNDRED EURO FIRE FUCK

I performed some sort of comedy, headless chicken routine, whereby I did a few circuits of the yard, entirely without purpose or logic, and then ran up to the front door and threw myself against it, shoulder first, like I've seen in films. Once, twice, three times. The door rattled, but remained intact. I stared at it, dumbly, rubbed my shoulder, kicked my flip-flops off, and sprinted to Vangelia's, the nearest house I knew to be occupied. I rushed into her kitchen, surprising the entire family as they were having their Sunday lunch, screaming incoherently about doors, fire and men.

'What?' Vangelia said, standing up.

'I'm locked out!' I managed. 'The fire is on!'

'But I don't have your key!' Vangelia cried, desperately. 'You didn't give me your key!'

'No key! I need a man to break down the door!'

Vangelia glanced at her son, Simos, a bulky man in his early forties and my unlikely hero of the day, and gave a nod.

'Go,' she commanded. And so poor Simos was forced to abandon his lunch and dispatched to save the crazy city dweller from her own silly self.

He didn't break down the door. Obviously. Being a man possessed of his senses (mine had evidently fled the scene), he assessed the situation calmly and arrived at a somewhat less hysterical conclusion.

'We'll just have to break a window,' he announced, cheerfully. 'And then you can climb in.'

And, armed like a Sifnos superhero with a long stick and the rug I use as a doormat (saving me, again, from my own silly self: my instinct, to use a rock, would have only led to a mangled hand), he smashed a windowpane, cleared the glass, turned the handle, and let me back in.

What a relief it was, to see the inside of the door again! Simos stood outside, beaming, and waved all my thanks and apologies away.

'Not a problem,' he said. 'These things happen. And if it happens again, you know what to do!' And with that, he took his leave of me and went back to his mother's lunch.

But I can't afford to smash a window every time a recipe calls for rosemary. I'm ringing the carpenter first thing tomorrow, to come and replace the glass and fit a handle on the outside of the door.

As day 7 comes to a close, and I sit here surrounded by balled-up tissues (a sign of my alternative health), I'm trying to draw some sort of positive message from this story, but I'm not sure there is one. Perhaps I could say that sometimes heroes can be found in the most unlikely places. Or that there is always a better way than throwing yourself against a locked door. Or I could just give this up as a bad day and a lesson learned, which is less about doors and more about solitude being challenging in ways that I hadn't expected or prepared for.

One thing's for certain, however: spontaneous cravings for rosemary are not to be trusted. If you ever feel such a thing taking hold of you, do not heed its call. It's the devil's work.

# Day 8

I was chatting to Susanne on skype, sitting at my desk. Antagonist was sprawled out on the sofa, examining her nails in a manner meant to indicate that she was bored, and a little pissed off. She doesn't like it when I talk to other people.

'You do know you're writing every day, don't you?' Susanne said.

'No I'm not!' I replied, categorically. A little defensively, even.

'Of course you are! You're writing your blog!'

'Oh,' I said, '*that*. That's not *writing*.'

Susanne gave me a look that was half confusion and half admonishment. 'It is!' she insisted. 'And it's wonderful!'

'Thank you,' I said, in a small voice, as Antagonist emitted a snort of derision. I told her to behave herself, in my sternest tone. Because *Susanne* is wonderful; having friends as supportive as this is wonderful. And Antagonist may get away with bullying me sometimes, but she's not allowed to mess with my friends.

The thing is, for all of her faults, I don't think it's fair to blame Antagonist for everything, and this paradoxical defensiveness is certainly not her doing. (I will resist the temptation of inventing yet another character; I've already been accused of schizophrenic tendencies once this week). It's all me, and perhaps I'm a bit of a snob, and I don't consider my blog *real* writing. I don't think of it as *literature*. I have this grand idea of the literary works that I will produce, and my blog posts just don't fit in.

I started this blog mostly as a measure of self-discipline, as a way to make myself publicly accountable, but I hadn't really expected that there would actually be a public to be accountable to. I'm surprised, every day, by how many people read my posts. I'm surprised by the comments, the honest, personal responses to the things I write. The expressions of support. It is incredibly gratifying, and moving, and valuable. Every day, there are moments when I question what I'm doing, and every day there is something – a comment, an email, a phonecall – that renews my faith in it and gives me the courage to carry on. People have told me they look forward to reading my posts every day. People have said that they can see their own struggles in the things I write about, and that it helps them, and even gives them hope. They have urged me to keep going, to keep writing. And I never expected any of this, but it's happening, nonetheless, and it *is* wonderful.

But is it *writing*? Is it *literature*? The Oxford dictionary defines literature as "Written works, especially those considered of superior or lasting artistic merit". Which doesn't really help. *Written works*: sure. But *superior or lasting artistic merit* is very hard to call. And *considered* by whom? A blog, on the other hand, according to Merriam-Webster, is "a Web site on which someone writes about personal opinions, activities, and experiences": nothing particularly offensive about that. Except that, by the very nature of the internet and the blog concept itself, *everyone* can be a blogger. Not everyone can be a writer. Maybe I am a snob, but I will not apologise for this opinion. Not everyone can be an electrician, or a politician, or an economist; each one requires a particular set of skills and not everyone has them. And writing is no exception. It takes a lot more than putting words down on a page to make you a writer.

And therein lies the paradox: Because I actually do have those skills. And even though I'm ready to dismiss my blog posts as *not writing*, I never just put words down on a page. I've been told, frequently, that I'm not a blogger: my posts for *This Reluctant Yogi*[iii], my yoga blog, have been criticised for being too long, too complex, too literary for the attention span of the average blog reader. And it's criticism that I accept readily: I've chosen the blog format for its immediacy and ease of use, but I'm not really *blogging*, as such. I put my entire self into everything I write, for both *Yogi* and *100 days*, exactly as I do when I'm writing a short story; I agonise over my choice of words, I edit and edit again. Each post takes me hours to write, and then I often dream about it at night, revising sentences in my sleep. I'll never attract the thousands of visitors that I, presumably, could, if my posts were shorter, snappier, a bit more reader-friendly. And I'm OK with that. Because I am a writer and though I'm not entirely free of vanity, it's not *hits* that I'm after, but *readers*. People who will read my work all the way through and won't mind that it's long, and who'll find something in it that touches them, directly.

Which, unexpectedly, is exactly what's happening. And perhaps wonderful Susanne is right, after all, and I can slowly, reluctantly, bring myself round to concede that what I'm doing *is* writing, and it's just as real and meaningful as those works of superior artistic merit that I will surely produce in the next 92 days, and beyond. I am writing every day, and people are reading, and if this crazy adventure of mine comes to nothing more than that, it will be enough.

In keeping with the tradition for long posts: day 8 isn't over yet. Because today was also the day my kickstarter project for *100 days* went live, and I cannot close this post without mentioning it. Susanne was with me, via skype, when I did it this morning; my hand literally shook when I clicked on the button to launch. I was incredibly nervous. But, once again, I was amazed by the support I got. There are five backers already, and my project was featured as a staff pick on kickstarter's "new and noteworthy" section. And so another countdown has begun: 28 more days to reach my funding target. If they are anything like today, there's no telling what might happen.

# Day 9

You know that phrase *things that go bump in the night?* In post-holiday Sifnos, *things that go bump in the night* are mostly donkeys. One donkey in particular: my new neighbour. He moved into the field adjacent to my house a few days ago, presumably to help clear (i.e. eat through) the dry grasses in preparation for sowing. Or maybe, it occurs to me now, this is where he actually lives during the year, and he's just back from his summer holidays, on another part of the island. Either scenario is just as plausible. In any case, the donkey spends his days happily chewing on grass, taking his exercise by running madly up and down the length of the field, and staring contemplatively into the distance. But it's what he gets up to at night that's interesting. You'd think he'd just go to sleep, but no: his preferred nocturnal activity seems to be bumping into things. Large, heavy things, judging by the thuds that reverberate through my walls as I lie, sleepless and sneezing, in my bed. Perhaps he suffers from insomnia, as I have for the last few nights. But mine is caused by my horrible, lingering cold, which has me twisting and turning and blowing my nose every thirty seconds; I can't think of what might be keeping a donkey up at night.

Donkey psychology aside, and following up on the unexpected challenges of living alone on a small island, I can now confirm that, yes, being ill is definitely one of them. I've always maintained that part of the reason people get married is to have someone fetch things for them when they're ill, and I could really do with a husband right now. Having to go out and get your own cough syrup and the ingredients for a cure-all chicken soup is hard enough in London, where there's bound to be a shop just round the corner, and a chemist not too far away. Not so in Sifnos. Here, getting to the chemist involves a rather substantial downhill trek, and an uphill return journey that the best of us struggle with at the best of times. And given my current affliction, and that I'm still a bit shaky on my left leg as a result of a fall in early August, I think it's safe to say I'm not the best of anything right now. But trek I must.

I won't be having chicken soup, however. I can't afford chicken soup. My budget for today is allocated to cough medicine, painkillers and fly spray and might just stretch, if I'm lucky, to a packet of Cup-a-Soup, if such a thing can be found in town. I'm also acutely aware that I'll still have to pay the carpenter for the new door handle and the broken window. I've toyed with the idea of offering him a massage in exchange for his work (the man needs it, with those heavy tools he lugs about all day) but I fear he night take it the wrong way; even the mention of "tools" sounds a little bit dodgy in this context.

On the topic of massage: Polyna is coming over to receive one on Thursday, and to give me another session of BowTech. Eleni spoke to her this morning, and she has pronounced my continued illness (a.k.a. alternative health) a good thing: it's the toxins leaving my body as a result of my treatment last week. Which I don't doubt; the symptoms started the day after my first session, and that's no coincidence. Bars or no bars, I've been holding on to a lot of shit that I didn't quite know what to do with, and all treatments of this sort have the potential of shifting things, often leading to some acute after-effects. I've seen it happen with massage, and it *is* a good thing. As well as necessary. I just wish my body would hurry up and get it over with already, because the endless coughing and spluttering and sneezing is driving me insane. And costing me a lot in toilet tissue; I went through an entire roll last night, and it ain't cheap. Also, my nose is sore.

I have been challenged enough for a day or two, please. I am ready for this wonderful, detoxifying illness to be over; I am ready for health of the conventional kind. I am ready for a good night's sleep, free of snot and donkey noises, and for getting up in the morning with a clear head. I am ready for the front door to be my friend again; I still glare at it suspiciously every time I pass it, and it gives me palpitations whenever I hear it shut, even though I'm holding the key in my hand. I am ready to pick herbs without fear. I am a little traumatised. But it's lucky, at least, that I decided yesterday that these posts count as writing because, with all the above factors at play, they're all the writing I've managed in the last three days.

I'm going to close this entry early. Eleni is hosting her final dinner party tonight; she's leaving next week – and then the hardcore solitude will begin. So I must attempt to make myself relatively presentable (i.e. not quite on death's door, but merely on the bus on the way there), and go over to give her a hand. Though my assistance may have to be in the form of moral support: I seriously cannot be trusted not to sneeze in the food.

# Day 10

I have a problem: I'm really inspired to write. I can think of nothing else. I sleep late, very little, and very lightly; sometimes I wake up in the middle of the night, with a half-formed thought trying to turn itself into a sentence (though, admittedly, this is often helped along by mosquitoes and/or coughing fits). I get up early in the morning, eager to start typing and deleting words on my screen. My computer is never off, and I'm never far from it. Today, I skipped lunch and anyone who's met me has probably just gasped with shock: I never miss a meal. This is entirely unprecedented.

You're baffled. You're scanning that first paragraph again, looking for the problem. *Inspired to write*, you read. Surely that's a good thing? Isn't that what you're there to do? You're thinking *she's lost it; the poor girl has lost her mind.* A little earlier than anticipated, perhaps, but it was inevitable.

I haven't: my mind is exactly where I've always kept it. But I'm just as baffled as you. Because there's something happening right now that I never saw coming, and it snuck up on me and it's knocked me down. And that's all I want to write about. Not my novel; not the half-written short story that sits in my "Writing" folder and taunts me with its unfinishedness. This.

I set out to do a thing for myself, a small thing, barely a blip on the radar of what people get up to every day. It was a big thing for me, maybe even monumental, but I didn't expect it to matter to anyone else. I threw a pebble in the lake that was my life, and stood back to wait for the little *plop!* and the sinking feeling, but the thing spread out, in concentric circles, with me bang at the centre. *What?* It's commonplace, to be at the centre of our own lives, and our actions often ripple out to those closest to us, but this thing is touching people I've never met before. It's taken on a life of its own and there I am, still at its centre, blinking stupidly.

But I'm not stupid. I know this isn't about me. I'm just a character in a story, the protagonist of this one, perhaps, but it's the story itself that people are responding to. I seem to have inadvertently touched upon something universal, our need to believe in dreams, and to believe that our dreams will come true. It's the Hero's Quest, the backbone of every story ever told. The details may vary, but the quest is always, fundamentally, the same.

And though I'm obviously into the story – I'm living it – it's people's responses that I find truly inspiring. Because in the ten days since I started this project, and in the two days since I launched the kickstarter campaign, I've been shown more support and kindness and generosity than I thought was in store in the world. People have literally gone out of their way to help me, stepped out of their own stories to join me in mine. Every day, they walk me a bit further down the path, saying nice things to me all the way. And more than that, more important, is that in starting along this path in the first place, in setting out to do this thing for myself, I seem to have made the path visible to other people. And in following my story, as I tell it, they are starting to make out a part of themselves, their own part in it. They may not be smashing windows to get past their locked doors yet, but they're considering the possibility. This is what's happening, and it's incredible.

I set out to do a thing by myself. I thought it was a lonely thing, but I have never felt less lonely in my life. There is no shortage of adjectives I could use: *Astonished. Astounded. Amazed. Stunned.* And then: *Grateful. Gratified. Moved. Humbled.* But I struggle to put the words together to express how I feel: *lost for words* is another one. And yet I try. This is all I want to write about.

So that's what I'll do, until I get the words right, or until the words run out. This story is everyone's story. And in writing my part in it, I've already achieved what I set out to do.

And on a metaphorical as well as a literal note: smashing a window to get past a locked door will only cost you 10 euro. Throw in another 5, and you have a brand new handle, so you can open and close that door, oh so casually, whenever you feel like it. It's a small price to pay, for getting what you want.

# Day 11

My front gate has a little voice. 'Hrndt-D!' it says. 'Hrvndd'. It's like a soft whine, like it's having a gentle moan about some chronic complaint; nothing too acute, and nothing it's prepared to do much about, but annoying, nonetheless. It scared the shit out of me this morning when I first heard it, and it continued scaring the shit out of me until I located its source, scouting the front yard with my heart pumping against my teeth. It only speaks in a certain wind, you see. An autumn wind, that I've never been here to experience before.

Or maybe it's the quiet. It's *very* quiet here. So quiet that you can hear a beetle shuffling about in the caper bush at the other end of the garden. A donkey chewing on a mouthful of grass in the neighbour's field. A cat sneezing. The front gate speaking in its whiny little voice. Or nothing; sometimes, absolutely nothing at all. It's incredibly peaceful and totally nerve racking in equal measures. This is island life in late September.

It's the newness of familiar things that surprises me, how they keep behaving in unexpected ways. How they're not just fixtures, the static background of my holidays, but living things, changing all the time. I've spent most of my summers on this island; twenty of them in this house itself. I thought I knew what it was all about. I thought I knew about the quiet; it's quiet enough, in July and August, when you're coming from London, or Athens, or any other city in the world. But it's a different quality of quiet now. *Now* is a different place altogether; I thought I knew Sifnos, but this is not the Sifnos I know.

Eleni and I went to the beach today; we both had headaches and stiff backs, and decided a quick swim might sort us out. It was warm, but the sunshine was patchy; there is an air of autumn that pervades even the most summery scenes. We went to the beach in Kamares, the port of Sifnos, where up to a couple of weeks ago the beach bars and restaurants were teeming with the tanned and the sunburnt, and you had to reserve a sun lounger in advance, and five ferries daily spilt tourists out onto the narrow quay, tourists laden with backpacks and suitcases and expectations for the start of their holiday, asking for directions to their hotels and stopping to point at things and blocking the road, and you had to fight for a seat on the bus.

Now a single ferry calls the island every day, and the frequency of buses has been cut down to half, but you can always get a seat. And the Old Captain Bar, which, earlier this month, had been taken over by twenty of my friends and family smothering each other in sun lotion and reading magazines, has but a single customer, a deeply tanned man in his sixties, pink sarong tied around his waist and flapping in the breeze, sipping a pint of beer and gazing contentedly at the mountains that frame the bay.

There are still tourists, but they are few and scattered and, no matter how far along their holiday they might be, there is a sense of wrapping up in everything they do. This is not a time of beginnings, not here, with the summer dying on the cooling sand.

'Let's get away from the old people,' Eleni says, as we search for a patch of sand to spread our towels on the near-abandoned beach. We look around.

'It's all old people,' I observe, not unfairly. 'Everyone else has gone back to work. It's just pensioners, and the rich, and (adding myself to the equation) the unemployed'.

Eleni gives a little nod but carries on along the beach, regardless, until we find a young couple that represents the under-30s population of Kamares on this day, and plonk ourselves a few feet away from them. The sand is cooling but it's still hot enough and it feels good against my skin. I lie back and stare up at the sky; the clouds drifting past the sun mean that I don't have to shade my eyes. It's not what I'm used to, but it's nice.

The end of summer has always terrified me. It almost makes me angry every time I hear people wishing each other "a good winter" as they part at the port. *What's the rush?* I want to scream. *It isn't winter yet.* And perhaps I thought, by staying here, in the land of summer, I might hold onto it for a little while longer. But you can't stop the seasons from changing. And this isn't the land of summer; it's just an island, and autumn has come. Summer is a time, not a place, and this place is moving on. And I can choose to stand still, obstinate and shivering in my bikini among the pensioners and the rich, or I can put some clothes on, exchange my flip flops for shoes, and follow Sifnos to wherever it might take me.

I wonder if the quiet will grow deeper as the days grow shorter, and I make my way, slowly, towards an island winter. I wonder how much darker the sky can get, and if new stars will appear. I wonder if the wind will blow from new directions, if its howls will have a different timbre, and if more inanimate objects will introduce themselves to me in voices I've never heard before. I wonder how many more familiar things will turn out strange, and if I'll get used to this happening, or if it'll keep taking me by surprise.

It isn't winter yet, but it is autumn. And I'm no longer on holiday, but I'm still here, the same but also different, behaving, like my surroundings, in new and unexpected ways. Not fixed, but changing; turning out a little strange. And I wonder how I missed it: that this is a beginning. I wonder how many more things I've missed, and what they'll teach me, when I finally see them for what they are.

# Day 12

I still think I may be crazy. This isn't Antagonist talking, and it's not self-deprecation, either; it's just an observation. Self-awareness is important, and I'm aware that my actions at the moment cannot strictly be described as sane: *based on reason or good judgement; rational or sensible.* I cross-examine myself, hold myself against an accepted model of a sound decision making process to see how I measure up. I try to look at the bigger picture.

Did I really consider the consequences of quitting my job and using all my savings to spend four months writing? And, once both the savings and the four months were almost up, did I reflect, carefully, upon my situation and my prospects before deciding to stay on a remote island past the end of the summer, without any income, for another four months? Did I come to the logical conclusion that this was the wisest course of action? Did I work out a plan for what I'd do after, what I'd do if this didn't work out? How I would cope if this all came to nothing, and I found myself back in London, in the middle of winter, with no job, no home and no cash to put up as a deposit? Did I really think it through?

Yes, and no. I agonised over these decisions. I stayed up, night after night, mulling them over in my head. Feeling breathless with fear at the possibility of staying, and breathless with fear at the thought of going back. I changed my mind a million times in the space of a single moment. I consulted my friends, tentatively broaching the subject in stages: *I'm thinking of staying a little bit longer. Perhaps I'll stay for a few more weeks.* 'Am I crazy?' I kept asking. 'Do you think it's crazy, doing this?' There was a process but it was neither rational nor sensible, and the answer that it eventually produced was not arrived at through reason and good judgement. It wasn't logical, but intuitive. Its wisdom, if it can be credited with any, was the wisdom of pure instinct, rather than knowledge and experience and the ability to put the two together and offer a considered argument. And in the absence of the usual markers for sanity: crazy. But also, I think, right.

Polyna came round to give me a session of Bow Tech and we talked, briefly, about what I'm doing, what's happening to me. She said a very interesting thing.

'I think,' she said, 'that this is a great opportunity to do what we should all be doing, and live day to day.' She paused to take a drag of her cigarette. 'You're doing it already.'

It was a revelation; another thing I'd missed. But that's exactly what I'm doing. It's all set up; I've set it up myself, inadvertently, through this journal. I've broken up my life into one hundred daily segments, a series of todays, each of them connected to the others but every one of them self-contained. I've done away with weeks and months and dates, and there's no more Monday, or Tuesday or Sunday: there's only ever today. And that's where I live. In writing these entries, I occupy each day fully, from beginning to end, because there has to be a beginning and an end to make a story. And that is, ultimately, what these entries are: one hundred separate stories.

So screw the bigger picture that we're constantly instructed to consider in everything we do. The bigger picture means worrying about January in September. The bigger picture means having to squint to make out the details of today. It makes the little things seem even smaller, and *that's* crazy, because its those little things that make our lives distinguishable from all the other lives, and our stories worth telling.

I suspect some of my friends do think I'm crazy but, to their credit, not one of them has said so. Their responses varied, but they were all, in the end, unreservedly positive. This is probably because they're all good and kind and supportive people, and they love me, and they're willing to indulge my whims with a smile and a shrug. But perhaps they could see, as I'm beginning to, that *crazy* and *right* are not necessarily mutually exclusive. That sometimes we need a little crazy to take us where we want to be. And I'm exactly where I want to be today. So I'm embracing the crazy, and sensible can join the bigger picture, and go screw itself. Sensible is still working seventy hours a week to pay rent for a tiny room it only ever sees at night, and crying in the staff room at work because it wants to be a writer. I have been sensible before, but today is day 12 and I'm happy.

And when my one hundred days are over and the bigger picture comes rushing back in, threatening to flatten all my little things with its far-reaching expectations and its wider implications, I will at least have had today. I will have moments to hold up to it and, maybe, bring today back into focus. And I will try to remember this, even if it means spending the rest of my life squinting to make out the details.

# Day 13

I want to take you somewhere tonight. I'll take you to
Vathy, on the southwest coast of Sifnos. A beach of
postcard-perfect beauty, all sparkling turquoise waters
and fine, golden sand, and enclosed, as if in a hug, by
mountains, to form a deep, tear-shaped bay. When Eleni
and I arrived this evening, the sun had just sunk behind
the mountains, out of sight, but still casting pinks and
oranges up into the sky and colouring the long clouds
that hovered over the horizon. There was no sound
except the gentle whoosh of the sea as it came in and
drew out. The water was silvery-pink and almost
completely still and we waded in, drawing ripples across
its surface. We bathed in the silvery-pink.

Afterwards, when we came out and changed into dry
clothes, the sun had set and the lights from the few
remaining restaurants along the beach were mirrored in
the water. It was just warm enough to sit there for a
little while, bare feet buried in the sand, looking out at
the mouth of the bay and the dark ocean beyond. We sat
in silence; there was nothing that needed to be said. One
of the restaurants had lit its outdoor oven and the smell
of wood smoke drifted over, carrying with it warmth and
melancholy both. There was no moon yet. A ferry passed
in the distance, all lit up. The sea whooshed in and out.
Nothing else happened.

I think I'm falling in love with autumn.

I mentioned self-deprecation in yesterday's entry, and I
am guilty of that. I struggle with compliments: I don't
know how to handle them, and my first instinct is to
reject the nice thing that's been said about me, to prove
that it somehow isn't so. I've been called "brave" several

41

times in the last few days. I've been called many things, but brave is the one that comes up the most. And perhaps I am. Even as I try to brush the compliment aside, to invalidate it with some argument, I know that it takes courage to give up the familiar and exchange it for the unknown, to swap safety for uncertainty and put all your money (both literally and figuratively) on a dream. But for doing this, for living this, for being here, I'm not brave. I am incredibly lucky.

# Day 14

I have just done A Thing. A very scary Thing, which also cost me £35. A Thing that means, officially, that I'm not going anywhere. I have just changed my return flight to London.

I hesitated before doing it. I picked a date almost at random, then stared at the page for a very long time, right hand hovering over my trackpad, credit card still tucked away in my desk drawer. CONFIRM, easyjet insisted. I clicked the button. I confirmed.

This is the second time I've changed this flight, which means this one journey from Athens to London has so far cost me a total of £250, if you include the £180 I originally paid for the pleasure of travelling in early September. It's like I'm on a mission to give easyjet all my money. It's been a fun game, but I think I might stop playing now. I'm flying back in January, and that's the end of it.

And the beginning, in a sense. I may be fourteen days into the project, but just over a couple of weeks ago all this was little more than an idea in my head, shared with a few friends only, and I still had a flight booked for September 24. I never really intended to be on that flight, but knowing it was there, knowing I still had the option took the edge off the fear. It was my get-out clause. It was the window I could smash if I locked myself out again; like one of those magic button door release gadgets, *in case of emergency, break glass.*

But I clicked a button instead, and now it's done. Now I've really done it.

Friends I've spoken to in the last week or so have asked me if I actually mean it: am I *seriously* going to stay on this island until December? Alone? Writing?

'Yes,' I assure them all, 'I seriously am. And since I've apparently announced to the entire world that I'm staying, I don't think I have a choice.' (I'm aware that a few hundred readers aren't exactly the *entire* world but, to me, they almost are and, besides, I like being dramatic.)

'Wow,' they say. 'You're brave (*crazy*).' That word again. There's often a pause, here, and then: 'Won't you get lonely? And what if it's cold?'

'You can call me,' I reply. 'And I might get an electric blanket; I've been told it's the best way to beat the damp.'

It's hot again today, so hot that, if I didn't know any better, I could believe it was still summer. It was overcast earlier in the day, with dark, heavy clouds straddling the mountaintops, but now the sky is clear and the flagstones in the yard are warm from the sun again. Only the quiet betrays the time of year: there is nobody around. There was a bit of excitement in the morning, with the church bells ringing for the Sunday service and a few of the locals marching past my door in their Sunday best (there still is such an outfit, here), but now their homes and Sunday rituals have swallowed them back up, and the village streets are deserted.

Eleni and I are going back to Vathy this evening, to have another sunset swim, followed by dinner in one of the beachfront tavernas. We have been planning this for a couple of weeks, looking forward to it with excitement, but also sadness. She is leaving the day after tomorrow, and this dinner is to be our farewell. We're having lamb chops and chips. This, too, we have planned well in advance.

So Tuesday will be another landmark in this journey; with Eleni gone, it'll just be me and my donkey friend next door. Who, incidentally, has been absent for the last two days, though Takis, his owner, assured me he'd be back. Takis runs the taverna where we're having our dinner tonight, so Eleni and I stopped by last night to reserve a portion of lamb chops. (Yes, you can do that. And it is not weird, it's wise.)

'Make it a good one,' Eleni said, while I, in the background – helpless glutton that I am – kept repeating the word "big". 'It'll be my last this year.'

Takis turned to me, beaming.

'So you'll be *all alone?*' he said, with far too much excitement.

'Yes,' I confirmed. 'Just me and your donkey. Though he seems to have abandoned me too.'

'Don't worry,' Takis said. 'He's just gone to help with carrying the grapes. He'll be back in a day or two, once he's done.'

This is a donkey in demand. He clearly cannot be relied on for company; his skills might take him away at a moment's notice. Solitude indeed.

It is official. There's nothing between me and the fear now, nothing to blunt its edges except doing what I'm here to do. There are no safety features built in, no magic buttons, and no get-out clauses. I do have a choice, and I'm staying here, for the next 86 days. Alone (mostly), and writing. Wow.

Yes. I'll get lonely and I will get cold. It will be dark, and windy, and it'll rain and I'll be confined to the house, on the edge of a near-deserted village. And, in case of emergency, I'll curl up in bed, with my electric blanket, and call someone, and maybe cry a little bit and ask them to tell me, again, that I'm not crazy, despite the fact that the only conversations I've had for three whole days have been with cats, and even the donkey is too busy to talk to me. I can see this happening; I can see it, clearly, in my head, as if it already has. And the funny thing is: I don't mind. I'm actually looking forward to it. All of it. Even being ignored by donkeys. And as much as it scares me that Eleni is going, just as I've committed myself – again – to staying, as much as it makes me sad because I'll miss her, I'm ready for the next stage to begin.

I'm not going anywhere.

And Eleni has just given me an umbrella, so I'm good for the rain, too. Which, I am told by the men who read the signs, is coming soon. And hard.

# Day 15

The men who read the signs are actually one man. His name is Leonidas and he's a taxi driver, and he is very wise. He foretells the weather for the coming year by reading the signs in the first six days of August, which the locals call *imerominia* (roughly translated: days-months). Each of those six days corresponds to two months, from September through to the following August, and reading them is a complicated art: a dry, hot morning on the 2$^{nd}$ of August doesn't mean good weather in November.

'Winter's coming early this year,' Leonidas declared, cheerfully, on a drive back from Chrysopigi. He didn't think this should put me off from staying; I'd have my electric blanket, after all. He was the first to dispense that piece of advice, and spent a long time describing the cosiness that can be derived from such a device.

The electric blanket has come up several times since, as has the imperative of attending the *panigiria*. *Panigiria*, church festivals held on saints' feast days and organised by local families or associations are, apparently, in terms of the island's social life, where it's at. They begin with a church service, followed by food and drink and much merriment in the form of live music and traditional dancing, and often escalate into wild parties that go on until the early hours of the morning. Not being at all churchy and lacking both the coordination and the desire to attempt any dance that includes choreographed moves in a specific sequence, I don't really see myself being a regular at these things. Despite being told I *must*. When I mentioned them to my friend Alexis, he laughed his head off. 'You'd hate it,' he said, and he's probably right. But perhaps I need to adopt a *When in Rome* sort of attitude, and open myself up to new possibilities. Although, having said that, what the Romans do, mostly, is ride around on scooters past beautiful piazzas, defying the laws of traffic and pausing only to enjoy pizza and pasta and gelato and cappuccinos, which are all delicious and not much of a hardship to embrace, whereas embracing sweaty strangers in an ecstasy of traditional dance and homemade spirits may require a bit more openness than I currently possess.

In the days and weeks before I made my decision to stay, I did a bit of what I came to think of as market research, with the product being me, and the object to establish whether there was a place for me in Sifnos. I took every opportunity to consult the permanent residents on what the island was like, off season, and whether they thought I'd survive. I was afraid I'd be dismissed as a city dweller, unequipped for the reality of island life once the souvenir shops had shut, but not one of them betrayed this opinion, and they were all, to the last man, positive and enthusiastic. A few shot me looks of concern when I revealed I'd be living in Eleimonas, alone, because the locals are free of our romantic notions of *reclusive author pursuing her art in isolated location*, and recognise my village for what it is: wilderness.

'Eleimonas?' they'd say. 'Alone?'

I'd nod, and mutter something about being OK on my own, at which point they'd recover and assure me, with renewed enthusiasm, that I'd be fine. As long as I attended the *panigiria*.

Other things I've found out: The supermarkets, along with the butcher's and the bakery, stay open throughout the year, albeit with limited hours. Most of the bars and restaurants close (it's happening already), but there's a secret café that opens only off season, and that's where the cool people hang out. If I am ever in need of workman's clothes, overalls and boots and suchlike, I can procure these items, along with 100% synthetic socks and jumpers, from something known as the Sifnos Cooperative, which also sells animal feed. The electrical shop up in Artemonas might stock the obligatory and much praised electric blankets, but nobody is entirely sure about that. And though my local supermarket actually sells organic pasta, pink Himalayan salt and, inexplicably, a range of Waitrose products, nobody stocks coconut oil. Which is a problem that may warrant a trip to Athens, for supplies.

Another thing I learned is never to get raped and murdered or otherwise require police assistance past the afternoon. The Sifnos police station is apparently only manned in the morning. After that time, all calls are diverted to the station on the island of Milos, about an hour and a half away on the boat, where the duty officer conveys your emergency, via mobile phone, to his Sifnos colleagues. As a woman now living alone at the edge of a village, in a house that feels very exposed, I do not find this particularly reassuring. I can just imagine how it would play out.

'Hello? Sifnos police?'

'Hello, this is Milos, conveniently located about two hours from your current emergency, how may I help?'

'I'm being raped and murdered in Sifnos!'

'Splendid! May I take your address?'

'SIFNOS! Katavati! Eleimonas! Turn right at the corner shop keep going past George the electrician's and Margarita's rooms and then it's left at Vangelia's house the one with the basil pot outside you'll see the church on your left keep going and it's the second house just after Mrs. Souli it's a grey gate there a bird-shaped knocker with a bell!'

' ... past George the electrician's ...'

Raped and murdered.

I think it's best, under the circumstances, that I confine all emergencies to the hours between 9am and 1pm.

On a positive note, however, the one restaurant in town that delivers stays open all year round, and they know exactly where I live. Perhaps they're the ones I should call if I ever encounter any suspicious elements loitering outside my home.

But the best insight into off season life came, hands down and uncontested, from Yiannis. Yiannis is an Athenian who owns one of the jewellery shops in town, and he and his wife and children have lived in Sifnos for many years now. I like Yiannis, mostly because he seems permanently amused by everything, which is an excellent default mode to be in. After responding, with trademark cheer, to my doubts and concerns, without a single mention of churches or dancing (for which I thank him), and declaring, in conclusion, that there was nothing to it, he began describing the contrast between town as I know it – so busy that people often come to a standstill outside his shop – and as it is in the autumn and winter months.

'You won't believe it,' he said. 'There's nobody around! It's like a ghost town.' And he went on to share the following story:

'I open the shop sometimes in winter,' he said, 'just for fun. Nobody comes. And there was this one evening and there was literally nobody, not a single person, and there hadn't been for hours. I was standing out here (just outside the shop, on the main path that runs through town), and I needed a piss. So I pissed right there – can you imagine? – right there, in the middle of the path.' He paused, to indicate the exact spot, with a huge grin. 'And I was King of Sifnos!'

I couldn't stop laughing all evening. And I think, bizarrely, more than anything else I heard during my market research, it was this story that convinced me I could belong.

Here's an idea: maybe I can claim this territory for myself in the most traditional way, skip the *panigiria* and go straight for peeing on the street. Men and dogs have been doing it since time began. And when in Sifnos.

So if there comes a day when I announce that I am Queen of Sifnos, try not to judge me too harshly. This is off season living; you city dwellers wouldn't understand.

# Day 16

It's funny how the weather likes to be symbolic sometimes. How it picks certain days that are heavy with meaning and throws its most dramatic effects into them, just to make sure you don't miss the point. Of course, this is an entirely subjective observation, placing me at the centre of the universe, and the weather acting out on my behalf. To most people, this is a perfectly ordinary day. To me, it's the day of Eleni's departure, sad because my friend is leaving, and signalling yet another end/beginning duo, with each side bearing its own implications and connotations. It's a day that means something, and the weather is awful.

It started last night, with the wind. It kept me up with its howls, its picking up of objects and throwing them noisily around, like a petulant toddler on a much larger, scarier scale, and its special trick of getting sucked into the chimney of the fireplace, in the room next to mine, and making this great roaring sound that you can actually feel as well as hear. If hell had a voice, I swear this is how it would sound. The house literally shook, every hinge creaking, every window and door rattling away, despite the fact that I'd gone round and secured them all.

It got worse in the morning. The clouds had arrived, but they were white, not dark, and very low in the sky, giving the day an eerie, ghostly quality, without the promise of release of impending rain. And the wind went nuts, blasting in from all directions, with gusts that ripped branches off the trees and rained almonds down on me whenever I dared stick my head out the door. It carried both of my drying racks off into the garden, and I had to chase after them, and fold them up, and weigh them down with rocks. The cats – two of them strays and one belonging to my neighbour, who seems to think feeding her cat sufficiently is a luxury she doesn't hold with – were all cowering in the yard, pressed almost flat against the floor, and giving bewildered little mews, which I could barely hear over the shrieking of the wind. I tried to feed them, but the bowl flipped over as soon as I put it down, and the food scattered all over the flagstones. I thought about bringing them into the house, but they won't come.

Just past eleven, Eleni called in a mild panic, to tell me there were no ferry tickets left.

'How's that even possible?' I said, pointlessly. This being the 23rd of September, a random Tuesday, neither of us had thought there was any need to book ahead. It turns out that, with the number of vehicle-carrying ferries now down to three a week, the freight lorries travelling to Athens from the four islands served by this line take up most of the space in the ship's garage, leaving very little room for passenger cars. By some miracle of fate, however, as Eleni was ringing around the travel agencies desperately and getting the same answer, there was a last minute cancellation and a ticket was secured. 'But it has to be collected by twelve,' Eleni concluded, in pleading tones. 'And it's a quarter past eleven!'

'I'm on my way,' I said. I threw some clothes on and legged it into town.

On the way back up, the day decided to test me. Despite its ominous start and Eleni's imminent departure, I was feeling quite cheerful: I held the miracle ticket in my hand, and a few rays of sunshine had broken through the cloud; you could see the colours of things again. As I skipped down the path, I noticed a tiny flash of ginger motion. It took me a second to recognise it as a kitten, another second to realise it was very, very unwell. I approached it cautiously and we both came to a stop. I crouched down and the kitten – I think she was a little girl – lowered her tiny body to the ground and lifted her head a fraction. She blinked with one, cloudy eye; the other one was grotesquely swollen and completely crusted over, that side of her face disfigured and her legs covered in scabs. She made tiny, spluttering sounds as she tried to breathe. I understood immediately and with horrible certainty that there was nothing I could do. She was one of those kittens that their mothers reject; cats are firm believers in the survival of the fittest, and this one wasn't going to make it. There is no vet on the island to intervene with that cruel law. All I could do was pick her up and take her home, try to clean up her eyes and pick the thorns out of her fur and feed her milk and tuna fish that she was too small and too weak to ingest, and I would watch her die. And I couldn't bear it. So instead I sat down, in the middle of the path, and we looked at each other, this kitten and I, and I wept. I must have been there for about ten minutes when a couple I vaguely know came along. I shuffled back to let them pass. The man shook his head and the woman, taking in the tears that I was uselessly trying to wipe off my face, paused.

'It's very ill,' she said. 'It's beyond help.' She said it kindly, as if that might give me comfort. And then they both nodded and carried on up the path.

The kitten still had her face turned to me. I don't know if she could see me, but she knew I was there. I reached out and stroked her head with a finger – she was too small for a whole hand – and she arched her neck to receive the touch. I thought again of taking her home, but I couldn't. I just couldn't do it. I knew she would die, but I couldn't bring myself to watch it happen. Perhaps that's the coward's way out, I don't know.

'I will remember you,' I told her, offering the only thing I could give her. A useless token for a little life that I cannot save. She looked at me and I looked at her. She blinked. And then, gently, slowly, she raised herself up and began to walk away. As if she understood. As if releasing me. Crying even harder now, I followed her example and stood on my feet and set off in the opposite direction. I didn't look back.

By the time I made it to Eleni's it was late and I was in pieces but I put myself together and delivered the ticket and then stood around, trying to look helpful, as she did what needed to be done to close up the house for the winter.

'Look,' she said, pointing to the furniture, tucked in cosily under sheets. 'They're sleeping.'

With the house locked up and a whole summer's worth of stuff loaded into the car, we set off for the port. I dreaded this journey, this driving at speed towards a parting, but Eleni, unexpectedly, turned it around.

'Goodbye car park,' she said, as soon as we'd pulled out. She turned to look at me. 'I do this,' she explained. 'Don't be alarmed.'

And so it went, for the entire drive to Kamares: Goodbye yellow cement mixer. Goodbye pile of stones. Goodbye dog on a lead. Goodbye horrible digger, destroying everything! Goodbye other digger, helping him. Goodbye sheep talking to each other. Goodbye rusty old car. Goodbye cat looking that way. Goodbye church on the side of the road. Goodby donkey. Goodbye man I've never met before.

It was absolutely brilliant. By the time we reached the port, I was smiling again.

I won't go in to the details of her leaving. There was a boat and she got on it and that was that. She's safely in Athens now, and getting ready to travel again on Friday, back to Turin, where she lives, and she'll be back next summer to say hello port of Sifnos, hello beach bars full of tourists, hello windmill, hello goat running across the road, hello car park, and wake the furniture up and bring her house out of hibernation. Refreshed and ready to fill up, once again, with people and bees and crumbs.

Some days are significant. Some days are symbolic. All days mean something. This was one of those days. It was just a day. The weather was bad, and I met a kitten I couldn't help, and my friend got on a boat and left. I cooked pasta in the evening, and watched a film. Just a day. Hello/goodbye. Beginning/end.

Goodbye Eleni who became my friend this summer and fed me fish and made me cushions and bought me cayenne pepper and told me stories and danced with me when I was happy and when I was sad.

And goodbye kitten.

I will remember you both: that you were here.

# Day 17

It isn't easy to see the good in people these days; they don't get many opportunities to show you. We each of us do small kindnesses for our friends and our family, with the occasional big gesture when it's warranted, and we don't give ourselves credit for being capable of much more than that. We retreat into our own lives, desperate to preserve the precarious balance that we've achieved to keep us going, and poised to protect it against anything that threatens to disturb it, or bring it into question. It sounds bleak, but it isn't; it's just 21$^{st}$ century living. It isn't easy.

We all have our dreams, but they are often sacrificed in the name of survival, of paying bills and getting mortgages and putting kids through school. They are put aside for another, better time, a "one day" when they'll be possible; we stash them away, and they often fester and make us bitter and defensive. We are all too easy with the criticism, all too ready to dismiss other people's dreams, to belittle them so they don't loom over us, mocking us with their out-of-reach possibilities. We respond with fear or anger or both, because we perceive them as attacks on our own choices and the dreams we keep secret in our heads.

I've seen a little bit of that since I decided to disturb the balance myself, and put my money where my mouth is, and try to live as a writer. There have been reactions ranging from the cautious all the way to the downright, stamp-on-your-dreams dismissive. Even my mum, who obviously wants the best for me, remarked, when I explained to her about the kickstarter campaign, that it sounded "a bit ambitious". She didn't think she was being negative, merely realistic. But our realistic often borders on the cynical and though I'm guilty of that myself, I still believe that we are all of us entitled to our dreams, as ambitious as they may be, entitled to living as if they are within our reach. And we owe it to ourselves to reach.

So that's how it began, for me, with reaching, but then it changed, and it isn't just about me anymore. Because, although there have been cautious responses, they were very few. And for each one of those there have been a hundred positive ones, a hundred that were unequivocally supportive. Because, contrary to everything I said above, I have been shown more good, more kindness and generosity than even I, the pathological optimist, could have dared to expect.

Because Richard and Sue built me a website to give my project greater visibility online. Because Katerina and Duncan, Eileen, Melina, Elly, Jill and many others have taken it upon themselves to campaign on my behalf. Because my mum has been converted, and is spamming all her friends, and Eleni has gone a step further, and is actually calling hers to demand that they pledge. Because Aliki sent me a care package full of thoughtful, perfect gifts. Because strangers and friends alike read what I write every day, and make the effort to get in touch and wish me luck.

Because, at the latest count, forty-nine people have backed *100 days* on kickstarter. Forty-nine people have taken the time to read my story, watch the most painfully awkward video ever made, fetch their credit cards and pledge their own, actual cash to support someone's else dream. Forty-nine people, all of them with dreams and frustrations of their own, some of them students, some of them unemployed, some of them expecting babies, some trying their best to make ends meet, and most of them, I'm sure, dealing with challenges and disappointments that I know nothing about, and yet every single one of them has put all that aside and stepped up to help me. Each of them has given me a step up so I can reach a bit higher.

This is much more than accountability, now: this is responsibility, pure and true and impossible, unthinkable, to ignore. I feel bound to all these people, in both senses of the word: a duty and a bond. I feel like we're all in this together and, of course, I'd want to feel that because the alternative is that we are, each of us, completely alone, and nobody gives a shit one way or the other; I actually received a message through the blog, to that effect. But I don't agree with that; I don't feel alone.

This solitude I keep referring to is not so much about being isolated on an island, or the Yorkshire Moors, or a cabin in Alaska. Taking my own circumstances as an example, I'm not so isolated at all: I have a phone, I have the internet, and there are still ferries running a few times a week that could take me to Athens if I needed a break for a couple of days. It is more the solitude of an inherently solitary pursuit, which is the process of writing itself, regardless of where you do it; a process only made valid by its conclusion and where faith is only ever placed in its final product, if you ever get that far. And even that, in this case, has been turned around, because what's happening to me is the rarest of things: I'm getting validation – readers! – *while I'm writing*, and they're putting their faith in me in advance. It's the impossible happening, and people being given money to write. People, as in *me*. Me! I may as well rename this project *100 days of getting more attention than I ever have before (or am likely to get again, in all my life).* This is a dream come true in the making, and we're 66% there. It's impossible. And it's happening. And it's about so much more than money.

Don't get me wrong: I want the money. I really want the money. I need it; that's why I dared launch a kickstarter campaign in the first place. And the "nothing to lose" principle that gave me the courage to try it no longer applies. I have a lot to lose. There is currently £1,670 pledged to *100 days*: a sum that would already make a difference to me, real money that people have given, freely and selflessly, because they believe in what I'm doing. And I refuse to let that go to waste. That would be a loss.

I've never been good at promoting myself; I have a fear of talking myself up. It's part modesty and part insecurity; it's a bit of self-deprecation, and a lot about Antagonist sneering and informing me, in her most condescending tone, that I'm embarrassing myself, and I should stop bothering the nice people and go back to my corner and be quiet. So although I've been doing what I can to promote this project, I've been holding back. But what I owed to myself is now a debt that's grown to include many others; because, as Nicos put it, in a comment on kickstarter: "You hold a bit of everyone's dream in your hands". So I figure it's time I came out of my corner. I put this thing out there, and I should have the balls to stand up for it, and see it through.

So this is me, and my newly-acquired balls: seeing it through.

# Day 18

There was something making a very strange noise outside my window last night. It sounded like a cross between a distressed kitten, an owl and a bat. I hope to god and all the angels it was just one of the three because, although I've braced myself to deal with extra wildlife during my stay in Sifnos, I quite categorically did not sign up for mutants lurking outside my window in the dark.

Also, my stomach was very upset. I mean, seriously pissed off. It was making some very alarming noises of its own. I'm not sure what I did to upset it, but I suspect it might have been the aubergines. I've got aubergines coming out of my ears at the moment. There are two aubergine plants in the garden, which seem to be going through some sort of ecstasy of fruitfulness and producing two or three of the things on a daily basis, and they hang there, all purple and shiny and swollen and screaming to be picked, and if I don't do it, the bugs will get them. On top of which Eleni gave me another bagful before leaving. I'm eating aubergines every day.

I'm going rogue tonight, however. I bought 400 grams of mince, and I'm treating myself to burgers and chips. With ketchup. Lots of ketchup. I crave ketchup; I crave simple, take-it-for-granted junk food: burgers and pizza and crisps from Marks & Spencer. I am so thoroughly sick of Greek taverna food. Which is convenient, actually, because I can never afford to eat out ever again and, besides, I have no one to eat out with. So, this season, I'll be mostly eating aubergines, at home.

I made a promise to myself a few weeks ago, when I decided to stay here. Conscious of the need to keep up a healthy level of activity *outside the house* (yoga on the patio and mad, solo dancing in the kitchen, both of which I practice regularly, do not count), the need to get dressed and go out and do something that doesn't involve staring at my computer screen, I promised I would take advantage of the fact that I now live within 30 minutes of the beach, and go for a swim as often as I could. Two of three times a week, at least. Even when I couldn't be bothered. Even when it got cold and windy. I shared this with my cousin Peter when he was here, and he told me that the water temperature actually peaks three months after the temperature of the air, which would make September and October ideal for swimming in the sea. No excuses.

I haven't really kept this up. I couldn't be bothered. It was a bit cold; it was windy. But I got up this morning, after a rough night of winged kittens and aubergine-induced discomfort, and it was a lovely, bright day, and before I had a chance to think about it too much (always my downfall), I'd thrown my bikini on and trotted into town to catch the bus.

I've always feared the melancholy of a holiday destination past the summer's end. Beaches tend to be the worst, all those recently vacated sun loungers and shut-up beach bars with the chairs stacked up, and the sudden abundance of space, all spelling out desolation, and a sense of something unfinished that finished too soon. A place that the summer left behind. I was nervous as I stepped off the bus.

It was exactly as I imagined. It was just before 10 o'clock, and I was the only one to get off at the beach; the other passengers, all five of them, were heading for the final stop, the port. One of the souvenir shops was open, multicoloured scarves and garish beach towels hanging limp and idle outside in the absence of wind, still hoping to be chosen by one of the few remaining besandalled tourists wandering around in search of breakfast. There was nobody on the beach, except for two distant dots, one red, one black, that turned out to be a mother and a child playing in the shallow water where the sea met the sand. The rows of umbrellas and sun loungers that people still paid for the privilege of occupying only a week ago had been dismantled and taken away, leaving behind a sparse ghost forest of poles sticking out of the sand. It was exactly as I imagined and nothing like I expected, and it was perfect.

This is the beach in late September: Instead of smelling other people's sun lotion, you can smell the sea. Instead of children's shrieks and too loud adult conversations and the constant bop-bop-bop of racketball games, you can hear the sea. You can see the sea, with no one running past you or standing in front of you or putting up umbrellas or shaking out towels or throwing balls about and blocking your view. And the water is warm, and it's all yours. Save from an old man in a bright green baseball cap doing his laps, and two dots, far away, building castles, the beach is yours. And there are fish: curious, silvery things that come up and nip you, and then bolt when you jump.

Just before dusk fell, I went over to Eleni's to water the plants. Grey clouds have gathered at the edges of the sky and made a half-hearted attempt at drizzle, but the rain doesn't want to come yet, and the plants are thirsty. It felt strange being there, with the house closed up and the outdoor furniture stored inside, and me on the outside dragging the hose from tree to tree and checking the lemons for ripeness. Eleni's barely been gone two days, but already you can feel this is an empty house. And the melancholy got me then, because, contrary to the beach, this is a place of summer, a seasonal thing, and now it's in limbo, suspended in time, a sleeping beauty waiting to be reawakened when the season changes, and changes, and changes again, and its fair-weather friends return. For the first time since Eleni left, I felt sad.

So I decided not to let the house drift into too deep a sleep, to give it a little nudge every now and again while I'm still here. I put the hose away and had a quick walk around the garden, picked up a couple of rotten pomegranates that had fallen off the tree, and swept up the leaves that had gathered by the front door. And then, as I stood on the patio in the back, taking in the view before I went back home, it occurred to me that I could do my yoga here. I brought my mat, rolled it out and did two sun salutations, and then I realised I was wearing the wrong shorts, which cut into my arse every time I tried to lunge, and that I didn't really feel like yoga anyway. So I laid down on my mat and just watched the clouds move across the sky for a while. And I hope Eleni will forgive me this trespass, because it felt right being there, keeping the house company, when melancholy has been its only other guest.

I think all of our disappointments come from expectations, the context that we build around everything we do, blocking our view. And the challenge for me, in being here, will be to disassociate these images, these places around me – the beach, the town, the bars that were open and are now closed, the locked up homes – with summer and its connotations, the people that should be here and the things that we would do, and just let them be what they are. Take them out of context, and see them for what they are. That way, there can be nothing missing and no one to be missed. There can be no disappointment, and melancholy can find another place to live.

# Day 19

Murder is not how I'd normally choose to start the day, but it had to be done. I'm sure people put up with a lot worse, but this fly that kept landing on me – cheek, shoulder, nose, forehead, shoulder, arm – and buzzing discontent every time I waved it away, before I'd even had my coffee, was driving me absolutely insane. So I killed it. I didn't feel bad. Actually, I felt a little bit bad, right after telling myself I didn't, because it was still a creature that was alive, and I took its life away as it lounged in the sunshine on my desk. I didn't like doing that. It was murder, and I plead insanity, and also the right of people to not be landed on, repeatedly, by flies.

It was mass murder, in fact, because there's never only one. So far, this morning, I've dispatched a total of five flies to that happy place where flies go when their time on this cruel earth is up. I'm becoming quite handy with the fly swatter. The trick is a steady hand and no hesitation. If you allow yourself to consider your adversary in a broader sense, if you let your thoughts drift to its tiny fly ambitions and its loving fly mother waiting for it at home, the game is lost. You just aim, and swat. The floor is strewn with the bodies of the dead, which might be just the motivation I need to do the sweeping and mopping that I've been putting off for days.

The killing spree gave me a thirst, so I made myself a fresh cup of coffee and settled down to enjoy it unmolested by inspects. And just then, the rain finally came, sending me into a panic of dragging all the outdoor furniture to the only covered bit on the side of the house and whacking myself in the shin in the process, only to stop again, completely, all of seventy-five seconds later. It's basically messing with me, is what's happening. And now the sun is out again, and I have a bruise.

OK, the sun is only out intermittently, and the wind is picking up again, and the rain may have retreated for now, but it hasn't gone very far. So, for all that preamble, guess what I won't be doing today. That's right: going to be beach. But Polyna's coming round in the evening, so I *will* be getting dressed. Which is something that's been troubling me, in fact: how do you maintain an acceptable standard of presentability when you know that nobody's going to see you? How do you still make the effort to get dressed every morning, to put on something other than what you wore to bed, or the same pair of shorts that you've been wearing, day after day, simply because you keep leaving it draped on a chair in the bedroom, night after night? How do you remember to run a brush through your hair and put on a pair of earrings?

The other morning, when Eleni was still here, I wandered out in my comedy shorts, hand-me-downs from an aunt – a garish floral print against a purple background – that I've adopted as my reclusive author uniform, and the top I'd slept in (no bra), hair sticking out all over place and bare feet. On my way back, after a brief chat with Eleni, I ran into my next door neighbour, an 85 year old woman in a stained housedress and plastic slippers, mucking out the chicken coops. Not a style icon by anyone's estimation.

'I should go get dressed,' I said to her, after she had detained me with her usual ten minute diatribe on the sorrows and sufferings of old age. 'I've come out in these random clothes…'

'Pah!' she said, and threw her arms up in the air. 'Don't worry about it. Nobody sees us here!' And she gestured to her own attire, in solidarity.

I did not find this comforting.

Making an effort with my appearance has never been my strongest suit, anyway, even in circumstances significantly more socially demanding than this. It's not that I am entirely free of vanity or insecurity, but it seems they are both idle qualities, not potent enough to force me into action. I've worn make-up a grand total of once this year: for my sister's wedding. And not successfully, either. My other sister, thirteen years younger than me, had to actually show me how to apply lipstick after I inexplicably ended up with red smudges on both my legs. She was very patient.

So this might be a challenge for me. Only this morning, when Jill suggested a chat on skype, I accepted her invitation on the condition that she pretends to ignore the state of my hair. She did an impeccable job, managing to sustain an hour-long conversation with me without once glancing past my hairline or betraying her alarm. She even went as far as complimenting my hair, which only speaks for what a good friend she is, because my hair is ridiculous and in urgent need of a cut. I suppose the fact that I'm still conscious of my looking like a crazy person means that I'm not quite there yet, and that's some consolation. But then again, it's only day 19, and 81 days is plenty of time for one to lose their grasp on personal grooming and hygiene, social decorum and common decency. This could get interesting.

In the meantime, while my grip on all those virtues is still fairly strong (by my own, not too exacting standards), I promise to call the hairdresser on Monday, and make an appointment. And this evening, in honour of Polyna's visit, I will actually open my wardrobe and select a different pair of shorts. And put them on.

The clouds are back, and they mean business. I walked Polyna to her car after our session, mostly for the sake of leaving the house, and also to buy a giant bag of crisps. I spent about fifteen minutes perusing the supermarket aisles, longingly touching things that I cannot afford (4 euro for a little tub of mixed fruit & nuts!) and clutching my precious bag of crisps to my chest, like an infant; so much for social decorum. In any case, by the time I stepped out onto the street, the clouds had closed in on us, turning the entire island into a giant sauna, with light effects thrown in. The result was spectacular, breathtaking for what it did to the sky, as well as on account of the fact that the air was as thick as treacle, and hot as a summer afternoon. It's all gone a bit tropical, and it's about to absolutely piss it down. Lucky I stashed the chairs away this morning.

On which note, I will wish you good night, and retreat to my sofa to eat my crisps and watch a film, and wait for the skies to break open, at last.

# Day 20

It's cold today, and I have no socks.

That's not entirely true: I have one pair of socks, but they're those little ankle things that you wear with trainers, which barely cover your heel and always, always start slipping down into your shoe as soon as you've taken two steps in them. They don't count. When I say socks, I mean SOCKS, thick, long and cosy, the kind that keep your feet warm.

I'm not prepared for this weather. When I made my suitcase, in mid-heatwave-stricken Athens in July, I was packing for summer. My wardrobe consists of vest tops, shorts, summer dresses, bikinis, flip-flops and sandals. The afterthought items – one pair of jeans, one pair of leopard print leggings, one long sleeved top, one cotton hoodie and my beloved, custom-made Converse – are my only saving grace, but they won't save me for long. My rationale, that I had no need for more than one pair of jeans anyway, because it wasn't as if I'd have many social occasions to dress for, was swiftly shattered by my mum this morning, like the illusion that it was.

'But what if you go out in the rain and they get wet?' she said anxiously. 'What if you need to wash them? What if you *spill* something on them?'

Which was a very good point: I spill things on myself all the time. Food, mostly. I will need a second pair of jeans.

I have a feeling Eileen is sending me some socks. OK, perhaps not so much a feeling as the fact that she pretty much said so. She told me she was sending me a goodie bag, and then she asked if I needed warm socks, and I said YES. This exchange came right after a coughing fit this afternoon, which itself was preceded by a whole morning of walking around in bare feet on ever-cooling ceramic tiles. So I was understandably very

69

enthusiastic on the topic of warm socks. So, yes, I think there's a good chance my goodie bag will contain socks. And if it does, I will wear them.

But I'm not ready yet. For all that I've said about seasons changing and seeing things for what they are, it'll still take a while to reconcile this – my summer home – with autumn, and winter. For all that I've said, I still don't understand why my feet are cold. Which may go some way towards explaining why, instead of putting the stupid little ankle socks on, I insist on walking around barefoot. I'm clinging to summer and socks equal defeat. As long as my feet are bare, the sun will come out again.

Or I will get pneumonia, or something old-fashioned like consumption, and have to be airlifted out of here in a helicopter because – that's right – there is no hospital in Sifnos. Which might be a good way to get myself over to Athens and pick up some jumpers and a few pairs of proper socks. I've never been in a helicopter; it might be fun.

Or I will get pneumonia and consumption and fail to seek medical attention because I am a new-age fool who believes telling yourself, repeatedly, that you're well will actually stave off disease and nevermind the fact that you're coughing up blood, and I will waste away, old-fashionably, and die alone, and they will find me amidst my blood-splattered tissues and they will say "If only she'd put on those ankle socks" and shake their heads sadly at this senseless loss of life and excellent talent. And I will be celebrated as a martyr for summer, and this blog will be published and become a bestseller, and my family will be inconsolable but significantly wealthier, and they will take to wearing ankle socks at all times.

The sun will come out again; the neighbour's son said so. He told me we'd have bad weather this weekend, but that it would be warm again from Monday. And if the neighbour's son said so, then it must be true, because he is A Local, and the locals Know Things. It's very likely that they Know Things simply because they watch the weather forecast on TV like everybody else, but I am choosing to ascribe mysterious powers of divination to the entire permanent population of Sifnos, and I am ready to default to their wisdom on any topic relating to island life (except the thing about attending the church festivals.) I can't tell you why, but I hold them in complete awe. These people say things like: "I saw the snake slithering down the path, and I followed it, but I didn't have my stick with me to kill it". And then advise you to get your own snake killing stick, for such eventualities.

I haven't got a stick, and neither will I be following the snake if I see it; I will be running like hell in the opposite direction, and nevermind what they say about me in the village. Luckily, the snakes are going into hibernation soon. But not all that soon because we're getting another burst of summer. Manolis said so.

I did some yoga this evening, a nice set of twenty sun salutations that made me forget all about the cold, and afterwards I got jiggy with it in the kitchen (Big Willie Style). I showered, and I put on my jeans and my brightest, neon orange top, in defiance of the darkness outside, added my hoodie to the mix, and Eleni's umbrella, and braved the elements all the way to town, and back, because I needed cigarettes.

And now I'm back, triumphant, with my cigarettes and a packet of biscuits. And soaked, through and through. My mum was right: there goes my one pair of jeans. I've changed into my leggings and a dry top and, fuck it, I think I'll wear the ankle socks as well. As exciting as helicopter rides and posthumous fame might sound, I think I'd rather stick around here for a little bit longer. I like it here, crazy storms and all. And they might say "She should have brought her killing stick

71

when she went walking in the dark in her ankle socks",
and shake their heads sadly at these city dwellers
getting it into their heads that they can handle island
life, and still have to airlift me to Athens to be treated
for snake bite, but at least that'll make for an interesting
story.

# Day 21

I've mentioned this to a few people, and their reactions have been understandably sceptical, but there is something strangely liberating about having no income at all. That sentence would still be entirely accurate if you were to substitute "liberating" for "terrifying", but it's no secret that freedom can be a scary thing, and no reason why the two can't be true at the same time.

In a sense, no income is better than low income. When you make just about enough to get by, the fear is a constant, nagging presence, a weight in your stomach or a pinch in your chest, giving passive-aggressive little coughs and rolling its eyes every time you consider going off budget. You live from payday to payday, always in dread of unexpected expenses, elated when the money comes in, frustrated when it inevitably runs out. Whereas, when there is absolutely no money coming in, the terror is total, and every day is just as terrifying as the next and the one before. It's a terror entirely free of anxiety or suspense, extremely reliable and unquestionably real. You have no choice but to give into it. And once you do, once you learn to embrace it, it really is liberating. And it teaches you a lot of things about what you actually need and how to make the most of what you have.

My friends know that I am a slave to food, and they are naturally concerned about how my current circumstances are impacting upon this essential quality. (I do think of it as a quality; I don't trust people who don't like food.) Iro sounded deeply distressed when I spoke to her last night.

'But do you have enough food?' she said. 'Are you only eating aubergines?'

'Aubergines are food,' I replied reasonably. 'I eat other things, too. But mostly,' I admitted, 'aubergines. I have a lot of aubergines.'

She sighed, and muttered something about making a list of items to send me.

This is what freedom looks like, from a certain angle: If you have aubergines, you eat them. Regardless of whether you feel like eating them, or feel like eating something else; you do not let them wilt and rot and then declare them inedible and throw them away. Leftovers are kept and combined into new meals. Stale bread is baked in the over and turned into rusks, or soaked in water and made into *gazpacho* soup. Ingredients are used sparingly: three frozen prawns chopped up small and added to tomato sauce for flavour. Salad is a weed that grows wild in the garden, and which I've taken to cultivating by shaking out the seeds back into the soil every time I pick some for my lunch. We call it *glystrida* and google informs me it's known in English as "common purslane", and can be eaten raw, added to stir-fries or boiled like spinach. I make Sifnos pesto with almonds from the tree and basil from my pots, and add fresh rosemary because I have so much of it (although I still don't trust the rosemary bush). I make tea from lemon verbena and fresh mint leaves. I sometimes walk to the other end of the village to pick fresh oregano from the side of the road. Lemons are scavenged from other people's trees; I have two of my own, but their fruit isn't ripe yet, and there are plenty of closed-up homes with lemons screaming to be picked, and with nobody around to pick them until next summer. And when the olives are ready, I'll pick those too, and attempt to make them edible. It's a long process of drawing the bitterness out first by soaking them in water, and then packing them in salt. This is not something I've ever done before, but I'm quite excited to try. And then I'll be eating olives every day. They're very high in protein, I'm told. They could almost replace meat.

Meat, at 11 euro per kilo, is a luxury I'm learning to do without – except on special occasions. Ditto for fancy ingredients like salami or those precious frozen prawns. As a comfort eater, I can only hope there isn't too much I'll need comforting from in the next couple of months. Frozen pizza, which has been used, in desperation, to curb my cravings for the real thing, has proven to be a luxury item as well, priced at four euro and twenty cents for a Margarita that tastes, mostly, of nothing at all. My attempts at homemade pizza dough have so far been 50% successful, on account of being cocky the second time around, and too stingy with the yeast, which meant my dough failed to rise. I ate it anyway. But Eleni has left me a couple of sachets of yeast, imported from Italy no less, and bought me a rolling pin when she caught me rolling out my dough with an empty jam jar, so I'm feeling hopeful on the pizza front.

Waste not, want not. Even potato peelings and onion skins and other such by-products of cooking are put to use as compost; I have taken to digging holes randomly in the garden and throwing them in, on the premise that they will improve the soil. I have no idea if this actually works, but it makes me feel all practical and at one with the earth and stuff, so I'll keep doing it. (Please nobody give me tips on home composting. I appreciate your kindness, but I'm really not that keen.)

The terror of having no income is too big to live in my stomach or my chest. It's the elephant in the room that I have learned to ignore while I go round chasing flies with my swatter. I live with it every day, and it hardly bothers me at all. It's very polite, except when it wants to make its presence known. And then it doesn't employ any time wasting passive-aggressive techniques, but marches straight up to me and whacks me across the face with its trunk. Or it sits on me. An elephant sitting on you is not so easy to ignore. It's very motivating, if nothing else. It makes it incredibly hard to breathe, but I do appreciate a straightforward approach. I like to know where I stand.

I stand here, next to my elephant, with a fly swatter in my hand and a generous supply of aubergines and edible weeds. I am very restricted in what I can do (and eat), yet I am free as I've never been before. I am terrified, but I'm not in the least bit stressed. Do you remember what that feels like? It's wonderful.

I'm not advocating the "no income" method as a viable choice for everyone; it's a very hard lifestyle to sustain, and the aubergines are bound to run out at some point. But there are many other ways to terrify yourself and find your freedom. And once you do, from this new angle, you will look at the terror straight on and see that it's a lot less terrifying than you imagined when you stood with your back to it, resolutely looking away. And you will stand by your elephant and put your arms around him, and ride him all the way to wherever you want to be.

I have to be honest with you, however: for all my big talk of freedom, some shackles can never be broken, and I will remain a slave to food for all my life. I'm happy to go along with this frugal existence for as long as it takes, but once I'm back in London and there's some money in my pocket, I'm dragging that ball and chain straight up to Angel, to eat the largest, spiciest burrito known to man. And then over to GBK for a burger and chips. And then perhaps I'll stop by M&S to pick up a bag of crisps for the way home.

# Day 22

Antagonist is back with a vengeance. She'd been away for a few days – I don't know where, and I didn't ask – but she returned last night and I could tell, as soon as I saw her, that she wasn't gonna be pleasant. She walked straight into my bedroom and accused me of being an impostor.

It was just after I'd read a lovely email, sent through the blog, by a girl in London who told me that my writing kept her company through the long, sleepless nights of new motherhood. It made me smile; it made me feel a lot of things that I can't quite put into words, because they're still so new to me. I was in bed already, and I was about to turn the light off on the day, and on that happy note, when Antagonist strolled in. She perched on the end of my bed and made a point of not looking at me. I waited for a while, and then I picked up my book and pretended to read.

'I see you're wearing ankle socks,' she said, breaking the silence. My feet were sticking out from the bottom of the blanket. I wriggled my toes.

'Yes,' I confirmed.

'Getting cold, are we?' she said, with obvious delight.

'A little,' I admitted meekly. 'But people are sending me socks and –'

'Yes, yes, socks and goodie bags and all kinds of nonsense. Aren't we popular.'

'No!' I stammered. 'I mean, it's really kind...'

'Kind!' she snorted. 'Stupid, more like. Being taken in by all this.' She made a sweeping gesture, drawing a circle with me at its centre.

'What do you mean?'

'You! Pretending you're a writer. Fooling all these people into reading your crap. Giving you their money! It's ridiculous!' She paused, gave me a twisted little smile, and lay back on my bed with her hands clasped behind her head. I sat up to make space for her, and hugged my knees to my chest.

'Does any of it make sense to you?' she continued, ponderously, gazing up at the ceiling. 'Have you fallen for your own hype?'

She propped herself up on her elbows and fixed me with her cruellest stare yet.

'Think about it,' she said. 'What exactly have you done to earn all this?'

I know I shouldn't let her get to me, but it's hard. She really knows her shit. Maybe she went away on a special seminar on how to crush my soul in new and inventive ways. Or a boot camp for bullies, helping them hone their skills. Whichever the case, she is very, very good at what she does. And what she does is finish off what I started. Because I don't need Antagonist to put me down; I'm perfectly capable of doing it myself.

Because I *have* thought about it, and it makes no sense at all. I am living a life that's completely new. I'm writing every day and strangers are sending me messages of support. People are sending me socks to keep my feet warm, so that I can stay here and succeed in what I'm doing. Of course it's ridiculous; it's completely unheard of! And I can't help but think, sometimes, when self-doubt gets the best of me, that it won't be long before I get found out. That it's only a matter of time before all these good people realise I'm just some girl on an island, writing some words, and I don't deserve any of this – their generosity, their support, their kindness, their warm socks; it's only a matter of time before I let them all down. That's why Antagonist is so effective, because in everything she says there is a little bit of truth. That must have been an excellent course she went on.

I couldn't think of what to say to her, how to offer any sort of defence. So I just sat there, with my knees pressed against my chest, saying nothing and staring at my hands, until she got bored and went away. And then I spread my legs out, tentatively, and went to sleep.

I shouldn't let her get to me, but her words still stung this morning. So I did some yoga. I did a coward's version of a handstand – feet up against the wall – to gain a different perspective, as my sister suggested. I pressed my forehead firmly against the floor in child's pose; I breathed deeply, in and out. I said my *Namaste* and thank you, and then maintained, several times, that *we're halfway there* and threw myself about to the rhythm of Bon Jovi's guitar. I brought this ritual to a close with a bit of Rage Against The Machine, for good measure. I felt a little better.

I was ready, now, to face Antagonist but, of course, she was nowhere to be found. I think she disappeared around about the time I started screaming *fuck you, I won't do what you tell me* and waving my arms around in her vicinity. She's a coward, like bullies tend to be. Also, she really doesn't like Rage Against The Machine.

But if she were here, this is what I'd say to her: It doesn't have to make sense. Sometimes crazy, impossible things stumble into being, and they make no sense at all. This is one of them. Writing is one of them. For all of the insecurity that's inherent in this thing I've chosen to do, there are times when I write something and I read it back to myself and I think, yes, OK, that's kind of good. Sometimes I recognise, reluctantly, that a rare, magical thing has happened, whereby these words I wrote, these words that are available to everyone, somehow became mine for a while, and I made them into something that people want to read. And that's nothing short of miraculous.

I'm not being modest, merely stating a fact. It's some crazy alchemy that allows this to happen, and I never take it for granted. Every time it happens, there is a moment of euphoria, a moment of perfect fulfilment, perfect peace. And then immediately after comes the fear. Because there is absolutely no guarantee that I can ever do it again. This might be the last time I write something worth reading. Every time might be the last.

So maybe I am an impostor and maybe I'll let people down, in that I've managed to pull this off so far, I did it yesterday and I'll do it today, but maybe tomorrow the words will not allow me to claim them for my own, and I will write something that no one wants to read. Or I will write nothing at all.

But if my writing kept someone company through one night, if it made someone laugh on their way to work, if it made them think, or cry, or do something slightly differently because they found some meaning in what I wrote – if any of that has happened even once, that's plenty already. The socks are an added bonus, and they just speak for other people's kindness, and make no comment on my popularity, or my talent, or anything I may or may not have earned. But I want to earn this kindness that's been given me, and I know of no other way than to carry on doing what I do. I want to deserve it.

But there is no hype, and I'm fooling no one; least of all myself. I'm just some girl on an island, writing some words, and it just so happens that I'm telling a story that people want to hear. For now. And I hope no one expects anything more miraculous from me than this, this daily attempt to make those words mean something. Because this I can promise you. In this, I will not let you down. And that's as far as my pretensions go.

# Day 23

Yesterday was a hard day.

It was the third day running that I woke up with a BowTech headache (they have arrived, without fail, on the day after each one of my three sessions so far), which no amount of my mumbo jumbo, "massage your temples and sniff this oil and trust in the universe" cures can shift, and it was really starting to get to me. The weather had been an obnoxious bastard for four days straight, four days of dull dawns and cloudy afternoons and gloomy, starless evenings, of rain and the threat of rain and the clouds of rain huddling around the sun like a rugby team. The humidity that everyone's been warning me about crept into the house, unnoticed, like a cat, and the remedy, opening the windows to draw it out, would only have resulted in more broken glass and another desperate appeal to the carpenter, with the wind having scored a mighty 9 on the Beaufort scale ("strong gale"). And the howling. I've used that expression before, casually, in conversation, *the howling wind*, but I'd never met the truth of it until now. I say "met" because this isn't weather, it's an actual, physical presence, and it really does howl. And howling I associate with wolves, which are very high on my list of phobias (jostling with cockroaches for the top spot, in fact), and though I know there are no wolves in Sifnos, I still can't help imagining a pack of them lurking outside my door. I tell myself to stop being a baby, but leave all the outside lights on at night.

And it was cold. Not ankle socks cold but put the heating on cold. Which I did, very reluctantly, and actually looking over my shoulder lest someone noticed and took this as yet another admission of defeat. The heater ticked into life and the house filled with that stale radiator smell that invokes winter like nothing else can.

Images of hats (which I don't have) and gloves (ditto) danced before my eyes, woolly harbingers of an evil yet to come. Which markedly did not improve my mood.

And as for cats creeping in, that happened too. I'd propped the front door open for a few minutes, and the neighbour's cat snuck in, and the first I knew about it was when she decided to press herself against my leg. I screamed and jumped and then the two of us fled in opposite directions. The momentum took me as far as the bedroom, where my brain finally caught up and, feeling very foolish, I came back out into the kitchen to find the cat standing in the doorway, looking thoroughly pissed off. She regarded me in a way that clearly conveyed the sentiment *What the fuck*.

'I'm sorry,' I told her. 'You snuck up on me. You can come back in.'

She conceded to do so, and took a leisurely stroll around the house, sniffing a selection of furniture items, while I entertained fantasies of her curling up on the sofa, purring gently, and keeping me company as I wrote. But of course she was straight out the door as soon as she realised I wasn't about to feed her.

Also, it was a Monday and though the days of the week mean very little to me now, I think some echo of the Monday Blues, the cumulative force of half the planet's discontent, still reached me here, in my workweek-free cocoon.

Cold, alone, confined to the house, blighted by headaches, terrorised by wolves and rejected by cats. And really struggling with my piece for the day, which wasn't helped by Antagonist going round leaving post-it notes with the word "impostor" in calligraphic script all over the place. It was hard.

It got better. I called Margarita to make an appointment for a haircut, as promised. She sounded surprised when I told her I was in urgent need of her help.

'You're still here?' she said.

I confirmed that I was, and she booked me in at 4:30.
I spent a very pleasant hour in her chair, as she
patiently dealt with the tragedy that poses as my hair,
and dispensed wisdom on essential items for getting
through the winter.

'If you have some money,' she began.

I shook my head emphatically, nearly losing an eye
to her scissors.

'If you *did* have some money,' she revised, 'you would
get a dehumidifier.' She held my head in place so I didn't
start shaking it again. 'Otherwise, you've gotta keep
airing the house. Get a draught going. Especially,' she
added cryptically, 'when the wind changes.'

'Electric blanket,' she offered later. 'If you only get
one thing.'

'But aren't they dangerous?' Eileen had warned me
of their propensity for bursting into flame. Thankfully
not while containing one's child.

'You turn it on one hour before bedtime. And turn it
off before you go to bed. Yes,' she concluded, 'forget the
dehumidifier. An electric blanket is what you need.'

I just cannot get away from those things.

We talked about what I was doing, and I amused her
with tales of socks being shipped from the UK. She asked
how I spent my days, and showed genuine concern
regarding the conditions of life up in my godforsaken
village. (Which is less than ten minutes away from
where we stood, but Margarita is a woman of town.)
Were there enough streetlights? Did I have a torch? I
should get a torch. Was there anyone around in the
neighbourhood? Would they help me if I needed help?
Was I eating enough? And did I go out at night?

I said no to that one.

'What, never? Not for a drink?'

'No. I have no one to go for a drink with.'

She paused, scissors aloft, and gently patted down a
rebellious tuft of my hair.

'You can come here for coffee,' she said.

She is a lovely woman, who cut my hair beautifully, mercifully short, so it won't trouble me for another month or so, and I'll really miss her and her excellent haircuts when I'm back in London, subjected, once again, to grumpy, over-styled teenagers who charge you £40 for the privilege of pointedly ignoring all of your instructions and giving you the layers you have expressly said you do not want. Margarita charged me €12, told me off when I tried to leave her a tip, and then asked me to write my name down before I left, so she could look me up on facebook.

At 10pm, after I'd spent four hours boiling and stirring and adding water to a stew of white beans that refused, point blank, to become edible (What is *up* with beans? Seriously.), I was saved by Christina, Eleni's sister, who called to tell me she had arrived in Sifnos and had brought supplies from my mum. She suggested we go for dinner, so I gave up on my stew and met her in town. We had pork souvlaki and chips, and then another portion of chips, and wine (Christina) and cigarettes (me), and a very lovely evening, which also served as my full quota of a social life for the week.

I came back home just before 1, to find that I had four new backers on kickstarter. As well two pairs of jeans, two thick, woolly jumpers, two pairs of leggings, and two pairs of socks – a Noah's Ark of essential clothing items, courtesy of my mum. I went to sleep happy, in socks that reached halfway up my shins. Respectable socks.

Today was good, too. I woke up with a headache again, but the sun was out. The wind was still going, but it had been demoted to a mere 6 or 7 ("strong breeze" / "high wind, moderate gale), so I opened all the windows, and the house felt fresh again. I killed the headache with Advil. I did yoga on the balcony. I fed my favourite of the three cats. (Not to the exclusion of the others; he was the only one around.) I finally did the laundry that had been collecting for days, on account of the weather conditions, and hung it out to dry. By the afternoon, the wind had died down to a gentle breeze. I had coffee and a couple of biscuits, sitting on the ledge in the sunshine. I had a chat with the neighbour over the wall from our respective yards, and it wasn't as excruciating as normal; old age and her bad hip only came up once. I watched the neighbour's cat's kittens playing for a while (though, to be fair, they mostly stumble into each other, fall over, and squeak).

But here is the best part: Just before dusk, I went over to the organic farm, on the off change that Nikos would be there, and I could buy some vegetables. (You normally buy your veg by appointment, but I didn't have his number). Nikos was there indeed, but he was leaving.

'I'm about to go meet the girls for basketball,' he explained. 'What do you need?'

'I don't know,' I replied helpfully. 'Some stuff?'

'I'll tell you what,' he said. 'I'll get you a bag and a pair of scissors, and you can help yourself.'

I've met the dude exactly twice before. But he waved my protests away, handed me the tools of the trade and off he went to meet his wife and daughters.

So I spent an hour exploring Nikos' crazy garden of delights, where vegetables grow in raised mounds rather than flat beds, and are all mixed up together, onions next to strawberries next to carrots next to giant silvery cabbages, and every mound features at least one tomato bush and a random sprinkling of flowers. I found the rocket amidst some orange blooms. I picked about a million tomatoes, of all shapes and sizes, sampling them as I went. I filled my bag to bursting with strange silver-green pointed leaves, similar to kale, which are apparently some type of New Zealand cabbage. I also found a single red chilli pepper, clearly destined to be mine. Nikos came running back at some point – he'd forgotten his daughter's bike – and found me bent over the rocket patch.

'I am so happy right now,' I gushed. 'I'm having the best time ever.'

'That's why I told you to do this,' he said with a smile. 'Psychotherapy.'

He was right: there was something incredibly soothing in being there, kneeling down on the soil, rummaging through foliage in search of chillies, picking vegetables with my hands. I can't imagine having any worries in a place like this; they'd get lost amidst the tangle of vegetables and flowers, and they'd never reach you.

Nikos stood and watched me for a moment, nodded, and was gone again. As I dropped the scissors off outside his door, I could hear them in the distance, at the basketball court down the hill: the ball bouncing against the floor, and the high-pitched shrieks and laughter of his girls. And this is a man who recently lost his main source of income: the restaurant he took over and opened this summer was shut down by the council, just as the tourist season kicked in, due to a licensing issue that he'd inherited from the previous owner. And yet he'll give a girl free psychotherapy and vegetables on credit, on his way to play basketball with his daughters, with a bicycle dangling over one arm.

And now I'm home and, after an additional two hours of boiling the crap out of it, my bean stew is finally, hopefully, ready to eat. So I will serve myself a generous portion and eat it slowly while I contemplate what to do with two kilos of tomatoes and whole tableful of leaves.

With all that soothing, I might have gotten a bit carried away.

# Day 24

October. This is officially uncharted territory now. I'd been here in September before, in its early days when summer still holds, but never in October or any month, in fact, between now and April.

I came in early April once. It must have been my last year of school, or the first year of university, circa 1996-97. The Easter holidays. We used to come for Easter often when I was growing up, the entire family packed tight in the car along with an inordinate amount of luggage and supplies, my sisters and I variably elbowing and kicking each other in the back seat all the way to the port, and then fighting over the bunk beds in our cabin and sticking smelly feet in each other's faces, as my mum and stepdad tried to come up with games to keep us entertained through the six and a half hour journey.

The Easter trips gradually became more and more infrequent, and at this stage we hadn't been for years, but I had happy, hazy memories of springtime Sifnos, of staying up late to attend the Good Saturday service and letting off fire crackers with the local kids in the churchyard at midnight. So I suggested to Aliki that the two of us go, and she agreed.

It was a mistake. We arrived in the afternoon, and it was bright and warm, and the air had the freshness of early spring. But in the house, winter lingered. I hadn't thought to ask our neighbour, Vangelia, to air it, as my mum normally did before we arrived; it never occurred to me. Aliki and I walked in, all smiles and dreams of our cosy escapade, and the cold was lurking behind the door and ambushed us and went straight into our bones. Everything was damp. *Everything.* Even the floor tiles had a sheen to them, as if they'd just been mopped. We sniffed the air suspiciously (damp) and tentatively patted various surfaces (damp). We opened the windows and took out some bedding that, on account of being folded up in the cupboard since last August, had graduated from damp to practically wet. A sense of foreboding began to infuse our naïve vision of this holiday, and we looked at each other in apprehension.

'It'll be alright, won't it?' one of us said.

'Of course it will,' said the other.

It wasn't.

It got worse. There wasn't enough day left to drive the winter out of a house that had been closed up for seven months, and as night fell the open windows only drew in more humidity from the air outside. Desperately cold and completely defeated by now, Aliki and I had given up on trying to save ourselves and submitted to our fate, and the evening found us sitting with our feet up on the single electric radiator, huddled together under a damp blanket, shivering and snivelling like babies. Eventually we realised we had to move or die, of despair if not pneumonia, and we layered up our inadequate, damp clothes and went into town.

Where everything was shut, and not a soul was to be encountered on the streets. Even the hotel was in darkness. We wandered around aimlessly, trying to get warm, until, like an oasis, we beheld the glow of the grill in the souvlaki restaurant. It was a tiny shop, with a single table inside, but it was open. We walked in, basked in the warmth of cooking meat for a moment, and then burst into tears. The owner, Katerina, who I knew vaguely from having purchased food from her on many a drunken summer night, looked up in alarm.

'Girls!' she said. 'Girls! What is it?' She came out from behind the counter and put her arms around us. 'What's wrong?'

But her kindness only made us cry even harder, and we were unable to speak.

'Sit down!' she commanded, indicating the only two chairs. 'Stop crying and tell me what's going on.'

We did as we were told and, eventually, amidst sobs, Aliki and I managed to convey our tale.

'Ooh,' she commented, shaking her head. 'That was a bad idea. You never ever go into a closed up house without airing it first!' Which was advice we could have used before deciding to arrive on the spur of the moment, but Aliki and I nodded remorsefully nevertheless, and promptly burst into another round of tears. Just thinking about that damp house was enough to set us off.

'Right,' Katerina said assertively. 'Let me sort this out.'

She picked up the phone and dialled the hotel.

'Stavros,' she said, listen. I have two girls here with a humidity issue and nowhere to stay. Will you please open up a room for them for the night because they're crying in my shop?' A pause. 'Thanks.'

She put the phone down. 'Give it ten minutes,' she said, and fed us chips while we waited.

Needless to say, Aliki and I were on the first boat out of there the next day. And I have not attempted another off season visit since. I stick to summer, and always make sure the house has been thoroughly aired well before I arrive.

I've seen Katerina many times in the intervening years, but she's never mentioned this incident; I don't know if she even remembers, but I will never forget how she saved us. And no matter how many souvlaki joints open on the island, and how highly recommended they come, I only ever go to hers. That's where Christina and I went the other night. They've moved to larger premises with many tables, inside and out, and they have a fancy printed menu now, but the people are the same, and they have my souvlaki loyalty forever.

And here I am now, in October, with November and December still to come, with cautionary tales of humidity being offered from all directions, and with crying in a restaurant as my only precedent for what might be in store.

October: breezy, sunny, relatively warm; the windows are open. A crew of two men is doing work on the exterior of the church; their voices and the clanging of their stepladder carry over in perfect clarity. The boy cat, my favourite, is lounging on the flagstones in the patio. His eyes are closed and he looks very relaxed. I go outside to collect the clothes off the drying racks. The neighbour comes out, muttering to herself as she bends over a flowerbed. She swears at invisible adversaries – *Oh, you're here as well? Go to hell!* – and waves a tea towel about. Sometimes, in the summer, she comes out in only her knickers, huge off-white things that reach up to her chest. She forgets that we're there, living, as she does, in true, permanent solitude for ten months of the year. I've been spared these displays now, on account of being here for so long, and of the cold. The bees are buzzing in the rosemary bush. I watch the boy cat spring up, dive into my peppermint and emerge, triumphant, with something large and green in his mouth, which he proceeds to chew on contentedly. I take a moment to be grateful for cats: that thing, whatever it was, could be hopping its way into my house at any given moment. The boy cat is my favourite because he is very polite. As the other two screech and scramble for my attention and whatever food I can give them, he just sits a little further away, looking semi-terrified and hopeful. He's a very large cat and he could take those pushy girls, no problem, but he always lets them eat first. He doesn't trust me yet, not completely, but I'm working on him.

October's alright so far. I greet it politely, semi-terrified but hopeful that none of the days and weeks to come will send me, whimpering, out onto the streets looking to be saved. But if it does happen, at least I know now where to go. And have a nice, big portion of handcut chips, too, while I'm there.

# Day 25

Round two with Antagonist, in the kitchen. I was doing the dishes, and she pulled up a chair, placed her elbows on the dining table and started drumming her fingers against the wood. Tap-tap-tap. I ignored her. There was no preamble this time. She didn't even bother to criticise my appearance; she went straight for the kill.

'Not talking to me then? No, of course not, you have better things to do.'

'Leave me alone,' I whispered, half hoping she wouldn't hear.

She heard. 'Oh! You want to be left alone now, do you? Getting tired of all the attention?'

I made no response.

'Yes, I suppose it must be exhausting, being so important and all,' she said reflectively, as if to herself. Tap-tap-tap went her fingers. And then stopped, abruptly.

'I have a question,' she began. I made the mistake of turning around then, sponge in hand. She gave a vicious but entirely genuine smile. She enunciated very clearly: 'Who the fuck do you think you are?'

It's a good question. Eleni and I talked about this, a couple of weeks ago. I have a habit of greeting any animals I come across – mostly cats, but also dogs and donkeys and sheep, if I meet any – with the question "Who are *you*, then?" They don't often reply. In most cases they run off, alarmed by the unsolicited attention, pausing only to cast bewildered looks at me over their shoulders, to make sure I'm not following them. I don't take it personally; you can't make friends with everyone.

'But that's a really hard question,' Eleni remarked, when I made this enquiry of a cat licking itself enthusiastically in the middle of the road. 'I mean, how would *you* answer that?'

'I'm not being existential,' I said. 'I'm only asking for an introduction.'

Eleni laughed.

'Besides,' I added, 'it can't be that hard for them. Look.' I pointed to the cat, which hadn't run off, and was now lost in an ecstasy of scratching its ear. 'I am cat.'

Another habit of mine is to use the word "pussycat" in situations that people find baffling. This term is not exclusive to cats but can be applied to any creature, humans included, that I find particularly cute and likeable. The most recent case featured a donkey. He was cute, and came up to me and let me put my hand on his muzzle.

'You're not a donkey,' I told him. 'You're a pussycat. Yes you are.'

Eleni, who was witness to this exchange as well, was beside herself. 'You're not a donkey!' she kept repeating, dissolving into a fit of giggles every time. It took her a while to recover, but when she did, she admonished me for giving the donkey an identity crisis.

Who the fuck do I think I am? How do you answer that, ever? I am one giant identity crisis but, then again, aren't we all? We are an amalgam of origins and wrong turns and destinations, of adjectives and expectations, of everything we've been to other people and everything we could be to ourselves, if and when and someday, soon; of the stories that we tell and the stories told about us, of the things we like and dislike and would like to be good at, and our failures; of roles inherited or chosen or earned, certificates, degrees, job titles and labels and definitions. Which is another thing I talked about recently, in an email exchange with Theodora: how it's the labelling that gets us into trouble. She pointed out, very wisely, that the Antagonists in our lives love labels, those neat, capitalised definitions that put us in our designated little boxes and make us excellent and defenceless targets. She's right. I had an Antagonist in the form of a boyfriend once, who took great pleasure in informing me that I wasn't a Writer, I was a Translator, and kicking me as I sat in my box, trying to work out how to get out. Was that what I did to the donkey? Was Eleni right? I meant it as a compliment, and, besides, I feel fairly certain that the donkey doesn't care one bit whether he's described as donkey or pussycat or vending machine. But I cared. The box labelled Girlfriend was vacated relatively soon after that, but I didn't write a thing for years.

Who the fuck do I think I am? I put it all together, the boxes and the labels and the ex-boyfriend and the existential cat and the donkey who'll carry on being a donkey no matter what I say, and I put my sponge down and walked to the other side of the table where Antagonist sat, and stood over her and offered her my hand.

'I'm Daphne,' I said. As if that had been her question.

She looked at my face in bewilderment and then at my hand in disgust.

'I'm not touching that,' she said. 'It's covered in slime!'

It was washing up liquid, actually, but I thought I'd let that go. I wiped my hand on my shorts and offered it again.

She took it, without a word.

I went back to my washing up and when I turned around again she was gone. I have a feeling she's looking up advanced bullying courses online as we speak. I'm gonna pay for this, I know, but it was worth it.

I'm Daphne. I am a cat person, but not much of a pussycat, unless you really, really like me. And I hope that'll do for now, by way of introduction. Let's leave the existential stuff to the cats.

# Day 26

Several people have suggested I have a Sifnos romance. There are numerous variations on how this would play out, but they all share a common theme:

A manly man, rugged and handsome in a rural kind of way; at one with the earth and the elements, wise in the ways of island life and good with his hands; strong and fearless but not macho, with a sensitive, intellectual side that he reveals in unexpected moments; principled and traditional – he knows how to treat a lady – but modern enough to take photos of said lady and post them, proudly, on facebook. He can be found occupied in some vague and rural manner on the fields, often with a book of poetry poking out from the back pocket of his jeans.

*I walk across the fields in search of wild oregano. I encounter a rugged, handsome man doing something rustic and important with a spade. Our eyes meet; the attraction is instant. He offers to read me some poetry and I submit, laying back in his strong arms, as dusk falls. We have some romance. He brings me bunches of fresh oregano, and shares poem excerpts on my facebook page.*

*I walk past the fields, on my way to the supermarket. I notice a rugged, handsome man doing something strange and elaborate with a shovel. I am intrigued; I approach and ask him what he's doing. He explains in a gruff but eloquent manner as he demonstrates. I am mesmerised by his passion and his strong arms. We have some romance. He sends me links to videos relating to his strange and elaborate occupation on facebook.*

94

*I stroll through the fields, and I am wearing ankle socks. I have not noticed the rugged, handsome man doing something rural and laborious with a plough, but he notices the deadly snake as it slithers its way to me. Before I know it, he has crushed it with his killing stick, and gathered me in his strong arms. We have some romance. He updates his facebook status with a philosophical quote about destiny, and tags me.*

*I cross the fields on my way home. I chance upon a rugged, handsome man engaged in some vague and essential way with a donkey. I approach and ask to be introduced. 'This is donkey,' the man says, and goes on to explain how donkeys have very gentle souls. He puts his strong arms around the donkey's neck, and reads me a poem he wrote earlier, on the topic of donkeys and their souls. I am captivated. We have some romance. He takes a photo of me and the donkey on his android, and makes it his cover photo on facebook.*

*I am lost in the fields, and night is falling. A rugged, handsome man abandons his manly and mysterious occupation to offer me his help. I fall, weeping with gratitude, into his strong arms and he guides me to safety. We have some romance. He posts on my facebook timeline: "You will never be lost again".*

Another thing all of these scenarios have in common (quite apart from a fixation with strong arms, which seem to be essential in the pursuing of a Sifnos romance) is a fatal flaw in their most fundamental presumption: the rugged, handsome man with the hands of a farmer and a poet's soul does not exist. I could roam the fields day in, day out, for the next 74 days precisely, but he would never be found.

This is a selection of the men I'm actually likely to encounter:

**Manolis**, the neighbour's son. Mid fifties, chubby. Enjoys wearing army fatigues and hanging out with his mother. Married, no children.

**Takis**, owner of restaurant, donkey and neighbouring field. Late fifties, balding, on the short side. Has unlimited access to lamb chops and chips. Married; not sure about children.

**Simos**, Vangelia's son, owner of hardware store. Mid forties, well fed. The man to call upon when you need a window smashed. Attached.

**Leonidas**, the taxi driver. Late fifties, semi-bald, very charming. Reads the weather and dispenses essential advice. Married, with grown-up children and grandchildren.

**Vangelis**, son of Leonidas, also a taxi driver. Age 24, rosy-cheeked and large. Very patient when driving my grandmother. Attached.

**Makis**, the carpenter. Mid forties, tall, pronounced handsome by the older generations of females in my family. Handy with power tools. Very relaxed sense of urgency and punctuality. Married, with children.

**Antonis**, the plumber. Early fifties. Pleasantly dishevelled in appearance, pleasantly sarcastic in personality. Very helpful when you've forgotten The Rules and flushed paper down the toilet. Married, with children.

**Post office dude**. Mid forties, bearded, friendly. Can generally be found relaxing with his feet up on the counter. Marital status unknown.

**Antonis**, the butcher, and the plumber's cousin. Early fifties, tall, impressive moustache. Often seen yielding a meat cleaver. Married, with grown-up children.

**Local crazy man**. Early fifties. Crazy looking. Wears three quarter length trousers and a captain's hat and enjoys being crazy in various locations across the island. Presumably single.

It's not looking good. But even if the fields of Sifnos were teeming with rugged, handsome men whose only ambition in life was to enfold me in their strong arms and read me poetry, the Sifnos romance fantasies would still never come to pass. Because what they all fail to take into account is the fact that I'm not available for romance. The part of me responsible for that sort of thing was long ago given to a particular man (who, in the interest of avoiding labels, will simply be known as M), and he has not given it back. Nor am I asking for it. He is not particularly rugged, and has never read me poetry.

He is handsome, however, and he does have strong arms. I have a shovel in the garden. Perhaps, if I could bring him over, hand him the shovel and get him to stand in Takis' field and look rural, we might be getting somewhere. There might just be some Sifnos romance yet.

# Day 27

My one-time boyfriend was wrong. He was wrong on many counts, but very manifestly on one topic in particular: I am not a translator.

When I quit my job as a yoga centre supervisor back in May, to embark upon four months of writing, I wasn't relying entirely on my savings and the kindness of the universe. I had a back up. I had been working as a freelance translator for the past seven years and though I was no longer doing it full-time, I still had a decent income from it. On an average month, I could earn between £300 and £800, in addition to my salary. The work was by no means guaranteed, but it did tend to arrive consistently enough, sometimes even to the point where I struggled to get through it, with 30 hours of translations added to my regular 40-hour week. So as big as it was, giving up my job and my life in London for a dream, I was fairly confident I wasn't going to starve. My savings and my freelance income would see me through to September, when I would return to London and get back onto my hamster wheel.

But the universe works in mysterious ways indeed, and as soon as I had done my final hour as a gainfully employed person, the translation work completely dried up. I didn't notice it at straight away; the first few weeks back in Greece went by in a haze, with me trying to adjust to a whole new reality, missing my friends in London and catching up with the ones in Athens. But as the weeks passed and no work arrived, a tiny seed of fear was planted and grew, in direct proportion to my ever-dwindling savings. It was a fear that was strangely dull, impotent almost; a lot more acute was the sense that I had been expecting it, that I had known this would happen all along. Even as I made decisions based on the relative certainty of this work, I had known. This wasn't a sensible move I'd made, it was a risky one, an all-or-nothing leap of faith, and it appears the universe took steps to ensure the ground below was clear of any bouncy surfaces. Faith, as it turns out, is a standalone thing; it doesn't come with securities. Or a cosy bit of income on the side, to tide you over in case your investment in it doesn't pay off. I told myself not to be paranoid, but I was right: in the months of May, June, July and August, I earned a grand total of £240. In the absence of other options, I decided to be amused by the situation and, with a wry smile and a nod to fate, slowly, to accept it.

By the end of August, when I began to contemplate staying here for the next few months, I was completely at peace with my lack of income and near-destitution. And when I made my decision this time, I did it knowing that there would be no money coming in, and I'd just have to wing it. The universe had been kind, after all, and provided a steady trickle of cash in the form of massage clients (though Eleni, who did my PR all over the island, had more than a hand in this, actually bodily assaulting people on several occasions, and informing them they needed my services), proving the adage about doors closing and opening, in some endless dance of cause and effect. And it showed me the truth of what I'd begun to understand: that it's no use trying to pile new stuff on top of the old; it'll all just topple over. You need to make space for the things you want – and I had plenty of space.

And then, last week, the work started coming in. And instead of the relief that any sensible person in my position would experience, all I felt was resentment. And another prickly, uncomfortable sensation that made my jaw tight and the breath catch in my chest, and it was so familiar that it took me a while to recognise it for what it was. Stress. And I realised, with sudden, shocking clarity, that I really had not been stressed for weeks. I have been scared, and upset, and worried and frustrated – all real, functional emotions, corresponding to actual situations and events – but I had felt no stress. And all it took was a couple of emails, innocently labelled "Texts for translation" but which, in my mind, appeared as OBLIGATIONS!, and I was back exactly where I started. It did occur to me, fleetingly, that this might be the universe testing me, throwing me a bone to see whether I would go for it and abandon my principles, or stand my ground. But my principles include, for better or for worse, a fairly strong work ethic, and I cannot let these people down. It's not their fault: it's just a case of mistaken identity. I'm not a translator, but they weren't to know.

So I'll do the translations, this time, but maybe next time I won't pick up that bone. Because I can't go back to where I started, and I will stand this ground I've claimed. I will protect it with everything I have, even if that means giving up jobs over and over again. I'll leave the space open, and I'll wing it.

I'm not a translator. When my ex accused me of that, he was failing – deliberately – to make a distinction between what we are and what we do. But sometimes, if we're lucky, what we are and what we do coincide, and what I'm doing right now is writing. It's all I want to do. And there's a petty part of me that wants to seek him out and tell him he was wrong but, actually, I have neither the time nor the inclination: I'm too busy doing what I am. Being what I do.

# Day 28

Living here, on my holiday island, off season is a bit like being a member of a secret club. Actually, no: it's like *applying* to be a member of a secret club. Membership is not automatic, and it's not open to everyone. There is a process. There are criteria for eligibility. There might even be tasks you have to complete, like when you join a fraternity as a pledge, to prove your worth. Or a sorority, in my case. Do sororities put their pledges through torture, too? I haven't seen any films about that. It's a frightening thought: girls are mean.

The locals have always been friendly, but it's a friendliness that only goes so far; it falls short of friendship. My family and I are accepted, to an extent, by virtue of having been around since the sixties, three generations making this island their summer home. We are greeted by name, and given eggs and cheese and vegetables from their gardens; we exchange gifts and neighbourhood gossip and the obligatory coffee and cake visits at the beginning and the end of our holidays. The honour of *You're alright, for Athenians* was bestowed upon us, unanimously, long ago. But we exist on the fringes of the community, at best; we are still seasonal people, and there are twelve months in the year.

So, as a pledge for the Secret Club of off season Sifnos, I may have one foot in the door, but the rest of me is still outside, and I've a long way to go before they let me in. In support of my application, I would like to mention certain parallels I've drawn between hardships that I've endured and low-scale hazing techniques that fraternities reportedly employ in the process of establishing a candidate's worth. It is my understanding (based entirely on bad American films from the nineties) that pledges are often required to dress in ridiculous outfits, and I am pleased to report I'm good on that score, and can add ridiculous hair to strengthen my position. Involuntary sleep deprivation has been thrust upon me on several occasions, thanks to donkey noises, flies, and the wind doing its pack-of-wolves impression. As for pledges sometimes having to go without showers, I must admit to a certain 24-hour period when there was very little contact between myself and running water. But I had done nothing physically strenuous, and I did not set foot outside the house, except to feed the cats, so I did not see the need. There has been no binge drinking, but there has been binge eating of aubergines, and that must count for something.

Nobody's tried to pee on me yet, thankfully (I'm under the impression fraternities do that a lot), although the peeing-on-the-street tale that Yiannis shared with me might be an indication of what's ultimately required in order to belong.

In fact, I now strongly suspect there was nothing accidental in this ostensibly casual narrative, and that Yiannis is actually a member of the Board of the Secret Club, tasked with carrying out preliminary checks on potential pledges, on account of his jolly and approachable personality and the strategic position of his shop, bang in the middle of town.

I further suspect that the oft-mentioned electric blanket is much more than a useful piece of equipment to keep you warm at night: it is a symbol, intrinsically linked to membership of the Secret Club itself. They would probably have it as their insignia, if only it were a bit more visually enticing. And it is not about drawing the humidity out of your mattress; it is about *commitment*. Owning an electric blanket proves that you are serious about staying around, long term, and dedicated enough to procure and invest in said item. Which would explain why everyone is so vague as to where I might get one. It's a test.

And, thinking about it, I'm sure the church festivals are not innocent either. Perhaps that's where the initiation rites take place, after the pledges, in their silly outfits, have consumed several shots of the ceremonial homebrew and a bowl of chickpea soup, and joined in the fevered steps of a complicated dance ritual that they don't yet understand.

I think I may have passed the initial assessment. Yiannis must have reported that I displayed neither shock nor disgust at the peeing tale and was, in fact, actively amused. He must have noticed the glint in my eyes that betrayed an openness to the weird and wonderful things I might experience as an off season resident of Sifnos, if not my natural predisposition to straight-out weirdness. I think he approved; he may have put in a good word with the Board.

They're warming to me. People who had so far acknowledged me with barely a grunt, if I was right up against their faces, now look me in the eye and speak. As I walk through town, the few shop owners who are still around sometimes wave. At the butcher's/grocery store, Antonis and his family point me to the good, local produce. In the square, the taxi drivers greet me with nods. Leonidas actually crossed the road to come over and say hello, and ask me how I was getting on. The post office dude, who, upon our first meeting just over a week ago, responded to my query about an undelivered package with 'Of course you haven't received it. I don't *know* you', now recognises me. He smiled when I walked in the other day. 'There's a yellow envelope for you,' he said, before I had the chance to ask, and handed it to me. The chemist remembers the stuff I've bought and keeps up with the progress of my cough. When Margarita, the hairdresser, invited me to pop in for coffee, I think she meant it. At Katerina's souvlaki place, where customers and staff now sit together drinking beer and wine, I am welcomed with a casual warmth that means a lot more than the careful attention they

103

show to tourists; it's almost a mark of approval. The delivery guy routinely winks at me. When Christina and I went there for dinner, Maria, Katerina's daughter, called us "girls", like her mother all those years ago, and lingered by our table for a chat after she took our order. When I went inside for a bottle of water, she let me take it out of the fridge myself. I think my status was elevated slightly due to the company I kept: Christina is an honorary islander, on account of her frequent visits during the winter, and her regular attendance of the festivals.

Takis, upon hearing my tentative explanation of what I'm trying to do here, got so excited that he invited me to come and stay in Vathy for a while. 'We'll give you a room to write in,' he said. 'And we'll be lighting the fire soon!' He then went on to tell me that, since I was sticking around, I could have the honour of naming his donkey (who is, apparently, a lady) once she returned from her business trip. Eleni, who was with me at the time, protested that she wanted to name the donkey too, and made some suggestions, but she was told, firmly, that she was leaving, and this was a matter for those of us staying behind.

And it isn't just Takis; most people I've spoken to have shown genuine interest in my writing, and asked some very insightful questions. Which shouldn't have surprised me, but it did. I still don't know what to expect from these mysterious locals. They're still as much of an exotic tribe to me, as I am a strange species to them. I sometimes feel like one of those colonials, uselessly holding out shiny objects to the natives, hoping to gain their favour.

And then one of the natives asks me to check out their group on facebook, and I am put back in my place: outside the door, swathed in my preconceptions, peeking in. And feeling like a bit of an arsehole, as well I should.

But the door is open. And from where I'm standing, the Secret Club looks like a very warm place to be, lit by the wood burning in Takis' fireplace. A place as ordinary as any other, that might become extraordinary once you stop proffering worthless trinkets and accept a cup of coffee and some cake. Where many weird and wonderful things might happen, and surprise you for all the right reasons, if you let them.

I have one foot in the door and still a long way to go before I'm invited in, but maybe, one evening, I'll push the door of the souvlaki place open, and they will all look up and nod, but no one will stand up to greet me. And I will pull up a chair and join them at their table, and have a glass of wine.

# Day 29

There was another writer here once, a few years back; an English man. Christina told me about him last week. He lived alone in a rented house in Kastro, the island's former capital, where a labyrinthine system of passageways and tunnels leads to the village's tiny adjoined houses, all enclosed within medieval fortification walls. The settlement is perched atop a steep, windswept rock overlooking the sea, from where the Sifniots of old could spot the pirates coming, and lock the village gates. These days, in the absence of pirates, it's a pretty cool place to be a writer.

This guy was a proper recluse. He kept to himself, hidden away in his quaint little house behind the castle walls for years, fully immersed in the solitary and mysterious act of writing. He was sometimes seen wandering around town, all wild facial hair and the distracted manner of the artist; he rarely spoke to anyone. He was a Sifnos celebrity.

'Surely you remember him,' said Christina. 'Everyone knew him.'

I didn't. But I mentioned him to my friend Alexis on the phone a few days later, when he asked if I was the only "foreigner" around.

'What happened to him?' he asked.

'Gone, I suppose,' I replied. 'He hasn't been seen for years.' Christina didn't know what had become of him, or his book; the tale of the English recluse had provided neither the happy ending nor the precedent I had hoped for.

'Maybe the wolves got him,' suggested Alexis, who had been regaled with the tale of the wolf-invoking wind. He's such a good friend; he always knows the right thing to say to ease my mind.

I've not been much of a recluse today. I have failed in my duties, both to myself and my bearded predecessor. I went into town, to check whether I had any post (I didn't) and exchange some more books before the bookstore closes for the winter. I spoke to several people, and encountered many more. My return journey coincided with the school breaking up for the day, sending hundreds of children of all ages hurtling down the hill and into my path. I passed a prepubescent Pied Piper playing Greek hip-hop on his phone, with a gaggle of tiny, primary school boys following in his wake, nodding their heads self-consciously to the tune. I stepped aside to avoid being swallowed up by a throng of teenage girls, all low-cut skinny jeans and aloof expressions. At the top of the hill, outside the school, the pick-up rush generated enough traffic to cause me to wait a whole minute to cross the road. It was a bit overwhelming. I dove into the supermarket, for a brief respite and a bag of crisps.

The rush had died down by the time I came out, and I made it back to the safety of home, having collected enough social interactions to last me a good few days. I said hello to the black cat, to re-establish my eccentricity, and settled down to do what a reclusive author's meant to do, and write. But my haven of solitude was invaded by an entirely unexpected foe: visitors. Not one, not two, but three of them. All in the space of a day. A screech of the gate, shuffling footsteps and a rattle on my door announced the arrival of the first one. I opened the door, cautiously, and Mrs. Souli, my next door neighbour, tottered in and plonked herself, and her trademark overpowering perfume, at my table.

'Ach, my poor legs,' she said, in lieu of hello, and stared at me expectantly.

I pulled up a chair. 'I have nothing to offer you,' I said apologetically. 'A glass of water, maybe?'

'I don't need anything. I can't see, I can't hear, I can't walk. What do I need? I'm old. Old people don't get given much, anyway.'

Cue fifteen minute rant on the evils of ageing, and society's failure to give back to the older generations, punctuated by cries of 'Ach!' and hip-rubbing, and my own feeble interjections of 'That's right' and 'It's a terrible thing' and variations thereof, depending on the complaint being voiced.

Just before she left, she spotted a jar of jalapenos that I'd just bought, to feed my chilli addiction in the absence of fresh peppers. She picked it up and shook it.

'Is it olives?' she asked suspiciously.

'No, it's chilli peppers. I like spicy food.'

'Hmm,' she commented, and tilted the jar from side to side, several times. 'What did you say it was?'

'HOT PEPPERS!' I bellowed, thinking perhaps she hadn't heard.

'Yes, yes,' she said, and placed the jar gingerly back on the table. 'I don't understand these things.' This is her favourite phrase.

I gave her a bagful of stale bread for the chickens, and she left.

Not twenty minutes went by, and the bird-shaped doorbell tinkled. I went outside, muttering *what the fuck* under my breath, only to find Kostas, former neighbourhood bad boy and my most favourite ticket collector on the summer buses, hanging over my gate, long arms dangling over the top, and a big grin just visible through the gaps between the slats.

'I'm gonna burn some shit,' he announced, referring, presumably, to the dried grass collected over the summer and piled up high in the field opposite. 'You may wanna shut your windows, so I don't smoke you out.'

I thanked him and he peeled himself off my gate and turned to leave.

'You're still here,' he said, as an afterthought.

'I'm sticking around,' I confirmed. He made no further comment. I heard the roar of the fire soon after.

I had lunch. I did some writing. I had a nap. I had a cup of coffee. I washed the pots from last night. And then – impossible! – footsteps, a cough, a knock on the door. And there was Antonis, the plumber, casually dropping in.

'I was in the neighbourhood,' he explained, redundantly; he lives exactly three minutes away. 'I wanted to talk about massage.'

I offered him water; he accepted. We both sat down and rolled up cigarettes and smoked them, and had another one of those insightful conversations about my writing that people keep surprising me with.

'So, how does this massage thing work?' he said eventually, and with a hint of timidity. 'My neck. Every time I move it, it goes crack.' I explained the benefits and limitations of the treatment and suggested we give it a try and see if it might help; he agreed, and we made an appointment for Wednesday. As I watched him leave, it struck me that this was a brave thing he'd just done. He's quite a gruff, manly man (pity he doesn't work in the fields), probably unused to asking for help, and it's touching that he'd submit himself and his knotted muscles to me, some random girl with a massage table. I felt a strange pride in him, this man that I barely know.

It's been two hours and there have been no further visitors. I jump up every time I hear a noise outside, but so far it's only been the cats. My admiration for the English writer has grown: the man was no fool in choosing Kastro for his dwelling. I could definitely do with some medieval fortifications and a good vantage point from which to spot the pirates as they approach. My visibility here is severely limited: they're upon me seconds after the tinkle of the bird, and then there's nothing between me and them but a wooden door. Which now conveniently features a handle on the outside. How

I am to achieve solitude under these conditions? How can I be a recluse, with all these visitors? I feel like I'm letting my predecessor down.

I shouldn't compare myself to him. He's set the bar too high, and I will always come up short, no matter what I do. Because, even if I were to barricade myself in for the next 71 days and refuse to speak even to the cats (but *pointedly*, just to score some extra crazy points), I could never achieve the dizzying heights of reclusiveness and eccentricity that he so valiantly claimed. It's the lack of facial hair, of course. It'll get me every time.

But if I were to grow a beard, even a tame, wispy one, like a teenage boy, I wouldn't need to live in a fortress. I think just one public appearance in town as the bearded lady author would take care of any potential visitors for good.

Except, perhaps, for Mrs Souli. She can't see very well, and the sprinkling of spiky hairs on her chin is not to be frowned upon. She'd probably think it entirely normal.

# Day 30

I wish I hadn't asked about the kittens.

I wasn't going to, but I ran into Mrs. Souli on my way back from watering Eleni's garden this morning, and she was blocking my path, and I could see she wasn't satisfied with just hello. But I couldn't bear another tirade on old age so soon, and I had used up all my reserves of polite nodding during yesterday's impromptu visit. I panicked, and blurted out the first thing that came to mind.

'How are the kittens doing?' I had been wondering about them; I hadn't heard their little squeaks for a few days, nor seen any of them doing their drunken kitten walk along the wall that divides our gardens, like they used to, before their mother came along to pick them up by the scruff of the neck and carry them to safety. And the mother herself had seemed anxious, and I could often hear her cry, in a frantic, mournful way that was too ominous to think about. I hadn't meant to ask.

'Gone,' she replied. 'All of them, gone.'

'Gone?' I repeated. 'Where did they go?' Allowing myself, against my intuition, to interpret her words as a call for action, a search and rescue mission that would culminate, via a short trek through the nearby fields and as far, perhaps, as the churchyard, to the mother being reunited with her kittens. They had just wandered off, that was all.

Mrs Souli gave me an impatient look. 'They died,' she said bluntly. 'They're dead. All of them, dead,' she clarified further, obviously thinking I was a bit slow, not quite familiar with the circle of life.

'All of them?' I said desperately. 'All four?'

'Four, yes.'

'But what happened?'

111

She didn't seem to understand the question. 'They died,' she repeated. And then, by way of explanation, or consolation, or simply stating a fact: 'They don't last.'

'Those poor kittens,' I stammered, close to tears.

'Yes,' she agreed shortly, with very little emotion. I shouldn't be surprised. Last week, when we exchanged a few words from our respective gardens, she told me she didn't like them.

'I only like the red one, a bit,' she confessed, as we both watched the tiny ginger and white cat playing by her feet.

'Shoo!' she said, as it stumbled against her leg; she obviously didn't like it that much. The mother, a black, ginger and white tabby with a strange face that grows on you as you get to know her, issued a deep, warbling sound – a warning, perhaps, or an order – and the kitten scampered off in her direction. She welcomed it with a lick across the face, and then nudged it away, gently, with her nose.

'Their poor mother,' I said now. 'I heard her crying.'

She shook her head sadly. 'Yes,' she said. 'Crying for her babies,' and her face was softer. She doesn't do kittens, but mothers is a topic she can relate to. 'It's a terrible thing for a mother,' she added, 'to lose your child.'

'Terrible,' I agreed.

'And she's very fruitful. She's had four litters this year.'

I was horrified. 'And all of them died?'

'Not all of them, no. Manolis took them to that restaurant, over by the mill. They feed them there.'

'That's good.'

'Yes.' She nodded. 'A terrible thing. When the young die. Not the old – the young. Before their time. But not kittens,' she added firmly. 'They just don't last. Nothing you can do.'

But there is, I was thinking; there are things that you can do. You can look after them, you can keep them safe. You can clean out their eyes and give them a box to sleep in. If they're ill, you can take them to the vet. Except there is no vet here, and I'm starting to understand it's because there is no demand. And those kittens didn't even look that ill; not picture perfect, perhaps, but not about to be snatched away by death, either, all four of them, in a row. In the city, you would fix them; you would do everything you could to fix them. In the city, four kittens dying is a tragedy; here, it's just some words you say, before moving on to something else.

'Ach, my hip,' said Mrs Souli. 'My regards to your mother.'

Death comes too easy here. It's part of the lifestyle. You have to slaughter the goats you breed. If your donkey gets too old to carry things, you have him put down. Dogs aren't pets, they're workers; cats are kept to fend off rats. Sheep die in the fields; birds in your back yard. You have special sticks for killing snakes. And the inspects, even just the insects. In the cities, we encounter them infrequently: a spider, a moth, mosquitoes on summer nights. If they get into our homes, we're squeamish about killing them; we try to find another way, or get someone else to do it. You don't have those options here, and it's every day. If a scorpion or a centipede comes scuttling in through your door, you don't hesitate: you slam your foot down and crush it, before it gets into your bed. If there are ants in the kitchen sink, you drown them in water and bleach. You swat the flies that buzz into your face and sit on your food; you keep the swatter handy at all times. You don't give it much thought, because, if you do, it's still killing. Death, here, is an everyday event.

And kittens, apparently, drop dead all over the place, and there isn't a thing anyone can do. They just don't last.

I'm not finding this educational. I'm not learning life lessons about death, or acceptance, or the impermanence of things. Death is not made easier by its proximity, or its regularity, or how ordinary it is. I'm not feeling philosophical; I won't turn into a Buddhist. This place, it's not teaching me to be stoical, or tougher, or more wise; it's just making me mourn kittens.

The mother cat wandered into the house earlier. I felt that I should treat her differently, stupid sentimental human that I am. But I think cats pick up on emotions, so I told her I was sorry, and bent down and scratched her on the head. She gave a little purr and went off, out the door and over the wall. I heard her crying again later, a little while ago. Crying for her babies.

But the saddest, the most merciful thing is, she'll forget long before I do.


A postscript to this day: I just reached my funding target on kickstarter. And what I wish, more than anything, is that Eleni were here to dance with me in celebration. Eleni, who has been with me in this right from the start, who probably checked my kickstarter page as many times as I did. She should be here, now.

I wish all eighty-six of my backers were here, and everyone who's supported me, so many people in so many different ways, during the last 30 days. It would get a bit crowded, so we might have to brave the wind and the cold, and take it outside. And we'd all dance together, in the moonlight, and probably frighten the cats.

But in their absence, I will put some very loud music on, and dance this out by myself.

And when the song is over, I will probably cry a little bit, and then sit down and have my dinner and watch a film, as if nothing had happened. Because none of this feels real.

# Day 31

There has been Sifnos romance before, of course. There was bound to be some: I've spent practically every summer of my life on this island. Discounting childhood infatuations and the summers of my early teenage years, which Korinna and I spent being aloof and semi-enthralled by local boys on mopeds, I can isolate three encounters that fall under the general category of romance. Only one of them was romantic; another involved the police. None of the three men were the least bit rugged, but one was admirably dishevelled and grungy, thus appealing to my youthful sensibilities, which, happily, did not stretch to being too bothered about personal hygiene, or the lack thereof. And of them became my stalker.

Giacomo was not particularly attractive. He was about as tall as I was, and slight, with a tiny waist like a girl's and shoulder length, scraggly hair. But he had sparkly eyes and a nice, big smile, and I was drunk. And bored: the friends I was spending the summer with were all in couples. He had been imported from Sicily for the summer, to work in Mamma Mia, the Italian restaurant in town. He spoke very little English, and the bar where we met was too loud for conversation anyway, but he nevertheless managed to convey, by means of energetic gesturing and sheer determination, that he was into me. I consented to a lengthy snogging session in a corner by the DJ booth.

When the bar closed and spilled us, bleary-eyed, out onto the street, Giacomo placed himself between me and my friends and uttered an entire phrase in English:

'Daph-neh,' he said, giving my name a passionate, if slightly whiny, Italian inflection. 'You come with me, *si?*'

I shrugged. 'OK.'

I communicated as much to my friends, and followed him.

As we started up the steps towards Ano Petali and his room, he took my hand.

'I'm not sleeping with you,' I warned.

'*Che?*'

'We're not having sex.'

'No?' he said, clearly taken aback. 'OK.' We took two more steps; he squeezed my hand. '*Poco?*' he suggested. 'Maybe a leetle?'

'No. Not at all. No sex.'

He sighed, and nodded sagely. 'OK. No sex.'

A few more steps, a tug on my hand.

'Daph-neh,' he said gravely.

'Yes?'

'*Pochissimo?*' He pinched the thumb and index finger of his free hand together, showed me the sliver of space in between.

'No!'

'OK.'

He tried anyway. In the room he shared with five of his colleagues (who had the good sense to reconvene to the kitchen, after greeting us with winks and Italian words I didn't understand), he tried and tried and tried. We spent a couple of hours engaged in a battle of wills and tangled limbs, until dawn broke and I declared this had been fun, but I was going home. I might have been a little cruel. Giacomo saw me to the door.

'*Ciao* Daph-neh,' he said, his shoulders slumped in utter resignation. But his expression was strangely but distinctly amused.

I thought that would be the end of it, but it was only the beginning. For the week that remained of my holiday, Giacomo was everywhere I went. He found us on the beach. He came to the bar every night, as soon as he finished work. He tracked us down in town one afternoon, as we strolled around looking at the shops. I was slightly disconcerted, but he didn't strike me as dangerous, and my friends thought it was hilarious, so we let him tag along. There wasn't much conversation to be had; we tried to include him as much as we could, and speak in English, but he mostly just nodded vaguely and randomly and we'd give up and switch to Greek. He didn't seem to mind. He seemed happy just being around, watching me with an expression of pure longing, and cheerfully resigned to the fact that there hadn't been, and wouldn't be, any further physical contact, which I had established by pushing his hand away very firmly the first time he tried to touch me. By the second day, he had decided he loved me, and our hopeless exchanges were punctuated by heartfelt cries of 'Daph-neh! *Ti amo!*'. I tried to explain that he didn't *amo* me at all, and it was probably only because I'd refused to have sex with him, but he wouldn't be deterred; he just smiled and said it again. At other times, he would just say my name, desperately, and shake his head.

We exchanged addresses before I left (this was the year 1996, when we still wrote letters) and, a month later, by which time I was living in halls of residence in Hatfield, forty minutes outside of London, where I'd just started a foundation in Art, I wrote him a few lines in the plainest English I could manage.

A few weeks later, I was having coffee in the kitchen with my friend and chatting about our coursework, when she suddenly stopped talking and fixed her gaze on a spot behind my head, with a puzzled expression on her face.

'There's a man outside the window,' she said. 'He's smiling kind of manically.'

I turned around, and there was Giacomo. Outside my kitchen. In Hatfield, Hertfordshire. Forty minutes from London on the train. He raised his hand in greeting.

'Ciao Daph-neh! I come!' he announced.

'Who's that?' said my friend.

'I think,' I replied carefully, 'he's my stalker.'

117

Giacomo had picked up a bit more English since the summer – he had bought a book and a tape and taught himself – and he managed to explain he was visiting London with his cousin, and thought it would be nice to stop by and see me.

'In *Hatfield?*'

'*Si*. Is where you live,' he replied, simply.

'And where's your cousin now?'

'London.'

'Let's go meet him!' I suggested, desperate to get him out of my house.

'OK.'

I gave him a cup of coffee and then dragged him to the train station and bundled him on the next train to Finsbury Park. I called Eileen to meet us there, for backup. And so it came to pass that Eileen, Giacomo, his cousin and I spent the day in London. We took them to Oxford Street. We took them to Hyde Park. We took them to Trafalgar Square and posed for photos with the pigeons. We had lunch in Leicester Square, a thick slice of greasy pizza and some wilted salad leaves on a paper plate for a pound; it was probably offensive to Sicilians, but it was all we could afford. We showed them the statue of Eros and the Houses of Parliament. They took photos of Big Ben. In the evening, we had a pint of English lager in a pub, and then I announced it was time to catch the train back home.

Giacomo insisted on taking me up to Finsbury Park. We said goodbye on the platform.

'It was nice to see you,' I said politely.

'Maybe I come again, before I leave?'

I shook my head. 'Maybe not.'

He nodded. 'OK,' he said. 'OK. *Ciao* Daph-neh.'

I never heard from him again. He had promised to keep in touch, but I guess his new-found English didn't stretch to the written word. Or maybe he just didn't love me anymore. I had expected him to turn up in Sifnos, but he didn't come the next summer, or the summer after that, and soon enough I forgot all about him.

Almost: I can never forget the last time I saw him, as my train pulled out of Finsbury Park. He was standing perfectly still among the last of the commuters, with that same expression of resignation and amusement on his face. It always makes me feel a little cruel.

# Day 32

Antagonist has acquired a thesaurus. She came in bearing it proudly, a huge hardback brick of a book. She sat on the sofa, put her feet up on the coffee table, consulted the index in the back, then flicked over to the desired page and peered at it with great concentration. I'm sure this was a tactic intended to create suspense, but it failed because I was too excited by the appearance of the book itself. Did she get it from Amazon? Did this mean I could order some books, too? I never got the chance to ask, however, because Antagonist had evidently found the word she was looking for, and tapped the page with her finger purposefully. She cleared her throat.

'Fraud,' she read. 'Charlatan. Fake. Phony. Cheat. Sham.' She turned to another page without looking up. 'Deception. Con. *Charade*. An act. A farce. A travesty!'

I knew where this began. It was a couple of days ago, and I just couldn't get my post for the day to work. No matter what I did, it resisted me. I would write a sentence, delete it, write it again. Get up, pace, make coffee, pretend I needed to pee. Feed a cat. Wash a cup. Sit back down, try again – fail. It was madly frustrating: I could see that the piece had potential, that it could be funny, that it could work. But it just didn't; the words refused to behave as I wanted them to. They eluded me, in every sentence I wrote, and rewrote. I fleetingly considered giving the whole thing up, and getting a job in McDonald's. I spent the whole morning this way.

By the afternoon, I was deeply depressed and my entire life was futile. I didn't feel like eating; I crawled into bed and snatched some sleep out of the claws of anxiety, which only left me more exhausted. And then, just as I was really about to give up and call the travel agency for ferry times to Athens, there was a click in my head and something shifted, just a tiny bit – just enough. I sat back down at my desk and started writing something else. And it worked. It was fine.

But I'd had the McDonald's moment, and Antagonist had picked it up and kept it safe. She has a collection of them, those moments of doubt, of despair, of cowardice, and she conjures them up, like magic tricks, to make me disappear and put me back in my place, at anytime she judges I've wandered off too far.

This, apparently, was one of those times.

'Pretend,' she continued. 'Feign. Make believe. Fake. Oh, there it is again! As a verb this time!'

I decided not to indulge her, not to fall for her tricks. Not to take her words in, and analyse them, and look for opposites to throw back at her. Not today. Today, I would just get on with my day. Between McDonald's and tortured artist, there's quite a lot of room for doing things. For example:

- I responded to six emails that had been sitting in my inbox for days. I wrote a few more: hellos to friends. I made a couple of phonecalls.
- I received The Gift Of Coffee. I went into the post office, and Post Office Man presented me, grinning, with two boxes filled to the brim with the precious capsules that I was fatally low on. Angels sung; I had been saved. I am learning that I can do without a lot of things, but I ain't living without my coffee. It's too cruel a fate. And now, thanks to the perfectly timed kindness of Spyros, my stepdad, I won't have to.
- I took photos of flowers. And trees. And clouds.
- I stopped by the supermarket, and procured chilli powder, smoked paprika and turmeric. Just to spice up those aubergines.
- I got a message from a lady called Nancy, who introduced herself as one of the editors on a Greek lifestyle site, telling me she had stumbled across my

project and liked it, and wanted to do a feature on it. And what did I think of that? What I thought is *what the fuck is going on?*, but then I filed it under "Your life is a bit surreal, just go with it", which is where most things are kept these days, and said yes, please.

- I made a cup of coffee without fear (thank you Spyros) and wrote 1,500 words on how *100 days of solitude* came about, as Nancy had asked. In Greek. Which was incredibly hard. I sent it off.

- I made another coffee, and started writing this piece.

I have not showered, or eaten, or done the washing up, and it's gone six o'clock. When would I have the time for my McDonald's job, with all this stuff going on?

'Where did you get that?' I asked Antagonist, who was still playing her word association game and searching for another variation of "fraud" to throw at me. 'Was it Amazon?'

'Yes,' she said suspiciously. 'Why?'

'Just wondered. Can you look up the definition of "antagonist" in it?'

She snorted. 'It's a *thesaurus*! It doesn't have definitions, it has synonyms. And you call yourself a writer!'

'Of course,' I said amiably. 'Maybe you could order a dictionary then, and look it up.'

'What for?' she spat, squinting at me angrily. 'I don't need a dictionary.'

She slammed her thesaurus shut and stomped off.

She doesn't need a dictionary, because she knows what it will say; I'm not the only one who's hurt by definitions. She's only here as an opposing force to me; without me, she would just *poof!* out of existence. And that can be my magic trick for putting her in her place, for once.

# Day 33

Korinna reminded me a few days ago that the word *wasser* featured prominently in our exchanges with the two German guys we met one Sifnos summer and then ran away with. This means "water" in German, so it was neither romantic nor significant in any obvious way, but it was definitely a prominent theme of this double, doomed romance. I do remember all four of us repeating it often and enthusiastically, *"Wasser!"*, but I have no idea how it came about. Perhaps one of them said the word as a bottle of water was passed between them; perhaps they were just trying to teach us words in their language and picked this one at random. I don't know; I honestly don't remember. I went on to have a long-term, long-distance relationship with Juergen – also doomed – so I remember a lot of things about him, but the origins of the *wasser* excitement elude me. Perhaps Korinna can shed some light.

I believe this was the summer of hitchhiking. Korinna and I had decided that we no longer wished to pay the bus fare, so we had taken to hitchhiking our way around the island. It made us feel grown up and cool, both qualities we aspired to. I had just turned sixteen, and Korinna was a couple of weeks short of her fifteenth birthday. My efforts towards cool consisted of wearing a lot of black, and Doc Marten boots coupled with short summer dresses; Korinna lived in Amsterdam, so she was cool by default. The hitchhiking fitted in nicely with our image. And it was easy: people would stop for hitchhikers in those days. Especially for two teenage girls in short dresses. To be fair to us, however, we only ever did it in the day, to travel to the beach; we knew better than to get into cars with strangers at night.

We met Juergen and Frank on the beach in Plati Yialos (*wasser?*); according to Korinna, they were throwing skipping stones and we were impressed. They were both seventeen, almost adults. We spent a happy afternoon lounging in the sun, smoking cigarettes and bonding over musical tastes and, apparently, German words. A plan was made to meet for a drink in the evening, and we all went our separate ways, to get changed: Korinna and I to our respective homes, and Juergen and Frank to the campsite at the far end of the beach.

We met them back in Plati Yialos at dusk, and were conveyed, by hired moped, into town. We spent the evening in the square, sitting cross-legged around the marble pillar of the war memorial, in a boy-boy/girl-girl pattern. We drank beer out of cans. Soon enough the configuration changed, boy gravitating towards girl to form couples. There was some awkward shifting around, and long boy arms placed tentatively on narrow girl shoulders, and I found myself leaning against Juergen's manly frame. He was very tall. There was some kissing. It was nice.

We were ambushed by our mothers when we got home. They were both at my house, sitting on the patio, which wasn't unusual in itself, but something about the way their both turned their heads sharply when they heard us come in spelt danger. They interrogated us in high-pitched voices.

'Where were you?'

'Town.'

'Who with?'

'Nobody!'

'Really.'

'Really! Why?'

'You were *seen*,' said Korinna's mum.

'Dorothy called,' my mum explained. 'You were riding on *motorbikes* with *strangers!*'

'They're not strangers! We know them!'

Our mothers, however, did not. Our behaviour was pronounced unacceptable, and the boys were deemed inappropriate, despite all of our protestations as to the goodness of their characters. We were expressly forbidden from seeing them again.

Naturally, Korinna and I decided, on the spot, that we were In Love, and there was no force great enough to keep us apart from our destiny. Not even mothers. We pretended remorse and acquiescence, and convened to my bedroom to decide on our best course of action. Which, according to our teenage logic, was clearly to elope. A plan was made to slip away early the next morning, meet by Korinna's house, and go to the campsite to deliver ourselves into Frank and Juergen's arms. We confided in my little sister, and instructed her she was under no circumstances to reveal what she knew, even if tortured. She was ten, and took her task very seriously. She was tortured, but she did not cave; it turns out it was Korinna's sister who gave us away.

It all went smoothly (Korinna tells me we actually *swam* across the length of the beach to reach the campsite, in order to avoid being spotted again, which I have no recollection of), and we arrived at the campsite to surprise Juergen and Frank as they slept in their tents, and announce that we were here to stay. To their credit, they took it quite well, and made sympathetic noises about the unreasonableness of mothers. Juergen sang "Get up, stand up, stand up for your rights", channelling Bob Marley as only a white German boy could, which made me feel noble and heroic, and entirely justified in this act of rebellion. The day was spent in hiding at the campsite, and in strategic talks about our next move, which, it was unanimously agreed, would be to escape to Milos the next day. All we had to do was stay safe until then, and freedom would be ours.

It wasn't to be. We were wakened from our broken sleep (the ground was very hard, and we were too excited) and dragged out of our respective tents at dawn by Korinna's grandmother, who was a very formidable lady, and not one you ever wanted to incur the wrath of.

She barely looked at us – we would be dealt with later – but Frank and Juergen were subjected to a lengthy and loud-voiced lecture on their irresponsibleness, much to the amusement of the other campers, who no longer minded having been woken up.

'You should be ashamed of yourselves,' she concluded. 'These girls are fourteen years old!'

Korinna and I protested feebly at this point, though, in her case, it was technically true. I had hinted at being seventeen, based on the fact that I'd already had my sixteenth birthday, a whole month ago. I didn't really see what the problem was, but Frank and Juergen looked a bit shocked. We had no time to explain ourselves, however: we were promptly and bodily inserted into the back of the police van, which Korinna's grandmother had arrived in, and driven home. And shouted at, a lot. And grounded forever.

It turned out, ironically, that Juergen really wasn't a stranger, after all. His mum had been a Sifnos summer regular for years, and closely acquainted with a friend of Korinna's mum. Which probably explains how I was allowed, eventually, to see him again, convince him that I wasn't fourteen, and embark upon a relationship that lasted, in an on-and-off capacity, for the next three years. And culminated in me lying in his bed, in a small town in Bavaria, with a temperature of minus twenty outside and the windows wide open because Juergen was afraid of germs, shivering and weeping from the cold, while the CD single of Toni Braxton's *Unbreak My Heart* played over and over again, stuck on repeat.

But that's another story, which, like many of the details of my Sifnos romance with Juergen, and the reason we liked the word *wasser* so much, will remain shrouded in mystery.

# Day 34

It's Saturday afternoon, and Manolis has just lit his wood oven. The smell of smoke and the heat from the fire drift into my house, and the wood crackles and pops in a rhythmic, soothing way, breaking the silence of the still, windless day. Soon, the wood will turn into coal and it will crackle no more; there will be no more smoke, only heat. That's when the pots will go in. The neighbours are bringing them already, mostly men, tasked with the carrying once their wives have done their bit.

The locals have chickpea soup on Sunday. Only on Sunday, because you can't make this in your kitchen at home. The soup, which is thick, like a stew, and tastes like all the homely comforts you can imagine, is cooked slowly, overnight, in clay pots with clay lids, in a woodfire oven. The women start preparing the chickpeas on Friday: they need to be soaked in water and bicarbonate of soda for twenty-four hours, to soften. On Saturday, they rinse them out and put them in the clay pot with some fresh water, onions and the seasoning of their choice. They add the lid and summon their husbands to carry the heavy pots to the oven. There's one in most villages, in someone's back yard, and they get the word out when they light them so the neighbours can bring their pots. Manolis has collected three so far, and he's lined then up next to the oven, to go in as soon as the fire has burnt itself down. In the summer, when my mum is here, he lets her know on Fridays so she can prepare her pot in time. He's said nothing to me since she's been gone.

I smell the smoke and come outside with my afternoon coffee. I sit on a ledge in the sunshine. It's cold in the house but out here the sun is still strong enough to warm your skin. I sip my coffee and watch some lazy clouds drifting across the sky. There are church bells and goat bells. A donkey brays. Somewhere, intermittently, there's a mechanical sound, but it's far enough to ignore. The wood crackles in the oven, and the men chatter with Manolis as, one by one, they come bearing their pots.

Tomorrow, our little edge of the village will come to life as, after church, the neighbours will arrive en masse to collect their chickpeas and bring them home, for Sunday lunch. I will watch them from my side of the wall, as I busy myself with some task or other; a few, the ones I know, might notice me and say hello.

I finish my coffee and go down the road to scavenge some lemons from the garden of an empty house; I want to make lemon cake. On my way back I run into Yorgos, Vangelia's husband, bound for Manolis' oven with his burden of chickpeas and a serene smile on his face.

'You must be enjoying yourself,' he remarks, after we've said our good afternoons. 'If you're still here.'

'I love it,' I blurt out. 'I've never been happier.' I drop a lemon in my excitement, and leave Yorgos behind as I chase it down the path.

In a break between pot bearers, I call out to Manolis over our dividing wall.

'Can I come and take some photos of the oven and the pots?' I ask.

'As many as you like,' he says. 'Why do you need to ask?'

'Well, I can't just walk into your house!'

He shrugs; he doesn't seem to think that would be a problem. The side door to the back yard is open, inviting the neighbours in.

I take my photos and then stand by the fire for a bit, until my face starts to sting from the heat. I stop to pet the cat, who's rolling around in a patch of sunshine.

'Next time you light the oven,' I say, 'will you let me know?'

'Oh,' he stammers. 'Of course. I just thought, with you being on your own...'

'I cook more than my mum, you know.'

'I didn't mean that,' he says quickly. 'Just that you'd have too many chickpeas.'

'Yes,' I agree. 'I'll just have to eat chickpeas all week!'

'You could put some in the freezer,' he suggests, obviously pleased that he's stumbled upon this idea. He smiles. 'I'll let you know.'

The pots go into the oven and the smell of smoke is replaced by the sweet, heavy scent of roasting onions. It wafts into the house and mingles with the smell of my baking cake. I fantasise about the chickpea soup I'll make. I might go rogue and add a few sprigs of rosemary, a dash of cumin, a pinch of chilli powder. I'll definitely have to freeze a few portions. I like chickpeas, but I don't particularly want to eat them every day for a week.

But I'll make a huge pot, regardless, enough to feed a large Greek family their Sunday lunch, because, more than chickpea soup, it's the ritual I like. Being let in on the secret on the Friday; the slow, careful process of lighting the fire on the Saturday, the camaraderie by the oven, the open door; the impromptu Sunday gathering of well-dressed churchgoers, as they crowd around the oven to collect their lunch.

I don't want to be the one watching them from the other side of the wall. I want to play, too. I want to be a part of this. I want to be one of them, in this small way, to stand in line with my neighbours and talk about the weather as I wait to receive my pot.

# Day 35

Alexis rates his overall experience of Sifnos as 98% fantastic. This is a cumulative score, based on several visits throughout the twenty years of our friendship, so it's pretty impressive, all told. The remaining 2% corresponds to the steps leading from my house down into town and, more significantly, back up from town to the house, and is described as "hell". To put this into better context: Alexis and I once crawled up those steps, slurring words of encouragement at one another, after consuming approximately 25 shots each of fuck-knows-what (we had placed our fate entirely in the hands of the friendly and creative barman) in a bar in town, on the last night of our holiday. And when I say crawled, I mean crawled, on our hands and knees; it's not a figure of speech. We could have been bitten by any number of scorpions and snakes. It's a miracle we made it home at all. And when we did, we really wished we hadn't. Death by scorpion bite (or alcohol poisoning) would have been a far kinder fate than what awaited us early the next morning: Moving Day.

This happy occasion involved packing up a whole summer's worth of stuff that included, indicatively, the personal belongings of a five-member family, plus any food items that hadn't been consumed, almonds we had picked from the tree, cheese gifted by the neighbours, and ceramics bought as presents and wrapped in sheets of newspaper that protected them not at all from accidental breakage, and then transporting all this to the car park and squeezing it into a medium-sized VW station wagon, along with two large, unruly dogs, prone to carsickness. The entire operation was performed, as a family tradition, in the least organised and most manic way possible, with optional but frequent outbursts of anger and/or despair. It was a wonderfully bonding experience, which Alexis had the good fortune to share on what was probably the worst hangover of his life. I have no idea how we got through it. Each round trip to the car, under a relentless August sun, laden with luggage and with cold, tequila-scented sweat running down our green-tinted faces, was punctuated by a brief detour for vomiting. Luckily my family was too focused on wanting to brutally murder each other and then throw themselves off a cliff into sweet oblivion to notice the condition we were in; that was our one saving grace. Although, having said that, there was no grace in any of it, and no salvation; there was only the endless lurching from house to car and back again, the carrying, the vomiting, and the world spinning round in a way it clearly wasn't supposed to. And Alexis and I grunting sounds of support and helping each other up when we collapsed under the weight of our load and our stupidity. Like I said: it was very bonding.

Those steps are the bane of my existence. They stand between me and civilisation, and mock me openly with their inevitability every time I need to go into town to collect my post or buy my cigarettes. It's not a long journey: I timed myself once and, on a good day, with no breaks, no social encounters and no stopping to talk to cats, it takes exactly 4 minutes to make my way down, and 4 minutes 51 seconds to get back up. The problem is, there is no *logic* to them. They are steep throughout, but that's the only consistent thing about them. Some are wide and some are narrow; some are too high and others are barely there at all; some are straight and some curve around when you least expect it; some have loose stones that trip you up and others have plants growing out of them. It's impossible to get a rhythm going. Alexis is right: they are the 2% that taints this island's perfect score; they are the Sifnos version of hell.

Apart from its satanic nature, I mention the passage into town for another reason. This brief journey – on average, four minutes and twenty five seconds each way – is one that I increasingly don't want to make. Not because of the steps, but because of the people; I'm finding it harder and harder to place myself among them. I went to the vegetable farm again the other day, and met Nikos, the farmer, and Marios, who works in one of the shops in town in the summer (now closed). We exchanged some words. And it was good; it was just about as much social interaction as I required. But going into town tests me a little bit. I feel exposed. I may be spoken to by any number of people, at any given moment, and I already find that slightly disconcerting. It worries me a little. I'm starting to question the wisdom of putting a girl with anti-social tendencies in a situation where she literally has to go well out of her way, and travel through hell, to make contact with other people. For a Londoner who usually thrives on the chaos of big cities and actually likes the Underground, I'm taking to this solitude far too well.

And what's even more worrying is that I'll have to take a trip to Athens soon. Alexis and Anna have just had their first baby, and I want to go meet him. I've promised. But I do wonder: if the town of Sifnos feels too crowded, what will Athens feel like? How will I feel when I step off the boat and I am catapulted straight into the giant, angry traffic jam that is the port of Piraeus on any given day, and the Metro, with my ribs exposed to the elbows of fellow passengers who have famously never understood the concept of personal space, and then the city itself, with its three million residents and two million cars, and motorbikes and buses and trams and trains and random people who stop you on the street to sell you ball point pens and tissues and tales of homelessness and unemployment. How will I cope with that, when having to nod at five people in a row feels like a challenge?

I promised to make this trip over a month ago and I was looking forward to it, before my 100 days began: it would be a nice excuse to break the solitude for a couple of days, to see my friends and family, eat proper pizza, get some essential supplies. And though all those reasons are still valid, there is a part of me that doesn't want to go. I like my solitude; I don't want it broken. I want to protect it, wrap it up in sheets of newspaper and store it somewhere safe. Breaking it might break the spell that Sifnos has put me under, the spell that allows me to write every day, and be this person that I am, socially inept and haphazardly dressed, but happy.

But I've promised and I'm going. I'll see my friends, eat pizza and get my supplies, and try to treat this as a part of my journey rather than a break from it. I'll try to remember that the spell is on me, not a place or a time, and I can take it with me, whenever I go, along with my laptop. I'll carry on writing and make those days in Athens count. But I may still add a couple of days to my total, anyway: that's how protective I've become.

It makes me nervous, but I do want to go: I want to meet Alexis' son. I want to sit with him and tell him stories of the things we've done, catch him up on everything that happened before he arrived, so he knows the people he's chosen for his parents. And I want to tell him about the steps: he needs to know what's in store for him when, years from now, he's called upon to help his dad and I up them, when we've had a few too many in town, and our elderly knees are too fragile for crawling.

\*\*\*

True story: a text message just came through on my phone, and I jumped. This does not bode well.

# Day 36

A shocking thing happened to me this morning: I woke up with an urge to go for a run. I lay in bed, stretching out lazily and contemplating my outfit – yoga leggings and my neon orange top, and proper, anatomically correct running shoes. Yes, I thought contentedly, I would walk into town to buy cigarettes, and then I would run all the way back up! I would listen to music! I would feel good! This went on for several minutes before I recognised it for what it was: madness.

There are certain fundamental things I know about myself, and one of them is that I do not run. Ever. Not even for the bus when I'm already late for work. Not even if all the hounds of hell are snapping at my heels and they haven't been fed for a week (though this has not been tested yet). I'm just not a runner. No matter how hard I try, I do not understand the point of it. I have been for a run once in my life, in the year 1997, when Eileen and I decided we were sporty, and we would run, uphill, from our flat in Finsbury Park to Crouch End. I made it as far as the end of our road, perhaps a hundred metres, give or take a few, and then stopped. I didn't even bother explaining to Eileen; I just turned around and walked back home. Slowly. I do not run: this is one of the few certainties I can rely on, in this ever-changing, unreliable life.

Just to clear up any confusion: the proper running shoes I mentioned belong to my mum (another of the world's most dedicated runners). I snuck them out of the bag she'd packed to take back to Athens at the end of her holiday, as I figured they'd be a more sensible choice of footwear than my flip-flops when the weather changed. My mum, please rest assured, does not miss them. But the point is, regardless of how it came to be in my possession, I had the running gear and I had actually imagined using it. It was very alarming.

It's been a strange few weeks, and being here is affecting me in many unexpected ways. But this I did not see coming. *Running.* What next? Team sports? Skydiving? Mathematics? I had a stern word with myself, and – just to make sure the madness did not take hold of me again – I put on a pair of jeans and my All Stars: the best my wardrobe could provide in terms of the exact opposite of sportswear. I would have worn a ball gown and high heels, if I had them. And in this highly precarious frame of mind I headed into down.

I felt much better once the fresh air hit me. I suspect I may have poisoned myself with the fly killer spray, which I applied liberally all over the house yesterday. I had no choice. The number of flies that descended upon me all of a sudden was borderline biblical. And they all had a death wish, which they wanted me to grant. It's not a role I am comfortable with, but I did what I could, swatting wildly and hopelessly at them like a dog chasing its tail, until, eventually, I gave up and resorted to the spray. Which certainly did the trick: when I came back into the house, fifteen minutes later (as per the instructions), there were dead flies everywhere. I am not kidding. I walked straight back out and went to the supermarket and bought a tiny version of a dustpan and brush, commonly used for cleaning your kitchen sink, just to sweep up the bodies. But anyway, it's entirely possible that, apart from wiping out an entire generation of Sifnos flies and giving me some serious headaches, the fly spray also has some hallucinogenic or personality-altering properties. Which would explain the urge to run. I was off my head. They really should put a warning on that thing. Yes, that's right: *apart* from the giant skull and crossbones, obviously.

In town, I ran into Christina, over from Athens for work, and spent a few minutes catching up. I invited her to lunch and we went our separate ways. I bought my cigarettes and started on my return journey and, I am pleased to report, I felt absolutely no urge to run. I took the steps up slowly, one at a time, pausing to notice yet another closed-up house, and those that were still alive, with open doors and cooking smells and radios playing and laundry flapping in the breeze, and when I reached the top of the hill, panting, I stood to catch my breath and laugh at myself. Running! What a crazy, drugged-up fool.

As I passed the playground, it occurred to me that I had no reason to be rushing back home. Christina wasn't coming for another couple of hours, and there was sunshine, and there were swings. And there was nothing stopping me from sitting on a swing in the sunshine for a little while. Does it sound obvious? It's not. We walk past things all the time, always on our way to somewhere else. This is one of the ways this place is affecting me: I am learning to stop. I stop to look at trees, or an interesting gate, or a derelict house. I stop to pick jasmine flowers, stroke a cat, or take photos of brightly coloured window shutters. I sometimes walk straight past a thing I would have liked to stop for, still hard-wired to keep going, save time, reach a destination; some of those times I catch myself doing it and go back. Those are good times; those are the times when I've won.

I don't always win. But this time, today, just as I left the playground behind and started on the path towards home, I turned right around and sat on a swing. Self-consciously, and with my feet planted firmly on the ground, but sitting on a swing, nonetheless. A few minutes passed, and I found myself pushing my toes gently into the ground. And then my heels. And then my toes again. I got a little swaying motion going, a tentative prelude to swinging, or a 36-year-old woman sitting on a swing and pretending she's not really into it, too scared to lift her feet off the ground and let go. Toes/heels/toes/heels, and the muted squeak of the hinges. I leaned back, experimentally, and looked up at the sky through the trees above. I made myself a little dizzy and lost my balance and my foot slipped and the swing jerked. And then I thought *fuck it*, and kicked. And I swung. I'd like to say that I soared into the sky, into the limitless blue, free of the worries that tether me to the earth, but really it was some average swinging on a rickety structure that now groaned in protest that it hadn't been built for me. But I did remember other times when I was small and light and it had felt like that. And I remembered the day when my childhood friend had flown off this exact same swing and landed on her face in the dirt, and got a scar on her cheek. Which made me very conscious of the age of the swing, so I let the motion wind itself down, and placed my feet back down on the ground.

Running and stopping aren't necessarily opposites. For some people, running might be their stopping, as long as they stop running *to* or *for,* and just run. There's a freedom to it then, a thing done without purpose or destination. Perhaps that's what my addled brain was craving when it urged me to go for a run. Perhaps my running is sitting on a swing. Keeping your feet on the ground is very wise, but you need to remember, sometimes, what it feels like to soar.

Being here is affecting me in many ways. And I think, perhaps, if I refrain from further solvent abuse, those ways will all be good. They might be alarming, like the urge to run, and they might be strange, but they'll be good.

# Day 37

I know where the hitchhiking went when it disappeared. It wasn't lost in the nineties, like I thought; it was hiding in off season Sifnos. It's been here all along. And I found it again today.

You can't take the sunshine for granted, and there have been too many sunny days I've missed. So I decided this morning that I would go to the beach while I still had the chance. I got as far as putting my bikini on, and then I did that thing I do, where I argued with myself that I didn't know the bus schedule, and I might as well just leave it for another day. But then I caught a glimpse of the sky outside my window, so impossibly, perfectly blue, and I made another decision: I would walk.

I loaded my rucksack with the essentials – towel, extra bikini to change into, pink hoodie top, book – and took the steps into town to post a letter and check the bus schedule for my return journey. As I was paying for my stamps, Post Office Man emerged from the back and handed me a package from Jo in London. I shoved it into my rucksack and took the road to the port.

There is no pavement along this road, it isn't meant for walking: it's carved out of the mountainside and it was made for cars. There is tarmac, and there are cliffs. It's bendy throughout, and very narrow in places. In one of those places, I heard a car approach, and I stepped aside and pressed myself against the safety railings to let it pass. The car slowed down.

I haven't shaken off the city cynicism yet; not all of it. As the car came to a stop, my first instinct was suspicion. The window rolled down and a kind old man asked if I was going to Kamares.

'Yes,' I replied curtly.

'Jump in the back,' he said. 'I'll take you.'

I said thank you but I wanted to walk. The man smiled, nodded his approval, wished me a pleasant walk, and drove away.

These things still happen here.

I walked. It took me longer than I expected. I walked and listened to music and took photos along the way and noticed things from an angle I hadn't looked at them before and stopped to note down phrases that came into my head and picked sage and oregano from the side of the road. A taxi passed me and beeped hello. I discovered the Grasshopper Quarter, a stretch of road about fifty metres long inexplicably taken over by dozens of the small brown insects that kept hopping into my path. Another car passed me, in the opposite direction. A cat leapt out of a bush and called out to her kitten in the field below. I walked, and it took me longer than I expected because I kept stopping, and also because every bend in the road failed to be the one that would finally bring me to the other side of the mountain and reveal the bay of Kamares down below.

I forget, sometimes, where I am; I forget that I'm on an island and what that means in terms of all that liquid blue, and what it does to the horizon. I stay in my little house, in my little village, and I look at the fields and the mountains and the sky, and I forget. But then, a final twist and there it was: my first glimpse of the sea. And with it another one of those moments when you have to stop and think, if you're that way inclined, of Cavafy and Ithaca and the true purpose of destinations. Or, if you prefer to rely on your own words, to just stand still and take it all in, the rugged, dry mountains on either side of you, and the sea in the distance below, wrapped up in flawless, cloudless sky, and try to find anything wrong with the world.

I arrived in Kamares at 12:20 and city girl kicked in again and starting making plans and apportioning time. The bus back to town was at 12:50, which gave me 5 minutes to get to the beach and take my clothes off, 15 minutes in the sea, 10 minutes to dry off, get changed and smoke a cigarette, and another 5 to walk to the bus stop by the quay, and make it back home in good time for lunch. And she picked up her pace with the determined air of someone who is excellent at achieving leisure and relaxation in the most efficient way possible. But Sifnos chick, the one who had stood on the road and looked at the bay from above, the one who sat on a swing, just laughed. 'Fuck your timetable,' she said. 'Fuck the bus. And fuck lunch.' She's not particularly eloquent, this Sifnos chick, and her manners could do with a bit of refinement, but there's no doubt she's the happier of the two.

So my disgruntled alter ego and I went to the beach and she watched in disapproving silence as I took a very long time to remove my jeans and top and hang them on a tree and spread out my towel on the sand and roll up a cigarette and smoke it contemplatively while listening to the whoosh of the waves. I went into the water and dove and swam and did a handstand and saw some fish and took my bikini top off and felt like a mermaid in my own, private ocean. When I came out, city girl sighed and shook her head, and we both watched the 12:50 bus pull in and pull out. 'Now look what you've done,' she said petulantly. 'There isn't another one until half past four.' I shrugged and opened Jo's package, and took out a pair of rainbow coloured woolly socks, and tried them on and had lots of fun taking photos of my feet in the socks in the sand, as I sat on a beach towel in my bikini. City girl did not share my amusement, or care for the point I was making about contrasts and things in unexpected places that fit, nonetheless.

I was going to walk back home, but I didn't. My All Stars had given me blisters (I should have worn my mum's trainers, but I was still frightened of the running connotations) and not even Sifnos chick was relaxed enough to attempt the uphill journey on sore feet. I walked to the far end of the port, where a taxi stood idle, and asked the driver if he was heading into town.

'I am,' he said. 'Let's keep each other company.'

I climbed into the back, and we introduced ourselves, and talked about the things we should have learned in school and those we learned instead (prompted by my confessing that I write in English, and his that he had never taken to it), and how we should never miss an opportunity to go to the beach, and the taxi business in winter, and how winter was still a long way off. He drove me all the way up to the entrance of my village, as far as a car can go, and only charged me half the fare. These things happen here.

There is much that is wrong with the world. The road twists and turns and it is long, and I forget, sometimes, about the horizon and the mountains and the blue. I forget where I am and I narrow my eyes and clench my fists when strangers approach me to offer me kindness, and when I stand alone on an empty beach I check the time in case there's someplace else I need to be. I haven't shaken it off yet, this instinct we have to annihilate our moments, to turn them into dust and build them into hours and days and weeks and months and years, just so we can look back and see all these piles of time that we've collected, burial mounds of dead time, because we didn't have the sense to live the moments that it's made of.

But there are times when I remember about the things that happen here, and that some things I thought were lost, like hitchhiking and random kindness and horizons, can still be found if I take the time to look in the right places. And never miss an opportunity to go to the beach.

# Day 38

I walked into the bathroom and clicked the light on and the lightbulb went pop and plunged me into darkness. And I thought: *the bathroom light gave up the ghost.* This is what my life is like these days: a never-ending narrative. Like déjà-vu, the phenomenon of remembering a scene as it happens, which neuroscience explains as sensory input that's taken a wrong turn and delivered to the bit of the brain in charge of forming long-term memories, my experiences are routed directly to the narrator, and processed as stories in the making.

This narrator is very fond of idioms. "Give up the ghost" is not a phrase I've ever used myself. I don't understand it. I know that it refers to dying or, in the case of inanimate objects, ceasing to function, but where does the ghost come into it? The implication seems to be that it was in there all along, and issues from the person or object at the moment of death; I can't help imagining the faint outline of a ghost lightbulb floating over the light fitting that used to be its home, and lamenting its brightness cut tragically short. But it doesn't make sense: the dead may become ghosts, but the living don't carry ghosts around with them, ready to be given up at the opportune moment. Etymological references suggest that when the word *ghost* entered the English language in this particular context, its meaning was closer to that of *spirit,* and it seems we have King James to thank for the idiom; according to his bible, Jesus was the first one to give up the ghost. Sinners who were smitten are also reported to have done the same; that's *smitten* in the biblical sense, although, come to think of it, people in love are always giving things up, and who's to say what that might include.

I won't allow the narrator to use such phrases. I am the subversive part of this partnership, the ambitious editor full of revolutionary ideas, who likes to go in and shuffle words around, and will not tolerate cliché and easy solutions. I am the educated one. I went to university and studied creative writing, and I was taught never to settle for the obvious description. I've also studied postmodernism and I am well aware of the death of the author and the impossibility of originality. The author has given up the ghost, and everything we say and do has been said and done before. But if all the words are borrowed, it strikes me that we should treat them with even more respect and strive to make the most of them, while we have them in our keeping. And not just take an idiom, like a ready meal from the supermarket shelves, and serve it straight out of the packet; we've got to shake it up a bit. That's why the editor likes shifting words around, whereas the narrator just wants to tell the story.

An article I read described déjà-vu as sensory input processed as "memory-in-progress". I like that. I think perhaps all of our experiences are memories in progress, in a sense. Stories in the making. The danger is our tendency to time-travel ahead to a point in the future when we can remember the thing that's happening right now. Much like our recent habit of looking at the world through cameras, capturing all our moments on digital devices rather than in our heads and in our hearts. Documenting our experiences to prove that we had them, reporting on our lives rather than living them. My narrator could have easily been guilty of that, of stepping out of the scene and searching her reference books for idioms to describe it, but it's a funny thing: the opposite is true. Through living my days one by one, as stories that I'm making, through always searching for the right words to tell them, I am more present in them than ever before. I notice the details, the tentative connections between things, the subtle undertones that turn a day into a story worth telling. I guess it's in the nature of the first person narrative: we may pretend distance, but we're always right there. We have to be, or there would be no story.

There is a device in fiction known as the unreliable narrator, the twist in the tale in himself, whose credibility is compromised in some way that makes the reader question how to interpret the story. Interpretation is also what concerns Mr Roland Barthes and the reason he kills his author; he claims that everything is "eternally written, here and now", each time it is read, and that the author's intentions or who he or she might be should play absolutely no part in what a reader takes away from a piece of writing. You write your story and then you give it up to the reader, and let them do with it what they like. You give up the ghost.

My narrator is extremely unreliable: she uses idioms willy-nilly, and makes things up all the time. She will do anything for the sake of a good story. Thankfully she doesn't speak out loud; she only makes suggestions in my head, like a theatre prompt giving me my cues out of sight. This, I feel, allows me to walk the line between sanity and mental illness, and call myself a writer. It is, however, getting a bit crowded around here. Between Antagonist, city girl, Sifnos chick, dead authors and unreliable narrators, editors, the occasional reporter or commentator, and the more elusive *me*, it's becoming increasingly hard to know which one of us is real, let alone sane, and who is telling the stories. But I suppose it doesn't matter, as long as the stories are told. And no one brings up any ghosts.

Speaking of which, they do, of course: the living carry ghosts around with them all the time. And it might not be a bad idea for all of us to be guided by King James and the smitten and dead authors, and give those things up.

As for me, specifically, I accept my death sentence but, in terms of giving things up, I prefer spirit to ghost.

I don't want my words to haunt you. But then again, my intentions don't matter and the words are not my own and everything is stories in the making being written over and over again, so I'm giving my spirit up, handing it over, setting it free. And you can make of it what you want.

This is day 38. It has been told.

# Day 39

I found a hairband left behind by one of my sisters on a window ledge in my bedroom. It is blue. It made me cry. This is their house, too, their summer home, and it's full of their stuff, and mine, and our mum's; stuff we all leave behind on purpose. But there was something about this little blue circle, unwound from Ariadne's or Margarita's hair and forgotten, so unobtrusive that it's been sitting there, on that window ledge, unnoticed for the past six weeks, that got to me. I could see my sister, one or the other, reaching back to untangle the elastic, placing it on the ledge and shaking out her hair, and then coming out to the kitchen to talk to me. It took me back to a moment when my sisters were still in the house and the hairband would be returned for, picked up again and twisted to make a ponytail. But they never returned for it. My sisters have other hairbands and this one was left behind to be found by me in mid October: a token to evoke their presence and invoke their absence, like a ghost.

We all leave stuff behind, on purpose. Mostly it's stuff that we want for next summer, clothes that can't be worn anywhere else, and Sifnos versions of everyday items: the Sifnos hairbrush, the Sifnos tweezers, the Sifnos flip-flops that have seen better days. Sometimes it's stuff that we don't want, and conveniently forget. In the room where my grandma slept, I found two plastic bags stuffed full of old newspapers. And people are always collecting pretty pebbles and interesting fragments of ceramic pots, and leaving them scattered all over the house. But as random as these findings might be, they are expected. Like our furniture and our kitchen utensils and the shampoo we all use and fight over, they are part of the house. We never question their presence; we take them as they come.

It took me days to sort out the house after everyone left. At first, it was obvious, practical things, clearing out the debris of an entire summer. Endless bedding and towels that needed to be washed and dried and returned to the cupboard. Empty bottles of shower gel to be thrown away. Cleaning out the fridge of everyone's forgotten snacks, and the kitchen cupboards of items in the wrong places, shoved in at random by too many people sharing a small house. Rice and pasta spilling out of open packets. Three separate, half empty bottles of olive oil. Crumbs everywhere. A bag of stale bread hanging off a hook.

Once all that was taken care of, and every surface had been scrubbed and bug spray applied to the appropriate places, I thought I was done. I stood back to admire my clean and tidy home, and went about the business of living in it. But, for all my scrubbing, it wasn't a clean slate. This house is built on layers upon layers of things that were once useful but have long ceased to be, and every time you try to throw something out someone will suggest it might be needed one day, and all the spaces that started off empty have been filled and filled again, and every time you clear a shelf someone comes along and puts something else on it because that's what we do with available space. And we all come here every summer and accept it, our beloved, dysfunctional house, because that's just how it is. We sidestep the obstacles and push the pebbles aside and that's how we live.

It took me a surprisingly long time to figure it out: the fact that things have always been a certain way doesn't mean they have to be. This revelation came to me in the form of frying pans. After weeks of struggling to get them in and out of their allocated drawer, it occurred to me that there were other spaces that could be used if I shifted a few things around, which would result in me not swearing out loud and kicking things every time I wanted to fry some food. So I emptied out all the drawers and cupboards in the kitchen, and put everything exactly where I wanted it. And then I had a very baffling moment, in which I stood in a kitchen that suddenly made sense, and thought *what the fuck have I been doing all this time?*

And when I looked around again, I saw a hundred things that were just as obvious as stale bread and dirty sheets, and just as unacceptable, once I'd allowed myself to question them. And I could tackle them in exactly the same way. Why spend my time endlessly pushing pebbles aside when I could just take them out into the garden? I started with that, and I carried on. I rearranged every cupboard and every wardrobe. I moved the furniture around, again and again, until I hit upon the layout that worked. I threw a lot of things out, and there was no one here to argue. I even cleared out some spaces that I haven't yet filled. I change something every day, and I'm far from done. Even now, I'm looking at the TV set that I never turn on, the TV set that is only here so my grandma can watch the news, and it bothers me, sitting there on its stand by my desk, but I haven't moved it. I might do it today. Tomorrow, it'll be something else.

I had a *what the fuck* moment a few weeks after I quit my job in May, and noticed how good it felt to not be running on stress. I had another one when I decided not to go back to London in September just because I'd said I would. Now, since I've been here on my own, I have them almost every day. Every time I do something that I'd denied myself before, simply because it wasn't what I did; every time I don't do something that I've always done, compulsively, unthinkingly, because I've always done it. Every time I sit at my desk to write, with another whole day ahead of me and no need to even glance at the time, because all of it is mine.

They are disconcerting, these moments, an odd combination of elation and shock. We are every day defeated by things we have never tried to take on. We take them as they come, without question, right up until the moment we question them, and understand that we don't have to live this way. And that's what shocks me: how I didn't know this before.

Making changes will always mean letting some things go. Some of them will be things that served no purpose and they will make space for those that do; others will leave gaps that ache and cause you to cry at hairbands. But we need those reminders, accidental or deliberate, of the things we've given up for the life we want, so that we can reach for a frying pan easily, at any time, or spend a winter alone on an island and be who we need to be.

And when I question myself and fall into the gaps, I will call my sisters on the phone and hear them say that I'm doing the right thing, and I'll realise it isn't a gap they've left, after all, but the space to miss them, a space to evoke their presence and be filled again when the time is right.

# Day 40

The wind changed last night. Faithful to the advice imparted by Margarita, hairdresser and off-season guru, I propped all my windows open and invited it in to do its magic.

This is a new wind. It's not the seasonal *meltemi*, the dry, north-westerly wind of the Aegean Sea that cools us down on August afternoons and carries our laundry off into the next field. It's not the nameless northerly wind that howls and rips branches off the trees. This one is blowing in from the south, a tropical wind rumoured to have set off from the Sahara and bringing us presents of desert sand. Soon, everything will be covered with a coating of fine, reddish dust. There are warnings on the news to keep our windows shut and avoid going out as much as possible.

My windows are open because Margarita said the wind will drive the humidity out. I don't mind about the dust, but this wind is wetter than a Turkish *hammam*. I can actually feel it on my skin as it whirls into the house and settles down, enveloping me in its warm, sticky tropical embrace. I imagine its journey from the desert up, swirls of dust travelling through north Africa and picking up exotic scents from the open markets and then crossing into the Mediterranean to be baptised in the heavy saltiness of the sea air before reaching me here, on my Aegean island, to say a brief, damp hello and moving on to Athens, to paint the cars red. I imagine it as a pungent, perfumed wind, both spicy and salty but, apart from a lingering mustiness, I cannot detect anything of Africa in its wake. I'm a little disappointed.

It kept me awake last night, this wind. It brought the mosquitoes back, for one, a feature of holiday Sifnos I was happy to leave behind in the summer. I had only just put my mosquito repellent away, a plug-in device that burns blue tabs to emit a strong, sweet smell that repels mosquitoes and people alike. The device was in the cupboard in the hallway; the mosquitoes were in my room. They approached me with their ominous high-pitched buzz, and feasted on my knuckles. I flapped about wildly and slapped my own face several times, in the time-honoured tradition of the half-asleep who will do anything to avoid getting out of bed.

Having failed to address the problem through self harm, I shrouded myself in my duvet, but the heat and humidity that were blowing in meant I was drenched in sweat within moments, and I had to throw the duvet off. A mosquito bit me promptly on the chin, and the wind coursing through all the open windows rattled and banged its way around the house. This isn't a howling wind; it's more the whooshing type. Except a whoosh is a gentle thing, whereas this wind expresses itself in the rushing, roaring sound of rapids, or the throaty baritone of motorway traffic. And it's just as constant. It doesn't gust, it doesn't stop, it doesn't vary its intensity: it just rushes through, powerful, determined, an unbroken line of single-mindedness all the way from Africa. I suppose it's an admirable quality in a wind, this constancy. It can certainly be relied upon to keep you awake.

But it wouldn't be fair to put all the blame on the wind and the mosquitoes. I am going to Athens this evening, and it scares me. The anxiety arrived as a tingling in my stomach yesterday morning, and it's been building up ever since. That's what kept me awake last night.

Of all my multiple personalities, I like Sifnos chick the most, and I don't want her tainted by the city. She's too fragile still, and I'm scared she might refuse to get on the boat. Or that she might slip away, unnoticed, as we're boarding, and I won't know until I reach the other side, and find that it's city girl that steps off the ferry in Piraeus. Because this is what happens, with certain places; they do that to you.

I've noticed it at times when I've been away from London for a while, and I step onto the Underground platform and feel the stale air against my face as the train pulls in, and I'm instantly transformed into a Londoner again. Fresh off the plane and already muttering passive-aggressively about people standing on the wrong side of the escalator. 'It's really not that hard,' I mumble, and roll my eyes, feeling at once righteous and put upon. And I don't mind that; in fact, I'm quite proud of being an arsehole Londoner. I've worked for it. And I'm actually one of the good ones. I will stop to give tourists directions when I spot them staring in near-panic at their maps, and I even smile at my fellow passengers on the tube; I just will not tolerate people standing on the left hand side on the escalators. Because it really isn't that hard.

It's different in Athens: I don't like the person I become when I'm there. We have a very complicated relationship, that city and I. It seems to disapprove of me, and I react like a rebellious teenager and behave badly. I feel suffocated by it. If Sifnos greets me cautiously, making no promises but placing its mountains at my feet and letting me draw my own conclusions, and London ignores me completely and lets me get on with things, Athens grabs me by the scruff of the neck, like a naughty child, and tells me I can't ride my bike until I've cleaned my room. And no matter what I do, I'm never up to standard; my room is never clean enough. No matter what I do, I can't make myself fit in. So I've stopped trying, and ride my bike elsewhere.

But it's still my city. I was born there, and I know how to navigate its streets. And I suppose it's survival of the fittest, because you can't bring Sifnos chick to Athens and let her wander around dreamily looking for jasmine flowers to pick. She'll be dead the first time she tries to cross the road. I'll have to be city girl to an extent, if I hope to survive the weekend without getting run over. But what worries me is this: if I leave Sifnos chick behind, will the writer still come along? And if I let her have a couple of days off, will she come back? Or will I return to an empty house, a city girl in Sifnos staring at a blank computer screen, with neither Sifnos chick nor writer to help me find the words to fill it, and visited by no one except the neighbour and her damaged hip, and Antagonist, when she's ready to say 'I told you so'? Is it really that fragile, this thing that I've been doing for the last forty days? Can it survive a weekend in Athens?

At around 4am I gave up and got out of bed. I rummaged around in the cupboard for the mosquito device, fed it a deadly blue tab and plugged it in. I applied coconut oil to my bites, and rubbed insect repellent lotion into every exposed bit of flesh. And then I went around and closed all the windows, one by one, and all the bedroom doors, and rolled up carpets to form draught excluders, and wedged my own door shut so it wouldn't rattle anymore. I got back into bed, and thanked Sifnos chick for taking care of all that. City girl couldn't cope with this shit. She'd just lie there, with the duvet over her head and the wind rattling and rumbling the hours away until dawn.

The blue tab released its sweet, terrible scent and, in the relative quiet, I fell asleep. And the girl who writes got up this morning, and went to her desk and has been typing words onto her screen ever since. I think she'd like to come to Athens, because I've promised her pizza and she's been subsisting on a diet of mostly aubergines for a while now. Maybe we can leave Sifnos girl here, to look after the house and open the windows if the wind changes again. Maybe we can bribe her with some treats from the big city to ensure she doesn't wander off while we're gone.

Maybe I could cut myself, and the writer, some slack. Maybe I can learn from Sifnos chick and relax a little, and bring this writer with me to the city and show her around, and have a slice of pizza and a drink, and trust that whatever it was that caused her to take over my life in the first place will still be here when I come back. And that it's not so fragile that it cannot withstand the tantrums of a petulant teenager and a few streets that are hard to cross.

# Day 41

I have become one of those people who write in cafés. The ones who sit there with their laptops, amidst the chaos of people queuing up to order coffee and eating blueberry muffins and fighting for seats and chattering about their jobs, and just tap away serenely on their keyboards as if they were alone in the world. I think this happens mostly in New York, and the people in question are impossibly cool, and their laptop is always a Mac. They order cappuccinos or perhaps double espressos, and then fail to drink them because they're so engrossed in the masterpiece they're committing to their screen before your very eyes.

I've always aspired to be one of them, but it's not entirely a joke when I call myself a reclusive author: I need almost perfect silence to write. I can barely tolerate background music, and other people are out of the question. I do have a Mac, so I'm good on that score but even so, I don't think I could ever pull off the level of cool required to join my fellow writers in Starbucks.

And yet, here I am, tapping away on the keyboard of my Mac, in a café in the port of Sifnos. I am drinking instant coffee because that's all they had, and *they* is a solitary man who seemed a bit taken aback by my arrival and told me he's just waiting for his business partner to take over so he can catch the 19:25 ferry to Athens, same as me. I might as well be alone in the world; excluding the man who's going around putting candles out on the empty tables and the two café cats, I am the only one here. And Enya is issuing loudly and atmospherically out of the speakers, which seems fitting, somehow. I am not all that engrossed in my work – missing my ferry for the sake of my art will only achieve the loss of 39 euro, and prove nothing – and this is not likely to be a masterpiece they'll talk about for years to come, and a beachfront café in the port of Sifnos in October is arguably as far as you can get from downtown Manhattan, or wherever it is that the cool people hang out. But let it be known that I am here, in a café, with my laptop, writing away. I am one of those people, if only for tonight.

I am travelling light, but appearances will deceive. My luggage is a large suitcase that contains a smaller suitcase, which is empty. I brought it into town on foot, and lifted it easily, one-handed, onto the bus, and carried it high off the ground all the way from the café to the port and onto the ferry, and the muscles in my arm barely twitched. I've attracted some curious looks, a couple of double takes. People must think I'm some sort of superhuman, sauntering around so carefree, swinging a giant suitcase as if it weighed nothing. Which, practically, it does. I confessed to Leonidas, who spotted me as I passed the taxi stand, and Vasiliki, Vangelia's daughter, who was waiting to collect someone from the boat. 'It's empty,' I told them. 'I'm going to Athens for supplies.'

The rucksack on my back contains my laptop, two pairs of knickers, my wallet and a scarf. That, and the clothes I'm wearing and my phone in the front pocket of my jeans is all I'm taking with me. This is more than symbolic: I don't really have that much to bring. I'm bringing an empty suitcase to fill up with things to take back. But it is symbolic, too. Something about wanting to leave as much of myself behind as I could, to stake my claim on the house and the life I've been living there and, conversely, bringing as little as possible to Athens. I don't want to encourage it, or give it the impression that I'm staying.

I am now a person who writes on boats. It's not particularly easy, but I'm determined. My tray table is too narrow and my laptop is balanced precariously on the edge, at a funny angle, and I'm having to hold the bottom with one hand so it doesn't topple over as I type. There are probably no more than thirty passengers in the economy class lounge, including the man from the café who is asleep with an eye mask on a few seats away, but there might as well be a thousand, for all the peace I'm getting. The obligatory screaming child is present, somewhere behind me, as is the shrill-voiced woman who has a lot to say. This is far from what I'm used to, my quiet desk looking out onto the garden and the blue-shuttered houses of the village beyond. Or even my candlelit table at the beachfront café, with Enya's ethereal vocals and the waves crashing against the shore below.

But I can feel city girl stirring, and I have to keep writing. I would like to put my laptop away, and eat the cheese pie I bought earlier and read my book, and maybe even sleep for a while, but I'm scared that if I do those things she will take over, and there's no telling what might happen then.

There's movement to my left and I turn around cautiously, expecting to see Antagonist with a smirk on her face, or a deranged passenger who is too keen for human contact on a boat full of empty space, but it's the writer who's taken the seat beside me.

'You can stop now,' she says gently. 'Just stop.' That's all she says. She puts her hand on my shoulder, and squeezes, and lets go. With her eyes, she indicates my laptop. I hesitate for a moment and then I flip the screen down and put it to sleep.

'I think I'll go smoke a cigarette,' I say.

It's very windy out on the deck, and a few resolute smokers are huddling in corners struggling to light their cigarettes. I get mine going and I sit on a bench to smoke it. The deck is lit by low yellow lights and everything else is black: black sea, black sky. We are crossing a stretch of open sea, far from any islands, and there is nothing on the horizon. The Saharan weather persists, and it's warmer up here than it is inside, and much more peaceful, despite the noise of the engine. I lie back on the bench with my feel dangling over the edge and stare at the black above.

When I return to the lounge, the writer is curled up sideways on her seat, asleep. She opens her eyes when I sit down and smiles at me lazily before closing them again. I slip my laptop back into my rucksack and take out my cheese pie and my book. I eat, but I can't focus on reading, and I can't get to sleep, either: it's too noisy and too bright. I put my earphones in to block out the hubbub of the lounge, and listen to music with my knees up against the seat in front. Every now and then, I glance over to my left, reflexively, to reassure myself of the writer's sleeping presence. I can't help it. It's like when you spend the night with a new lover and you keep waking up to check that they're still lying there, beside you. I'll get used to her in time. In time, I might even take her for granted. I might come to expect that she'll be there, wherever I am.

I know that the writer is me. I know I'm Sifnos chick, and city girl, and even Antagonist. I know that I am all these people, all at once, and I shouldn't need to give them names and voices and personalities, and have them tell me the things that I do or do not want to hear. But I need them still, and names are powerful things. With a name I can summon them or dismiss them, and that's a very old kind of magic, and I need it still. I need the magic to make sense of all that's happening. Perhaps one day I'll just be me, a person who spent a winter in Sifnos, a person who once wrote in a café, a person who talks to cats and stops to pick flowers and knows how to use her elbows to claim her space on the Athens Metro, and can tell you the best place to get a burger in every London borough, and which bus to take to get there. And I won't need to split myself a hundred ways to reconcile all this. I'll take it for granted.

In the meantime, there is a writer asleep in the seat next to me and she is mine and we are going to Athens.

# Day 42

At Monastiraki station, on our way to Piraeus, my mum and I met the speaking train information service. She manifested in the form of a short, squeaky girl. We were debating how long the train journey would take. I said twelve minutes; my mum argued for much longer.

'Fine,' I conceded. 'Let's say fifteen.'

The speaking train information service leant into our conversation, unsolicited.

'I will tell you,' she said. 'It takes just under ten minutes from here to Kallithea, around two minutes between each station. From Kallithea to Moschato, it's just over two minutes. Another two or three minutes to Faliro, and then let's say four or five to Piraeus.' She paused. 'So that's approximately eighteen minutes altogether, from Monastiraki to Piraeus.' Another pause, presumably to allow us to digest this information. 'I know this,' she added. And stepped back.

My mum and I exchanged a look, muttered out thanks, and got on the train. I checked the time, 13:14 at the moment of our departure, and kept an eye on it on my phone throughout the journey, determined to prove her triumphantly wrong when we reached the port in fifteen minutes or less. We arrived at exactly 13:32. I slipped my phone into my pocket and kept my mouth shut.

It was an interesting journey, with on-board entertainment that consisted of a varied line-up of beggars and buskers: almost every stop introduced a new, exciting act.

**Thissio:** Middle-aged lady, handful of ball point pens. She speaks in the passionate, rising and falling tones of a traditional lament. 'Good evening my good people. My (genderless) child has emphysema and also blah-blah wrong with its aorta and needs to have an operation. I cannot afford to pay for its personal care so I am selling these pens for thirty cents each.' Said pens are thrust in passengers' faces. 'Please. God bless you. Only thirty cents. Please. For my child.'

**Tavros**: Ten-year old boy, large accordion. He moves through the carriage, sounding a series of seemingly unconnected notes. He approaches each passenger individually, presses the accordion against them, and says 'please'.

**Petralona - Kallithea**: Intermission. Small girl in pushchair tosses full cup of frappuccino-type drink, grenade-style, onto the floor. It explodes, splashing several bystanders and creating a fast-expanding puddle that moves threateningly towards people's feet and luggage. 'It looks like poo,' she observes happily, while her mother attempts to mop it up with tissues donated by other passengers.

**Moschato**: Man in late twenties, pronounced limp, no other props. 'Hello guys. I lost both my parents is a traffic accident ten days ago. I am now homeless and I'm sleeping at the port. I have no one. Give me some change, guys, for a plate of food. I'm all alone. Come on, you guys, just a bit of change.' As he passes the beverage-throwing girl, who is now out of her pushchair and squiggling like a worm in her father's arms, he breaks into a huge, genuine smile that lights up his face. I notice he's quite attractive. I'm still very confused by his back story.

Public transport featured heavily in this short trip to Athens. It began on the Friday night, when I stepped off the boat in Piraeus. I had braced myself for the shock of noise and traffic at the port, but I hadn't accounted for the weekend revellers. The train station was busy, but I got a seat, cloaked myself in what remained of my Sifnos mellowness, and settled in for a brief and painless journey to the centre. The sudden proximity to the girl in the seat next to me and the knees of the man opposite brushing against mine made me a little nervous, but I was coping well enough, for a recluse. Up until Kallithea, when the train doors flew open, much like the gates of hell, and all the youth of Athens descended upon me, dressed up and perfumed, and draped themselves over my suitcase. I felt the prelude to a panic attack bubbling up in my stomach. 'Get a grip,' remarked city girl, compassionately, but I just clenched my fists and took shallow breaths all the way to Monastiraki.

It was the final stretch of the journey, all two stops of it, on the Metro, that broke me. I stood in the middle of the carriage, straddling my suitcase and with my rucksack exposed on my back, jostled by a million over-excited Athenians, and I realised, with a mixture of curiosity and horror, that I'd been touched by more people in the last ten minutes than I'd seen in an entire month. I gave city girl a nod, and she jumped in.

'Touch me and you die,' she growled at the assorted youth around us, and cleared a space wide enough to breathe. She spent the rest of the journey assessing danger and glaring menacingly at anyone who as much as glanced in my direction or brushed accidentally against my bag. When we reached our destination, she picked up my suitcase and rammed it into people's legs, causing them to part like the Red Sea, begrudgingly but with more respect than they'd show someone asking politely to be let off. I was extremely grateful to her.

Another notable journey was the one to Alexis' house, when I got on the wrong bus and found myself travelling through residential streets I'd never seen before. The only other passenger took against the earrings I was wearing, which featured the Hindu goddess Lakshmi. Through narrowed eyes he informed me that the only true god was our lord Jesus Christ, and quoted several passages from the Bible to illustrate this point. I argued that we all have our own ways and our own beliefs, and we're just doing the best we can, but this did nothing to pacify him. 'You are lost,' he told me. He was right. When he got off, the driver asked if I was OK; the man had recently joined a cult, he said, and I should pay no attention. We had a short philosophical discussion, and then he drove me past the end of his route, to a place I recognised. Alexis picked me up in his car. 'I thought you said you knew your way around this city,' he said with a smirk. City girl told him to fuck off, and proper balance was restored.

My mum had to help me onto the ferry: I am no longer travelling light. The suitcase that I lifted oh so casually on my way to Athens is now an unbearable burden that will most likely kill me before I reach my longed-for Sifnos home. The task of getting it all the way there is so impossible that it's almost funny; in fact, I actually stopped to laugh a couple of times en route from my mum's house to the Metro station, as I dragged the thing for three metres at a time and understood, with perfect clarity, that it couldn't be done and that I'd have to do it, anyway.

There's a saying in Greece that goes: "There is no such thing as *I can't*; there is only *I don't want to*". By the time we reached Piraeus and I was faced with another fifteen minutes of bearing this cross on rickety wheels through portside traffic, I quite resolutely did not want to. We stopped a cab and explained to the bemused driver that he needed to convey us 800 metres down the road to Gate E9. It was the best 5 euro I ever spent.

We managed to get my suitcase onto the luggage racks on the ferry, and then my mum walked me upstairs, to the second level open deck. We found a bench and sat down and pretended to be relaxed, and even joked about my mum accidentally coming to Sifnos with me, if the boat happened to set sail while she was still on it. We kept this up for about ten minutes and then she bolted up, hugged me, and left.

163

There were a few of us up on the open deck, chasing the sun around. In Piraeus, we all started off in the shade, fighting for occupancy of the few benches that were protected from direct sunlight. As soon as the boat left the safety of the port and the wind hit the deck, a game of musical chairs began as, one by one, we all abandoned our shaded benches for the nearest available spot in the sun. Every time the sun shifted, so did we. I managed a few fifteen-minute naps before having to move again, adding another layer of clothing each time, but I eventually ran out of both clothes and sunny spots, and gave up. The 20th of October is clearly not the time to attempt to sleep on the open deck of a moving boat. Another important lesson in off-season survival: bring a sleeping bag, or be prepared for the sticky plastic seats and glaring strip lights of the economy lounge.

As we came into the port of Kithnos, our first stop and still close to three hours away from Sifnos, I snuck into the first class seating area. There wasn't anything particularly special about it, but it did have spacious airplane-type seats and it was quiet. And empty: there were perhaps eighty seats in there, and seventy-six of them unoccupied. I felt resentful of a world where seventy-six seats must remain empty just because a piece of paper says so, and in a gesture of protest, and also because I wanted to read my book in greater comfort than that afforded by the economy lounge on the level below, I claimed a seat for myself. I sat stiff and straight backed for the first few minutes, poised for getting caught and ceremoniously evicted back to the plastic chairs, where I belonged. But city girl, who had chosen not to follow my mum back to the city, even though I'd given her the option, whispered defiance in my ear. For all of her faults, she is not easily intimidated, and she'll claim her comforts where she can get them. Emboldened, I arranged myself in my best approximation of nonchalant entitlement, kicked my shoes off, and laid back to enjoy my book. No one paid me any attention at all.

Towards the end of the journey, I went outside to smoke a cigarette. And it occurred to me, as I stood on the deck, moderately cold and windswept, lit by the glow of the lounge that I'd just left and that appeared so cosy and inviting now, and looking out at the dark sea and the very faint lights of Sifnos in the distance, that there is something in me that thrives on a bit of adversity. I like comfort, but not all the time; I like to struggle for it sometimes. I like getting lost and being found. I like windswept decks and warming my hands on a cup of stale, ship-brewed filter coffee. I like a clandestine seat in the first class lounge and a suitcase that's impossible to carry. I like a bit of roughness in my seas; if it's all plain sailing, I might not even notice that I'm going anywhere.

Perhaps we're all like that, and we need the adversity to remind us that we're entitled to a comfortable seat and to spending 5 euro on a two minute cab ride because we just don't want to carry that heavy suitcase anymore. And that we are, each of us, doing the best we can, no matter what our back story might be or which deity happens to be dangling from our ears.

# Day 43

It's hunting season in Sifnos. Shots have been ringing out all day, echoing across the fields and scattering birds. I'm getting used to them now, but they were quite shocking the first few times: the contrast between an almost total silence and these blasts that shatter it is too sharp to ever recede, completely, to background noise.

You see empty shells in the summer sometimes, half-buried in the ground or lying on the side of the road, colourful plastic tubes with rusting metal caps, but you never hear shots. Each one that is fired now puts me in mind of the single shot that signals the beginning of a race, or the gun salutes used to mark important occasions. I think there might be something in this: that the launch of the hunting season and the off season coincide, and there's something ritualistic about those shots. I came back from Athens last night, and it feels different now, somehow. I have bought an electric blanket, and I am here to stay. And they are firing their guns to say: this is when it all truly begins.

Leonidas picked me up from the port. He lifted my suitcase into the boot of his cab, and I threw my new electric blanket, still in its box, in after it.

'Ah!' Leonidas exclaimed, interrupting me mid-rant about the heavy suitcase and its useless wheels. 'You got one!' He picked up the box and examined it carefully before giving a slow nod and placing it back into the boot. 'Yes,' he said, 'this is what you need.'

'I'm very excited,' I admitted and, eager to impress him with my commitment to island life, I went on to tell him, as we drove up the mountain towards the town, that I'd also ordered a dehumidifier to be delivered next week. He made noises of approval, and gave some advice on positioning the device for optimum effect. We drove in silence for a while after that, a comfortable silence as he negotiated the sharp bends in the dark roads and I took in the new feeling of homecoming that these same roads now evoked.

'How has it been?' I said at length. 'What did I miss?'

Leonidas thought for a while. 'We had a northern wind on Sunday. It cleared the air nicely,' he reported.

'Good,' I said. 'That's good.' It felt like the right thing to say, although the northern wind is the one that gusts and howls, and it's really not my favourite. I didn't mind having missed out on its latest visit. 'I'm glad to be back,' I added. Which was true.

Leonidas drove me as far as the road allowed.

'I wish I could take you further,' he said, as he placed my suitcase at my feet.

'Me too,' I agreed, wistfully. 'I really wish you could.'

I paid him and said good night. He paused before getting back into his cab.

'Enjoy this,' he said. 'Be happy.

'I will,' I said.

I am.

I waved goodbye and took the long, dimly lit path home, dragging my suitcase over broken cobblestones and donkey shit, on wheels not equipped to deal with such terrain. It lurched and wobbled and toppled over several times and crushed my foot, and the screeching, dragging noise it made sent one of the neighbourhood dogs into a panicked frenzy, and she darted out of her house and followed me, yapping madly, for about fifty metres, which didn't really help, but it did make me laugh. It took me almost twenty minutes to cross a distance that normally takes less than five, and I arrived at my front door stooped and twisted like a goblin, and with aches in every part of my body that I knew were only the precursor to the pain that would come in the morning, and I didn't even care. I was home.

It feels different now. Newly scary, but good. With the trip to Athens behind me, there is nothing left but an uninterrupted stretch of days and weeks and months, all the way from here to December; unbroken, and mine. It's just me and the island now, and there's no denying that winter is on its way. It's in the quality of the light and the smell of the soil. It's in the chill that permeates the house, the damp that took over in the two days I was away, despite the refreshing northerly wind. It's in the wind itself, no longer here to cool us down, but here to tell us that it's time to close our windows and huddle up upside with a hot cup of tea. It's time to turn our electric blankets on.

I think maybe going to Athens and coming back was some kind of test that I passed. I think Leonidas got in touch with the Board of the Secret Club and reported on my electric blanket, and my dehumidifier, and the fact that I gave the correct response to the wind. I think it's them out there now, firing their guns to say: welcome.

# Day 44

Contrasts. Let's say between a shopping trip to your local Sainsbury's in London and vegetable shopping at the organic farm in Sifnos. A weekday in late October, 6pm. Let's say that weather conditions are roughly the same: overcast and drizzling, with a moderate wind in Sifnos and London colder by a few degrees. You leave the house, probably through several doors, lifts, stairways and carpeted hallways. You step out onto the street, into the harsh, artificial glow of the ever-necessary streetlights and neon shop signs. You walk along the pavement, around puddles and rubbish and broken glass, past traffic lights and zebra crossings and people waiting for the bus. Cars zoom past; a police siren sounds in the distance, coming closer. You reach Sainsbury's: sliding doors and a sudden blast of hot air from the overdoor heater. The security guard ignores you.

You leave the house and step into the yard. The almost tree rustles in the wind and rains a few dry leaves over you. You walk down a path carved into the mountainside by the stream that used to flow through here in winters long ago, before the village blocked its way, and onto the main road. The streetlights are not on yet. In the eerie pre-dusk light, you walk in the middle of the road, past olive trees and fields being prepared for the winter crops and six goats and a single car. You reach the farm; you call out the farmer's name.

You take a basket and make your way methodically around the aisles, hot to cold and brightly lit, while generic pop music plays in the background, and the self-checkout lady screams 'Please scan your items'. You squeeze past shoppers and baskets and pushchairs to reach shiny tomatoes in plastic packaging, and 100gr bags of baby rocket leaves for a pound. You put some other items in your basket, mesmerised by stickers and labels and 3 for 2 offers. You queue up for the self-checkout; you scan, you bag, you feed your card into the slot, you pay, you take your receipt as instructed. 'Thank you for using Sainsbury's self check out', says the lady machine. You exit through the sliding doors; the security guard ignores you.

Nikos comes out with his sleeves rolled up to his elbows, and a dusting of flour across his front. 'We're baking cookies,' he explains, and hands you a pair of scissors and two plastic bags. 'Not that many tomatoes left,' he warns. 'You'll have to rummage around.' You make your way slowly from patch to patch, separating tomatoes for salad and tomatoes for sauce, snipping handfuls of rocket leaves just above the roots, and pulling beetroot straight out of the soil. You go on a treasure hunt for chillies, and discover three different types. You get a mild rash on your arm and mud all over your shoes. You take two bags full over to the house, and rap on the kitchen window. A dog jumps on you and leaves wet paw marks on your jeans; Nikos comes out and tells him off. You return his scissors and he glances at your bags. 'Just give me a fiver,' he says. Transaction now complete, you chat about homemade cookies versus the store bought kind, and how having no money enables you to think in different ways, and then Nikos slaps his forehead and disappears into the house. He emerges a few seconds later, holding out a cookie. 'I almost forgot!' he says. It's still warm, and tastes exactly like a home baked cookie should. You say so, and Nikos beams. 'I'll be starting on the winter stuff from next week,' he tells you as you're leaving. 'Spinach, lettuce, radishes. It's gonna be amazing!' You pat the dog, and three cats follow you to the gate, to see you out.

You rush home through traffic and people and noise, carrying heavy bags full of things you didn't intend to buy. You stop in the corner shop to top up your Oyster card. The shopkeeper grunts in greeting. 'Fifty pee charge for credit card payment,' he barks; you accept this with a nod. You collect another receipt, walk along pavements, cross a few roads, unlock several doors, and you're home again. You unpack your shopping, as is, into the fridge, freezer and kitchen cupboards. You put the TV on and stick a buy-one-get-one-free pizza into the oven. You top it up with rocket, which is washed and ready to eat and one of your 5-a-day, and just a tiny bit slimy.

You make your way home back up the empty road, swinging bags full of fresh vegetables, in a silence punctuated by the tingle of sheep bells and the occasional gunshot. The streetlights have come on, but they are few and far between, and the mountains are dark shapes against a multicoloured sky. You pick some oregano from a bush. At the bottom of the path that leads up to the house, you encounter a man finishing up some roadworks. 'Good evening,' he says. 'Hello,' you respond. You smile, he waves, and you carry on. You notice some pink clouds, and stop to take a photo. You reach the house sweating and out of breath, and kick leaves off your doorstep so they don't blow inside. You put some music on and spend an hour washing soil and bugs out of your vegetables, and drying it, and swaddling the leaves in paper towels, like babies, to keep them fresh. You cook the squishy batch of tomatoes with some garlic and the fresh oregano you just picked, to keep in jars for later, and boil some beetroot for dinner while munching on spicy, crunchy rocket leaves.

My sister called me last night, as I was rinsing out my rocket leaves and the tomato sauce was bubbling away on the stove. 'What are you doing?' she asked, so I told her about my vegetables and my shopping trip. 'Well,' she said, 'I've just left work now because it was so busy, and I had a flu jab in my lunch break.' It was just past 7pm in London and, sure enough, there was a siren screaming in the background. 'I'm just saying,' she added. 'About the contrast.'

She wasn't complaining, and I don't pity her: my sister has a lovely life. She has good friends and a wonderful husband and she buys organic vegetables from the farmers' market and she does yoga and meditates to keep the sirens out of her head, and on Sundays she cycles over to the market in Columbia Road to buy flowers to decorate her quirky, sunny flat. On top of which, she has a giant Sainsbury's within ten minutes' walk, where she can get just about anything she might conceive of, and more, seven days a week. I know that life; I used to have it too – not the same but similar, in the fundamental things. But the contrast between that and this makes us both pause in our conversation and shake our heads in wonder. Because my life, now, is made up entirely of those moments that my sister has to snatch out of different life, a life that can easily become all about plastic packaging and concrete pavements and automated transactions under harsh neon lights, if you let it. She has to fight for those moments, to seek them out and carve a space for them in her every day, whereas I just stroll out of my house and pull rocket leaves from the ground with my hands, as a hilltop cemetery becomes a work of art against a backdrop of cloud and setting sun.

And while I love London and large supermarkets and doing my shopping without having to exchange a single word with another human being, and I know I will return there one day and I'll be glad that I can buy bagfuls of rocket for a pound at any time of the day or night, I cannot believe that this contrast should go unremarked. I cannot believe that muddy vegetables and homemade cookies and pink clouds don't do something to your soul, or whatever it is you call the thing that gets you out of bed each morning.

And I know that this kind of life is not sustainable in the long term, but I'd like to think that I can bring some of it with me, for when I'm getting out of a different bed. My soul may have to make do with clouds in greyscale and cookies that come in a box, but maybe I'll remember about the alternatives, and the contrasts that make us pause in conversation, and about putting those moments in your day so the sirens don't drown out your thoughts. And when I go to Sainsbury's, maybe I'll smile at the security guard and sometimes even queue for the cashier rather than the self-checkout, and take my time to get back home, and seek out places where I can look upon some kind of horizon and the dark shapes of buildings against a lighter sky, and pause to shake my head in wonder and make the contrasts a little less sharp, before rushing back to my frozen pizza.

# Day 45

I have made a mistake. I have put a load of laundry in the washing machine, and I know what's going to happen now: I will live with damp clothes hanging stiff off the clothes horse for a week. They will smell bad, and they'll make the house even colder, drawing more humidity in and laughing at my sad little storage heaters.

I cannot take them outside. The wind has gone insane. I thought I'd met all its different personas by now but this, again, is new. According to my grandfather and my grandma who, perched on opposite sides of my family tree in their separate living rooms, like to keep an eye on the weather for all of us, and panic accordingly, there are high winds all over Europe. My grandma called to inform me that there was a cold front coming into Greece, and went on to express her concern about my uncle's trip to somewhere particularly northern this weekend, a place neither of us could place on the map, but vaguely understood to be mountainous and cold.

In a later phone call, my grandfather reported that this was another southerly wind, and as high as an 8 or 9 on the Beaufort scale. 'At least it will be warm,' I remarked, pretending knowledge. 'No,' he corrected sternly, and employed technical terms about pressure and weather fronts to demonstrate why this particular southerly wind would in fact bring the temperature down even further. I understood nothing, but my grandfather was a vice-admiral in the Greek navy, commanding actual ships in the war, so I wasn't about to argue. 'Don't leave the house,' he advised. I assured him I would not. We then progressed to an analysis of the weather in London, and the question of whether or not my sister should be leaving the house. I pointed out that she had no choice and it was reluctantly conceded that she could, provided she took the appropriate precautions. These weather-related phone calls are a common occurrence. The Greek news programs are notorious for sensational reports, which have often turned flooding in the South West of England into an imminent danger to me, as I strolled through the streets of London, unaware that the Thames was about to burst its banks, or a huge tidal wave was on its way from Cornwall and would arrive to flatten the city any moment now. Assorted grandparents would place panicked calls and if I failed to answer, it was immediately assumed that I had drowned/blown away/been crushed under the weight of a fallen building. 'There is a hurricane in London!' a grandparent would scream down the phone, and I would look out of my window at the drizzle and the leaves rustling gently in the breeze, and promise not to leave the house. Similar fun was had by all around the time of the London bombings, except then even I, for all my bravado, could see the merit in staying put.

Doing laundry was a mistake, but I was running out of clothes and I never had that many to begin with. Shedding some of my vanity is all good and recluse-appropriate, but it can be taken too far. Neglecting to look at yourself in the mirror is fine, but wearing the same, increasingly smelly clothes for three days in a row is teetering on the edge of problematic. And it's very easy to do, especially when most of your other clothes are in the laundry basket. So I allowed myself a moment of delicious vertigo, and then stepped back from the edge and threw everything into the washing machine. I am now attempting to dry my clothes in the spare bedroom, in the little heat emitted by the storage heater on the wall. I know all this will achieve is warmed-up humidity and condensation and, to make things even worse, I've gone against local wisdom and closed all the windows, practically barricaded myself in, because this wind is not curative, it's fucking scary. And I'm sure it would dry my clothes nicely if I could nail the rack to the ground, although, having said that, one of my chairs has ended up in the neighbour's field, and I have no idea when or how it got there, so I won't be taking this thought experiment any further.

My grandfather was right this time. I should have listened to him, but I broke my promise and left the house. I didn't have much choice: I needed to go to the supermarket for essentials like water, olive oil and washing up liquid. I also needed to leave the house for the sake of leaving the house because, left to my own devices (which is entirely the case) I am liable to forget there is a world outside my door, albeit one made up of 2,000 residents, most of which are taking their grandparents' advice and staying in. Just like wearing clean clothes and maintaining a basic level of personal hygiene, it is important to periodically expose myself to social interactions and practice the art of using full sentences to communicate with other human beings. (Chatting to the boy cat as I serve him his lunch doesn't count: I know this.)

It wasn't too bad on the way there. I had to dodge a few stray bits of trees that flew randomly into my path, but the wind was behind me, and its efforts to lift me off my feet were actually helpful in getting me up the hill. There was a sense of adventure, of courage in the face of adversity that I enjoyed. Not so on the way back. There is a stretch of path, the first part after you turn off the main road that runs through the village, that my grandparents, on one of their early visits to Sifnos in the sixties, had termed Siberia. The nickname lives on: this place is a freezing cold wind tunnel even at the very height of summer. Imagine it now in late October, with a crazy, chair-stealing wind coming straight at you with relentless force; imagine pushing against it with a rucksack containing a 6-pack of 1.5 litre bottles of mineral water, one litre bottle of olive oil, a kilo bag of flour, five large onions, a loaf of bread and a bottle of washing up liquid. With dust in your eyes, and large leaves slapping you in the face, and more bits of trees threatening to impale you from all directions. It was not one of my better ideas: I had neatly crossed over from courageous to stupid. I survived, but only just.

I confessed to my grandfather later. He was disappointed by my recklessness, which he did not think justified by the need to procure supplies, but was appeased, to an extent, when I promised anew to stay in until the weather improved. 'I have learnt my lesson,' I said, to please him, and told him about my chair flying off into the next field. He was not amused. 'It's very cold in London,' he said gravely, moving on to international affairs. 'I haven't been able to get hold of your sister. I hope she's OK.'

I lied. I fully intend to go into town and check my post. The weather has not improved and is, in fact, markedly worse, with rain having joined the wind to prove my grandfather right. I'll wait it out for a bit, but chances are I'll get rained on at some point during the journey, and return home with more wet clothes to add to my collection. And if I carry on like this, I'll eventually run out of dry clothes entirely, and then I really won't be able to leave the house. Which means my sister will be getting all the phone calls.

I cannot wait for my dehumidifier to arrive. It is the most excellent, magical machine, which even has a special setting for drying clothes indoors. It's interesting, how many things you learn you don't truly need, only to be blindsided by other things that you never even knew existed and now find you suddenly and absolutely cannot do without. And how the weather, that harmless favourite of British bus stop chat and the source of all of my grandparents' fears, is actually a practical issue in places like this. It isn't graphics on an interactive map on the news, or a factor in deciding what clothes to wear and whether to take your umbrella out with you; it's right there, on your doorstep, all around you, shaping your day and stealing your furniture and taking over your decisions. And messing with your personal hygiene. When Leonidas mentioned the wind the other night, he wasn't making small talk; he was reporting on the weekend's most significant event.

So this new life of mine will be ruled by the weather. I will be guided by it, and pander to its whims, and try to be sensible and keep myself dry. Right up until my dehumidifier arrives. But once it's here, I might whack it on that special setting and recklessly go outside in the rain, and stand in it, and maybe even dance, and let it soak me through and through. Once, just one time; just because I can.

# Day 46

Sometimes all it takes is a short walk, a bit of sunshine and a song.

I woke up late this morning, and upset. I was having a nightmare about kittens in plastic bags and it was such a disturbing image that it took me a while, upon waking, to reassure myself it was just a dream and let it go. My first act of the day, before I'd even made it to the bathroom to brush my teeth, was to crush a centipede with a flip-flop, which reminded me of another fun fact about humidity: how these dudes really like it. When I tried to boil water for my coffee, I discovered that I'd managed to burn my electric kettle in my effort to remove the limescale last night. I'd poured vinegar into it, and then boiled it, and it overflowed and the water seeped into the cables and short-circuited the thing: this morning, it was dead. My day had not begun well.

I boiled water in a pan and made my coffee and I knew, before I'd even taken it over to my desk, that the thing I dread the most had finally happened: I had run out of things to say. I turned the computer on, but didn't even bother to click on the Word icon on my desktop, like I do first thing each morning, and watch it bounce happily as it loads the document entitled "100 days". I could not face the sight of all those pages full of words that I've written, and the blank one, the first of an infinite number of blank ones, under the heading "Day 46". I just leaned back in my chair, sipped my coffee, smoked a cigarette and stared idly at the screen, and waited for my uninvited quests to arrive.

Susanne asked me a while ago how I managed to find something to write every day. The answer I gave her, the honest answer, is I don't know. That was about twenty days into my one hundred, and I'd gotten away with it for all that time, and then I got away with it for another twenty-five days since. But that's what it feels like, a lot of the time: like getting away with it. Because I get up every morning and sit in front of my computer and the words come and I write them, and I cannot explain how this happens; I don't know where the words come from or where to go look for them if they don't. And I've gotten away with it so far, somehow, by some crazy voodoo, but the fear has always been there, along with the elation, that one day it will stop. And all the words I've written before will mock me, and there will be no more. I will have nothing more to say: no more to write.

They came, one by one: self doubt and self pity, defeat, futility and a paradoxical sense of vindication, Antagonist wearing some sort of party hat, several critics bent over black leather-bound notebooks, and the people who recruit for McDonald's, with forms and clipboards and balloons. There was also an old friend, the urge to crawl into bed and pull the duvet over my head and let the world pass me by; most people call her depression, but she'll answer to any name, as long as you're willing to let her in. They all crowded around me, pulling up chairs and squeezing on sofas, and there was an atmosphere of mounting anticipation in the room, a morbid sort of excitement, as they all fixed their eyes on me and waited. Someone cleared their throat. Antagonist smiled encouragingly and nodded. One of the McDonald's people proffered a balloon.

I looked at them, and out of the window, at the dark clouds smothering slithers of blue sky.

'Excuse me,' I said, standing up. 'I have to go buy a new kettle.'

This isn't a story where something profound happens and everything gets turned around. I don't meet a sage or an unlikely guru, or even a bent old lady with a headscarf and unexpected words of wisdom, or a man on a donkey who knows exactly the right thing to say. I don't have any revelations or stumble upon the answers, only to realise I had held them in my very hands all along. There is no twist in the tale, just a twisty, damp road that led me to a shop called Vicko, where a cheerful lady sold me the last electric kettle she had in stock. And also a doormat, which has become a necessity since the rain began, and two plastic soap dishes. I paid for these items and put them in my rucksack, and left. Nothing happened, nothing more than that.

As I took the road back home, I became aware of a jingling sound coming from my bag. I slipped it off one shoulder and dug out my phone, which had decided, by its own accord, to open up iTunes and play some music. I shrugged, and put my earbuds in: the song was *Romeo and Juliet* by Dire Straits. I walked and I listened, and, by coincidence or design, the sun chose that moment to push through the clouds and the day was suddenly, tentatively, bright, and I looked to my right and saw the sea. And that was it. That was all that happened.

If someone asked me about my day, I wouldn't have much to say. I got up, I killed a bug, I had a cup of coffee. I bought an electric kettle and cooked risotto for lunch. The neighbour's cat came to see me and I petted her for a while and she purred, which made me feel really good, but I wouldn't mention it to anyone asking about my day. I wouldn't mention any of those things, because none of them are important. And I wouldn't say anything about how a song and a walk and the sun actually did turn my day around, because I wouldn't know how to explain it. And I wouldn't bring up the incredible beauty that I saw all around me, images that, like those pink clouds the other evening, are the antidote to the urge to hide in my bed: we don't talk about such things to each other. The words would sound inadequate or, worse, contrived. So if someone asked me about my day, I would say nothing much. And yet, from all those insignificant, inexpressible things that make up a day when nothing happened, here are the words that came. I didn't go looking for them, I wouldn't know where to look, but I went to buy a kettle and I found them, nonetheless.

I was going to do some yoga yesterday, but then I remembered I'd put all my yoga clothes in the wash and they were now hanging, wet, in my spare bedroom. So I decided that I couldn't do yoga – with regret, because I really wanted to, but there was obviously nothing I could do, because my yoga clothes were wet. And then I laughed at myself, and put a pair of cotton leggings on – the ones I wear to bed – and a random top, and spread my mat down, and did yoga.

I short-circuit myself all the time, and those guests of mine, this morning, had handwritten invitations. I suppose it was a bit rude, walking out on them like that, when I'd gone to the trouble of asking them around. They were still here when I got back, chattering among themselves; they went quiet when I walked in. I stood at the doorway and looked at them all, gathered together, all the reasons why I couldn't and wouldn't write. And then I laughed at myself, and went to my computer, clicked on the Word icon, and waited patiently for my document to load. When I turned around again, my guests had dispersed. All that was left was a McDonald's balloon, and Antagonist's party hat, lying on its side on the floor. I turned back to my screen. I scrolled through thousands of words until I came to the page headed "Day 46". Not blank: just waiting to be filled. I began to type.

Sometimes all it takes is a walk and a song and some sunshine. Sometimes, not always. There will be times when it's a lot harder than that, and there might come a day when I do no yoga and write nothing at all, but it won't be because I don't have the right clothes or because the words are not where I expect them to be; there are ways around those things.

Sometimes you've gotta treat an empty page like an empty day that started badly, and put stuff into it until it adds up to something worth telling, and be brave enough to talk about the beauty that you've seen, even if it makes you sound like a fool. Sometimes you've gotta laugh at yourself and stop asking people you don't like to stop by and welcome the words, wherever they might come from. And let the voodoo or the inspiration or the obstinacy or whatever it is that puts words on the page do its thing, and be glad, as you type your last full stop, that you got away with it, once again. Perhaps getting away with it is all you can hope for, when you strive for such improbable, inexplicable things like turning days when nothing happened into something that somebody might read.

And then laugh. You've gotta laugh.

# Day 47

I love the new ritual of turning my electric blanket on every night. I do it as the day nears its epilogue, twenty to thirty minutes before I want to go to bed. And then, when I climb in, it's the loveliest thing. The air in the house is getting chilly, I can feel it on my face, but the bed is reliably warm and the duvet heavy on top of me. I sleep very well.

Another nightly ritual is the music. I confessed to Eleni a couple of months ago that I knew nothing about classical music; I was vaguely interested – listening to classical music fitted in with my idea of how a writer lives, along with finally reading James Joyce's *Ulysses*, which, I'll admit, I haven't been brave enough to tackle yet – but I didn't know where to start. She was shocked, and offered to remedy this situation by introducing me to one piece of music every night. We did it that same evening, and a few times since: I would go over to her house and we'd have a cup of cardamom tea and she would play the piece she'd chosen for me. She might say a few words before, about the composer or the musicians or the piece itself, and what it meant to her, but once it began, we'd listen in silence. Then we'd finish our tea and go to bed. We didn't do it every night; sometimes we forgot, and sometimes social things got in the way but, since she's been gone, she's emailed me a title and a composer, without fail, every evening. And every evening I make a cup of tea and listen. It's often cardamom tea, because Eleni gave me the box when she left, but not always. I want to make it last.

I do a lot of listening these days. The rain has come, and there is no longer any sky between the clouds. It's been raining non-stop since last night, and with the rain has come a whole new range of sounds that I need to identify

184

and file away as harmless or act upon, accordingly. There's the splatter and drip of falling rain itself, and the sound it makes as it hits the fields all around and is soaked into the soil, which is duller than its city counterpart, and quite soothing, if you tune into it. There's the patter of raindrops against the windows. Then there's the gushing of the water collected on the roof and diverted through pipes into the cistern below the house, and the gurgling and sloshing as it flows into this underground pool, amplified by the acoustics of the cavernous, half-empty space. This one took me a while to figure out: it sounded like there was a waterfall actually inside the house, and I spent a good fifteen minutes going from room to room, in utter bewilderment, before I remembered the cistern directly below the kitchen area. This, too, is a good sound, once you know you're not about to be flooded out of your home.

Not so good is the fact that there actually is a little waterfall inside the house: it appears in my bedroom when the rain hits from a certain angle. The water rushes through the gap beneath the balcony door and trickles down the steps and pools on the floor, and then begins to spread ominously out towards various cables and electrical outlets. This does not please me in the very least. Constructing a makeshift dam on the outside had no effect, so I've resorted to stuffing the gap with a pink towel, and hoping for the best.

There are many other sounds apart from those introduced by the rain. There are one-off sounds, and periodic sounds, and constant ones; there's always something humming or buzzing or crackling, somewhere in the house, and I'm not always able to identify the source, or assess the level of danger it presents. This makes me very nervous. There are too many new or unfamiliar appliances, and I don't yet know how they behave, or how likely they are to kill me.

I have a deep mistrust of electrical appliances as a species, these ostensibly innocuous devices powered by a lethal force that I do not understand, and my recent misadventure with the kettle did nothing to assuage my fears. And all of a sudden I'm having to contend with three storage heaters and one free standing electric radiator that I've never used before, the new kettle, and an electric blanket that I've been warned may spontaneously burst into flame. Nevermind that the latter promises "Overheating and Overcurrent protection" on the box, and that the lady who sold it to me assured me it comes with a warranty; what good is a warranty if I'm consumed by flames as I sleep? So I'm keeping a close and suspicious eye on all of these appliances, and, even though I'm growing fond of the electric blanket and the comfort it brings, part of my nightly ritual is switching it off completely and unplugging it from the wall before getting into bed. Despite the instruction manual informing me that it's perfectly safe to leave it on its lowest setting throughout the night.

My rituals are like punctuation marks in my days. I switch on the blanket: and now bed. And the music is like a parenthesis, a space in the narrative where you can bring things in from the outside, and so, within those brackets, Eleni and I sit together on my sofa every night, with steaming cups of cardamom tea, and listen. This often coincides with the twenty or thirty minutes it takes for the electric blanket to warm up the bed, and together these two rituals put some syntax into days that are otherwise deliciously, deliriously open ended.

And in terms of how a writer lives, this might be it: with days understood as grammatical constructions and the largely unpunctuated *Ulysses* on the bookshelf, waiting to be read, sometime, as Mozart's *Requiem* plays in the background and, in a footnote, Eleni gets up from her sofa to make another cup of tea.

# Day 48

I know a man with a flying Bentley and he's going to fly it all the way to Sifnos. This is not science fiction: in the world this man lives, a world I travel to sometimes, flying Bentleys are just as possible as any other mode of transport. I have long ceased to be surprised.

We originally thought he should go for the next model up, the all-terrain Bentley, suitable for journeys on land, air and sea. This is not too difficult to achieve: apart from the standard engine (which is anything but standard, obviously, this being a Bentley), the all-terrain model is also equipped with two powerful propellers, suited to both aeronautical and seafaring purposes, and a set of fins that, at the touch of a button, unfold into wings, enabling the vehicle to float on the waves or glide on the clouds, respectively. It really is wonderfully simple. And comes with soft leather seats and a bitching sound system, as standard.

The all-terrain Bentley is a pretty advanced piece of technology, but it's not the top of the range. That would, of course, be the space model, aimed at the universally minded traveller who doesn't want to wait until the moon shuttle is ready to take bookings from the general population. It is still in the development stages, and a prototype is available for purchase, for which there is a waiting list. Early adopters are required to sign a disclaimer because the space model is limited in its functions: it is capable of launching into space, like a rocket, and then joining the orbit of one of a number of preselected planets, by killing the engine at the right moment (the car's sensors pick this up, and a red light flashes on the panel behind the steering wheel to warn the driver), but no provisions have yet been made for further navigation or returning to earth. Very few of these prototypes have been released, but they are out there, circling the planets up above; with a telescope, you can sometimes catch a glimpse of their taillights as they go round.

I'm sure this man could get himself right at the top of the waiting list for the space Bentley if he wanted to; he has a way of getting what he wants, perhaps because he figured out, early on, that it's essentially just as easy as not, and it's simply a question of what you put your energy into. He doesn't need to, however. He lives in a spaceship, and he can take himself up to the stars whenever he feels like it. He does that sometimes. But he comes back, with stories to tell.

We had settled on the all-terrain model, but then we realised we had fallen into the trap of conventional thinking. We were approaching the question in terms of a standard journey from central London to the village of Eleimonas in Sifnos: the drive to the airport, the plane ride to Athens, a cab or train or bus to the port, a journey on the ferry to Sifnos, and then the final stretch of road up to the house. Land, air, sea. But, of course, the beauty of a Bentley is that you can park it right outside your home and take off from there, flying it high above the London skyline and through the clouds, over the seas and mountains and cities and valleys of Europe and all the way down to Sifnos where, guided by the blue dome of the church next door, you can land it directly on my roof. There's plenty of space up there for a Bentley, and the beams are strong; they can take the weight.

The flying Bentley has been ordered, in black, with tinted windows and heated seats, and a jack for plugging your iPhone directly into the built-in sound system. When it is delivered, he will pack a small bag and throw it into the boot, put some music on, switch the mode from "drive" to "fly", and he will soar into the sky. He will be spared the traffic on the North Circular, and the discomforts of easyjet, the chaos of Athens, the indignity of the blue plastic seats of the economy lounge on the ferry and the long, cold wait for the off-season bus, and he will arrive in style, uncreased and smiling, in time for dinner.

This is not science fiction, and it isn't fantasy. It's just the way it is. There is a world where everything is possible and that's the world I'd like to live in. Where getting what you want is just as easy as giving up on it. Where a man will fly his Bentley all the way from London to Sifnos and land it on my roof. He will come into the house and unpack the few items he brought in his bag into the space I've cleared in the wardrobe, and we will sit together in the warmth, while the engine of the Bentley cools down on the roof above. We might fly it to the beach every now and then, to spend some time looking at the sea, but mostly we will stay at home, together but a few feet apart, in a silence that contains all the words, and I will write stories about the lives we live on earth, while he thinks about his next trip up into the stars.

# Day 49

It's funny how there can be sunshine through the windows on one side of the house, while on the other side it's as dark as hell on doomsday. I watched an introductory video on mindfulness meditation a while ago, and it said to remember that, no matter how bleak the day might be, above those clouds the sun is always shining; there was a little animation of a bright, happy sun to illustrate this point. The image stayed with me, and it's a good image to keep in your head, if you can, but it's not always so easy to take it out of there and apply it to your bleak day, when the window you're looking out of is dead set on doomsday.

Hell on doomsday might be marginally more cheerful, actually. There are bound to be fires, and those are bright, colourful things, and warm. Perhaps you wouldn't share this point of view if you're one of the sinners being purged upon them, but as a resident of a small Aegean island on a dark, damp October evening in an increasingly cold house, I long for the comfort of an open fire. A fireplace and a bathtub: that's all I would wish for, if I could wish for stuff.

It's true, of course, about the sun always shining. The sun is always shining somewhere, even on the darkest days, even at night. You see it when you fly out of Heathrow on a reliably gloomy, English day that you haven't really thought about too much because it's the standard state of affairs, and it's no good dwelling on it. The plane takes off and within moments it rips through the clouds and all of a sudden it's glorious sunshine, so intense that it hurts your eyes and makes the skin on your face tingle, if you have a window seat.

I'm all for positive thinking, but I don't generally find this comforting; I mostly find it irritating, that this beautiful warming brightness is up there all the time, and we can't see it. That such a powerful force as the sun can be blocked out by something as insubstantial as clouds. Floating condensation, invisible vapours made visible by cooling air: clouds are little more than an optical illusion. They are practically non-existent. You could just blow on them and they'd disperse. And yet they look so solid, especially when seen from above: impenetrable.

I went into town in the early evening. It's gotten really dark since the clocks went back, and it was pitch black already at six o'clock. I needed to get a couple of things from the chemist and the bookstore, but not urgently; mostly, I longed for lit-up places, for the yellow glow of indoor lights that looks so welcoming from the outside, and the possibility of walking in. At the chemist, I fell into conversation with the girl who works there. She's in her twenties, with short hair dyed intensely red and a ring in her nose, and the restless air of someone who's seen a few things and has an appetite for more: if you have a notion in your head of what a small island girl is like, this isn't it. But then again, our preconceptions rarely match the truth; I'm learning this here, anew, every day.

She asked me how I was getting on, and I gave her my standard, enthusiastic response: coming up to two months, and I love it. She seemed surprised.

'I'm struggling,' she confided. 'I'm thinking, maybe, of leaving.'

She told me it's been seven years since she lived in Sifnos full time; she'd been away in Rhodes and Athens, and this is her first winter back.

'I'd forgotten,' she said. 'It's so quiet. I need people. I need life.'

I told her how it feels, sometimes, when you walk through town, and it isn't like all the people have left but as if no people had ever been there at all, never walked those streets, never stepped into those shops and bought jewellery and ceramics and the traditional drawstring bags, never queued for the bars and the restaurants or sat on the steps outside the ice-cream shop watching the crowds go by. It isn't a town deserted; it's a town that never was. I told how I was on the phone to my mum the other night, as I crossed through town on my way home, and I lowered my voice to a whisper, instinctively, so as not to disturb it.

'Exactly,' she said, and described a similar scene – boarded-up shops and that profound stillness – at the port. 'Ghost town. I can't stand it.'

I nodded. I could see her point of view: she is standing by the doomsday window, on the wrong side of the clouds, and the outlook is bleak. I tried to he helpful.

'I think it depends on how you look at it. Think of me: I feel incredibly lucky to be here, and all my friends keep saying how jealous they are. Maybe think about it from their side, how they'd be here if they could. And we are.'

'Yes,' she said, 'maybe.' But far from convinced.

'And you can always leave,' I added. 'For me, that's my safety net, that I can leave at anytime. That's why I'm so happy to stay, because I always have the choice. You can leave whenever you want.'

This made more sense to her; she smiled. 'I can,' she said. 'You're right. I guess it's not too bad.'

Maybe she needs to leave; maybe she needs the city, now, as much as I need the ghost town. We're not all the same. But I wanted to show her the sunshine window, get her to turn her head around and look, and make her choice. I don't know if it helped, but I tried.

My little sister Margarita called me later, and she told me that she'd like to spend some time in a place like this, a holiday place, out of season, haunted by the ghosts of summer. That the idea of it really appeals to her.

'You've got to see it,' I agreed. 'You can't imagine it unless you do.'

'I want to,' she said. 'I want to come.'

It's funny, how it's all a matter of perspective, of where you place yourself and which window you look out of. Of whether you're an islander feeling trapped by the deserted streets, or a city girl freed by all the empty space and the quiet. Or, like my sister, drawn to the melancholy of a place caught in between the seasons, for the novelty, for a change. And whether, when the outlook is bleak, you can think of the clouds as a metaphor for all the things that block your view, and how insubstantial they truly are. And then, on those days when the darkness is all around, whether you'll keep standing by the window, looking out, trying and failing to imagine the sun, or if you'll know to put your heating on and turn on all the lights in the house and make your own brightness and fantasise about an open fire and a hot bath, and wait it out.

# Day 50

My life is a piece of writing in progress, and it has just gone postmodern. There is a raven in my garden, and the critics have pronounced it intertextual.

In postmodern literary and cultural theory, intertextuality, derived from the Latin *intertexto,* "to mingle while weaving", is the complex interrelationship between works of literature; quotation, allusion, parody and plagiarism; the shaping of one text's meaning by another. It's borrowing ideas and phrases from other sources, drawing upon the tales that came before to construct your own. And my story, it seems, is woven with strands of poetry and legend and myth, encyclopaedic citations and other people's imaginations, all coming together to shape the meaning of my days. Everything is connected.

It began with Edgar Allan Poe's *The Raven.* Eleni stumbled upon the notion that perhaps Poe had also spent 100 days of solitude in Sifnos, in an attempt to do some writing undisturbed, and his loneliness was broken by the unexpected advent of the ominous Raven, much like mine has been interrupted by the unsolicited visits of Mrs. Souli, her bad hip and her disdain of my jarred jalapeno peppers.

Unlike the Raven, Mrs. Souli does not perch above my door; she waltzes straight through it and plonks herself down on a chair and shall not be moved until the appropriate time for a neighbourly visit has elapsed. Unlike the Raven, who at least has the decency to only croak "nevermore"[iv] intermittently, Mrs. Souli has a lot to say. Nevertheless, when it comes to unexpected visitors, I can certainly see the parallels between Poe's plight and mine. Especially considering the raven's reputation as a bird of ill omen, and the fact that Mrs.

Souli has never once crossed my threshold without bringing news of at least one death, recent or remembered, in what, in her unwritten book of rules, counts as light-hearted neighbourhood gossip.

There are often ravens in the garden. Or maybe they're crows. They're part of the same species, and I'm no birdwatcher. In any case, they are big and black and noisy, and not particularly graceful. One attempted to land on one of the smaller branches of the almond tree the other morning, but he was too heavy for it and the branch bent and nearly threw him off. He became very flustered and flapped his huge black wings in a manner that indicated he was offended, and gave several loud croaks before flying off to settle on the electricity wire at the other end of the garden. There are often one or two of them up there, sitting still, keeping watch, and occasionally reporting things to one another in their high, piercing voices.

There are smaller birds, too, sparrows or robins, nervous little things that twitter, unseen, from within the trees, and sometimes materialise in the garden or the yard, hopping around and pecking at insects. There are doves that travel in flocks, alighting en masse upon the fields and then taking off again, always with a sense of great urgency and a flurry of synchronised wings. And there are eagles and falcons, gliding soundlessly in the air over the mountains, in that majestic, swooping way they have. They frighten me a little. They don't come to my garden. But I did have a seagull stop by one day; it looked really confused and didn't stay long.

Neither Mrs. Souli nor the ravens have so far tapped on my door upon a midnight dreary, but moths do tap on my windows every night. They throw themselves against them with desperate but relentless determination, hoping, always hoping to reach the beautiful bright light on the other side of the glass. They make so much noise, often closer to a thud than a tap, that it took me several nights to accept that it could possibly be produced by such flimsy creatures. I kept going round, peering through windows and doors, expecting to see a person or a cat or something, anyway, more substantial than a handful of moths. Even now that I know, there are still times when I get up to check.

According to Greek mythology, ravens used to be white, and they were associated with Apollo, who, among his many other talents, was also the god of prophesy. He was not above petty sentiments such as jealousy, however, and he sent a white raven to spy on his lover. When the raven returned with news that she had been unfaithful, Apollo turned his rage upon him, and scorched him black. The phrase "don't shoot the messenger" had obviously not been invented yet, or Apollo was too pissed off to care. Despite this unfortunate turn of events, Greek mythology is one of the few traditions that regards ravens as symbols of good luck, as well as the messengers of the gods in the mortal world.

Sifnos, incidentally, is known as the island of Apollo, and its capital, Apollonia, is named after him. Poe calls his Raven "prophet"[v], and I am a writer whose loneliness is broken by uninvited guests. There are references from Wikipedia in this piece, and dictionary definitions quoted verbatim; the moths tapping on my window at night are both real and a parody of Poe's *Raven*, and the poet's broken loneliness in the second paragraph, and mine here, is an allusion to the poem itself, or perhaps plagiarism of the same.

Perhaps, then, I should embrace the intertextuality and, when Mrs. Souli descends upon me next, I could cry "leave my loneliness unbroken"[vi] in direct quotation of Poe, and draw a neat, postmodern circle around all of us: myself, and the poet, and my neighbour, and the god Apollo, and the ravens, and the midnight hour moths. But I don't think Mrs. Souli will appreciate being sent away in verse, and all I am likely to achieve is her shaking her head vigorously and muttering 'I don't understand these things', before launching into another tale of a neighbour's demise. Upon reflection, given the choice between the two, I would go for the Raven.

There is a raven in my garden now. He croaks loudly, repeatedly, as if to make a point. Perhaps he comes to bring me luck; perhaps a message from Apollo. Perhaps he comes to perch above my door: *only this and nothing more*[vii]. Everything is connected.

# Day 51

Depression came. She came to tell me to go my bed. She came with the storm but, like the storm, I had felt her rumbling approach long before that. She likes to give warning, build up the anticipation, set you up for the plunge into her horrible anticlimax, the flatness she brings that neutralises everything into nothing.

The day before, the Tuesday, was symbolic, and there were signs of her already. It was a national holiday, *ohi* day, the day of no, and it completely passed me by. On the 28th of October 1940, Benito Mussolini delivered an ultimatum to the Greek Prime Minister, Ioannis Metaxas: allow the Italian forces free passage into Greece, to occupy certain strategic locations, or there will be war. Metaxas refused but, contrary to popular misconception, he did not just say "no"; he responded in French, the diplomatic language of the day, and said: *'Alors, c'est la guerre'*. Then, it is war. But the Greeks love slogans and battle cries and, in contrast to their everyday conversation, they like them punchy and to the point. And they couldn't very well take to the streets shouting stuff in French; they had their national pride to consider, especially on a day like this. So *Alors, c'est la guerre* became a resounding Greek No!, *ohi*, a short, two syllable word of pure defiance, and that's the word they chanted, in their thousands, when they spilled out on the streets of Athens, until their throats were raw. And then, there was war.

There are parades on *ohi* day, and marching bands, and bunting, and the Greek flag flies everywhere. The children gather in the village square, dressed in white shirts and navy blue skirts and trousers, and march proudly through town, and the officials make moving speeches about the courage and integrity of the noble race of the Greeks. All this took place on Tuesday, and I

198

missed it, cooped up in my house on top of the hill, typing away on my computer. When I passed through town in the evening, all that remained was the bunting, a long row of blue and white flags flapping about in the breeze over the empty benches in the square.

I felt her approach in the late afternoon, after the celebration that had gone ahead without me. Nothing too obvious, but there was a restlessness that often preludes her arrival. I dressed myself in several layers and stepped out into the final vestiges of the gloomy day. I would walk, I decided, down to the ring road and follow it round in a big circle, all the way to the supermarket, past the playground and back home; it would take about an hour. This was not a road I'd walked before. You wouldn't do it in the summer: it's too busy with cars using it to bypass the traffic at the centre of town and, like most of these island roads, it makes no provision for pedestrians.

I should have known better than to expose myself to all that nothingness; I should have known I was making it too easy for her to find me. I had counted on quiet roads, a peaceful, contemplative walk to settle me down, but I'd forgotten about *ohi* day, and I got more than I bargained for. There was nobody around, only stillness and, every now and then, the parked up vehicles of everyday labour, abandoned only for this one short day of celebration that seemed to stretch, infinite, into the future and the past. This is a small island, but the emptiness made it seem vast, and it was exciting at first, like a child suddenly free to explore all the secret places that adults usually guard, but then I became acutely aware of my own smallness in comparison, and the feeling turned to awe.

It wasn't loneliness, but the actual, physical fact of being completely alone. I let myself think about it and it frightened me. A donkey stuck his head over the fence as I was passing by, and I jumped so far that I found myself on the opposite side of the road before I realised what had happened, felt immensely silly and crossed over again to pat his muzzle and apologise. I walked on, and I could hear my footsteps on the tarmac, a dog barking, echoey, in the distance, a birdcall, the dry rustle of creatures low in the grass. Nothing else, no other sounds: nothing mechanical, nothing human. An eagle circled overhead. The shadows grew deeper. A single motorbike drove past, and the noise it made seemed completely absurd in the ever-expanding stillness.

It was a good walk, despite the fear; it made me feel alert and alive. But I should have known better than to walk alone, when she had warned me she was coming; I was too easy to find. And she came to me, like a bad fairy, and sprinkled me with her flattening dust. I took the emptiness home with me, and into town, later that evening, when I met Christina on one of her flying working trips, for a bite and a glass of wine. The process had been set in motion, and all the warmth and the unexpected company could do was stave off its inevitable conclusion for a time. I had exposed myself, and I was infected.

And so the day of *ohi* passed me by, and then came Wednesday, and depression. She came with the storm, and I surrendered without a word. As the rain began to fall, I felt her twisting me up inside, turning me inside out, and then she was there, with her soothing, hypnotic voice. 'Just lie down,' she said. 'Just give in, and lie down. There is nothing else to do.' I surrendered and took to my bed, and she came to tuck me in, full of tenderness and gentle words, like a nurse for the terminally ill. Palliative care, with no hope for recovery. Just give in to it. There is nothing else. I closed my eyes, and went to sleep.

When I woke up, the storm had been and gone but depression lingered, her heavy flatness making it hard for me to move, like a stiff old blanket that she'd laid over me while I slept. I kicked it off, and shook some life back into my limbs, enough to carry me listlessly around the house, pretending activity by making tea. Depression lingered, and whispered desolation.

The Greeks are always being defiant; we're always looking for things to be defiant about. And when it comes to inventing battle cries, we are truly undefeated, the most notable of all being the immortal two words uttered by Leonidas of Sparta in response to the Persian King Xerxes' demand that they lay down their arms and surrender: *molon labe*. Come and get them. The man had balls.

I had mislaid mine for a day, the day of defiance: I'd been a bad Greek, and let it pass me by. But then I found them again, a day late. I found my defiance, but not as I expected. I found the saddest, most embarrassing, most heartbreaking Greek songs I could think of, and played them loudly, standing up in the middle of the room, and cried, for no reason whatsoever: for nothing. And I surrendered in defiance, and I said no, a day late, but just on time. It wasn't war, it was guerrilla warfare; dirty tactics and sad Greek songs and Leonidas' words, paraphrased for the 21st century: bring it. Bring it the fuck on.

There were no flags and no fanfare, but it was a celebration, nonetheless, because as I cried over nothing, I realised I had nothing to cry about, and that made me laugh. Depression slunk off, taking her blanket with her, and I turned the music off and drank my tea, and painted my toenails red. Leonidas winked, and the Greek Prime Minister said some stuff in French that I didn't understand. And the day ended, and Thursday came.

# Day 52

Mythology spills into life again and here, in Sifnos, the stories of Apollo and Daphne, Daphne and Orpheus and Orpheus and Eurydice all come together to the soundtrack of Pink Floyd.

I had forgotten about Apollo and Daphne, but living on Apollo's island and thinking back, this morning, on another Sifnos romance of the past, I was reminded of my mythological namesake. Daphne was a Naiad, a freshwater nymph, and daughter of the rivergod Pineios. According to the myth, arrogant Apollo made fun of love god Eros and his trademark bow and arrow, telling him, in effect, to leave weapons to the big boys, such as himself. Eros, twisted little bastard that we all know him to be, responded to this insult by taking two arrows, one of gold to induce love, and one of lead, to incite hatred, and shooting them through the hearts of Apollo and Daphne, respectively. Apollo was seized by a helpless, passionate love for Daphne and she, in turn, couldn't stand the sight of him.

Apollo pursued her relentlessly but she was having none of it and kept eluding him, until Eros intervened and Daphne realised she was about to be cornered. She appealed to her rivergod father to save her and he cast an enchantment to transform her, where she stood, into a bay laurel tree. Her skin turned to bark, her legs grew into roots that burrowed deep into the ground and her arms became branches laden with fragrant bay leaves; Apollo caught up with her and tried to enfold his tree-shaped love in a desperate embrace, but those same branches shrank away from him in disgust. Undeterred and fiercely loyal, Apollo vowed to keep Daphne safe and honour her, and used his divine powers to give her eternal youth. And this is a true story, it has to be, because the laurel tree is evergreen, and its leaves are used in wreaths to crown the head of leaders.

The story of Daphne and Orpheus is also true, if a little less mythical, and it takes place in the town of Apollonia, whose streets are lined with laurel trees. Daphne, in this case, is a bored nineteen-year-old girl, back from her first year as an art student in London and trapped in the relative hell of a family holiday. Orpheus is a boy of eighteen, fresh out of school, with greasy, grungy shoulder length hair that often falls over his eyes, and a guitar.

His mythological counterpart was a legendary musician, famed for his soulful playing of the lyre that could enchant men, women and inanimate objects alike. Orpheus fell in love with Eurydice, another nymph, and this – unlike Apollo's doomed love – was, happily, reciprocated. They married, but on their wedding night Eurydice was bitten by a snake and sent down below, to the land of the dead. Hades, lord of the Underworld, and his wife Persephone, worn down by Orpheus' incessant lyre playing, agreed to let him come into their realm and fetch his wife back to the land of the living. There was a condition: Orpheus must walk ahead of Eurydice and lead her out of hell without once looking back until they had both crossed the threshold. Orpheus lost faith at the last minute and turned his head, to catch one final glimpse of his love before the darkness claimed her forever.

Nothing so dramatic for Daphne and Orpheus of 1997, but he did save me from boredom, temporarily, with his guitar. I knew him, vaguely, from school: I think he was on the same school bus as me, and also had a fling with a girl in my class. I ran into him in town one evening. He was sitting on the low wall around the village square, feet dangling over the edge, strumming his guitar. I stopped and said hello.

'Sit,' he said.

I sat.

'Do you like Pink Floyd?'

I nodded. And without further ado, Orpheus launched into the opening chords of *Wish You Were Here*[viii]. As the intro was nearing its end, he turned his head towards me and fixed his eyes on me from behind a curtain of dark hair.

'Sing along,' he said.

So I sang.

Tentatively at first, unused to the sound of my own singing voice in public, unsure of how it matched his, and I kept looking over at him for reassurance, and he kept giving these little nods of encouragement in response, and our voices came together on that song, his low and raspy and mine higher and trembling a bit, and somehow it worked.

And when the song ended, Orpheus rested his guitar flat on his lap, laid one hand on top of it to keep it steady, and placed the other on the back of my neck, drew me in and kissed me.

I kissed him back.

And thus began my most romantic of Sifnos romances that turned me, for a few summer nights, from Apollo's Daphne to Orpheus' Eurydice, with busking thrown in.

That first kiss: the way he just claimed it, as if there was no question that it could be denied. I didn't remember Orpheus being that assertive at school; I didn't remember much about him at all, except that he existed in the margins of my social life, an awkward kid who played in a band, a little too greasy for my liking. But there was something mesmerising about him now, and I knew even then that half of it was an act, but the other half was genuinely captivating. He smelt musty and manly and vaguely unwashed: skin, sweat, cigarettes and mildew, in a heady combination that made me press up against him for more. And he was a good kisser, deep and unrushed and fully committed to it – which is a bit of a deal breaker when kissing is all you are doing. But more than anything else, I think it was the music that did it; it was his golden arrow. Like the other Orpheus of myth, he could charm the pants off you with his guitar. Although I would like to point out that this observation is part conjecture and part unfulfilled desire, because my pants, though they were fumbled with, stayed firmly on that summer. Ours was a romance of serenades and slow, torturous kisses, and an achey longing that it never occurred to us to act upon. We would just pull apart, flustered and breathless, and sing another song.

I don't know how we graduated from that first semi-private performance of *Wish You Were Here* in the shadows of the square to busking, with a plastic cup by our feet, in the most prominent locations in town. I have no idea what possessed me, what emboldened me to do it. Orpheus identified as a musician, but I am not and never have been a performer of any sort. But I sat beside him, leaning back against walls and lampposts, with my knees drawn to my chest, outside bars and restaurants and shops, and sang with him, every night. I can only explain it through legend, a legend I didn't know about at the time, and say that I had fallen under a spell.

There was nothing original about our choice of songs. It was mostly guitar-led ballads, and Pink Floyd's *Comfortably Numb*, and *Yesterday* and *Let it be* and a few other Beatles' favourites. The repertoire varied slightly from evening to evening, but we always did *Wish You Were Here*, at least once, and often a second time, as our final song before we collected ourselves and our profits, spent the latter on ice-cream and beer, and found a dark corner to kiss in.

I never loved Orpheus but I have loved that song, deeply and unfalteringly, ever since. I no longer associate it with that boy or that summer, but it began then, when we sang it together, and meant every word.

Being teenagers, I don't know what we thought we knew about lost souls, but we put ours into every word we sang, and for those few moments that it lasted every time, we really felt it, as if we had written the lyrics ourselves.

It's been almost twenty years since that summer, and I've met some lost souls in that time, and lost mine more than once, and traded beauty for convenience, and compromised for the easy things instead of fighting for the worthy and the hard, and I have sung *Wish You Were Here* from inside my fishbowl, looking out at a distorted view of the world through the thick, curved glass. I know now a little of what those lyrics mean.

But it seems that I have spilled out of my bowl, and found new ground in the old, and come to a place where I can see myself on the other side of that song and choose the things that matter this time around. And I don't know if it was myth or legend or enchantment, the lyrics of a song or something else entirely that brought me where I am, but I do know that it's here that it all, somehow, comes together. And yes, by now, I do think I can tell.

# Day 53

'It's Halloween,' Eleni told me on the phone last night.
'Did you light a candle?'

'What? No. Why?'

'You should light a candle and place it by the window. You never know what might come in, on a night like this.'

I thought about it. 'I have my aromatherapy oil diffuser on, which is lit up and changes colours. Does that count? It's by my bedroom window.'

'I'm not sure,' Eleni admitted. 'I'm making pumpkin with paprika for dinner,' she added. 'I've burnt it a bit.'

We both agreed, without quite knowing why, that this was appropriate.

Halloween. All Hallows Eve, the night when the spirits of the dead wander the earth. Another day I missed because I was absolutely convinced, all day yesterday, that the date was the 30th of October.

'It's the 31st,' Eleni corrected. 'It's tonight.'

'That's funny,' I said. 'I've just been writing about lost souls.'

'It's Halloween,' Eleni repeated, as if that explained it. But I hadn't known.

It was a dark night, moonless and cold, and I had been sufficiently spooked on my way to the supermarket, up the deserted, windswept path, intermittently and insufficiently lit by pale street lights that somehow make the inky blackness in between seem even deeper.

'There are so many weird noises,' I told my mum, whom I'd called for company on the walk, as trees shook their branches threateningly at me from the shadows - and I think they were elms.

'You sound different,' she said, and I could tell by her tone that she was concerned.

'I'm the same,' I assured her. 'I'm fine. But this is different. It's kind of savage, you know? Wild.'

'Even the locals say so,' she agreed.

And I remembered how Mrs. Souli is always telling us about the darkness, about the absence of light in the neighbourhood, and how nice it is when we turn up and put ours on. I never knew what she meant, until now.

On Halloween, they say, all journeys must be completed before sunset, but the sun sets at half past five, and I didn't know what day it was, and I went out at 7:45. I needed to buy baking paper. My granddad was displeased. I called him on the way back and he worked out, by the way I was slightly out of breath, that I was walking. His voice rose in panic and anger.

'What are you doing out at this time of night?' he demanded.

'It's eight o'clock,' I pointed out, with a laugh.

'No it's not!' A pause, while he presumably checked his watch. 'I don't care what time it is! You shouldn't be out, it's dangerous!'

I looked around, at the blackness and the ghostly lights and the shadows whipped about by the wind, but I'd had my moment of weakness, my accidental Halloween, and I was feeling brave again by now.

'Don't worry,' I told him. 'It might sound scary, but there is nothing bad here at all. It's probably safer than any other place I could be.'

He wasn't convinced, I know; he never will be, but these are my darkened streets and I'm the one who walks them, and I can't expect everyone to understand.

No one knows exactly how Halloween began. Some say its origins are purely Christian, the eve of the feast of All Saints, a time to remember the saints and the martyrs and the faithful departed. Others trace its roots back to pagan harvest festivals, and the Gaelic Samhain in particular, which is celebrated from sunset on the 31st of October to sunset on the 1st of November, halfway between the autumn equinox and the winter solstice, and marks the passage from the bright days of summer and harvest season to winter and the darker side of the year. This is a time when fairies slip through the cracks and walk among us, and the dead revisit their homes and are offered food at our tables.

On Halloween, the veil between words is thinner and fire is important. Candles are lit in Christian graveyards to commemorate the souls of the dead, and the pagans light bonfires to ward off evil spirits. And in a house in Sifnos, an oil diffuser flashing pink and green and red and blue stands guard at the window to keep the darkness out. Accidentally, because I didn't know about lighting candles until Eleni mentioned it, and I didn't know it was Halloween. And I still don't know if it counts, because it isn't fire, it's just brightness that you plug in, and maybe the spirits don't recognise electric lights but only living, dancing flames.

But I wonder if any of it is really accidental. I didn't know about Halloween yesterday, and I spent the day writing about lost souls. And I didn't know about Samhain either, not until this afternoon when I did some research, but this morning I was out in the garden, patting the soil into beds and planting seeds for winter.

I think some things are woven into the fabric that we're all made of, and a lot of what we dismiss as accident or explain as coincidence is just the natural way of everything falling into place to form a pattern that was drawn long ago. And maybe on Halloween, on certain days during the year, it's us, on this side, that break through into other realms, and tune into something bigger than ourselves, something that is ancient and unstoppable, like the passage of seasons and the changes that it brings. This is a Christian island, but it was bonfires they were lighting yesterday, not candles for the dead; bonfires to burn the last of the summer away and prepare the fields for the cold months ahead. There were no masks and no pumpkins and no rituals, but these people celebrate what's important in their everyday ways.

And maybe some of their ways are rubbing off on me, or maybe it's the water or the wind or the soil I was kneeling on this morning, but it seems I've fallen in line with the pattern, and it wasn't an accident. And maybe tonight I'll place a light in my window deliberately, a comfort for my neighbour and a beacon to invite the spirits in, and then I'll set the table for all of us to eat together, because the darkness outside frightens me only a little, and there is nothing bad here at all. It's the safest place I can be.

# Day 54

I woke up to actual sunshine this morning, thick stripes of it across my bed. I sprang up, all excited, and rushed to the living room to gaze at the sun through the three large windows along the east-facing wall of the house, just in time to witness that dulling over into gloom again, like one of those fade-in/fade-out transitions in films.

I know I share my home with multiple personalities, most of them rude and badly behaved, and talk to cats frequently and without shame, but it's this weather that's schizophrenic. Or maybe he's just spoilt; he simply cannot make his mind up.

*Sunshine?* Yes!

*Cloud?* Great!

*Cold?* Yeah baby!

*Rain?* Sure!

*Wind?* Fuck yeah!

But he can't have it all, and neither can I, and more often than not it's the sunshine that gets sacrificed. Fade to black.

Sunshine is the least exciting of the weather phenomena. Of all his toys, he likes wind the most, and I can see why. It's the most expressive and the most powerful. Sure, he can do interesting things with rain, he can soothe or drench or drown you, but with the wind he can whip up some pretty impressive storms and raise waves as high as skyscrapers, which are just as effective. With wind, he can shift the clouds to wherever he wants, rip trees out of the earth and knock down buildings. He can make hurricanes, and typhoons, and men cower, helpless, in doorways, and some excellent sound effects, too, to scare girls as they lie in their beds.

I can't say why I think of the weather as male, but I'm sure I'm right. The ancient Greeks knew this too. Their lives were ruled by the whims of Aeolus, keeper of the winds, who was very much male and also openly schizophrenic. There were three of him strolling in and out of Greek mythology, all with the same name and same function but different parentage, separate but connected, and neither the most dedicated of mythographers nor the dude himself could tell them apart. There is a precedent, it seems, for schizophrenia in the weather. It's hereditary.

I sat on a bench in the square with Sonia the other day, under a dull, grey sky, and watched her smoke a cigarette. Sonia rented our house last year, and I was the first one in after she left in July, temporarily handing it over to us for the summer, to return in September. I don't like her. She is arrogant and self-important and a bad, careless tenant, and her patronising, proprietary air, which allows her to tell me things that I already know, and talk about "our beloved island" and this lovely, flawed house she was lucky enough to call home for a winter as if she were the uncontested authority on both, does not extend to looking after the latter. I walked in to find the house unloved, with cobwebs on all of its windows and open packets of food in every cupboard, and all our things moved around haphazardly and without permission, and a pot full of mouldy pasta, like the opposite of a welcome home, in the kitchen sink.

She had a monster of a dog (as evidenced by the size of the steel chain she tried to leave behind, twisted around the trunk of the almond tree), who routinely ran away and killed chickens and sheep and landed Sonia at the police station on several occasions, and also chewed through our front door, actually tearing chunks out of it while his owner, presumably, stood aside and watched. There was also a panel missing from the balcony door in the room I sleep in ("my bedroom", she called it). When questioned, she was completely unapologetic about both and, with regards to the broken panel, she calmly retorted: 'That wasn't me; it was the wind.'

'Well, in that case, maybe we should ask the wind to pay the carpenter,' my mum and I remarked caustically. But later, when Sonia was gone. And good luck pinning Aeolus down, anyway.

We also had a very bizarre conversation during the handover in July: she took me to the garden, and showed me a stick propped up against the drystone wall.

'This is my stick,' she said. 'Please make sure it's here when I come back.'

'Your stick?' I repeated, really struggling to comprehend what was going on.

'Yes,' she said patiently. 'My stick. Please make sure nobody takes it, or throws it away. I want it back.'

I blinked, stupidly, and looked at the stick in question and the girl apparently charging me with its care, with her hands on her hips.

'I'm sorry,' I said. 'You want me to look after your stick for the next two months?'

'Exactly,' she replied, and smiled, as if that settled it.

'You do realise this house will be full of people coming and going over the summer, and that we're actually having a wedding in this garden, right here?'

'Sure,' she said, slowly, with a hint of a question mark at the end, like she couldn't quite see what any of that had to do with her stick.

I realised then that this was one of those battles you walk away from, and nodded amiably. 'I'll do what I can,' I assured her. 'I can't imagine anyone will bother with your stick, but I can't promise you I'll be watching over it the entire summer.'

'Try,' she said curtly.

I made her clear the cupboards and take her chain with her when she left, but I didn't bring up the mouldy pasta; I think mostly because I couldn't quite believe she'd left it there in the first place.

I don't like this girl at all, but I had to meet her to collect some money she owed my mum; she had agreed, reluctantly, to cover part of the cost for repairing the damage caused by the dog and the wind. So we sat together on a bench, and she smoked her cigarette and gave me unsolicited advice that I didn't need.

'There's a path on the side here, past the bakery, that will take you straight back home.'

'Yes,' I said. 'I know. I use that path all the time.'

It was as if I hadn't spoken.

See up there?' That's the church of Saint Eleimonas, the one that's by the house.'

'Yes,' I said. 'I know.'

'I'll show you the path in a moment,' she added, magnanimously. 'I'm going that way anyway.'

I gave up. 'OK,' I said. 'Thanks. That's helpful.'

'Of course,' said Sonia, not at all humbly; Sonia who has lived in Sifnos for a total of 13 months and had only visited, briefly, a couple of times before. I wanted to smack her straight across her smug, self-satisfied face. 'And how are you getting on?' she asked, benevolent guru-like.

'Great. It's all good. Except I'm getting a little tired of the weather.'

'What do you mean?'

I pointed vaguely at the clouds, and made a sweeping motion to indicate the gloom all around. 'I don't mind about the cold, but I need some light.'

She gave a short, condescending snort. 'What are you talking about? There's light. This is light.'

I wished I still had her stick, so I could beat her with it.

In July, after I'd spent two days cleaning the house and bringing it back to a self that it recognised, and

214

apologising to it for the company it had been forced to keep, and dancing joy back into it, with music as loud as my portable speakers would allow and all the windows and doors open, to drive Sonia's residual energy out – another thing she tried to leave behind, I told my mum in no uncertain terms that that girl was not coming back to live in this house. She agreed, but we are both huge chickens when it comes to confrontation, and dreaded having to tell her. We were spared: we summoned her to discuss the damages and, after arguing coolly on every single point, she casually mentioned she wasn't planning on returning. Which meant that the house was free for me to claim as my own, when I changed my mind in August and decided to stay. And the stick, incidentally, did survive the summer, only to be snapped in two when I locked myself out of the house and Simos used it to smash the window and let me back in, thus avoiding breaking down the new, 700 euro door that had been fitted to replace the one Sonia's dog had eaten. It's beautiful, how it all falls into place.

Late this morning I went into town to buy cigarettes. There was a patch of sun on that same bench in the square, so I sat down for a while, with my legs stretched out in front of me, watching a slow Sunday life unfold in the interactions between the few residents that were around, and savouring the warmth on my face, coming and going. And I thought: screw you, arrogant, argumentative girl – this is sunshine. Fading in and fading out, but this is it. This is what I meant by light.

And then the weather, or one of the three multiples of Aeolus, opened his fabled bag of wind and blew a long, thick cloud over the sun, and made a mini twister of leaves and pine needles and dust dance wildly across the flagstones in the square, and I got cold, and stood up to leave.

I followed the path home – my path – that I've been walking up for years, keeping my eyes on the church that would guide me, if I needed guidance, back to the house – my house – that I love despite its flaws. And I thought: thank you, careless, unreliable girl, because I wouldn't be here without you.

# Day 55

Boy Cat and I had a bit of breakthrough the other day. I was out in the garden, kneeling in the dirt by the new bed I'd just made, and poking holes into the soil with my finger, about five centimetres apart, to drop individual beetroot seeds into them. I was so focused on this that I didn't notice Boy Cat approach, but his quiet, black and white presence must have registered somewhere because I looked up, and there he was, a mere five feet away. He was sitting perfectly still, with his tail curled up neatly around him, watching me. He was poised to bolt at the first sign of danger, and he still had that nervous look in his eyes, but there was curiosity in there, too. I could almost imagine him saying "Whatcha doin'?" if he were a less timid cat; a little snort of a laugh escaped me at that thought, and his eyes swivelled in alarm.

'Hello,' I said softly. 'I'm planting beetroot seeds.' His tail twitched, but he stayed put. 'We've also got spinach and carrots over there.' I lifted my hand slowly to show him, and he followed it with his eyes. 'Isn't that exciting?'

He didn't respond. I went back to poking my beetroot bed, and then sweeping the upturned soil over the holes, and patting in down gently, with the smoothest movements I could manage, protecting both my beetroot babies and this new, fragile intimacy between girl and cat. This was the closest he'd ever come to me, and I wanted it to last.

'I'm going to get up now,' I warned him when I was done. 'Would you like some food?' He backed away as soon I started to move, and he was well out of the way and watching me nervously from a ledge before I'd even fully righted myself, but he hadn't fled, exactly, more like walked away really fast. It stung a little bit, but it was progress.

'Come,' I said. 'I'll get you some food.' He followed at a safe distance, and waited until I'd filled his bowl and gone back into the house before eating.

Margarita asked me if I thought the locals were different with me now.

'Maybe,' I said. 'In small, subtle ways. I think they're starting to take me more seriously, the longer I stay.'

The guy at the kiosk knows what brand of tobacco I smoke now, and he just wants to know how many, and I no longer have to say my name at the post office when I go in to check for post. Loukia, the butcher's wife, sent me home with half a kilo of mince and a debt of 6 euro because she had no change to break my ten, and laughed when I promised to come back and pay her the next day, and various acquaintances drive by in cars and on motorbikes and wave and toot their horns, when they never used to do that before.

There is, perhaps, some kind of shift towards acceptance, but I think, to an extent, there is also a truth in my jokes about pledging for the Secret Club. Everything worth having is earned in some way and I think this is essentially about trust. We are fair weather friends, all of us who come here for the summer. We swan around with our tans and our faraway city airs, we claim ownership of patches of land and trees and piles of brick, we dip in and out of a life that we consider genuine and quaint, and pick up colloquial expressions that sound strange on our lips to show how well we fit in. We observe the local customs, dance at the festivals and cook our chickpeas in authentic clay pots, but we bolt at the first sign of danger, or rain. We are not to be trusted.

And I have started off as one of them, the untrustworthy. I may have stuck around for a while now, but it's not been long enough. Just like Boy Cat keeping his distance from me, checking me out, the locals are vaguely curious, standing five feet away, waiting to see what I will do.

When I run into people I haven't seen for a while, since the fair weather days of summer when my presence was unremarkable, when I was still one of those who would leave, they are always surprised. We exchange hellos at first and then they pause to take me in, in my raincoat and my scarf, brighter maybe than the average Sifnos outfit, but still just another resident of the village, going about her business on a chilly autumn day.

'You're still here?' they always say.

And I always give the same reply: 'I'm not going anywhere!'

Always the same line, and always with the emphasis on *anywhere*, because I can't imagine anywhere else I'd rather be. I can see that it pleases them, that it makes them smile. But it isn't a line; it isn't a compliment designed to make them like me. It's just the way it comes out, every time, because every time I'm questioned I realise, afresh, that this is how I feel. And perhaps that's precisely why they smile: because it's genuine. Because I'm not pretending to be one of them, or going out of my way to fit in. I'm just here, like they are, doing my thing. Perhaps it goes some way towards earning their trust, breaking that five foot barrier. But there is still a way to go, and I'm sure there's an edge of doubt in the smiles they give me, a hint of amused indulgence. *Let's see how long you'll last*. Perhaps October smiles are different to November smiles, and the smiles I'll get in December, if I'm still around.

I don't think Boy Cat will ever sit on my lap and purr, or even let me touch him. But he sleeps outside my door most nights, and spends his days lounging in the deck chair that I've left out especially for him, although it's getting slowly destroyed by the rain. And perhaps the most I can hope for is that he doesn't run away from me when I come out to feed him; perhaps five feet is as close as we'll ever be, and it might just be close enough, considering where we began. And perhaps December smiles are as far as I'll ever get with the locals because, no matter how long I stay, it'll always be temporary and full acceptance, I expect, is not a matter of months.

But then again, there was another breakthrough this afternoon. Mrs. Souli stopped me as I was going past her house. She was standing on the path right outside her door, presumably on her way to somewhere, with a cardigan hanging loose over her shoulders. She peered at me myopically, or suspiciously, or both.

'You're the girl next door,' she said.

'I am,' I confirmed.

'My eyes... But listen, next Saturday, he might be lighting the oven. Might be. God willing. And the weather. If you want to bring a pot.'

'Great,' I said. 'Thank you.'

'What? I can't hear. I can see your mouth moving, but I can't hear a thing!' She stepped closer and leaned forward, proffering her ear.

'THANK YOU!' I bellowed. 'THAT'S VERY KIND!'

'Yes,' she said. 'It's not certain, but god willing. You get your chickpeas anyway. We'll talk again.'

She turned around, drawing her tattered cardigan tight over her chest, and limped away up the steps. And I was about to leave, too, when something bumped against my leg. I looked down to see her cat, looking up at me eagerly.

'Hello,' I said. I bent down and scratched her behind the ears. She purred.

Distance is not an issue with those two. One of them barely knows who I am and the other mostly likes me for the bag of Whiskas I keep in the cupboard by the door, but they seem to accept me in these capacities: probably neighbour, possibly friend. And I might be joining the chickpea queue at Manolis' oven this weekend, god willing, and the weather. For a few moments of a Sunday morning, I might be one of them in some small way.

There might be chickpea oven conversations that I can join. There might even be chickpea oven smiles, for all I know.

# Day 56

The life we see here in the summer, the life we know as Sifnos, is neither quaint nor genuine, as it turns out: it's little more than a performance put on for the benefit of the tourists, a show that runs for approximately three months out of each year. But come the end of the season, the set gets taken down and the props put away and discarded programs fly about in the wind and are trampled underfoot, and that's when real life begins.

The roles we have cast the actors in – taxi driver, butcher, restaurant owner – are shed like cocoons and out come all kinds of creatures; they leave their natural habitats, the contexts in which we have learned to understand them, and turn up in the most unexpected places.

Vangelis, taxi driver junior, is loading boxes onto a truck at the port; a couple of days later, he drives through the village in a forklift. His father, no longer folded behind his taxi wheel, is tending to his fields on the north side of the island. Antonis the plumber is also the Vice Mayor and presides over meetings before rushing off to fix someone's burst pipe. Bus conductor Kostas hires himself out as burner of summer debris, leaving scorch marks in the fields is his wake. A café owner runs the bookstore; his waitress sells me lightbulbs at the supermarket. The hotelier in town keeps bees, and the stonemason's son, who apprentices with his father in the summer, cracking stones with a hammer and hauling bags of concrete, is building himself a reputation as an excellent cheesemaker. A bus driver is standing high on a stepladder, whitewashing the outside of a house; another of the taxi drivers pops up in a crew of three redecorating a small hilltop church. A shopkeeper leads a herd of goats into a fenced-up field, as his wife leads a gaggle of kindergarten children to the playground across from the school. The supermarket delivery boy drills holes along the side of ring road to install cabling. Only the post office people stay put.

Beachfront restaurants close up and reopen in obscure locations and the lights in the seaside villages go off, one by one, as their residents move inland to their heated, winter homes. The houses in town empty out as the tourists they've been sold to go back home, and the outskirts come to life. Three buses are lined up on the side of the road by the high school building and gradually become part of the scenery. Winter landscapes emerge out of the dry fields of summer and the beach is a foreign land. The place we know as Sifnos all but disappears. With a dizzying sense of disorientation, you can catch glimpses of it, vague allusions to familiar things, if you really try, but it's an entirely different picture you're looking at once you open your eyes. Like one of those optical illusions where you can see another image if you bring your gaze out of focus, it reveals itself for what it's been all along: a trick. If you were to be plucked out of summer Sifnos and dropped straight into this, without transition or explanation, it would make no sense at all: nothing is the same. Nothing is where you expect it to be.

"Things in the wrong places are terribly exciting". This is Eleni's phrase, coined a few weeks ago as a potential subject for her artwork that she let me borrow, for inspiration. It's odd: although we're far apart, she in Turin, mixing up paints in her studio, and I in Sifnos, playing with words on my screen, our lives seem to be running parallel, and we often stumble upon the same themes in our work. Perhaps that's because there is only a finite number of themes available in the world, in different variations and disguises, and we are all eventually drawn to them through our individual paths, or because of some alchemy of friendship that developed between us during our long summer together. In any case, nothing is accidental, and things in the wrong places recur, separately, for both of us.

My Kindle turned up in the wrong place today. It was ordered by my uncle as a present almost a month ago; it left the Amazon depot in Germany in good, German time, and then took itself off somewhere, and no amount of tapping its tracking code into all possible websites gave any clues as to its whereabouts. For the past three weeks I have made myself a nuisance to post office and courier staff alike, turning up every couple of days and insisting that they check, again, for my mysterious package.

This morning's venture looked like it might yield the same non-results. I spent ten minutes at the courier office with both the man and woman who work there, all three of us speculating on where my package might be, based on a rumour that it was sent through DHL.

'If that's the case,' the man said gravely, 'then it should have been delivered here. It should be here by now.'

He offered me a large, unclaimed box addressed to someone called Grace, in desperation, which I politely refused; they both shrugged apologetically, and wished me luck.

At the post office, Post Office Man No. 3 looked through the delivery slips and shook his head. I was about to leave when Post Office Lady interrupted.

'I think there's something in the back,' she said.

'Yes,' came the disembodied voice of Post Office Man No. 1. 'It's here.'

And it was: my Kindle, in its Amazon cardboard box, and with a very prominent DHL sticker on the front, gone rogue though the postal system to arrive, unexpected, at the Sifnos post office.

'How strange,' the lady remarked. 'I can't imagine how it ended up here.'

I think Eleni knows and I am beginning to discover that there are no such things as wrong places. There are only things and places in endless combinations, people and things in places that you wouldn't expect, and a shift of context to allow for their presence there. And that is exciting because it means that everything is always where it should be, and that things could turn up, somewhere else, when you've given up hope. And that you can put yourself anywhere, at any place at all, and that's exactly the place where you'll belong.

# Day 57

I woke up this morning with an urge to move things around.

Actually, that's not true: the urge came last night, as I lay in bed reading a book on my new Kindle, and I suddenly decided I was no longer happy with my bedroom. My bed was creaky and uncomfortable and I absolutely could not tolerate it a moment longer. My only option would be to move to another room, the one my mum uses as her bedroom in the summer, which has a newer, sturdy, non-creaky bed with a decent mattress. Yes, I thought, that's what I'll do. First thing in the morning. I went back to my Kindle, and pretended to read.

Five minutes later I was up, standing at the doorway of my potential new bedroom and frowning at the configuration of the furniture: it just wasn't right. Something about the position of the bed bothered me; I would have to change it if I were to move into this room. But there was something niggling at me, some echo of a reason why that wouldn't work. I chased it around my head for a while, but it kept eluding me. I went back to bed and turned the light out.

At a quarter to midnight I gave up and got the tape measure out. This wasn't a wise move: all it did was turn the niggle into a very clear memory of having done this before, at the end of the summer. And having established then, just as I did again now, that my fantasy of the bedroom's layout and its actual dimensions did not match, and the only way to move the bed to a satisfying position would be to take it apart. It wouldn't work. I went back to bed, practically twitching with frustration, and lay awake for far too long, rearranging furniture in my head.

I took the bed apart. I did it as soon as I got up in the morning; I didn't even have the patience to finish my coffee. Bleary eyed but determined, and with a stiff neck that I blamed on the bad bed and that turned my irritation into a duty to myself and my myoskeletal health. I took the bed apart and put it together again, where I wanted it, and moved all my stuff from the one room to the other, and made some improvements in my new wardrobe, and decided my old bedroom was now my yoga room, which was an unforeseen outcome of the room switching and it made me happy. I stood still for a moment, taking in the good work I'd done, and then I started on the rest of the house. It was my biggest overhaul so far. And now nothing is where it started off this morning, and I'm exhausted, but my neck seems to be fine. And the beast of moving things around has stopped roaring and settled down on the rug that I've just placed in front of the heater in the living room. It seems content for now: pacified, if not at peace.

I don't know what it is with me and rearranging furniture. Every space I occupy is an ongoing puzzle that I have to keep putting together, forever shifting the pieces around to find a perfect fit that never seems to last very long. Perhaps I'm an idealist, convinced that things can always be improved. Perhaps it's due to an innate restlessness that urges me to seek change upon change upon change, without respite; the same restlessness that caused a psychiatrist to suggest to my grandma, when I was little, that I might have ADHD. (I do not. But she still brings it up, darkly, when I annoy her with my fidgeting.) Perhaps it's a form of wisdom, the understanding that nothing is fixed and nothing is permanent, that everything is in constant flux, mirrored, bizarrely, in the configuration of my furniture and the impermanence of their placement in any one location. Or perhaps, conversely, it's a stand against the impermanence of things, a territorial instinct to move things around and make my mark on the place, to say: *I am here. This is where I am.* Which feels increasingly pertinent here, now, the more time goes by, and my solitary adventure in Sifnos settles into ordinary, everyday life. This house is morphing, gradually, into something like a permanent home, and I'm taken aback, sometimes, when I catch myself thinking of it as where I live rather than where I'm staying for a while.

Which is a good thing, in the light of the following exchange I had with the lady at the courier office a couple of weeks ago.

**Me**: 'Good morning. I'm expecting a package.'

**Lady**, shaking her head: 'It's not here.'

**Me**: 'But –'

**Lady**: 'Oh, sorry! I mean, I've got nothing. No packages at all at the moment.'

**Me**: 'Shall I come back tomorrow, then? Do you get deliveries every day?'

**Lady**: laughs wholeheartedly.

**Me**, confused: 'Why are you laughing?'

**Lady**, inexplicably amused: 'Every day? We get none! There are no boats!'

**Me**: 'What do you mean *there are no boats*?'

**Lady**: 'There are no boats! None coming, none going. No boats!'

**Me**, a little scared: 'Like, no boats, *ever*?'

**Lady**, relenting: 'Well. Hang on.' Turns to her screen, types something in. 'OK. No boat tomorrow. Nothing on Friday. Nothing on Saturday. There might be one on Sunday, possibly, but we don't know for sure. Definitely nothing on Monday.' She looks up, smiles. 'Maybe come back sometime mid next week, and we'll check again.'

**Me**, nodding but concerned: 'Are you telling me we are basically marooned in Sifnos?'

**Lady**, with a smile: 'Basically, yes.'

Which is fine, unless of course you happen to conceive of the notion that you might want to leave, and you can't.

Not until the Wednesday after next, possibly; nobody knows for sure. But as long as you banish all thoughts of leaving from your mind, completely, it's absolutely fine.

It's fine, because I don't particularly want to go anywhere. But that doesn't mean that I haven't, on and off, slipped into fantasies of throwing myself off a ledge and breaking something – an arm, perhaps, not a leg – in order to warrant being transported to Athens by helicopter. The risk, of course, being that I might end up in Syros, which is where the nearest hospital is. And which is a beautiful island, actually, but that's hardly the point, when you've broken your own arm for the purpose of *leaving* an island.

'I know a man who hired a helicopter to fly him to Athens once,' Spyros told me, referring to a time, many years ago, when he'd spent a few weeks in the Sifnos winter. 'He was in a hurry and there weren't any boats, so he just called for a helicopter and it took him home.' He paused, reflecting. 'I think he had a meeting or something. He couldn't wait.'

'Don't be ridiculous!' I said. 'Who does that? Who has five grand to spend on a helicopter ride because he cannot wait?'

He named a well-known shipping magnate.

'Oh. Yes. That's who.' I changed the subject and made a mental note to keep my eyes open for appropriate ledges to fling myself off.

The word "permanent" seems to have grown a little heavier since I used it last, so I think I'll just put it down for now, on the coffee table, and move it later, if I need to. I'm sure it's technically possible to get claustrophobic on an island made almost entirely of space, where the horizon stretches out endlessly in all directions, but I don't feel that, not yet. I won't be breaking any bones to get to Athens. And since I'm not a shipping magnate of any reputation, large or small, I suppose helicopter travel is out of my reach. But I can wait. And maybe, for now, I'll go to my new yoga room and ease myself into some slow, grounding postures, and then meditate on that favourite phrase of mine, *I'm not going anywhere,* and the implications of the other one that goes: *be careful what you wish for.* And laugh, like the lady in the courier office; looking out on a boatless horizon, stuck in Sifnos and amused.

# Day 58

Jesus is installed in my house and He is performing the miracle of extracting water out of thin air.

I don't mean to offend anyone, but to me this machine is the Messiah. He came in the hours of darkness, causing gladness in the hearts of many as the late and long anticipated ferry, wearing a halo of bright lights, heralded its arrival by a single long hoot on its horn, shattering the deathly silence of the small island port. The men who lifted Him out of the hold and into their truck didn't recognise Him, disguised as He was in his box, but they were innocent in their ignorance. They treated Him well and delivered Him safely to the Sifnos Post Office, as had been written, thus earning their place in heaven in my, slightly unorthodox, book.

His coming was prophesised by text message. It arrived on Monday, in the capital script of all important announcements: DISPATCH OF ORDER NG500050748 TO SIFNOS POST OFFICE. THANK YOU FOR YOUR COOPERATION. I stared at it, disbelieving, and made the pilgrimage into town.

'I've had a mysterious message,' I told Post Office Lady breathlessly as I flung myself over her desk. If she was alarmed by my frantic manner, she didn't show it. She smiled – she and her colleagues indulge my constant demands on their time with the patience of saints – and took the phone I was holding out for her inspection. She squinted at the screen.

'What does it mean?'

'You have been sent something through our courier service,' she deciphered. 'It should come with the Wednesday delivery.'

'If there are boats.'

'If there are boats.'

I resorted to prayer, and my prayers were answered by Post Office Man No.1. In fact, he went further than that, and called me himself. The phone rang this morning, and he spoke in the voice of the prophet, and he said:

'You have a little package.'

'A *little* package,' I asked carefully, 'or a biggish one?'

'Well...'

'Does it look,' I added impatiently, 'like it might be a dehumidifier?' Proof before belief, I know, but it's a necessary part of this tale.

'Yes!' he said. 'A dehumidifier. That's exactly what it is.'

*Excuse me!*, boomed a celestial voice, sounding a little offended. *That's Jesus, actually, you're looking at right now*. But luckily it was only in my head. I like Post Office Man, and I wouldn't want him to think I'm judging him for his blindness.

'Thank you!' I gushed. 'You've no idea how happy you've made me!'

He laughed.

'I'm on my way.'

Ten minutes later I was standing at the desk with a signed delivery slip, waiting for Post Office Man to re-emerge from the back with my package.

'Daphne,' he called and I turned to the doorway where he stood, with a shock of pleasure that he'd used my name, and I fleetingly thought that maybe this prophet/sinner and I could be friends. But then he said 'It's here,' and all earthly concerns were erased from my mind when I beheld Him, all aglow, as the sun shone upon his glossy box.

SUITABLE FOR FLATS OR 4/5 BED HOUSES!, He cried.

WARMS THE AIR AS IT DRIES!

CONTROLS DAMP AND CONDENSATION!

ALLEVIATES CAUSES OF ALLERGIES!

LOW NOISE – 38dBA!

ECO FRIENDLY DESIGN! NO REFRIGERANTS!

Hallelujah. Praise the lord.

I took him in my arms (there was a handle on the side of the box, but it was broken) and carried his LIGHTWEIGHT DESIGN, ONLY 6.4 Kgs! body all the way up the hill, as church bells rang.

I am not judging my Post Office friend: once I too was blind. It was Margarita of Apollonia, patron saint of good haircuts and badly insulated houses, who opened my eyes to the possibility of this blessed, damp-free life. It was she who first spoke the word, *dehumidifier*, but I doubted, and I said I'd get an electric blanket instead. But the lord is merciful or, as they like to say in Greece, *God has*. And what he has, mostly, in Sifnos, is some very persuasive ways of making you change your mind. He has cold wind and he has rain pouring through gaps under your doors and he has humidity creeping into your bed at night and that deep chill that you cannot shake off no matter what you do, that turns your fingers to ice in the middle of the day. So I opened my eyes and I opened my heart and I opened my wallet and got my credit card out, and let Jesus into my life.

He's here now, in the centre of my home, performing miracles and making a LOW swooshing NOISE - 38dBA, which, I swear, is the sound of a thousand angels flapping their wings.

# Day 59

I've been talking to the moon since April. That's eight moons so far, larger or smaller depending on the rotation of the earth, but all of them full: that's when you talk to the moon. And it was full again last night, smaller than it's been in recent months, and high up in the sky, but bright enough to cast shadows. I went outside and stood in its light, tilted my head back, and talked.

Susanne got me started on this; she was the one who first mentioned full moon rituals. All you need to do, she told me, is find the moon, look up at it, and tell it what you want out of life. And the moon will make it happen. There is also a crystal involved, traditionally, but, in the months since April, since the first time the moon and I talked, I've come to understand that's not important. It's isn't about the crystal; that's just a prop. It isn't about the fullness of the moon or even the moon itself. It's about the words you choose. The story that you tell.

My sister and I taught a yoga and creative writing workshop together last January. It was a New Year Intentions workshop, whereby we would let go of the year gone by, and set our intentions for the one that had just begun. My sister started by getting us all to create a *sankalpa*, the yogic version of a new year's resolution, but kinder. This is a positive phrase, expressed in the first person singular and in the present tense. A simple example: "I am happy". Once you create your *sankalpa*, you plant it in your mind, meditate on it, repeat it to yourself (silently) like a mantra, until it becomes truth. In this instance, we also wrote it down on a bit of coloured card, and tucked it under our mats. My sister then led us through a sequence of yoga postures and breathing exercises, and then it was my turn.

So I stood up in front of seven people (or, more accurately, sat cross-legged on the floor, this being a yoga workshop) and talked to them about the power of stories, the stories we tell ourselves and those that other people tell about us, the grand narratives that we accept or struggle with as universal truths, and the smaller, personal ones that we create to define who we are. And then I asked them all to think back to their *sankalpa* and imagine the person they'd be if it were true. The changes that would have to be made, the things that would have to be in place, added or subtracted or moved around, and the sort of life this would give shape to. I asked them to imagine that person and that life and write about them, in the third person, as if writing a story. To write a day in the life of who they'll be, when everything they want for themselves has come to pass.

I made the same suggestion to Susanne the other day, when she was planning what to tell the November full moon. Susanne was the one who warned me to be specific, to leave no room for misinterpretation, but she was being a little too vague this time.

'Let's think of this in practical terms,' I said. 'Imagine you're asking someone to go to Selfridges and buy you a dress that you've seen. You wouldn't just say "I want a blue dress" and send them wandering up and down the aisles to bring you something that loosely matches that description. You'd tell them the brand and the size and probably the item number, and which department to find it in, to make sure you get exactly what you want.'

'Huh,' said Susanne. 'You're right. Maybe I'll write a list.'

'No,' I said, remembering the creative writing exercise. 'Don't write a list. Write a story.'

If I were to give that exercise to myself, this is the story that I'd write:

Sunshine filters through the curtains in Daphne's bedroom, and she wakes up. It's coming up to half past seven. It's been months since she's set an alarm, but she always wakes up early, excited for another day to begin. She stretches, eases herself out of bed, and pads over to the kitchen to turn the coffee machine on so that it warms up while she brushes her teeth and washes her face. She doesn't bother with brushing her hair, she just gives it a quick ruffle and it's fine, but she always puts earrings on. She gets dressed, makes her coffee, and takes it outside. Two cats appear from two different directions and meow for her attention.

'Good morning,' she says. 'Be patient. I'll feed you in a bit.'

The cats settle down on the flagstones, not too close to each other, and follow her movements with moderate interest. Daphne sits on the ledge bordering the neighbour's field and turns herself around so her legs are dangling over the edge and she can let her gaze wander over the mountains that are growing greener by the day, and the shapes they make where the clouds overlap their peaks. It's breezy but not windy, and there's an autumn chill in the air, but it feels like there will be warmth in the sun later in the day, when it climbs higher up in the sky. She sips her coffee and smokes her first cigarette and goes back inside. The cats lift their heads expectantly.

'I haven't forgotten,' she tells them. 'I'll be right back.'

Once the cats have been fed, she takes what's left of her coffee over to her desk, and turns her computer on. She spends a few hours writing, getting up periodically to make a fresh cup of coffee or stretch her legs and look out of the window. Around mid morning, she takes a break and goes out into the garden. She checks on her new vegetable beds – she has planted spinach, beetroot, rocket and carrots – and kneels down to pull out a few weeds. In the rocket bed, hundreds of tiny, bright green shoots are breaking through the soil, reaching for the light. She brushes them, gently, with the tip of a finger, smiling at the thought of the home grown rocket salad she'll have one day, soon. She'll water them later, this afternoon, when the sun is on its way back down.

She writes until lunchtime, which is no longer a particular hour in the day but exactly the moment she feels hungry; today, it happens to be at 1:34. She cooks a slow risotto with red onions and cherry tomatoes and some finely chopped purple-green curly leaves that she picked herself at the organic farm down the hill. She throws in a handful of prawns for flavour, and a few springs of fresh rosemary and mint from the garden. She eats, washes up, and has a short nap, to put a pause in her day.

The sun is still shining when she gets up, just after 3, so she decides to go for a walk. She follows the ring road through the mountains for a while, gets barked at by three surprised dogs who are unused to the sight of pedestrians, and turns off into a path she's never taken before. The path leads her past the island's landfill, where huge metal bins are lined up in rows and mountains of rubbish are waiting to be sorted and buried. She stops a while to take it all in and wonder how it's possible that even this is beautiful here. She takes some photos, for proof, and moves on.

Her route now takes her past winter trees and twisted branches and the straight lines of fields in the process of being ploughed, and brings her to the back of the village, a side of it she's never explored. She walks slowly, noticing colours and shapes, catching glimpses of mountain or sea framed in the gaps between houses, looking out for signs of life: a motorbike propped against a wall, heavy clotheslines catching the last of the sun, the tinny sound of a radio, the murmur of conversation, fried onions, smoke drifting out of chimney and snatched by the wind. The light is growing dimmer as she turns a corner and finds herself back in familiar territory. She walks another ten minutes to the supermarket, and buys two lightbulbs and a packet of plain flour – she has just decided she'd like pizza for dinner.

At home, she makes the pizza dough and sets it aside in a large ceramic bowl, close to the radiator, to rise. She waters the garden, makes a pot of tea, and settles down at her desk for another couple of hours of writing. When she's done, she rolls out her mat in her yoga room, and goes through a few sun salutations and some stretches that her body's asking for. Afterwards she puts some music on, as loud as it will go, and dances around the living room and the kitchen until she's out of breath. She has a shower, puts her clothes back on and calls a couple of friends, pottering around the house while she's talking to them, tidying up and moving things to better places, as these occur to her.

When she feels the first twinges of hunger she checks her dough, which is warm and fluffy and risen to perfection. She rolls it out on the kitchen table, sprinkles it with olive oil, and turns the oven on to preheat. She calls her mum as she tops her pizza with fresh tomato sauce, red chillies, capers picked and pickled in the summer, salami and grated cheese. Twenty minutes later, she eats her pizza on the sofa, watching an episode of a TV series on her computer. After dinner, she makes a cup of fresh mint tea and smokes a cigarette while listening to tonight's piece of classical music, chosen and sent by her friend Eleni every night. This ritual complete, she locks the front door, turns off the lights and goes to bed. She reads for an hour or so, and drifts off to sleep.

This is how I'd write it; this is exactly how I live. This isn't just a story told or written: it's a day taken out of my life. The *sankalpa* that I scribbled on my bit of coloured card in January was "I am a writer", and this is the story of the person I would be. I don't have everything, but I have everything I need. And I would, eventually, add some friends in the room rather than on the phone, the chance to cook them dinner or have them put their hand on my shoulder, and maybe even some Sifnos romance, but this is basically it: the shape of a life, imagined and lived. So last night, when I talked to the moon, when I stood in the light it cast and looked up, I had nothing to ask for. I just looked at it and said hello, and thanks. I don't need to tell the moon stories, not now. Now I'm writing my own story every day.

Susanne wrote hers last night and she told it to the moon. She read it to me this morning. It wasn't the kind of story that sends you wandering through department store aisles, flitting from rack to rack, head pounding and eyes burning from the harsh bright lights, reaching for anything that looks like it might fit and making the wrong choices. It was the kind of story that gets exactly what it wants and, in writing it, Susanne could finally see what that was. She wrote herself into a life that fit. I don't know if the moon will intervene, but the pieces of that life will come and settle around her.

Stories are powerful, and they won't be stopped. Just like my rocket shoots pushing up through the soil, they will break out into the world one way or another. Stories need to be told; that's what they're made for. And if you don't tell yours, someone else will. And if you tell it the wrong way, that'll be the narrative that you've written yourself into. So tell your own story. Tell it the way you want it to be told. Tell it to your friends. Tell it to the moon. Write it down, and tell it to yourself. But tell it.

# Day 60

It's Saturday and that means, *god willing*, it's also chickpea day: the day when I will be invited to enter Manolis' hallowed wood oven and place my pot in the queue. This is very exciting.

Preparations began on Thursday evening, when I took a bag of chickpeas out of the cupboard and slapped it bang in the middle of the kitchen table, so I wouldn't forget. Mrs. Souli had paid me one of her impromptu visits earlier in the day and confirmed the plan to light the oven on the Saturday. She then sat down on a chair and started to rub her hip. In a desperate bid to escape yet another retelling of the fable of the wise man who declared, upon being questioned, that the heaviest thing in the world is, in fact, old age, I asked her to talk me through the chickpea preparation process. She was happy to oblige; she feels compelled to pay me these visits, as good neighbourly conduct dictates, but really struggles for something to say to me, with my strange city ways and fancy jarred goods and all.

'You put them in water on Friday, and soak them overnight,' she began. 'At least 24 hours.'

'Don't I need bicarbonate of soda?' I asked, having heard a rumour to that effect.

'No soda,' she said sharply. 'Just water.' She paused, to make sure I was following; I nodded. 'Then you strain them on Saturday, and put them in your pot with your onion and your salt and your olive oil. And some bay leaves. Do you have bay leaves?'

'I do,' I lied, refraining from telling her that I intended to steal them from a neighbour's garden.

'Then you add your rainwater, just enough to cover the chickpeas.'

'Can't I use the tap?'

This elicited a frantic head-shaking response. 'It has to be rainwater,' she said firmly. 'But Manolis can add it for you, when you bring your pot. He's good like that, my boy.'

I confirmed the goodness of Manolis and thanked my neighbour for her advice, hoping to bring this visit to a polite close.

Mrs. Souli shrugged. 'Ach,' she said. 'And now to get out of this chair.' She made a great show of placing both hands on the table and hoisting herself up, only to stop midway, and sit back down. 'They once asked a wise man what the heaviest thing in the world was. You know what he said?'

I know. But wasn't it a wise man, also, who said "hell is other people"?

It's windy again today and something must have fallen on Boy Cat, because there was a loud bang and he came limping past the front door, just as I'd opened it to feed him, looking even more alarmed than usual. He placed himself gingerly on the low wall by the rosemary bush, lifted the injured leg up at a funny angle and stared at it in confusion.

'What happened?' I asked him, but he wasn't forthcoming with a reply. I looked around for the object that caused his injury but couldn't see anything distinctly out of place so I gave up and poured some food into the cat bows. I've had to weigh them down with stones because they kept blowing away and clattering around the yard and scattering cat biscuits shaped like three-petaled flowers all over the place, with the cats chasing after them, which can't be the most relaxing of dining experiences. Now they have to eat around the stones, but they seem to be managing; it's all about adaptation. Though I really wish Boy Cat would come inside, where it's warm and his bowl would stay put, and I could say soothing words to him about his injured leg.

It's windy and suspiciously warm and the dark, heavy clouds are low in the sky, and the weather talk has started up again.

'Storms!' my grandma announced excitedly. 'Terrible storms are coming! They said so on the news!' The news is the undisputed authority on everything, and trumps even the evidence of your own eyes.

'And the other thing,' she went on, 'what do they call it? When there are cars on top of other cars.'

'Hurricanes?'

'That's it, hurricanes. They showed the cars on the news. Although,' she added, 'that wasn't here, it was somewhere else.'

'So we won't be getting hurricanes in Greece, then,' I said, trying but failing to keep the sarcasm out of my voice.

'But we will,' my grandma insisted, unfaltering in her faith. 'They showed it as a warning, so we could see what it looks like.'

'That's very thoughtful of them,' I said, insincerely, since I'm entirely sure the citizens of Athens would notice if a hurricane came tearing into their city, with or without the help of the TV news. They probably wouldn't stand around pondering "What *is* that? Might it be that thing they showed on the news, or something else?", as the twister ripped their homes from their foundations.

My grandma caught on at this stage. 'Are you being sarcastic?'

'Yes,' I admitted. 'Sorry. I just think they might be exaggerating slightly. Although,' I added, relenting a little, 'it does look like it might rain.'

'That's good,' my grandma pronounced, confidently. 'They need the rain in Sifnos. As long as it's not the kind that puts cars on top of other cars.'

I'm fairly confident that the cars of Sifnos will remain unstacked, but what concerns me is that Mrs. Souli named the weather as a deciding factor in the lighting or not of the oven, right after god's will. She didn't, however, specify what conditions would mean that the oven cannot be lit. The wind doesn't seem to be an issue: they are still lighting fires in the fields all around, which, I have to admit, makes me a bit nervous. But if not the wind, then what? The rain? What sort of weather qualifies as unwilling? This might be cynical of me but I suspect that, in most cases when the ovens don't get lit, it's actually god that's unwilling and the weather gets the blame. Perhaps god sometimes just doesn't want the people of Sifnos to eat chickpeas, and we are famously not meant to question his will. He works in mysterious ways, after all: it's not like we haven't been warned.

There must have been something about people drowning on the news as well, in some weather-related tragedy, because my granddad managed to repeat the word no less than six times in a three minute conversation. After assuring him that I wasn't about to drown in my hilltop home, I tried to steer the subject away from the weather by stupidly mentioning that my sister was spending the weekend in Geneva.

'What?' my granddad bellowed, instantly switching to panic mode. 'What is she doing that for?'

'She's visiting her friend who lives there,' I replied meekly, berating myself for having forgotten, once again, that no topic is safe with a 92-year-old man who sees danger in everything.

'But *what for?*'

'Um,' I said, unable to come up with a better reason than the one I'd just stated. 'It'll be a nice break for her,' I provided, desperately. 'She works hard.'

'Is she going by airplane?'

'I guess so,' I replied, but tentatively, because I didn't know the precise nature of the danger my sister was in. 'Or maybe by train?'

Sharp intake of breath. '*Train?*' No, not a good answer.

'Actually, I'm sure she's flying. Definitely. She said so.'

My grandfather sighed. 'I just don't understand why you people insist on doing these things,' he lamented.

'But they are good things,' I pointed out, uselessly. 'Travelling is one of the good things in life.'

'Not when people are drowning,' he retorted.

Old age is heavy indeed. The question is who gets to carry it.

I was so excited about chickpea day that I went on my bay leaf scavenging mission first thing this morning, and then spent the intervening time glaring at the chickpeas in their bowl and poking at them at random intervals to test their softness, as they soaked happily away, oblivious to my growing impatience. Once a full 25 hours had elapsed, I drained them and tipped them into my clay pot, along with the obligatory onion, olive oil and salt. Contrary to neighbourly advice, however, I decided to give my first foray into this Sifnos culinary tradition a Moroccan twist, and have added turmeric, cayenne pepper and paprika, and a sprinkling of coriander seeds.

My pot is ready, on the table, and the light is fading outside. There is no sign of Manolis yet, and no telltale scent from the oven, either. But the weather hasn't gotten any worse, so I'm hoping god is in the mood for chickpeas this weekend, and the oven will be lit as planned, and it won't be long before Manolis calls my name over the wall, as is his habit, and tells me that it's time. And I will carry my heavy pot up there, and ask Manolis to add the rainwater, as if I knew all along that's how it's done; as if I do this sort of thing every day. Casually, as if I hadn't been holding my breath for this moment since Thursday.

# Day 61

This is the story of a car that fell out of the sky and a ship that sails the seas, two cities, one island, a man and a woman in the right and wrong places, and a pot of chickpea stew cooking slowly in the embers of a woodfire oven overnight. I will tell it exactly as it happened.

The flying Bentley took off from London and ran out of fuel, mid-air, and M had to crash-land it in Athens. Which is where he is now. While I am in Sifnos. It is Saturday evening, and there are no boats from Athens to Sifnos until Monday; the Bentley is scheduled to return to London on Tuesday. These are the facts; they do not bode well for Sifnos romance.

So much for fucking Bentleys. The car is obviously faulty; there must be something wrong with the fuel gauge, or the tank itself. I will be suing Bentley, no question about it. I will be writing them a very strongly worded letter in the first instance, expressing my shock and profound disappointment, before engaging the services of a solicitor to seek legal redress on my behalf. Emotional distress, and the waste of a perfectly good, homemade pizza that I was in the process of enjoying when the tragedy occurred, and which is now stone cold. Those bastards should count themselves lucky that M is such a skilled driver and was able to bring the vehicle onto the runway without injury to himself or others, and that he was fortunate enough to be flying over Athens International Airport at the exact moment his engine cut out. It could have been a lot worse; it doesn't bear thinking about.

After a lengthy discussion, during which nobody suggested to anybody else that they should have perhaps consulted the boat schedule before randomly landing in Athens on a Saturday afternoon, and nobody at all said the words "remote island", "November" or "what the fuck", it was agreed upon that M would be spending the night at my sister Margarita's flat, and directions were issued for getting there. Several options – including a flight to Santorini and a seven hour boat journey from there to Sifnos – were explored and rejected, as was the possibility of hiring a helicopter, if one found himself with a few thousand euro to spare. One didn't. Though I'm sure we could claim it back from Bentley, when we win that lawsuit.

I went over the schedules again, in desperation.

'There's a boat that'll get me to Athens tomorrow evening,' I said, 'if you insist on flying back on Tuesday.'

'Can't you get here any sooner?'

'Yes. I could break my leg and be airlifted in a medical helicopter. But I won't be doing that, I'm sorry.'

M conceded, reasonably, that this was fair enough. But it still left us with the question of what we'd actually be doing, instead.

'So you're stranded in Sifnos,' he remarked.

'No,' I said. 'You're stranded in Athens. I'm exactly where I'm supposed to be.'

But I will leave here, still. I will leave my electric blanket and my rituals behind, and I will leave food out for the cats, and I will travel to Athens tomorrow. I'll spend the night there, and on Monday morning I will go shopping for things I need and things I crave, and some interesting snacks for the journey back home, and then M and I will catch the boat together in the afternoon, and sail to Sifnos.

This is not a twist. In this story of people and places and connections missed and new ones forged across a map of

246

Greece, the answer was simple in the end, as it almost always is. It happened like this:

A city, an island, and a telephone line conveying options and possibilities and considerations, back and forth, between the two; a pot of chickpeas, soaked and seasoned and waiting to be cooked, and a wood oven sending out smoke signals that got lost in a thunderstorm that was most unwilling. And Manolis calling my name over the wall.

'I'm making chickpea stew,' I told M when I came back in. 'It's just gone in the oven.'

'I'm getting the boat on Monday,' he said.

And thus it was tacitly and mutually agreed that Tuesday could just as well be any other day, and if the Bentley is determined to stick to a plan as faulty as its fuel tank, then it can fly back to London on its own, and good luck to it.

So tomorrow I'll collect my chickpeas and put them in the fridge to keep them fresh, and then I'll make my way down to the port and travel to Athens, where a man with a broken Bentley awaits in my sister's flat. I could just stay, and eat my chickpeas warm out of the pot, and let him make his own way here on Monday night, but I won't be doing that. It would be as senseless as breaking my own leg for a helicopter ride. Because I'm quite fond of this man, as it happens, and though people could have checked with other people before doing stuff, one solitary boat trip is a small price to pay for another, with company and snacks, and chickpea stew waiting for us on the other end. We'll just have to heat it up when we get home.

# Day 62

I am on a boat sailing through the Aegean sea, and time
stands still, five hours into a six hour journey that will
never end. I go outside, impatient, hoping for a glimpse
of the lights of Athens in the distance, but they are not
there. And then I walk to the other side, and I find them.
It's disconcerting: total blackness on one side and all the
lights of mainland Greece twinkling away on the other,
and this boat in the middle, sailing between the two,
offering both options but not having to choose. I look at
the lights for a while but then I go back to the side of
black, to smoke my cigarette there. Blackness is rarer
than light, and your eyes don't have to make any
decisions. You can let your gaze settle on nothing, and
focus on everything else.

Time will play its tricks, but all journeys will end. And at
the end of this one, I will take the train to a northern
suburb of Athens, and walk up a street that I've walked
a thousand times, and I will ring a doorbell that I've
never had to ring before, and M will let me in to a flat
that used to be mine. A flat that is still almost mine, in
big ways and little ways. In the furniture I bought and
collected over the years that I lived there; the fridge and
the washing machine that were a welcome home present
from my grandma; the colours on the walls that my
sister hasn't painted over; my mosaic cupboard handles
in the kitchen and the threadbare bathroom rug and my
rainbow chandelier and my plastic pasta strainer and
my books on the shelves. And M is there now, stretched
out on the sofa I put together myself, its red cover faded
and stained in places, but still comfortable, or standing
on the balcony on this mild November night, taking in
the smells and sounds and sights of Athens. My sister's
flat; my flat. The flat I once shared with another man,

with traces of the past still clinging to its corners like dust that you missed when you were cleaning, but untainted – and made new tonight, when M opens the door.

I will ring the doorbell and he will stand in the doorway with the hallway light shining behind him and let me in, and it will be completely strange and completely ordinary, both. Kind of like the ship and the darkness and the light, and all the things worth speaking of at all. Where opposites coexist as entirely equal possibilities and there is no contradiction, and you can drift from one to the other but you don't have to choose. You don't have to decide anything. There is nothing to decide, because it's all there.

There is light on both sides now. No choice: I am in Athens. And in all the years I've been away, all the times I've left this city and come back, I've never been happier to be here. And that says a lot about a lot of things, things I might have to spread out and examine at some point, but right now what it means is that I'm exactly where I need to be.

# Day 63

You can deny the existence of Tuesdays but sometimes one of them sneaks up on you. And so it was that Tuesday came and M got on a plane and flew back to London. I could be dramatic and add that he took my heart away with him, but we don't do that; we don't take things away from each other. Planes fly and people come and go, and everything stays where it should be.

He didn't stand in the doorway and let me in after all. I rang the doorbell and nothing happened. He tried to pick me up from the train station and wandered off in the opposite direction and I found him halfway up the road. I had given him directions earlier, in case he wanted to explore the city during the day, and it seems one of us doesn't know the difference between left and right; it's debatable which one it is and it doesn't really matter anyway, because we still managed to meet somewhere in between. And we both stood outside the door and he unlocked it and we walked in together.

This is where words fail me; this is where I come up against all the things I can't express. Like when you lie on a sofa with a man and listen to him talk about psychology and website optimisation and karma and stock prices all at once and you're completely taken over by a feeling that you cannot name and you want to laugh and cry at the same time and all you can do is look at him and smile. Like when he goes off on tangent after tangent after tangent and you follow him as best you can, because there's nowhere he could take you that you don't want to go. And when you tell him that you're lost he says 'You're still here; we're still together', and it no longer matters where that is.

I could talk about Sundays and Mondays and Tuesdays, endless cups of tea and a flat that we almost never left. I could tell you how I subsisted entirely on endorphins for 48 hours and never once looked at my phone or the time. I could use words and say things and I could equally say nothing at all, for all the good it would do. This is where I'm tempted to resort to melodrama or cliché or metaphysics. This is where I invoke concepts I don't quite understand, like quantum, hoping that science can explain the things I can't. This is where I say, in a pause in conversation, 'I'm just wondering what sort of karma it was that led me to you'.

There are Sundays and Mondays and Tuesdays, cups of tea and tangents and conversations, science and metaphysics, karma and cliché and communicating vessels that always balance out, and there are words you can use, like love, like left and right and up and down, but I wouldn't know about any of these things. This is where I stop trying; this is where I lie back on the sofa and look at a man and smile. This is where I am, no matter where that is.

You can deny time and put one hundred days into a single Monday and turn left instead of right, but Tuesdays will come and words will fail and love will always be one of them: don't bother. And heart is just the name we give to a place where we keep those things we can't express. And if he happened to take mine with him when he left, on this Tuesday, I wouldn't even notice. I have no use for it when he's not around. So Tuesdays will come and planes will fly, but nothing will be taken away. Nothing that matters.

In the taxi on the way to the airport, just as the control tower came into view, M turned around to me and said: 'I ruined your one hundred days.'

*No*: you made them.

And that, on this Tuesday, is the best I can do with my words.

# Day 64

Back to my chickpeas, then. Back to my rocket and my spinach shoots. Back to exchanging greetings with Manolis over the wall, as we both tinker in our respective gardens. Back to Boy Cat, who seemed happy to see me in his own, reserved way; back to the Black Cat That Coughs, who ran up to me yesterday, coughing and meowing, before she remembered that she's scared of me and ran off in the opposite direction. Back to the hum of my dehumidifier, the ticking of the heaters as they come back to life, the window shutters rattling in the wind and the little alien cries of the geckos talking to each other across the ceiling beams. Back to the smell of damp soil and fires burning in the fields. Back to the electric blanket that keeps my bed warm.

Back, with bruises on my skin, and with a crick in my neck because I insisted on resting it against a man's shoulder at a funny angle all through the night. Back with a good supply of coffee and coconut oil and stories that will last me a while. Back home.

'What's the weather like?' Susanne asked me yesterday.

'Grey,' I replied dramatically, 'to reflect my mood.' But then I laughed, because I didn't mean it; I have all the colours here that I need. I don't need to look out the window to find them. And the sun will shine again: it's what it does.

Wednesday night was warm and windless and I felt a sting of emotion as the ferry glided, with its door lowered, up to the dock. There were few lights at the port, very few people, four lorries lined up along the quay waiting to board and the dark shapes of the mountains in the background, their outline picked out by the moonlight. It was a melancholy scene, a place subdued,

253

but the emotion I felt was joy, and gratitude for this little island and its quiet welcome, the way it lets me slip back in, like I belong.

I had arranged for Vangelis to pick me up; the buses are now only running on weekday mornings, to transport the kids to and from school. There were five taxis at the rank, their drivers sitting close together on the low wall behind, in the shadows, smoking and sipping coffee out of polystyrene cups. I squinted desperately at them, trying to pick Vangelis out of the line-up, my short-sighted eyes straining in the low light. He stood up and raised his hand, the tip of his cigarette tracing a line in the darkness and pointing, like a wand, to his car.

'I thought you were bringing someone,' he said, looking around for my missing person.

'I was,' I replied, and explained about ferries and planes and Tuesdays and how a trip to this place, under pressure, just didn't feel right.

Vangelis nodded in agreement: you don't bring stress to our island, you come here to leave it behind. 'Probably for the best,' he offered. 'He might have struggled with the quiet and the isolation.'

I smiled to myself. 'He can take it,' I said. 'He'd love it. He's like me.'

Vangelis laughed, amused, perhaps, at the thought of there being two of us solitary weirdos, just as he's starting to get used to me.

'In that case,' he said, 'tell him to come back, and stay.'

He's getting used to me, I can tell. He still finds it strange that I choose to live here on my own, without seeking company, but he seems to accept me now, and our small talk is growing bigger.

He drove me to the end of the road, and turned around in his seat as I was about to get out. 'You're in trouble,' he said. 'This island has got you under a spell.' He grinned. 'You'll find it hard to leave.'

I smiled to myself all the way home, nodding in agreement: you don't come here to leave, you come here to stay.

'But what about the chickpeas?' Eleni asked this morning.

The chickpeas will keep. They're in the fridge and they're still fresh, and I will eat them for lunch and for dinner, on their own, and with rice, and in a salad and, if there are some left over still, I'll throw them in the blender with lemon juice and tahini and turn them into hummus. They won't go to waste; nothing ever has to.

Don't get me wrong: it's always good to have another weirdo to share your chickpeas with. And electric blankets are no match for pressing yourself against another person to keep warm at night. I woke up looking for M this morning, and the solitude that has only been a word so far became an absence in my bed. Susanne and Eleni aren't asking about the weather or the chickpeas; they're asking how I feel, because they know I'm made of very soft materials and everything that happens leaves an impression on me. And that's exactly how it should be, because what kind of shapeless thing would this life be otherwise? And absences are only the product of presences, because you cannot miss what you've never had, and I've had a lot.

So my answer is this: The weather is fine, and chickpeas taste just as good when you eat them on your own. I feel nothing but gratitude and joy, and if a little melancholy seeps it, that's food for writers, and we often go looking for it in the grey, quiet days. Don't worry: the sun will shine again and cars will fly and Manolis will light his oven many times over the next few months. I am soft, but not dented. This life is moulded by the people and things that we press ourselves into: sometimes missed, but not missing. Nothing is missing at all.

I have a lot. I have an island that lets me call it home, and neighbours who notice when I'm coming and going, and the acceptance of one cab driver at a time. I have spinach and rocket and carrots growing in the garden, and coffee and coconut oil to last me for a good, long time, and a pot of chickpeas all to myself. I have colours enough for all the grey days this winter can throw at me, and an electric blanket to keep me warm. I have all the words I could ask for and new stories to tell, and the solitude I've chosen, until I choose to break it again. And that absence in my bed is not a gap that needs to be filled, it's only the space claimed by a man who puts bruises on my skin, small tokens of much larger impressions. And he will glide back into it, like a ship on a windless night, when the time is right, and I will welcome him quietly, like he belongs.

# Day 65

This is a new twist: my days, it seems, are now themed; yesterday certainly was, though I didn't see it straight away. I got up in the morning feeling flat. I had slept badly the night before, and every dream I had featured an electrical appliance malfunctioning or failing. Electrical appliance anxiety is not uncommon in my life, but this particular bout was partly self-inflicted, the result of a game I played with M on Sunday night. The other part was due to a horrifying revelation that he made, inadvertently, the day after, whilst jabbing at electrical wires with a screwdriver that kept lighting up to indicate that they were live.

Being, among many other things, a professional electrician, M went around locating and fixing faulty switches in Margarita's flat. So far so good: both of them were pleased. But then I came along, and decided to play the game of listing reasons why M should come to Sifnos with me rather than catching his flight back to London. And the dangers of electricity were too compelling to resist.

'My bedroom light keeps going off at random, no matter how many different bulbs I give it.'

M nodded. 'That'll be the connection.'

'And then there's this extension socket that says *Dzt*,' I added.

'It buzzes?'

'No. It's not a buzz. It's a *Dzt*! It's not a good sound.' I meant every word of this, by the way; that extension terrifies me. Every time it utters that little sound, I'm convinced it's about to burst into flame. I give it a wide berth whenever I walk past it, and often glare at it from a distance, though I'm not sure what I expect this to achieve.

'Oh,' said M, with a hint of concern. 'Perhaps it's overloaded.'

'See!' I cried triumphantly. 'I am obviously in grave and terrible danger, and it's is your professional duty to come and save me from flickering lights and extensions that say *Dzt!*'

He agreed that this was, indeed, the case and, satisfied that I had made my point vis–à–vis electrical emergencies, I moved on to more traditional tactics: enticement and bribery.

'What can I give you?' I asked.

'What have you got?'

'How about some gum?'

He gave me a puzzled look. 'Gum?'

'I don't know. People like gum.'

He shrugged. 'Go on.'

'What if I dance for you?'

'Would it be a sexy dance?'

I thought about this. 'I could sway my hips,' I said, 'in what I consider to be a sexy manner but no, in all honesty, probably not.'

The Dangers of Electricity was a good game to play while I lay in my sister's bed, safe in my electrician's arms, but then I came back here on my own, and the extension socket still said *Dzt* and M wasn't around to save me. I glared at it. 'Don't do that,' I pleaded, but it ignored me. I decided to take action. M had advised against running too many appliances off a single extension, and his word is gospel, so I moved things around to reduce the load and consigned the offending extension to a different plug, out of the way, where I at least couldn't hear it if it insisted on speaking. 'There,' I said. 'I don't need no electricians. I can manage perfectly well on my own.' I went to my bedroom and flicked the switch. Nothing happened. I sighed, and turned on the bedside light.

The revelation wasn't part of the game. It came later, when M discovered yet another faulty light switch in my sister's living room. He pulled it out of the wall and it was now dangling from several exposed wires of various colours, and he was poking at it with a screwdriver. In bare feet. I danced around him – not sexy in the very least – wincing and whimpering every time his fingers came close to the wires, my hands balled up into fists in white knuckle terror, scanning the room for wooden objects I could whack him with if the need arose, and asking inane questions.

'Are those wires live?'

'Yes.'

'Do you have to stick your hands in there?'

'Yes.'

Inspiration stroke, and I ran to the bedroom and came back brandishing his sandals.

'What are those for?' he asked, still poking at the gaping hole of death.

'They're plastic! You must wear them!'

'Put them down, Daph,' he said gently. 'It's OK. I'll be fine.' He smiled at me and I felt marginally calmer, but still refused to let go of the sandals.

And that's when he said it, the phrase that shook my entire belief system to its very core. Casually, apropos of nothing, except for the fact that he was fiddling with live wires in barefoot nonchalance.

'You know, electricians don't have a clue what they're doing half the time.'

'No,' I said faintly. 'Take it back.'

'What?'

'You don't understand: to me, you are god. When you stick your hands in electrical sockets, you are god. I have to believe you know what you're doing. Do you understand? To ordinary people, electricians are gods.'

He laughed; he doesn't understand. What to me is an absolute miracle, a death-defying feat of pure magic, to him it's just what he does. And he carried on doing it as I watched, transfixed, still holding out the sandals, a votive offering to gods that I refused to believe did not exist.

Afterwards, when the switch had been fixed and the living room was bathed in light and I had been talked into relinquishing the sandals and joining him on the sofa, M turned to me with a grin.

'So I'm a god then, am I?'

'Shut up,' I said, maturely. 'I don't like you. You're not getting any gum.'

The theme of the day wasn't electrical, though it may seem that way. A likely interpretation could be that it was about powerlessness, or failure, or both. I spent the night helpless against failing appliances, an ordinary person lost in the realm of the gods. And when I woke up in the morning, I failed to start up. I felt hollow: not drained of energy, but more like the energy had been gouged out of me, violently, leaving me sore and empty inside. My limbs were heavy and tender, my eyes stung, my face tingled, and I was cold and shivery, despite having turned on every single heating appliance in the house. Staring at a blank page on my computer did no good: my head was as full of words as it always is, but they were all lying flat on their backs, like dying insects, refusing to engage with each other or with me. I didn't have the strength to summon them, to raise them up. I could barely get myself to sit up straight. I idled the day away, wandering listlessly around the house, crawling from bed to sofa and back again.

I think it was the helplessness I felt when I stood next to M in my sister's living room, clutching that pair of plastic sandals to my chest, with the gods falling off their pedestals and no one left to pray to for his safety, that caused the electrical nightmares and set the theme for the day. But I didn't make the connection until the afternoon. It all came together then, gods and electricians and ordinary people, terrible revelations, failing appliances and my own flat, faulty state, forming an unlikely circuit that buzzed and intermittently said *Dzt*, a loop that began and ended with me.

It happened as I lay on the sofa with my laptop balanced on my knees: my screen grew a shade dimmer, the dehumidifier stopped humming, and the lights went out. I froze as my frazzled brain tallied up the number of appliances making demands on my behalf upon the Sifnos electrical grid. Four heaters, one towel warmer, one dehumidifier, one laptop, several lights. I heard M speak the word "overload", the divine admonishment in his voice as he repeated the commandment I had failed to observe: *thou shalt not run too many appliances all at once.* The extension socket had warned me; it had been saying *Dzt!* but I hadn't listened. I had brought this on to myself, and I would now be plunged into darkness for all eternity, with no heating, no wifi, and no gods to appeal to for salvation.

Some latent wisdom told me to unplug everything, before leading me to the fuse board where I established that none of the switches had tripped. This confused me, as it indicated that perhaps I wasn't to blame for the electrical disaster that had befallen me. I stepped outside, but the daylight, faint as it was, still held, and it was too early for the streetlights to have come on. I was about to go back in when I noticed movement through the branches of the almond tree.

'Hey, Manolis!' I called out. 'Have you got power?'

'Yep,' he replied. A pause. 'Nope. There is no light.'

A powercut, then. Not divine retribution. A time when the gods become as ordinary and powerless as the rest of us, and darkness and light and wifi signals are placed in the hands of elusive and abstract forces such as public power supply companies, which are very unlikely to answer their phones on a Saturday afternoon.

'So what do we do?' I asked Manolis. 'Just wait it out?'

'Yep. Light some candles and wait it out.'

I laughed to myself then, because I'd put it all together and a candlelit vigil to my fallen electrical gods fitted in nicely; the circuit was complete.

The power was back on by the time I'd dug out my tea lights; the powercut lasted all of ten minutes. The lights shone again, brighter than ever before, and the modem twinkled back to life. I plugged my heaters, one by one, into their sockets and switched the dehumidifier on. I went outside to speak to Manolis.

'It's back,' I announced.

'Yep.'

'Does this happen often?'

'Not really, no. But it just needs a break every now and again, you know? A rest. And then it comes back on.'

Perhaps the theme wasn't failure, after all, but regeneration. Perhaps all of us, my appliances, the Sifnos electrical grid, the gods and I, needed a break, a reboot to restore us to full power. Perhaps we were all a bit overloaded, and we ignored the signs. Or maybe I just had the flu and some nightmares and there was a powercut – no circuits, no connections, no theme. In any case, all appliances are behaving well today, and I feel much better; I don't remember any of my dreams.

I can see M sitting high on his pedestal, twisting a screwdriver between his fingers, his bare feet dangling over the plastic sandals that he refuses to wear. I can see him laughing at me and my electrical anxieties and the wooden objects that I wield to protect him from things that he doesn't fear. And as long as he's up there, doing what he does, I know that I'm safe. I don't want him climbing down for no good reason.

So I would like to assure him that there are no emergencies here, and no one that needs to be saved. The extension is probably still saying *Dzt*, unheard and out of sight behind the sofa, and there's no telling what the bedroom light will do when I flick the switch, but it's fine. We're all doing fine. I don't want to play the game anymore; it gives me nightmares. I would further like to confess that I have no gum and I can't dance and, in terms of enticement, all I have to offer is myself. And other people's plastic sandals, if the need happens to arise.

# Day 66

I was invited to dinner at my uncle's house last night. Actually, that's not entirely accurate: I was an afterthought, and invited to join my family in the short break between dinner and dessert, and that's only because I happened to call my mum at that time. She was still chewing when she answered the phone.

'Are you eating?' I asked.

'Yes. Hang on.' There was some shuffling down the line, and then my uncle's voice on the other end.

'So we'd like to invite you to join us for dinner,' he said.

'Wonderful,' I replied. 'Haha.' I instinctively glanced around my empty, quiet house, slowly filling up with the scent of my chickpea stew heating up on the stove.

But then he said those two terrible words: 'On skype.'

'What have I ever done to you?' I muttered.

He laughed. 'Just answer the call.'

'I can't wait.'

I didn't have to wait very long. A tablet was found and a video call came through from Margarita's account.

'Yey,' I said by way of greeting as I clicked the button to answer. My sister's face appeared on my screen; she gave me an apologetic smile before turning me around to join my family at the dinner table. They were all there: my grandma next to me on the right, looking everywhere but at the screen that Margarita was holding up; my mum, bent over her plate; my uncle Dimitris in the distance, at the head of the table, his face arranged in an expression that clearly expressed the message "Did you think you'd get away?" I raised my eyebrows at him; he smirked. On the other side, Ariadne, guest of honour, on a weekend visit from London, and finally, to my left, Natalia, my aunt, conveying sympathy with her eyes.

The kids had left their seats and were running in circles around the table, their heads bobbing up excitedly and then disappearing from view, to appear again, seconds later, in another part of the room.

'Isn't it marvellous, this technology that brings us all together,' I said flatly. Everyone spoke at once. 'I don't know what I've done to deserve this,' I added; I heard Margarita laugh.

There was a bit of commotion then, and I was treated to a close-up of my cousin's ear and the inside of his mouth, accompanied by rustling and screaming, and closely followed by a shot of Margarita's nostrils.

'This is not making me nauseous at all,' I commented.

'Sorry,' came my sister's voice, and I was righted up again.

'She can't see us,' somebody said.

'She doesn't want to see us; she wants to see the food. Show her the food.'

I was about to protest, but then I thought better of it: these people know me. 'Yes,' I said. 'Show me the food.'

The camera panned over the table, giving me glimpses of largely unidentifiable, half-empty dishes.

'So what did you have?'

Assorted family members called out menu items: Salad! Soup! Chicken! Potatoes!

'We're having ice cream for dessert!' screamed my cousin Ivi.

'Ice cream!' repeated her brother, as the top of his head appeared on my screen. Another commotion and a lot of jerky movements and grunts and then his voice, 'Woo! You're on a rollercoaster ride!', as the tablet was thrust up and down and sideways in what, I have to admit, was a very convincing simulation. I begged him to stop.

'Cosma!' Margarita said sternly. 'Give it back to me!' A struggle, my cousin's high-pitched protests about how unfair it all was, and stillness. My grandma's face now filled the screen.

'Talk to her,' my uncle urged.

She looked straight at me. 'Coocoo!' she said.

'Yes. Coocoo indeed.'

She smiled, delighted, and raised up both hands to wave. I did the same, and Margarita moved the camera around the table to reveal my entire family following suit, waving at me with both hands.

'Does that mean we're saying goodbye?' I asked hopefully.

'No,' said Dimitris. 'We're just excited to see you on our television. Like the Queen.'

I gave them all a royal wave. 'How gratifying,' I said.

When we had all waved at each other for long enough, I cleared my throat and asked for their attention.

'Guys,' I said, 'which part of me choosing to isolate myself on a remote island gave you the impression that I enjoy group chats on skype?'

They laughed, and so did I, because I didn't really mean it. It was kind of nice to have them all invade my quiet home, for a little while.

Just before I was released back to my solitude and my chickpeas, I managed a quick chat with Natalia.

'How's the writing going?' she asked.

'Good. I just finished today's piece. It took me all day!'

She seemed to ponder this. 'So,' she said, 'you're writing every day, about your day, and you spend the whole day writing...'

'Yes,' I said. 'Don't dwell on it. It's all getting a bit philosophical. Like a chicken and egg sort of situation.'

Natalia laughed. 'You could be the guru of all writers!' she suggested. 'Writing about writing about writing.'

And that's as far as we got with the philosophy, because just then another bobbing head nearly knocked the tablet out of Margarita's hands and it was unanimously agreed that it was time to bring the session to an end. We all waved again, and then they were gone.

The guru of all writers: I like that. I wonder what such a position would involve, and if writing about writing about writing is qualification enough to apply. I think the recluse thing should work in my favour, and I have more than a few examples to offer in support of my eccentricity and social ineptitude. I'm sure my family would be more than happy to attest to that, especially given my less than graceful participation in last night's skype session.

A problem I'm likely to encounter is niceness: the guru of all writers cannot be nice, or especially approachable. Such a role should encompass all the essential qualities writers are known for, and being a bit of an arsehole is unarguably one of them. I would also have to be unpredictable and hard to reach, frequently disappearing for days on end, on account of the muse having paid me a visit. Living along on a remote island certainly puts me in good stead – a cosy flat in central London doesn't strike me as the appropriate dwelling for a guru – but I suspect both my isolation and the remoteness of the island would have to be exaggerated slightly, and wilderness and hardship strongly hinted at. In my dual capacity as guru and writer, I believe a certain amount of suffering for my art is to be expected.

Do gurus have disciples, or followers, or students? I think I'd call mine students, and also refer to myself as a student at times, to reinforce the point that we are all of us always learning, and being taught. My manner wouldn't be gentle; that quality has been claimed by the gurus of the spiritual realm. As the guru of all writers, I would be edgy and bit manic sometimes; at other times, I would drift away, mid-conversation, stare contemplatively into the distance, into faraway worlds of my own making, and then, sometimes, pull out my ever-present notebook and scribble feverishly and illegibly in it for several moments. I would not apologise for this.

I'd really have to work on my persona, to achieve that unique blend of humility and arrogance that separates the gurus from the ordinary humans, and to develop the ability to convey how modest I am about knowing everything there is to know. I would contradict myself often, to keep things interesting. I would pursue many tangents, introduce several twists; I would be my own unreliable narrator, keeping my public guessing all the time. I would have to learn to express myself a lot more vaguely, and insist, if questioned, that this is a deliberate tactic, to encourage people to think for themselves. I would make references to "the death of the author" and other obscure literary theories, and explain how all our words are open to interpretation; I would invite my students to interpret mine in accordance to their own, personal contexts. I would employ complex and abstract terms to mirror the complex and abstract nature of life and literature. I would master the art of speaking while saying nothing very much at all and, conversely, making my long and frequent silences heavy with meaning. I would be silent often. And brooding; as the guru of all writers, I would have a lot to brood about.

I would sometimes speak exclusively in similes and metaphors, but never use euphemisms: I would always say *fuck* and *dead* instead of *sleeping together* and *passed away*. I would become known for my sharp tongue and my sharper wit and people would fear and admire me for these qualities in equal measures.

When in conversation with my students, I would always challenge them, perhaps even taunt them a little with my superior intelligence and extensive vocabulary. I would always correct their grammar; I would be fair but strict, and that would be my gift to them. If anyone made the mistake of sending me written correspondence which was misspelt, badly punctuated or employed text talk, I would publicly humiliate them, for their own good.

I would preach respect for the English language; I would advocate subversion and unconventional techniques, but only when the student had fully mastered the correct usage of the language and the formal elements of writing.

I would have to provide a certain number of inspirational quotes that people could then post of facebook for their friends to like; that seems to be important. I'd also need to set up a dedicated twitter account, or, better yet, get one of my students to take care of that for me; they would be honoured, I'm sure. I might also purchase one of those new .guru domains, so anyone looking me up online would be in no doubt as to what I am. They'd just type in www.daphne.guru and there I'd be.

The guru of all writers: I think I could pull this off. Once again, however, I come up against the problem of facial hair. A wispy growth would certainly not cut it in this case. It would have to be a full on beard, and probably long enough to weave into braids, with multicoloured beads and bells attached to the ends. That would be the sort of beard the guru of all writers should sport. Is it fair to be excluded from this simply because I am a girl? Should I be denied my calling and deprive my would-be students of my wisdom on account of gender alone? It's an undeniable fact: statistically, most gurus have beards. Perhaps I could be the exception to the rule, controversial in my lack of facial hair; perhaps, in addition to the guru of all writers, I could also be the voice of female gurus everywhere, discriminated against because of their eager, hair-free faces. But that sounds like a lot of work, and it probably wouldn't leave me much time for writing, what with all the placard-making and naked protests I would have to organise.

It also occurs to me now that being the guru of all writers would involve public appearances, in one form or another. I would have to agree to a number of interviews, albeit rare and on my own, exacting terms. The phone would ring far too often, and I would have to answer it sometimes. And, at the very least, I would have to make myself available to my students, in person or – horror of horrors – on skype. I would have to set up group sessions with them, whereby they'd all gather around a table, much like my family last night, eagerly awaiting the face of their guru to appear on the screen, ready to receive my teachings and clutching notepads in which to take down every single one of my important words. And I would say: 'Guys, which part of me being a bit of an arsehole misanthropic guru living alone in total isolation on a remote and savage island gave you the impression that I want to chat to you on skype?' And they would laugh, because they'd think I was joking. But they'd be wrong.

I don't think I'm cut out for gurudom, after all. I don't think I have what it takes. I don't belong in the limelight, but in the dim light of my desk lamp, writing my words down without knowing if they'll be important to anyone at all. I think I prefer the quiet of my home being invaded, as an afterthought, by people who love me and don't really listen to a word I say. I think I might be destined to remain exactly who I am, nice and approachable, even though I don't always answer the phone, only a little isolated and eccentric in very small ways, beardless and studentless and the guru of no one, quietly learning every day how to better be me.

# Day 67

There was an earthquake last night. In fact there were two, a few minutes apart, just after 1 in the morning. I was awake, but I didn't feel a thing. But the epicentre was in the Bay of Evia, up by the mainland, so perhaps the tremors didn't reach us all the way down here, in the Cyclades. I am a little disappointed: perversely, I quite like earthquakes; I like the drama of them.

Greece is prone to earthquakes, and we grow up knowing that the earth might move. I remember earthquake drills at school; I remember being told how to evacuate the building in an orderly manner if there was time, and how to curl up under our desks, on our knees and with our hands over our heads, if there was not. I remember about doorways being the safest, sturdiest parts of any building. You wouldn't think it, perhaps, but if everything else collapsed around you, if the ceilings caved in, doorways might be the only thing left standing. It's a striking image that I always keep in my mind: a free standing doorway amidst the rubble, as the dust begins to clear.

Earthquakes fascinate me. I think it's something about their inevitability and our powerlessness against them; all those seismologists watching their fancy instruments, monitoring movements and predicting possibilities, yet there is nothing they can do to stop an earthquake when it comes. Something about the irony of it, that the ground that we walk on, the solid ground beneath our feet, is not solid at all. Deep down in the belly of the earth something is always shifting, tectonic plates like puzzle pieces always moving around to find a better fit.

There have been two major earthquakes in my lifetime. The second one, in September 1999, I missed. I was in London. But I witnessed its aftermath, a few days later: refugee camps in the outskirts of Athens, and colour-coded crosses marking buildings and homes: green for safety, yellow for structural damage requiring repairs, and red for those that couldn't be salvaged, that had to be taken down. My mum's house was green; my dad's yellow, and there were cracks in the walls. Crosses also marked the graves of the victims: 145 people were killed, 2,000 injured, and 50,000 lost their homes. The earthquake had lasted exactly fifteen seconds.

The first one, in February 1981, I claim to remember, but it's most probably a false memory, created by several retellings of a story that has now become family myth. It happened at night. My parents woke me up, carried me out of bed in my pyjamas, and we fled the house in my granddad's Citroen. My dad's parents were also there, in their own car. They had obviously been advised to stay clear of buildings, make their way to open spaces away from the densely built up city centre, so we got into the cars and drove. Apparently, upon seeing both sets of grandparents, I understood this to be some sort of occasion, and occasions, in my limited experience, were happy and involved food. I was two and a half years old, and life was as simple as that. Half asleep but excited, I said the only thing that made sense to me: 'Since we're all together, why don't we go somewhere to eat?' It must have made them laugh, my take on this disaster that had shaken us out of our beds; it must have relieved some of the tension of not knowing, as we drove away, if they'd have homes to come back to. I can almost hear myself saying those words, this famous quote; I have no doubt that it happened as told, but I think it's the telling of it that masquerades as memory, putting words in my mouth. I do remember being in that car, however, bundled in the back seat of the old Citroen; I remember it's dry, dusty smell that I can still summon now if I concentrate very hard; I remember the darkness and the glow of the headlights of the cars behind.

The worst thing about earthquakes is the noise: it comes just before the tremor itself. It's a deep, guttural groan, the very foundations of the earth pushing against each other, and everything we've build upon it screaming in its effort to stay upright. It's a sound unlike any other you've heard before but you know it, instantly, for what it is: a primeval alarm system that makes all your hairs stand on end. Then comes the shaking and the rattling, the clatter of objects banging against each other, the crashing of things falling off tabletops and shelves, which is much less frightening because you know what's happening by now. 'It's just an earthquake,' you say, and wait it out. Perhaps you go around pushing things back from the edge, or stand under a doorway like they told you in school. But it's just an earthquake, and it will pass. And then it'll just be a thing to talk about with your friends. Did you feel it? Did it wake you up?

There was a minor one a few years back, when I was living in Athens with an ex boyfriend. He wasn't Greek and the earth moving was nothing but an idiomatic way to describe good sex. The earth hadn't moved for us for a while. But then, in the early hours of the morning, it did. I was woken up by the bed creaking as it shuddered along with the building and the earth beneath. I opened my eyes and saw my ex staring at me in wide-eyed terror.

'What the fuck is that?' he shouted.

'Oh, it's nothing,' I replied, perhaps a little insensitively. 'It's just an earthquake.'

'*Just* an earthquake?' He threw himself out of bed and stood in the middle of the room, arms thrust out as if to fend off invisible attackers, trembling with nervous tension as the ground beneath him shook.

'Get back into bed,' I said. 'It'll be over in a moment.'

'No fucking way! It's an *earthquake!*'

'Fine. Then go stand under the doorway if you must do something. The middle of the room is the worst place to be.

He actually complied, which was a first; he really resented being told what to do. A few seconds later it was over, just like I'd said; the plates had found a new fit to try and, with a little sigh, the earth settled back into stillness. I lifted my head off the pillow to look at my ex, cowering in the doorway, clutching the frame and glaring at me accusingly as if the events of the last few moments had somehow been my fault, and it occurred to me that I really didn't want him back in my bed. The earthquake hadn't shaken me, but this did.

'You might want to stay there for a while,' I said cruelly. 'There might be another one. They often come in twos.'

Things come along and shake up our lives, and there's no science to monitor their movements. There might be warning signs, but we often ignore them and even when we don't, there's little we can do to stop the ground from shifting beneath our feet. It's hard not to think this way in the wake of an earthquake; the symbolism of tectonic events is too potent to resist. The ground might look solid but underneath the surface, our lives are just as restless as those plates, always pushing puzzle pieces around to find a better fit. And when the ceiling caves in, that's when we realise we'd been living tentatively in structures marked with a red X, unsalvageable, because we didn't have the courage to demolish them ourselves. Sometimes it takes an earthquake to wake you up.

You can't stop the earth from moving; all you can do is wait it out. But once it's over, once the dust has cleared, you can open your eyes and bring that image to your mind: the free standing doorway, a passageway amidst the rubble. A way out and a way in.

# Day 68

The Greek language makes no distinction between solitude and loneliness; the word for the both is the same: *monaksia.* It's odd because it's praised as a rich, expressive language, one that knows to separate romantic love (*eros*) from its other manifestations, and yet it won't allow you solitude without being lonely or loneliness in a crowd, unless you explain yourself.

I'm having to explain myself a lot, to defend my solitude from the loneliness it implies. It happened with my mum the other night, when I took her with me on that solitary night-time walk to the supermarket and counted, for both of us, the number of lights I could see on the way. '*Monaksia,*' she said, more for herself, to understand why I was feeling overwhelmed, and I had to clarify that yes, it was the fact of knowing, of being surrounded by the evidence that I was, almost, completely alone, *solitude,* but no, it wasn't loneliness. It isn't easy to explain and even harder to understand because this, again, is a matter of interpretation and perspective, and maybe for my mum, for many people, solitude and loneliness are one and the same. Even harder because *monaksia* can also be translated as desolation, and desolation is not a straightforward word either; it has connotations far darker that the picture I described.

Before I came upon an English translation, I thought the title of Gabriel Garcia Marquez's novel was "100 years of loneliness". That's what the Greek version told me. I was intrigued and wanted to read it, but I sometimes referred to it, in jest, as "100 years of misery". Pre-emptively, because 100 years of loneliness is a heavy sentence; it doesn't foretell of much joy. And it wasn't too inaccurate a description, as I discovered when I finally read the book, some ten years ago, in English. I knew, by then, that it was about solitude, but it was a solitude that failed to protect the characters, that failed to make them happy, and it brought loneliness and desolation too. I read a copy belonging to my friend Sabrina, which I spotted on her shelf one evening, and remembered it was a book I'd always said I'd read. I asked if I could borrow it, and Sabrina refused; she gave me *Love in the time of cholera*, instead, and insisted I read that first, as an initiation to Marquez, before moving on to *100 years*. I did as I was told, and handed *Love* back to Sabrina a week later, to be officially deemed worthy of *Solitude*.

I don't remember much about it, except that it wasn't light-hearted, and that the utopian town of Macondo, founded by Jose Arcadio Buendia as a new beginning for himself and his descendants, is proven to be a mirage, a dystopia, as seven generations of the Buendia family suffer the same, predestined misfortunes and history repeats itself in cycles. But a surprising detail that came back to me this morning, more significant perhaps to me than to the novel itself, is that Jose Arcadio Buendia believes Macondo to be surrounded by water; Macondo, the setting for *100 years of solitude* and Buendia's promised land, is an island.

One hundred years of solitude on a fantasy island – isolated, if only in its founder's imagination. One hundred days of solitude on the island of Sifnos, served only infrequently by boats. And, once again, history repeats itself in the details, surprising, because I had no memory of the island connection when I paraphrased Marquez and wrote myself into this story. But perhaps, like in Marquez's novel, everything that happens is written somewhere and all any of us are doing is endlessly acting it out. Everything that happens has happened before.

It's hard to avoid thinking that way when you find yourself living a life of magical realism, where several stories, yours and other peoples, true or imagined, constantly overlap. When a girl I've come to know in the last few weeks, who contacted me through the blog, told me in her first message how she used to dream of moving to a Greek island to write a novel, with the main character called Daphne. When there's actually a novel, written by Alexandra Belegrati[ix] and published in Greece in 2011, entitled (in loose translation) *It had to be that way*, which is about a woman who gives up her life to spend a winter in Sifnos. And when its author, who wrote to me in utter disbelief when she stumbled upon my story, confided that the novel was part wish fulfilment for her, a change of life written instead of acted out, and served as the gateway to her quitting her job and becoming a full-time writer. How can I separate myself from these stories when they all seem inextricably linked?

The concept of an island is symbolic, but islands no longer exist. What solitude can I claim when, even on my loneliest of walks, I can call my mum and have her walk every step beside me? What isolation, when invisible networks put the entire world on my computer screen? This island may be real, a mass of land surrounded by water, but its connection to people and places and things does not rely on ferries calling at its port. Solitude is a decision we make, and loneliness might be implied, but it doesn't have to be chosen; it's just one of the interpretations available.

It might be surprising, but history repeats itself in the details, whether we remember them or not, and there is always a girl on an island somewhere, and the title of Alexandra's novel could also be translated as *Everything happened as it should*. It was written that way.

# Day 69

This place is incredibly beautiful. I just can't get over it, no matter how much time passes; I can't get used to it. It gets me every time I leave the house.

I had to go to the bank this morning. I wasn't looking forward to it; I don't think anyone does. But I had to go pay a cheque in, a cheque that I'd finally managed to snatch out of the very reluctant hands of the National Museum of Contemporary Art, for a translation I'd completed in April, after a full six months of waiting, hinting, cajoling and eventually threatening. My mum collected the cheque on my behalf, and attempted to pay it in to my account; she queued for forty-five minutes only to be told, firmly and unapologetically, that it needed to be paid in by me in person, and at my account holding branch. No explanation was offered for this bizarre requirement; the cashier dragged her gaze over to the next person in the queue, and my mum was dismissed. I picked up the cheque when I was in Athens last week, with a vague idea of trying my luck in Sifnos, but I wasn't feeling hopeful: banks are banks, and rules are rules, no matter where you are.

I was a little stressed when I set off, pre-empting the failure of my mission and a bit resentful of the fact that this cheque was imposing upon my schedule-free, obligation-free existence. But you can't hold on to these feelings here. The walk into town, that four-minute clamber down the steps, made them disappear as soon as I lifted my eyes and looked: Sifnos, my dry island of sun-scorched brown, has burst into green.

'This isn't winter,' commented Nikos the organic farmer the other day, as we both scavenged around his vegetable patches in search of beetroot for me to take home. 'It's more like spring.'

It had looked like rain earlier in the day, but my visit to the farm coincided with a full hour of warm, glorious sunshine. I got so hot I had to take my jumper off. 'I know it's bad for the crops,' I confessed, 'but I like it.'

'I know,' Nikos said. 'I like it too.'

We both squinted up at the sun, and brought our hands up to shade our eyes so we could look at it for a little longer.

In Alpha Bank, Sifnos branch, the manager said good morning and held the door open for me, and the cashier greeted me with a smile, as if we were old friends. I didn't have to queue. I went straight up to her and asked to pay a cheque into my account. She took it from my hands, peered at it, and handed it back. Here we go, I thought.

'This was issued by the National Bank,' she said. 'Why don't you just go over to them and get it cashed straight away?'

'Can I do that?' I asked, suspiciously. This wasn't at all what I'd expected.

'Of course! If you leave it with me, it'll take three days to clear.'

'But the cash will be going into this account, anyway,' I insisted.

'So go get your cash, and we'll pay it in, and it'll be in your account this afternoon.'

I stared at her. 'Really?'

'Oh,' she said, and smiled. 'I see. This isn't Athens. We don't torture you for no reason.'

I went up to the National Bank, which is housed in a tiny white building with blue doors and windows, its entrance lined up with potted geraniums and basil. No queuing there either. The cashier made small talk while she processed my cheque: where do I live, what do I do, how's it all going? She gave my ID card a cursory glance, counted out my cash, told me to have a good day, and sent me on my way with three hundred euro in my pocket and a skip in my step. Literally: this place makes me want to skip. Sometimes I do it without even noticing.

There was a queue in Alpha Bank the second time around, in that there were four people standing by the desk, and I wasn't served straight away, but that's where the similarities ended. If it weren't for the cash exchanging hands and the signatures asked for and received you'd hardly know there were business transactions taking place. Everyone looked really happy to be there, and in no particular hurry to get anything done, which, paradoxically, meant that everything got done quickly and efficiently. They were all on first name terms and their banter was on the side of teasing. I stood a little further away, basking in the unexpected warmth I'd just walked into, but not quite part of it, with a stupid smile on my face.

At some point, the cashier leaned over her glass partition and waved an envelope full of cash over a man's head. 'I'll give it to someone else,' she warned.

He was looking the other way and he didn't hear. I touched him gently on the shoulder.

'There seems to be a fat envelope for you,' I said.

He smiled and thanked me, and turned around to collect it. The cashier bopped him on the head with it before handing it over.

My transaction was over in seconds, with many smiles, one signature and no trouble at all. I thanked the cashier for her advice before I left.

'I love Sifnos banking,' I told her.

She winked. 'We like things easy here,' she said, and then turned her attention to another customer who'd just walked through the door. 'Maki!' she called, and came out from behind the counter to give him a hug.

Banks are banks and rules are rules, but where you are does matter, as it turns out. There are other places, where things are exactly as easy as they are.

On the way back home, I caught one of those glimpses of sea that still take me by surprise. There were clouds on the horizon, but I could still make out Paros in the distance. This is what gets me every time: the fact of being on an island. This is what I can't get used to. It's not something that can be experienced or understood intellectually; it's something that happens when you stand somewhere high up and you see it, and you remember, in your soul, that you're surrounded by the sea. That you are disconnected and connected at the same time, isolated on this little floating patch of land, but look: there's Paros straight ahead, so close you could almost reach out and touch it, and Folegandros if you turn to the south, and the blurry shapes of Ios and Santorini, on a clear day. Connected and disconnected by the sea.

I went to pick Eleni's olives in the afternoon. She told me very sternly last night that I ought to immerse myself in the agricultural element of Sifnos life, and though I protested that I'm being all kinds of agricultural in my garden, she does have a point: I've been meaning to pick the olives, but I've been lazy.

They come off very easily, the olives. You only have to touch them and they fall into your hands, as if they were waiting for you to come along and collect them. I'd told myself I'd only pick a few to begin with, just the lower branches, but I didn't want to stop. Every branch released another handful of firm, shiny fruit, and I went into some kind of olive picking meditation, and all the thoughts tumbled out of my head as easily as the olives dropping into my bucket when I opened my palm to let them go. There was nothing to think about: I only had to look, reach out my hand, tug gently and receive.

There's something in all of this, a secret that can change your life. I don't think it's about olive picking in particular. We can't all go around picking olives off trees. There aren't enough olive trees in the world, and even if we were to plant more, fill the earth with olive trees shimmering silver in the sunlight and heavy with fruit, that wouldn't be the point. And I'm sure there are olive pickers out there who are unhappy. Who dream about an office and a desk, about wearing a suit and picking up a phone and telling their secretary to contact so-and-so client, and could she please get them a coffee once that's done. And that secretary dreams of running a B&B in the mountains with her daughter, while the daughter is a dancer in her heart, and longs for the applause of the crowd as she stands in the beam of the spotlights on a stage somewhere, and takes a bow. And a girl who does that every night wishes she could take her make-up off and curl up on the sofa with a book, and with no one staring up at her.

And another girl in London, who only wants to write, who has never dreamt of living on an island or picking olives off trees or kneeling on the ground and gently teasing weeds out of the soil, becomes a writer by doing all these things. And she will leave them behind, eventually, her island and the trees, the seeds she planted, the pink clouds she saw and the glimpses of the sea, the winter springtime and the moments that made her want to skip, but maybe she'll remember them in her soul.

Because the point isn't living on an island, or picking olives off trees; the point is how we dream of other things, and that we can find them. The secret is to look, and see. Reach out, tug gently, and it'll all fall into your hands. Stand somewhere high up and be surrounded by whatever's there. It doesn't matter what it is, as long as you're part of it.

This place is incredibly beautiful. I say it often because it needs to be said. I don't want to get used to it.

Maybe I'll remember.

# Day 70

I just encountered Manolis sauntering down the path
with a huge shotgun in his hands. We said hello and he
began to walk away, the gun not remarked upon. I
couldn't let it go.

'Are you going hunting?' I asked.

He stopped, looked down at his gun as if he'd only
just noticed he was carrying it, shrugged.

'Yeah,' he said, a little dejected. 'I'm looking for
thrushes. But there aren't any around. This weather...'
And he waved the gun about, drew a large semicircle
around himself with it, to indicate the unfavourable,
unseasonal warmth and sunshine that was keeping the
birds away.

I managed to say 'Um,' and made a face that
expressed absolutely nothing, because I couldn't bring
myself to be upset that there weren't enough birds
around to shoot. Nor that it was warm and sunny; I'd
spent the day walking around in a vest top, and my skin
had begun to give off that earthy, sun-warmed scent,
that summer scent that had been chased away by the
wind and cold and rain of October.

But then I looked at this big, awkward man, a man
divided between a mother and a wife, between the duties
of husband and son, who spends more than half his time
– every morning, every late afternoon, until it's dark –
keeping his mother company, a man whose wife probably
isn't waiting for him at home when he returns, although
she's there, with his dinner cooking on the stove and a
nod for when he walks through the door. I saw him
standing there, on the path, in his beloved army
fatigues, rocking back and forth on his bulky, scruffy
boots, self-consciously holding a shotgun behind his back
with both hands; I saw a little spark, a glimmer of
eagerness in his eyes, how he only wanted, for a little

while, to go off and play. To go traipsing through the fields, not a son, not a husband but a man alone, with his gun and the flutter of birds in the trees. And I relented.

'Have fun,' I said, and I meant it.

The shy, grateful smile he gave me stung a little.

Question: who am I to judge? Wrong question: who is anyone? Biblical references to stones and casting them come to mind. Manolis is not a bad man, no better or worse than any other man. He is kind, and he is gentle in his gruff, awkward way. He has a special, soft voice that he uses with the cat when she bumps against his legs and he doesn't think there's anyone around. He looks after her kittens, cleaning out their crusty eyes and feeding them antibiotics in the hope of staving off the illness that claims litter after litter, although he's done this too many times and he knows how it's likely to end. And when he needs release, he likes to shoot birds with his gun.

Winter is late to come, and it's confusing the birds. It's messing with their migratory schedule. I looked it up: the birds of Northern Europe use the islands of the Aegean as a transit station on their way down south; halfway to Africa, they stop in Sifnos for a rest. They make their temporary homes in the olive trees, and the men come out with their shotguns and hunt them. But it's too warm this year, and they haven't come. And I can't pretend to be upset. I like walking around in a vest top in November, and keeping my windows open. I like knowing that those shots I hear ringing out in the afternoons are probably aimed at nothing. I want the winter to take its time coming. I want the birds to stay away, stay safe up in the north. I want the men to come home empty handed.

Question: Am I any better when I chase flies with my swatter? When I bring my foot down on a centipede? Is there any redemption in the fact that I apologise to them after I've done it? That I say to them 'Sorry dude, but you were going to bite me'? That I feel bad? Because I do. I feel bad, but I still do it. I bring my foot down and crush them, before they get the chance to crawl into my bed.

There are two spiders living in the house, that I know of. One of them has made its home along the skirting board in the living room; the other one likes to hang out in a corner of my bedroom. I leave them alone. Geckos run up and down the ceiling beams, mostly unseen, but I hear them talk to each other at night. Beetles shuffle in often, and I trap them under a glass, slide a postcard that I keep for this purpose underneath, and release them back into the garden. The same goes for crickets, though they are much harder to catch, and they make me nervous with their flittering. I do what I can. I'm a good person, not better, not worse than any other. Is that the question? Who's better? Who's worse?

If you were to stand me next to Manolis, strong and rough and armed with a shotgun, preying on little birds for sport, if I stood next to him with my bug-saving postcard and my centipede guilt, I'd look good. If you stood me next to a gentle, lonely man living his life for others, who only wants some time to be himself, if I stood there, killing flies just because they bother me, you'd have to think again. And if the two of us, with our excuses and our innocence, were joined by M, the man who recently spent three nights trapping mosquitoes in a jar so he could release them outside and spare their lives, if Manolis and I stood next to him, we should both be stoned to death.

Except that M doesn't judge; he just does what he does. He doesn't carry stones to throw at you. He showed me his hands, and there was nothing there. And when I came across Manolis and his shotgun, for all my goodness, I had been holding a stone. Turning it around in my hand, testing its weight, its impact when it hit its target, big man with a big gun going after little birds. I didn't even know I'd picked it up. I looked down at my hands, the way Manolis had looked down at his shotgun, and was surprised by what I held. Ashamed. And then I let it drop. I let it go.

I hope Manolis has fun. I hope the warm weather lasts. I hope that winter is late to come. I hope I can wear my vest top in the sunshine for as long as possible, and that the birds stay safe up north. But it's the natural order of things that winter comes and birds migrate and men hunt and kill and bugs get trampled underfoot so they don't bite you. And all those things will happen, but we'll try to be good. We'll nurse sick kittens that are destined to die and keep an old woman from being lonely, we'll rescue a beetle from drowning in the sink and leave spiders alone and crumbs for the birds in the garden, and we'll be kind to each other. So that we can stand side by side and hold our hands out, empty of stones to cast, empty of things that bring us shame, and understand the hardest thing of all: that we're all just doing what we can.

# Day 71

I didn't feel like skipping today. No: today I found enlightenment, and I danced on the street. Right in the middle of the main road, halfway between Apollonia and Kamares, I danced to the Ramones. And I felt only a little embarrassed when a car came round the bend and caught me at it. I gave the driver a sheepish look and a nod and carried on dancing until the song was over. He probably thought I was crazy. But what's crazy is not dancing on the street. This is what I learned today.

It was a day of cloudy sunshine and I decided to walk to the beach. I haven't done it for a while. I had no ambition to get into the water, only to walk, and think, and then sit on the sand and look at the sea. So I set off with trainers on my feet and music in my ears and I walked.

It never gets old, this journey. There's always something new to see, and a new train of thought that you can ride in your mind while your feet follow the curve of the road, round and round through the mountains, through patches of shade and patches of light, until something inside you gives a little shudder and releases, and you're free. Until something bursts open and you dance on the street, and that's when you learn how crazy it is that you'd never done this before.

This enlightenment that's on everyone lips these days, that people seek in theories and books, in yoga studios and silent retreats, in deprivation and denial and dogma: it isn't there. It's in having the freedom to walk to the beach in the middle of the day, and the clarity to see it for what it is. I found enlightenment on the road between Apollonia and Kamares, and it was easy, and it didn't cost me a thing. And meditation? Meditation is looking at the mountains. It's walking for the sake of walking. Meditation is not getting rid of all thoughts; it's making space for the ones that matter. It's listening to the waves on an empty beach. It's rolling around in the sand, not sitting still and straight backed with your eyes closed, because the stillness you need is inside. And it can't be so fragile that you're too scared to move, too scared to open your eyes in case you chase it away.

Somewhere between dancing and arriving at the beach, I saw a dead cat in the grass on the side of the road. Killed by a car. There was no blood on it, no obvious marks of death: it looked exactly like a cat lying in the grass but I knew instantly, even from a distance, that this was a lifeless thing, fur and bones and nothing else. The cat inside was long gone, chasing crickets amidst rows of purple cabbages in the valley below. I wanted to look away; I didn't want my joy tainted by tragedy, I didn't want to carry the burden of a dead cat on my walk. I wanted to turn away from the sadness and pretend I hadn't seen it, but I didn't. I forced myself to look for as long as I could stand it, because happiness isn't about ignorance or oblivion or turning your face away; happiness, I think, is what survives the tragedies. It exists alongside the sadness, not despite it. And death only happens because we are alive. So I looked at the lifeless thing in the grass; there was a fly buzzing over it in circles, but it wasn't as morbid as I'd feared. I said a few words in my head for the cat that had once been inside, and carried on walking. I took nothing with me, no burden of death, but the cat that had lived bounded up behind me for a while, before leaping over the safety railings and disappearing in the fields.

But ignorance is bliss, and sometimes you walk past a dead cat and someone says 'Don't look'. And you stiffen up and pick up your pace and keep your eyes resolutely ahead, but it's pointless because you know exactly what's there, you have the picture in your head, and you're carrying it with you as you walk away. But if you were to look, you'd only see a dead cat. When you look, it's no worse than you imagine. You might see it, but you don't have to take it with you. You can choose what you carry, and what you leave behind. We're capable of so much more happiness than we know.

Today I found enlightenment on the road between Apollonia and Kamares, and it didn't look like much. It looked like orchards and cabbage fields and rock faces covered in moss. It looked like a cat killed by a car. It looked like a girl walking to the beach, a girl dancing in the middle of the road. It looked a little crazy. It felt like freedom, and joy. And that was all. That was the grand revelation that you won't find in books or silence or discipline. It doesn't sound like much but if you listen carefully, you'll always hear a song that makes you want to dance.

Dancing on the street's not crazy. What's crazy is trying to capture freedom with rules, and how we make our lives so small that there's no room for dancing. That we're too scared to look, too scared to move, that we have so little faith in joy that we stifle it with stillness. We are capable of so much more joy than we know, and we kill it with fear and stillness. I mean, fuck: when you suddenly find yourself dancing in the middle of the road, how can you ever go back to sitting stiff and straight backed with your eyes closed, summoning a revelation that you've already had?

We are alive, but that isn't a condition that defines how we live. You can be a cat lying in the grass or a lifeless thing on the side of the road; from a distance, they look exactly the same. You can get up and leap over the safety railings and run through the fields and roll around on the ground, or you can lie there, stiff and still, and wait for the flies to come. What's crazy is how often we choose the latter.

# Day 72

This happened to me one evening in late October: I was walking home from the supermarket. It wasn't very late, probably around seven, but it was one of those days when night comes early and the darkness feels heavy, somehow – a little ominous. There was no moon and the clouds were cloaking the stars. I walked alone, in total silence. I could hear my footsteps, the rustle of the plastic carriers containing my shopping, the occasional rattle of my house keys as they knocked against something in my bag. My breath, in and out. The far cry of an owl.

And then, on this black October night, on a narrow, cobbled path snaking through the quiet whitewashed houses of a Greek island village, completely out of place and time, the tinny, terrifying sound of a wind-up music box playing *Jingle Bells*. Slowly, in the process of winding itself down. Like I'd stepped out of my life and straight into a horror film. I don't scare that easily, but my legs went numb.

If this were a film, this is the point when you'd sit up on the edge of the sofa and bring your hands up to your face and hold your breath and urge the fool walking all alone in the dark as the music box plays its deadly notes to *run*. Because everyone knows what that sound means: someone's about to be hacked to pieces. If this were a film, it would be a low budget production, unimaginatively entitled *Horror in Sifnos*, and featuring a crazed killer posing as a friendly neighbour who likes to chop up his victims in small chunks and stuff them in clay chickpea pots, with bay leaves and spices, and bring them to the oven on Saturdays, to cook slowly overnight. He is caught when the well-meaning owner of the oven opens up one of the killer's pots to add rainwater to the chickpeas. But this particular scene in only halfway through the movie, and you know this girl doesn't stand a chance. She will run, but it'll be too late. And you'll shake your head and wince and scream as the dark form of the killer detaches itself from the shadows and pounces upon her with his hacking instrument of choice, but really, she only has herself to blame. That's what happens to fools who walk alone in the dark while the music box plays. Everyone knows where that storyline leads.

I didn't run, but I walked a lot faster, equally frightened and amused, but not laughing yet, not until I'd made it home and all the shadows along the way had proven themselves to be just that. And then I laughed. Because the whole thing was entirely surreal. But once I'd taken my shopping out of the bags and my legs felt solid again, a new fear sent a tingle up my spine: *Jingle Bells*? Crazed killers I can deal with, but that music box was evidence of something much more terrifying, much more unfathomable than chopped up humans in clay chickpea pots: Christmas in Sifnos.

I've known it was coming for a while. I think it was Eleni who first mentioned it, Christmas and Sifnos in the same sentence, but I just couldn't get them to fit. I shook my head like a stubborn child and said *No*, because it couldn't happen: it was one step further than my imagination was ready to go. I've come to terms with the changing of seasons; I've opened my eyes and seen the island in many different lights, the different shades of green and auburn it's dressed itself in, the way the sunrise and the sunset have moved across the horizon and how the moon now hangs in another part of the sky. The last few weeks have all but erased the pictures of summer Sifnos from my mind. They no longer stand next to what I see and ask questions, but have faded quietly to the background, waiting for June, while I fall in love with October and November. And December is around the corner and I'm excited for what it might bring, but I've known that month in other places, and I know what the jingling means. Christmas is coming to Sifnos. And I'm not ready yet.

Christina and I had our monthly dinner date a couple of nights ago. We went to the souvlaki place as always, and Maria wandered over, called us "girls" and took our order for pork chops and chips. As we waited for our food to arrive, I noticed our table had been decorated with a large red plastic flower that glittered in a very suspicious way.

'That looks a bit Christmassy,' I remarked, without thinking.

'It is Christmassy,' replied Christina, matter-of-fact. 'And there's a Christmas tree.'

'A *what?*'

'A Christmas tree? With lights and baubles and all that? Right there.' And she pointed. And there it was, just like she'd said. With lights and baubles and all that: a Christmas tree. In Sifnos.

I'd known it was coming, but my denial had allowed me to walk into this place and see nothing but the salt and pepper shakers and the menu and the custom made ceramic ashtrays. But there was a tree in the corner, right across the door I'd walked in through, and Christmas flowers on every table, and festive green tablecloths, and sparkling lights and toy Santas hanging from the walls. I felt lightheaded.

'Isn't a bit early?' I said weakly.

'Nah,' said Christina. 'This is nothing. Wait till you see the nativity scene in the square!'

'What?' I cried, panicked. 'Now?'

'Not now. But soon.'

It was cold today. The winter's tired of playing games with us and there is no more hide and seek. I went into town on my cigarette run, with my jacket zipped up as far as it would go and my scarf round twice around my neck. I kept my hands buried in my pockets and wished

I'd worn a hat, although it feels too early when three days ago I was picking olives in a vest. The few people I met moved differently: they've all adopted that hunched up shouldered, chin tucked in stance of winter, and strolling has given way to striding as we all gravitate towards the warmth.

It feels too early but it's late November and it's late. And December is around the corner, and it will be Christmas soon. Soon, the decorations will go up on the streets, and there will be a nativity scene in the square and the children will start getting excited and people will be wishing each other happy holidays. And I will be here, and I will see it, Christmas in Sifnos, and then I will have seen everything.


As we were leaving the souvlaki place the other night, leaving the warmth and the shimmering lights to step back into the night, I put my hand on the door handle and said 'Into the darkness, then'.

Katerina and her husband laughed. 'It's not that bad.'

'It is, up where I am,' I said, and I described exactly where that was.

'Oh my,' Katerina said. 'She's right. It's OK up to the well, but from then on it's pitch black. And there's something about the houses along that path,' she added, turning to me. 'They seem to loom, you know? It's all kinds of spooky up there.'

'Thank you!' I said, gratified. 'It is a bit scary sometimes. But I know what everything's supposed to look like by now, so as long as nothing's out of place and none of the shadows move, it's fine.' I gave them my bravest smile.

They both laughed again, but then Katerina's husband turned serious, and put his hand on my shoulder.

'You know there's no danger here, don't you?' he said softly. 'You know there's nothing there to fear.'

I know. And I don't scare that easily. I will continue to walk alone, along these quiet, darkened paths, stroll deeper into winter and stride towards the warmth. I will follow my storyline and everything will look like it's supposed to and nothing will be out of place. There will be no horror in Sifnos, and December will come and bring what it may. And my legs might wobble a bit, sometimes, but as long as the shadows keep still and the music box stays unwound, it'll be fine. Sit back on your sofa and uncover your eyes: the worst thing that can happen here is Christmas.

# Day 73

The lights flickered and died. The dehumidifier bleeped and flashed red, twice, in protest, and turned itself off. The lights came back on, briefly, with a buzz, giving out a strange yellow glow, and then trembled out again. The phone gave a single, desperate beep. And then nothing. Darkness. Silence. Powercut, round two.

I thought I was a veteran. I thought it would be ten minutes, like last time, and all my appliances would start humming again. The battery of my laptop took over and I sat in semi-darkness, in the dim light given off by the screen, sipping my cooling coffee and typing away. Calmly, a little smugly. Like this was a game that I knew how to play.

Half an hour later the coffee had run out and my coffee machine was a dead thing, plugged into nothing. I had no internet access, and my feet were getting cold. The game was no longer fun, and someone had clearly changed the rules along the way. I grabbed my keys and went on a reconnaissance mission around the neighbourhood. No lights on at Mrs Souli's, no radio sounds. I walked on, to Vangelia's house, and heard voices coming from the kitchen downstairs. The door was ajar; I pushed it open and stuck my head in: darkness.

'That answers my question,' I said, in lieu of hello.

'No power,' confirmed Yorgos, as Vangelia motioned me to sit down. She had the phone pressed against her ear. 'Daphne's here,' she said. 'She has no power either.' She glanced at me; I drew a flat line with my hand. 'No, I haven't called them yet. Yes, you call them and let me know.' She hung up without saying goodbye.

I was still standing up by the door, watching Yorgos eat his breakfast at the table, with my shoulders hunched. The ceiling is so low that it grazes the top of my head if I stand at full height.

'Sit!' Vangelia commanded. 'That was Sophia. She'll call the electricity people. You want coffee? I'll make you coffee.'

There are few certainties in life, but one of them is that there will always be a pot of Greek coffee brewing in Vangelia's kitchen; she had one on the go now, bubbling away over the blue flames of her little gas stove.

'It's lucky I have this thing, isn't it? And an extra one, see?' She tapped the spare canister, on display on her kitchen counter. 'What coffee do you want? I only have Greek.'

'Greek coffee would be lovely.'

I pulled a chair up to the table and Yorgos looked up and passed me, inexplicably, a knife. 'It's got honey on it,' he announced.

'Thank you,' I said, and placed it down in front on me. It was soon joined by a napkin, a large wholemeal rusk, a biscuit and a chunk of bread torn off a loaf.

'Eat,' Vangelia urged, with each new offering. She pushed the butter in my direction, nearly knocking the rusk into my lap. I picked it up and took a bite.

'What else do you want? Cheese? I have more rusks in the freezer.'

'Nothing, Vangelia, sit down, please.'

She did, but her bum had barely touched the chair when she bounded up again. 'But your coffee!' she cried. She poured the fragrant, frothy liquid into a cup, and slammed it down on the table. 'You want milk?'

'No, thank you. I don't drink milk.'

Vangelia nodded, and immediately surrounded my coffee cup with three tins of condensed milk, two of them opened. 'Have some milk. I have milk in mine.' She crumbled an entire rusk into her own cup, while simultaneously chewing on a buttered slice of bread. 'I have low blood sugar,' she explained.

The phone kept ringing and reports coming in from different parts of the island that they, too, had no power; Vangelia filled each of them in on all the previous conversations and what each person was doing, if anything, to resolve the issue. In between answering the phone and flitting around the kitchen in search of more random food items to place in front of me, Vangelia told me how she hadn't slept the night before because of the ache in her back.

'It's because you never sit still,' I offered, and sat back in my chair and sipped my gritty coffee while she unloaded about doctor's appointments and tablets that don't help, and how, between her housebound mother and her husband and the goats and the chickens and her children dropping in looking to be fed, she never gets a moment's rest.

Once the tirade was over, I cautiously broached the subject of massage, and how it might be good for her back. Cautiously, because I was afraid she'd either look at me blankly, or dismiss it as fancy city nonsense. It felt good to be invited into her little dark cave of a kitchen and her confidence, drinking Greek coffee instead of espresso, and forcibly eating rusks; it felt almost like friendship, and rejection would hurt. She surprised me.

'Would it help?' she asked eagerly. 'And can you do that?'

I said yes to both. 'Just come round, whenever you have some time. I'm always there.'

'Yes,' she said. 'I never see you. I never see anyone. I know nothing about what goes on in Sifnos.' Just then, the phone rang again, and the woman who ostensibly has nothing to do with Sifnos life stood right at the heart of it, where I've always placed her, and provided yet another update on the powercut situation. 'It's all of us,' I heard her say. 'We have no light. Sophia, and George, and Daphne down by the church, and Vangelia.' She rattled off a few more names, promised to call if there were news, and turned back to me.

'Where were we? Yes: it's good to know you're here. Someone told me you'd left, I don't remember who. But I said no. She's one of ours, I told them. She's not going anywhere.'

And of all the things she gave me this morning, of all the treats she placed in front of me in welcome, this was the one that meant the most. I wanted to hug her, but she didn't know what she'd given me and she'd be taken aback. I only smiled.

I took her gift with me when I left, along with a biscuit wrapped in a napkin that she had forced into my hands as I stood by the door. I went home to sit in the dark and the cold and wait, patiently, for the power to return. Not smug, not quite a veteran, just another name on the list of those without light, Daphne down by the church, another resident of an island ruled reluctantly by Queen Vangelia from her kitchen, where powercuts are a social occasion and there is always a pot of Greek coffee on the go.

# Day 74

My mum needed yoga last summer. She probably needed a lot of things besides yoga, things that I knew nothing about and things that I couldn't give her even if I did, but yoga was the one thing that I could nudge her towards without losing my balance; I could hold out my hand and guide her without losing my own place. I kept holding out my hand, but she wouldn't take it.

I knew she needed it like I know myself to sometimes avoid the things that will help. To take to my bed and pull the curtains tight against the sunshine when I need to step out of the house and feel it on my skin. I do that. I turn away from the hand that's held out to me, turn away from the light and hide in my bed. And when I'm in there, I won't jump out and throw myself into the daylight just because someone's standing over me with a hand outstretched, insisting that this is what I need. But maybe, if they were to come into my room and draw the curtains open halfway and sit on the edge of my bed and wait, maybe then, slowly, one limb at a time, I'd come out. And my mum wasn't going to go from stress to mat in one leap, and what I thought was nudging was perhaps pushing too hard and she was putting all her weight into it so she didn't get knocked over. My intentions were good, but I was asking for too much. I kept my hands to myself and tried another way.

There are three bedrooms in this house. In the winter, one of them is used for storage. In the final days, before we leave, we pile everything in there that we want out of the way. Tools and tins of paint and bits of wood that might come in handy and empty boxes and boxes full of stuff and the outdoor furniture and spare sets of cutlery and crockery and baking trays that don't fit in the cupboards and extension cords and mosquito repellent machines and extra sheets and clothes that we don't want to take home and a sprinkling of screws and a notebook and some bottles left behind in the bathroom and a cracked mug full of marker pens and dry food that will keep until next year and some crumpled up receipts and a hat and the spare pillows and the speakers that we plug into our computers and a handful of pebbles from the beach and cable that no one can identify and a business card from a restaurant and some orange clothes pegs and an opened bag of tealights and a new box of washing powder and three lamps without bulbs and a vase and some change in a bowl.

I was the first one in the house last summer, and the storage room was piled up high, higher than normal, because there had been a tenant in during the winter. I opened the door on the day that I arrived, took one look, and closed it again. It was too much.

'That room,' I told my mum, 'that's your mind. There's too much stuff, and you don't even know what's there anymore, only that it's stuff that you wanted out of the way. And you keep adding more stuff on top, more stuff that you don't want to deal with, and you can never relax because even with the door closed, you know it's there.'

She nodded.

'And what you're trying to do is tackle it all at once, this huge pile of shit. You keep opening the door and looking at it and closing it again, because it's too much. You wouldn't even know where to start, but you know it would take a whole day to clear that room out. You'd be in there all day, bruising your hips against corners jutting out and with stuff falling on top of you and you'd skip lunch and miss dinner and stay behind when we all go to the beach. No wonder you keep the door closed.'

'But why are you all going to the beach?' my mum interrupted. 'Why aren't you helping me?'

'It's a *metaphor*,' I said pointedly. 'It's *your* room of crap.'

'Oh. Right.'

'I have one too,' I assured her. 'A room full of crap.'

'OK.'

The point I was trying to make was that you can't tackle the room all at once. You have to break it down. In my first week in the house last summer, I only went into the room when I needed something I couldn't find anywhere else. I kept calling my mum, asking for things. 'If you haven't found it, it'll be in the room,' she said, every time. And I'd go in and find it and put it back in its allocated summer place, and like that, bit by bit, I cleared the room, in time for my grandma to move in.

'And that's what yoga could do,' I concluded. 'If you stop looking at it as this huge thing you have to take on all at once, and just do a little bit, a few minutes every day, it'll be like going into the room and taking out one item each time. That's what it can do, make a little bit of space in your head each time, take one thing away that you don't need in there. And slowly, over time, you'll clear out the room. Bit by bit. And then you can leave the door open and stop dreading it every time you walk past.'

One night, during my first week in the summer, the mosquitoes came. They hadn't bothered me the first few nights, but now they were here and they were buzzing around my face and biting my knuckles and I couldn't sleep. I knew the mosquito repellent machines were in the room. I knew, because I hadn't found them anywhere else. I hadn't searched because I hadn't needed them so far. And now I did and it was the middle of the night and the room was piled up high with shit and I was too scared to rummage around dark boxes where, I imagined, all kinds of multi-legged creatures lurked, so I choose what I perceived to be the lesser of the evils, and gave myself up to the mosquitoes.

In the morning, sleepless and bad-tempered and covered in bites, I went into the room. I looked at the pile of crap, sighed, knelt down and lifted a lid at random.

And there they were, three of them: the mosquito repellent machines.

And that's another metaphor, about how all of our clutter stops us from getting to the things that we need. All these dangers that we perceive, the terrible fears that we install in our imaginations, how they stop us from even trying. How all the clutter, all the crap we pile up in these rooms of ours stop us from searching for the good things that are there.

On the way home from the supermarket last night, I felt incredibly happy. It wasn't that vague, generalised happiness that I almost take for granted now; this was a happiness that was very specific. I was happy about something in particular, but I couldn't think what it might be. I searched my day for the big thin    gs: something that happened, something I'd done, some achievement that would justify this euphoria. But there was nothing, nothing that stood up to that height, only another day of vague, generalised happiness.

And then I remembered: it was chilli peppers. Two whole handfuls of them, red and firm and shiny, in my bag. The supermarket had brought in a fresh batch of chilli peppers, for the first time since late September, and I had bought some. And that was it: the source of my happiness. I was happy because of chilli peppers. It doesn't sound like much but when you're happy, that's as big as any big thing you care to name.

I've made some big moves in the last few months. I've shaken things up and brought things down and moved them around, and got rid of a lot. But I wasn't lying to my mum this summer when I told her about my own room of crap. This summer, I still had a room full of crap. Despite my big moves, for all the things I left behind, this I took with me.

But there's space now in my room. The clutter is gone. I keep the door open so I can go in anytime, and put things in there that I want to find. It didn't happen overnight, nor did I waste a day bruising myself to clear it out. But bit by bit, day by day, with each ordinary day of vague, generalised happiness when nothing big happened, one by one all the things I didn't need were taken away. With each ordinary day of a life that had once seemed extraordinary, the small things slowly came to light. And there is space now for them to be as big as they truly are. And when there's space enough for chilli peppers to make you happy, that's when you know you're doing something right. And your room is where you keep the things that matter.

# Day 75

Day 75 feels significant, somehow. A landmark. Three quarters of the way there, and twenty-five days to go. Only twenty-five. I don't want it to end.

One hundred days was an arbitrary choice, or a romantic one, perhaps. I liked the sound of it, and the connection to Marquez. In any case, from where I stood seventy-five days ago, it looked like forever. I protested whenever anyone referred to it as a challenge, but it was; it could have been. It isn't. I wish I'd called it *two hundred days* now. Or simply *days of solitude*. Or *days*. No numbers, no definitions. No countdown.

This isn't a challenge: it's easy. So easy that it brings almost everything into question, the concepts of easy and hard, possible and impossible, and the misconceptions upon which I've been building the limits of my life. But we don't trust easy: easy is boring and unworthy; hardship is noble and admirable. It won't do to glide through life with a smile on your face. There needs to be a certain amount of suffering to validate your achievements. *Nothing worth having comes easy*: this is our culture. A culture that sets up challenges for us every step of the way, that urges us to overcome, always overcome.

I didn't start off knowing I could do this. Seventy-five days ago I had no idea how it would turn out. I didn't start it as a challenge, but I expected it to be hard. I was wrong.

'I couldn't do what you're doing,' Susanne told me the other day but I think, from where I'm standing now, seventy-five days into the easiest thing I've ever done, that she might be surprised.

Seventy-five days and the only time I've ever wanted to be anywhere else was that Saturday afternoon when M

was in Athens and I was half an ocean away. Seventy-five days and not one of them has felt too long. Seventy-five days and as many stories that turned out different than I thought.
I will be lonely. (I'm not.)
It will be scary. (I like it.)
I can't write every day. (I can.)
I will get bored. (Not once.)
I don't dance. (I do.)
I'm not a writer. (I am.)

It's a disconcerting thing, to be surprised by yourself. To allow yourself to be surprised. To step outside the margins of your story, the story you've been telling yourself so far, and go further. To actually get to know yourself outside the story, and be surprised.

A few years ago, I was going through a hard time and I was depressed. Alexis called me as I lay on my sofa in Athens, pinned down by self-pity.

'What's the matter with you?' he asked.

'I'm depressed.'

'How come?'

I snorted, bitterly. What a stupid question, I thought; did he really not know me at all?

'That's just how I am,' I replied curtly. 'I'm always depressed.'

Alexis laughed. 'What the fuck are you talking about? You're never depressed! You're one of the happiest people I know.'

I bristled; I actually took offence. I was about to protest my depression, to build my case up with evidence, but when I looked for it I came up empty-handed. I was so shocked by this that I forgot to be defensive, and for a moment I saw myself through my friend's eyes, saw the person he'd been seeing for the past fifteen years of our lives, and she wasn't who I thought. I wasn't depressed: that was just a story I'd created back in school, a persona I'd cultivated when

305

depression equalled depth and intelligence and stood you apart from those shallow, giggly girls who thought of nothing but their nail polish. Unsuccessfully, as it turns out, since I was the only one who'd fallen for it. A moment, but it was one of the most defining in my life: I was thirty-one years old, and I'd just discovered I was happy. I peeled myself off the sofa, and Alexis and I went for coffee.

Depression isn't cool, and happy isn't shallow, and nothing worth having is hard. Nothing comes easy except the things that belong to you. An easy life is what you have when you're living the way you're supposed to, whichever way that might be. When you stop overcoming and just glide. And it isn't boring in the very least: seventy-five days on, I can tell you that.

I got a message from a man who lives in Naxos, 365 days a year he said, and he challenged me. How about, instead of this, I try one hundred days without a computer and without a phone, writing in pen on sheets of paper? How about I see what that is like? I replied that this would require a level of insanity that I don't feel I've earned quite yet. But the point is: you never know. And you never will know, unless you allow yourself to be surprised. From where I'm standing, outside the margins of the stories that made things hard for me, this is the only challenge worth taking on, the only thing you need to overcome. Everything else is easy; everything is easy when it's right.

# Day 76

I slept very well last night, on account of the fact that I forgot to switch my electric blanket off, which meant I didn't wake up freezing in the early hours as has been the norm in the last few nights, since winter arrived. I forgot to switch the electric blanket off and it did not burst into flame overnight, and I woke up warm and uncharred this morning, for which I am thankful. And thus began my Sifnos Thanksgiving. Waking up, alive, is always a good start to the day.

We don't celebrate Thanksgiving in Greece. It's not on our calendar, but we hear rumours of it, of Americans gathering round dinner tables to fill up on turkey and pumpkin pie and be thankful for stuff. I have a very vague understanding of the origins of this holiday, other than that Pilgrims and Indians are involved, so I looked it up. In a tale that seems to be as much myth as it is history, the first Thanksgiving dinner was held in Plymouth, Massachusetts, in 1621, when the Pilgrims invited the Indians to join them in a feast, giving thanks for the Indians' help and the colony's first successful harvest. The Pilgrims had arrived in the area the previous year, entirely unprepared, and the local Indian Wampanoag tribe had taken these crazy white people, the "coat men", under their wing, and shown them the ropes and how to grow things, so they didn't starve to death. It's a nice story and I hope it's true, in part, even though it's part of a bigger story, and sadly, unarguably true, where the colonists slaughtered the natives all over America, and stole their land and weren't at all thankful.

I slept well last night, but I had a dream about my friend Ali, a vivid, elaborate dream that went on for what felt like hours, and whose details escape me now. I woke up missing her. I haven't spoken to her for months. We have drifted apart in the last few years, which is stupid because whenever we get together I can't think of a single reason why. I had sent her an email a few days ago, when I heard a song that reminded me of her, but she hadn't replied.

I went to my desk, still reeling from her presence in my dream, with the intention of sending her another message, urging her to get in touch. I sipped my coffee as I checked my email: all junk. And then, with a discreet ping, a new email dropped into my inbox. I clicked on it, both shocked and completely unsurprised, and read Ali's message. My second thing to be thankful for, today.

Perhaps I'll host a fantasy Thanksgiving dinner tonight. I'll be the Pilgrim and the locals can be the Indians. I have no turkey, but they can share my chicken soup; I took a chicken breast out of the freezer last night, for that purpose. It won't be much of a feast, but it's a large chicken breast and if I chop it up really small there should be enough for everyone to get a taste. I'll add onions and rice and potatoes, and cook it all in a big pot of broth. I'll also make a salad with lettuce and radishes from the garden, to celebrate the harvest, and flavour the soup with lemons from my tree. The locals can bring offerings, too. Though I hope none of them will bring dead deer, like the Indians reportedly did, or little birds shot out of the trees. But I wouldn't mind a few eggs, or a bit of cheese.

Manolis can come, and his mother, and his wife, if she's not at work. Antonis the plumber and Makis the carpenter. Vangelia and Yorgos and their children, Vasiliki and Simos, if they're free. Margarita the hairdresser, and Post Office Man No.1, and Loukia from the butcher's. The entire souvlaki family, mother, father and daughter, and the cashier from Alpha Bank. The girl from the chemist, and the guy at the kiosk who remembers what tobacco I smoke. The two sisters who run the supermarket at the top of the hill. Nikos the farmer and his wife. Polyna, of course, if she's around. The man who advised me to plant rocket and spinach and sold me the seeds. I am thankful to all of these people, these and many others, and I would like them to come round tonight, and sit down at my table and share my chicken soup, and be the natives to my coat men, the ones who have taken me under their wing and shown me the ropes.

I am the coat men of Sifnos, even though the coat I wear, a blue rainproof jacket with fleece lining, was purchased right here a few weeks ago. I walked into a shop I'd barely even looked at before, a shop I've walked past hundreds of times but never deigned to consider entering, where two women were watching a cooking show on a large TV set mounted on the wall. I went fearfully from rail to rail, keeping a safe, aloof distance from the garments on display, convinced that there was nothing there for me, with my high city standards. Until, right at the back and hiding amidst an alarming amount of faux fur, I found exactly what I was looking for, and in my size. Which was, apparently, XXL, and made by the excellent brand MISS PASSION.

'You're lucky,' said the lady behind the counter. 'It's the last one.'

It fits me perfectly, my Sifnos jacket, made in China.

I got another email from Ali later this morning, all in capitals and full of exclamation marks. *Sit Down* by James had just come on her radio, and that's a song that reminds her of me. Of times long ago, when we saw each other every day, and danced the nights away in shady London nightclubs. Of singing along with plastic cups of lager in our hands, of sitting down on the dirty, sticky floor whenever the chorus demanded it. *Sit down next to me.*

Life is up to its tricks again, and two songs and a dream bringing Ali and I together today are no coincidence, but today being Thanksgiving is. It means nothing to me. I have the same objection to Thanksgiving as I have to Valentine's Day. Shouldn't we be thankful and in love *every day*, instead of saving it all up for special calendar occasions? We get together, on these holidays, and stuff ourselves with food and exchange our gifts, and we forget what we're there for, and we forget to be thankful for the fact that we're there and together at all. We don't say thank you enough. We don't write love letters. We wake up every morning and don't notice we're alive.

I am thankful and I am in love. Today, on this day that is just an ordinary Thursday on the Greek calendar, and tomorrow, and the day after, and every day that I wake up, alive. And I'll have my fantasy dinner, tonight and every other night, and I'll invite everyone, because it's a fantasy and everyone will fit, everyone I'm thankful to, everyone I'm grateful for, everyone I love and have loved in the past, the friends I talk to every day and the ones I haven't spoken to for months, and we will all sit down together and share my chicken soup, Pilgrims and Indians and natives and coat men, crazy white people all of us, regardless of what shade of skin we come in, who would do well to remember that we're lucky to be alive. And say thank you and I love you, while there are still days.

# Day 77

I was recognised in the supermarket last night, the smaller of the two at the top of the hill. I had just been to the larger one for basics – a six-pack of mineral water, light bulbs, olive oil – and stopped by here on the way back for a couple more things. I was in my own little world, a place I inhabit more and more frequently these days, with very few distractions to lure me out. I found the items I wanted, a bag of crisps and a single lemon, and placed them on the counter by the till. There was nobody there. A couple of customers were milling about the aisles and one of the staff, a pretty, dark-haired girl wearing the store's light blue uniform, was arranging vegetables on the shelves with a small smile on her face. I stood by the till and waited patiently, happy to stretch out this moment of nothing to do, enjoying the easy-going pace of the Sifnos shopping experience, the fact that the till is left unattended and nobody feels the need to rush to your service.

Eventually, the girl put down the box that she has just emptied of lettuce, kicked it to the side and approached me, beaming.

'Bravo,' she said.

I was completely confused. I looked around me, looked at my crisps and my lemon on the counter, the position of my feet on the floor, trying desperately to work out what I'd done that deserved praise. Had I placed my items in a way that pleased her? Was she complimenting me for standing out of the way and not making a fuss about waiting to be served?

'I read your work,' she explained. 'It's very good. Well done.'

I must have blushed; I felt my cheeks grow hot. 'Thank you,' I gushed, taken aback and flattered and

311

moved and embarrassed, all at once. 'That's really good to hear.'

'I left somewhere too,' she added. 'To come here.'

'Where did you leave?'

'Athens.

She's been here for a year now, she told me. It's going well.

'So you're happy?'

She took her time to answer. 'I feel good in myself. You know?' I nodded. 'I think that's what matters.'

It's funny how you can find an affinity with strangers; how I recognised something in this girl's open, smiling face, and she recognised me as someone who might know what she meant. We said no more to each other. Another blue-uniformed lady came along to take my payment, and the girl went back to restocking the shelves; I waved at her as I left. She didn't even tell me her name. But my brief meeting with her had me smiling all the way home, and her words stayed with me for much longer.

To feel good in yourself: that's what matters. I think I know what she meant. I don't know what her background is, why she left Athens and what brought her here. I don't know her dreams or her ambitions, what she hopes for in the future and what she's left behind. I don't know what fulfilment she gets from working at the supermarket or what else she might be doing or what she did before, but her smile – even before she spoke to me, as she arranged vegetables on shelves – told me that her words were true. It was the calm, unobtrusive smile, almost private, of someone who has nothing to prove. Who's found something much more valuable than a career or money or any other measure we use to estimate success: herself.

People are always finding themselves these days. They're finding themselves mostly in faraway, challenging locations: it seems that half the population of the Western world has misplaced itself somewhere on the Indian subcontinent or thereabouts, judging by the number of people who travel there to search. It's a bit like the gold rushes of the late nineteenth century, except now we're panning for spiritual revelations instead of gold, and return holding ourselves – found! – as a trophy, high up for everyone to see.

I have nothing against people finding themselves in India; I just don't think there's any need to go that far. I think the journey is in the decision to make a change, and once you make that decision, you're just as likely to come across yourself two streets down from where you've always lived as in an ashram in Kerala. Or you might find yourself in a small supermarket in Sifnos, smiling contentedly as you stack the shelves. And you can do it like this girl I met yesterday, quietly, with dignity, without the drama. Without expecting anyone to come up to you and say well done.

It's not about a place or how far you travel: you can't get away from your shit by buying miles. You can travel all over this world, climb every mountain and dive in every sea, but it'll follow you, wherever you go. But you can find yourself at any place, any place you happen to find yourself, any place you happen to be. Once you decide to change what needs changing, you can go anywhere at all. You could find yourself anywhere, and that's where you'll be. Feeling good in yourself, with nothing to hold up as a trophy and nothing to prove.

The sky today is white and the cloud-topped mountains put me in mind of the Alps, though I've never seen the Alps up close. It isn't cold, so I went outside with my afternoon coffee, and stood on the ledge at the end of my garden and looked at the fields below. And I knew what the girl meant, to feel good in yourself – wherever you stand. I came here for my summer holiday; I didn't come in search of revelations. I wasn't looking for myself in Sifnos but, apparently, this is where I am.

# Day 78

The Dippy Hippie insisted that I open the windows this morning. She said we needed to get some energy flowing through the house; she sensed it has stagnated, she explained. I rolled my eyes, but I indulged her. There's light outside, not sunshine exactly but brightness, and the breeze is just below the window-slamming threshold. It's not a bad idea, to get some air in here.

The Dippy Hippie is another one of my alter egos. She's in charge of alternative health, positive thinking and my overall spiritual wellbeing. She's the one who dabs me with essential oils and mixes up mysterious potions when I (don't) have a cold, and mumbles mumbo-jumbo at the full moon. She frowns every time I take a painkiller, but she's harmless. She's also in charge of yoga, ever since that other persona of mine, the Reluctant Yogi, went missing; I guess her reluctance finally got the better of her. So it's the Dippy Hippie, now, who spreads out my mat and gives me meaningful looks, on those days when I get stiff and achy from being bent over my computer and forget to do anything about it. Writers aren't known for good posture. I'm a bit reluctant, but I'm grateful to her for trying.

I haven't seen Antagonist for a while. I wonder what she's up to. I thought she might turn up this morning, when the Dippy Hippie started going on about stagnant energies. Next to crushing my soul with her bare hands, she likes nothing more than mocking anything she perceives as vaguely spiritual, and the Dippy Hippie is a perfect receptacle into which to pour her sarcasm. She just leaves herself wide open. But, this time, Antagonist did not take the bait. It's not like her at all; she must be doing something very important.

The others are still around. Sifnos Chick has really come into her own recently, and she keeps us all safe when we forget where we are and become a danger to ourselves. She is the enforcer of The Rules of island life, which include: never drink the tap water, never make crumbs, never flush paper down the toilet, and never, ever put your shoes on without shaking them out first. I forgot that last one the other night, when I went into town to meet Christina, and I could feel a faint sting in my shoe from the time I stepped out of the house. I wasn't too concerned, but Sifnos Chick got herself into a state.

When you feel a sting in your shoe in Sifnos, you always check!' she shouted, but it was too dark on the way down and it would have been pointless, so she made me take my shoe off as soon as I arrived at Christina's house. There was nothing there. 'But there could have been,' Sifnos Chick said darkly. 'You never know what might crawl into your shoe.'

She's always trying to get us to go for walks, and she spends a lot of time in the garden, where the beetroot seeds have now sprouted tender, reddish shoots. City Girl sometimes joins her, though she doesn't like to get her hands dirty or mud on her shoes. She sits on a chair in the patio, or a ledge if it's dry, and watches Sifnos Chick being rural while telling her tales of city life. She's bored, and twitching for excitement and the sound of traffic, but she's adjusting, and she's taken it upon herself to teach Sifnos Chick about crossing roads in Athens, for the next time we all find ourselves there. There was a time, after our last visit to the city, when she became a bit depressed, but I promised to take her to London in January, and that put the smile back on her face. She loves London, and she's started telling Sifnos Chick about the sirens, and the Tube, and all the supermarkets we will visit, where you can buy beetroot in a packet, already cooked. Sifnos Chick just stares at her blankly; she can't see the appeal in any of those things.

The Writer is mostly seen leaving rooms as the rest of us enter them. She sighs deeply, dramatically, and mutters, and glares at whoever it is that's disturbed her peace, and then she gathers up her notebook and pen and marches out pointedly, to reconvene with her Muse elsewhere.

I think I miss Antagonist a little. Also, her absence makes me nervous; I can't help imagining she's planning something big, some unexpected twist in this tale of ours that will turn everything around and reveal her to be the Hero and me nothing but a misguided fool, right before the end. I tried to summon her the other day, to goad her into appearing, with the words I thought could never fail.

I positioned myself at my desk, placed my fingers on the keyboard and said 'I'm a writer', three times. Three times is how spells always work.

'Actually, I think you'll find I'm the writer,' protested the Writer, looking up from her notebook.

'Shut up, you,' I said. 'I'm trying something.'

'Fine,' she replied, irritably. 'I'm busy, anyway. Just try to keep the noise down; I'm *writing*.' She's getting more cantankerous by the day. She made a great show of flicking through pages, and then, with a sigh, she stood up and walked out, leaving me on my own. Antagonist never came.

The rest of us seem to have found some tentative balance, a way to coexist, despite our differences. It has been known, of an evening, that we all sit together around the kitchen table in relative peace.

'Shall I manifest some dinner?' the Dippy Hippie might suggest, and City Girl will snort.

'Will it be raw organic leaves sprinkled with chia seeds and dressed in pee extracted from an Indian guru?' she'll say, and Sifnos Chick will gaze wistfully out the window, at nothing because it's too dark, and tell us all how she can't wait until the rocket is ready to pick and what a wonderful thing it is, living off the land.

And City Girl will retort that she just wants a burger and chips, 'For fuck's sake!' and 'Who's a girl to sleep with to get that sort of thing around here?' and Sifnos Chick will appear to actually be considering this question, as the authority on all things local, while the Dippy Hippie will giggle and urge City Girl to try visualisation, to create a picture of the burger and chips in her mind, and meditate on it.

'It can be just as rewarding,' she'll add, with a twinkle. I think she's learning the art of taking the piss.

At this stage, I might offer to make pizza, topped with rosemary from the garden and with chia seeds baked into the dough: would that please everyone, how does that sound?

And the Writer will say: 'I don't need to eat. I am an artist. I feed my soul with words,' or something to that effect, but then she'll have a slice, anyway. She likes pizza. We all do.

I wonder how this story will end. I may be the one writing it, but I'm no good with plot, so I tend to just let things happen and take me where they will. Characters in stories soon take on a life of their own and dictate their own outcomes, so all I can do with these people around my table is watch them and let them find their way. But I do wonder about Antagonist: where she's gone, what she's up to, whether she'll return. I wonder if there's a showdown still in store for us, a battle between good and evil, if she'll return with some superweapon to destroy me once and for all and provide a climax to our story, or if she'll just slip, anticlimactically, into the footnotes and be forgotten as the days slowly run out. Or if the twist in our tale is that she'll stroll in one evening, casually, as if she'd never been away, and join the rest of us at the table, and take a slice of pizza, and only mock us a little for our assorted weaknesses, and maybe even smile.

It isn't like her, but it could happen. You never know with stories, how they might end.

# Day 79

Boy Cat is hurt. There is a huge, gaping wound in his neck, dripping blood. His paws are pink with it; there are thick drops, a trail of where he's been, on the flagstones and in his bowl. He looks alright. He doesn't meow like usual – a low, tuneless Boy Cat meow that makes me laugh – but he comes to the door, waiting to be fed.

'Not this again,' I say when I notice the wound. 'What have you done?' He doesn't tell me; he just looks up at me with that mixture of caution and hope. I shake some food into his bowl; the drops of blood – fresh, bright red – make me feel sick. I watch him come and take a bite and, like a coward, I go back in the house. There's nothing I can do.

It's probably some sort of abscess. He had the same wound in the same place in the summer, when he first showed up in the garden, checking us out from a distance. We left food out for him and called him the see-through cat, on account of the size of his wound. It looked really frightening but he seemed to be coping, so we left him to it and hoped for the best. We weren't too attached. It's never a good idea to get attached to the strays you feed in the summer. Especially ones with huge, gaping wounds in their necks. We've learned this over the years. These cats come and go, and you can't dwell on where they've gone when, one day, they don't come back.

But I let my guard down, and he kept coming, and it's no longer summer. I'm attached to him now; he's my Boy Cat. I feel completely helpless. I play vet in the absence of an actual vet on the island, but it won't do any good. I can say it's probably an abscess that burst, and google backs me up: apparently, cats often develop abscesses, caused by bacteria from the bites of other cats. Boy Cat is a fighter, so an abscess seems like a

319

reasonable diagnosis. But neither google nor I can treat him. Even if I had the antibiotics and the needle and the courage to do what needed to be done, he wouldn't let me get that close.

I'm attached to him; I've come to rely on his presence. It's been good having him sleep outside my window, hearing his funny meow greet me when I step out of the house in the morning. Earning his trust, slowly, one day at a time, with each sprinkle of food I add to his bowl. I've grown to love him, slowly, from a distance, the careful distance he keeps between us, but smaller than it used to be. Close enough to love him, but still too far to help. He won't let me touch him, won't let me clean his wound. He's my Boy Cat and he's hurt and there's nothing I can do.

This is the life I've chosen, this winter, at this place where the rules of summer no longer apply. I've let my guard down and I've become attached; I've come to rely on things, and these are the things that I might lose. Where cats come and go and things come and go and people come and go that you've grown to love and you can never know, when they go, if they are coming back. And there is nothing you can do but hope for the best, and that they'll be there, when you open your door in the morning, the cats and the things and the people that you love; unharmed, unhurt, waiting. That they'll go and they'll come back.

This is the life, in any place, at any time. You let your guard down, and things come to you, and these are the things that you have gained.

# Day 80

My sister Margarita called me yesterday. 'I've been thinking about your writing,' she said. 'How it's changed. It's like you've gone to a place and you've looked around and you've found somewhere to sit, and that's your little corner now, and you really like it.' She paused, and I considered myself, where I was sitting as I talked to her, in my cosy corner where the sofa meets the wall, surrounded by cushions. 'I don't mean Sifnos. Obviously you like being in Sifnos; it shows, and you say so, all the time. But I mean with your writing. It feels like you're very comfortable, where you are. Settled.'

It's funny how thinking in metaphors runs in our family. It's funny, too, that I've been feeling it recently, this sense of settling in, of being settled, but it took my sister's words to make sense of it. I've found somewhere to sit: a strange way of putting it, maybe, but exactly right.

'In the beginning,' Margarita added, 'it was like with someone who've just met, and you're a bit nervous and you don't know what to say, so you keep making jokes to break the ice. But not now. You know what to say now.'

Boy Cat's found somewhere to sit, too. I didn't see him all day yesterday and I was worried, but he was waiting outside my door this morning, and he meowed and hissed and he's no longer dripping blood. He had his breakfast and I had my coffee standing in the patio as the clouds cracked open and sunshine broke through and surprised us both. I finished my coffee and went back in, but I left the door open. Before long, Boy Cat approached and stepped over the threshold.

He stood in the doorway for a moment, his eyes flitting nervously from me to the room at large, assessing how likely I was to jump him and what other dangers might be lying in wait in this new place. And then, cautiously, he padded in. He didn't sniff table legs and corners as cats normally do; he just walked around, looking. He took his time. He disappeared into the bedrooms and emerged a few minutes later to do a final circuit of the kitchen table before coming to a stop at a spot near the front door, a rectangle of sunshine on the ceramic tiles. He lowered himself down, folded his front paws under his head and blinked. He wasn't exactly settled, admittedly; he was on stand-by, ready to flee, which he did when I got up from my desk to make a second cup of coffee. But he came back and found his spot again, and sat there, in his unreliable patch of sunshine that faded and brightened with the clouds. He stayed for about half an hour, until his busy cat schedule took him away to his next engagement.

It's funny, this process of settling, how it takes its time, how you can't rush it. It's funny how the lives of a cat and a girl can run parallel and provide us with new metaphors through which to make sense of ourselves. How that spot by the door has been there all along, but you can't just take a cat and place him there. He has to look around and choose it for himself, and then he'll sit. And he'll settle, eventually, when he feels comfortable.

And how long it was that I spent standing in doorways and anticipating dangers, how many years of looking around, walking in circles, doing circuits around myself, before I found somewhere to sit. Before I knew myself well enough to stop making jokes. Before I knew that I had something to say.

# Day 81

My classical music education continues, and Eleni's choice for me on the evening of the first day of December was a piano piece by Mendelssohn entitled *Romance sans paroles*. She sent it late, this morning, with apologies, and I said I'd listen while I drank my coffee. It was slow and soulful and evocative, but I didn't pay it nearly as much attention as I should have; I didn't close my eyes and let the notes do what the composer intended. I was distracted by the title: romance without words. The sort of claim that's guaranteed to get my mind churning. I couldn't focus on the notes because I was thinking of the words, which is ironic. I had to listen to it a second time, to hear the romance that was there.

Romance without words: you can't make such claims if you're a writer. You can't claim anything without words. Composers could get away with it, maybe, and artists, and then only if you forget that music and art are language systems, just like language, with notes and images playing the role of words. But there is no leeway for writers: words are our words, and without words all we have is a blank page. Which is very postmodern and you could put it in a gallery and have people gaze at it reflectively as if they could see something there beyond the blankness, and pretend to understand your intentions, but it wouldn't be writing, it would only ever be a blank page. And you'd have to give it a title, make a claim: *Writing without words*, which are words. You could make this claim and maybe get away with it, but you'd never get away from the irony that it entails.

And ordinary people, those who claim no particular capacity as writer or artist or composer, can they have romance without words? Can they claim love without saying it? I'm an ordinary person. I've sat in silence and in love and felt no need to say the words, but they've been said at some point, or written, and they're a token that you can give, and I don't understand the value of holding back when it's yours to give and you want to give it. It's like walking past a shop and seeing a teacup in the window that your friend would like, and going in and buying it for her, spontaneously, and then taking it home and storing it in a cupboard, out of sight. And expecting your friend to know that you thought of her and bought her a teacup that you never gave. It makes as much sense as wanting to say something and not saying it: none. The words are ours to give but not ours to keep; they're not for holding back or storing in cupboards. Intentions don't reach people on their own. They need a title, at the very least.

Words are often accused of being easy but, actually, they're not. Some words are really hard to say. It's hard to say I love you. I love you is a door that you open for someone to walk in or walk away. Or hesitate on the threshold, wordless, staring down at the mat that says COME IN.

We have good reasons for not saying it. We have pride and self-preservation and ancient survival instincts and this modern culture that has a fear of open doors. We only open our doors when someone comes knocking on them. We want guaranteed outcomes, we don't want to stand there like fools by our open doors with no one walking in. We want romance without words, and without risk. Like a game of Taboo, where some words are forbidden and you have to use other words to get your teammate to guess what you actually mean to say. And if you say love you lose. So you say it in roundabout ways and hope you'll be understood without breaking the rules, hope that they'll guess at love and you will win the game without saying the words. But I don't think love should be guessed at, or hinted, or presumed. It should be given because you want to give it. Love isn't for holding back. It isn't ours to keep.

You can win the game of Taboo if it means that much to you. You can buy teacups and store them away. You can wait for people to come knocking on your door before you open it. You can give them a blank sheet of paper and expect them to read love. You can get away with all of this, and risk nothing, but you can't get away from words.

Mendelssohn couldn't get away from words either; he called his composition *Romance without words*, which are words. And whether or not he saw this title as ironic, he knew enough, at least, to make a claim. And if he meant his *Romance* as a token for a lover, as I imagine, I'd like to think that she read that title and heard the notes as he'd intended and stepped inside his open door, instead of standing on the threshold and listening to the music drift out, a slow, soulful piece evoking something that couldn't reach her, and closing her eyes and pretending to understand.

# Day 82

Yesterday I became entirely self-sufficient. I attained this lofty state by the process of successively making myself happy, making myself cry, self-soothing and giving myself a cookie that I had, of course, made myself. This was preceded by having changed a potentially dangerous lightbulb and baked my own bread, all in the space of a single day, in which I had absolutely no need of other people.

I was warned, when I decided to stay here for the winter, about spending too much time on my own. About getting too comfortable in my own company. About becoming too self-sufficient. Is this what they meant? I make my own entertainment. I make my own bread. I make my own bed and I lie in it, alone. Has it gone too far?

For a while, a few years ago, my sisters and I had taken to using the term self-sufficient as a synonym for weird. When one of us behaved a little strangely, or said things that only she understood, when she seemed too happy in her own company or kept herself a little too amused, the other two would turn to each other, nod gravely, and pronounce her a bit self-sufficient. Loud enough for the third party to hear, and protest.

The lightbulb incident was a proud moment for me. I was frightened of it. It's an outdoor light, right above the front door. I'd changed the bulb a few weeks ago, but it had gone again, too soon, and this made me suspicious. With all the rain, I imagined, perhaps water had leaked into it, causing some terrible and potentially life-threatening electrical calamity.

I sought help. I contacted M and described the frightening lightbulb. He asked for a photo so I climbed on a chair and took a couple of shots, and waited for his diagnosis. It came, half an hour later: a typical case of a very old light fitting.

But in the meantime, I had stepped back on that chair and changed the lightbulb. I'd made sure the switch was off and I was wearing rubber-soled shoes. I checked the light for evidence of water and found none, though I did discover a dismembered bug inside the glass casing. I scraped it off, swapped the old bulb for the new, screwed the cover back on, tightly, flicked the switch, and made light. All by myself.

Later, when the sun had gone down and the new 100 watt bulb shone brightly over my front door, I put some music on and danced. I danced with joy and with abandon, knocking into furniture and tripping over the rug and then, completely without reason or warning, I burst into tears. 'This is a bit worrying,' I thought as I sobbed into my hands, still swaying gently to the music. Once both the song and the crying were over, I sat myself down on the sofa, made myself a cup of tea and fed myself a cookie from my latest batch: studded with raisins and raw cacao nibs, and flavoured with orange essential oil. 'There, there,' I said, patting myself on the back. 'You're OK.'

I reported this to Susanne in the evening.

'I don't think it's worrying,' she said carefully. 'You've just getting closer to yourself.'

'Perhaps,' I said, 'a little too close.'

I'm not protesting: I am a bit self-sufficient. I can spend hours, days in my own company and not get bored. I can make myself laugh, make myself cry, make myself feel better, and make myself dinner. I can put myself to bed after a long day, and read myself a bedtime story. And I'm not that frightened of lightbulbs, if I'm honest. I have changed lightbulbs before and I will change lightbulbs again, and no one need know about it. I don't need help, most of the time. But sometimes I ask for it anyway.

I might be self-sufficient but I'm not self-contained. I don't begin and end with myself. Despite appearances, despite the circumstances that I've chosen and protect, my life is other people. I might not see them, I might not even talk to them that often, I might be happy to spend weeks only with myself, but I wouldn't be myself without them. I might have fought for solitude, moved away from people to find the space to write, but without them I'd have nothing to write about. Nothing to say.

So when I changed that bulb and the light came back on, I immediately informed M of my achievement. I thanked him for his help, and added that his presence is still required, that he still needs to come and save me from myself, though both of us know that I don't really need saving. I don't need saving from the weather, but my granddad soothes his own fears by telling me what to wear in the rain. I asked Polyna for advice on curing olives, because she's done it before, though I know all the information is online. I sometimes ask my friends for their opinion when I've already made up my mind. I call my mum and ask for things that I could easily find if I looked. I let my grandma tell me how to make a dish I've made a hundred times before.

I have no need of other people, but I need my people in my life. And asking for help, sometimes, is an invitation, a way to bring them in, to keep them close. To remind them, and myself, that we don't live this life on our own. We might be self-sufficient, but we're not self-contained. And if we begin and end with ourselves, the middle bit is filled with the people we've chosen, unsolicited recipes and advice you don't really need, frightening lightbulbs and unnecessary raincoats and gardening tips, and if we need to get away from it sometimes, it's only because we know it's there, and it's this middle bit that makes a life; the reason we ever have anything to say.

# Day 83

I have decided to defy local advice and spend Christmas here, alone. Despite being expressly warned against doing so. It was Vangelis who issued this warning when he last picked me up from the port.

'I can see that you've got a good thing going,' he praised me, 'but don't get any ideas about Christmas. That's when it gets really hardcore. Everyone that you see here now? They'll all be gone.'

This is an island that relies, largely, on tourism, and the locals need to be around for Easter and the summer season. Christmas is the only holiday they can get away, and they do.

'I know you,' Vangelis added, making me smile. 'You're thinking about it. Don't do it.'

But do it I will. I think all the praise has gone to my head and is making me reckless. Only last week, I was pronounced an authentic Sifniot, by a man who is a Sifnos tradition in himself: Marios, proprietor of the legendary general store "A Bit Of Everything". The shop is closed for the winter, as the locals have little need for postcards of chisel-chested Greek lovers smirking seductively against a background of bright blue sky, but Vangelis lives in the back, and I saw him coming out of his door one morning, on my way to the square. I stopped to say hello.

He did a double take. 'You haven't left?' he said.

I shook my head and stood before him, with my arms held out, to demonstrate my continued presence on the island.

'Your family?' he asked.

'Long gone.'

'But you have stayed. You're an authentic Sifniot, you are.'

High praise indeed. And that's not all, because, two weeks ago, I can now reveal, I was admitted to the royal court of Sifnos by peeing on the beach. There was no ceremony, on account of the fact that there was nobody around to witness this act, which is also the reason I was able to perform it. I had walked six kilometres to the port, and had enjoyed three cups of coffee in quick succession before leaving the house. My bladder dictated the rest. I found a bush and I crouched, and I became Sifnos royalty. Not Queen: you don't get the crown for squatting behind a bush. But a lady-in-waiting, at the very least. Despite my most unladylike behaviour.

It's true that the island empties out over the Christmas holidays. Polyna confirmed it. She was telling me about a soup kitchen she and some friends will run for two weeks from mid-December, to provide meals for those in need. They started it last year and sixty people turned up daily; this year, they expect closer to a hundred.

'But if there are that many people that need help, wouldn't it make more sense to do it once a week throughout the year, instead of two weeks running over Christmas?' I asked.

'You'd think,' said Polyna, 'but the neighbours help them out during the year. The neighbourhood takes care of them. But they all go away for the holidays, and these people have nothing to eat.'

A sad fact, but also a happy one: for fifty weeks out of the year, there is such a thing as a neighbourhood here.

My neighbourhood is empty already, so I don't think I'll notice much of a difference. I'm pretty sure Mrs Souli won't be going skiing for her holidays, and neither will Vangelia. All the shops will be closed for a couple of days, so I'll have to get my supplies and cigarettes in advance, but I think that's it: my Christmas, planned.

I think I like the idea of the 25th of December being just another day. 'It might be liberating,' Eileen said when I told her; I think it will. It'll be like an extra day in the year, a day added to my calendar, almost brand new: Christmas without Christmas, a day I've never had before. I don't like Christmas. In my experience, it's been a day of *have to*, of dry turkey and presents that no one really wants. I love my family, but I can eat with them on any other day, and, besides, I have no presents to bring. I was thinking of going down to Kamares and picking sage from the side of the road: there's a long stretch just as the sea comes into view where it grows wild and in abundance. I could hang it up to dry, and make bouquets and tie them up with ribbon; I think they'd make nice gifts. But I can give them later, it doesn't have to be Christmas. They'll keep.

I think I'd like to go into town on Christmas day, when everyone, those few who haven't left, will be at home eating dinner with their families. To see Sifnos all decked out and twinkling for Christmas, with not a soul on the streets: that's an image I'd like to have in my head. An image to come back to when I need something rare and unusual to counteract the hectic tedium of ordinary life.

I don't like Christmas, but freed of the *have to* we might become reconciled. I might look at the decorations that are already appearing outside the houses, strange and colourful against the white, and see effort and beauty. I might look at the twinkling lights and just see twinkling lights. If I stripped it of its meaning, it might come to mean something else. Maybe I'll come to like it, the 25th of December, reimagined. Maybe I'll even take some sage bouquets over to Mrs Souli and Vangelia, or bake some cookies in the shape of stars. Maybe I'll go up to Artemonas, to the annual Christmas Village, and wander around and look at ornaments and trinkets and smile, and wish people a happy Christmas.

It doesn't have to be Christmas. I can get together with my family and friends on any day, and eat, and give out sage instead of presents. But I think I'd like to reclaim this day, the 25<sup>th</sup> of December, just this once, stripped of its meaning so that it means something to me, at last. Even if it's just a day when I had nothing much to do, and had to do nothing: that's better than turkey and presents. That's liberating. Against local advice, I'd like to give it a try.

# Day 84

Do you remember the tin can telephone? Also known as "lovers' phone", this was the children's toy version of an early mechanical telephony device, whereby sound is converted to vibrations and conveyed along a solid medium, to be reconverted to sound at the other end. I remember playing this game as a child, putting together the telephone by connecting the bottoms of two paper cups with a length of string and then standing at opposite ends of the same room, with the string taut between you and your playmate, and talking into the cups. I remember how exciting it was, to cause sound to travel along the string and reach your friend, waiting eagerly with a paper cup against their ear. To make your voice heard across the room.

This morning, I clicked a button and my friend appeared on my screen and it wasn't exciting; it was just our usual coffee date on skype. I clicked a button and a kitchen in Sweden came into view and Susanne, still bleary-eyed and wild-haired, stood by the stove boiling water for her coffee, while I sat at my desk in Sifnos, coffee already made, and rolled a cigarette and told her about the clouds that had descended overnight. There was no string, and our voices were heard across a continent. This is our tin can telephone, today.

We're living in a sci-fi fantasy and there will come a day when we'll all be assigned our own, unique IP addresses and communicate with each other over wireless networks. This is the Internet of Everything, and it'll make our connections more relevant and more valuable than ever before. Or so Cisco claims.

The Internet of Things: I'd never heard of before until this morning, when M suggested I check it out. We'd been having a conversation about programming languages, with me pointing out how their names always sound grand and vaguely mysterious while he earnestly tried to learn one of them, the awe-inspiring Objective-C. But the Internet of Things and its evolution, the Internet of Everything, where people can play the part of things, are in a league of their own. 'It could almost be a story title,' I commented to M, missing the point entirely. I can't help it; my mind is wired to pick up on words.

I'm not tech-stupid. I can stumble my way through some relatively advanced concepts and not hurt myself on the cutting edge. I can handle most computer crises, and I can even write a bit of HTLM (one of the least grandly-named languages, but fascinating, still). But if you talk to me about the Internet of Everything, you've gotta know that I'll miss the point. I'll give a cursory glance to the technological implications, the possibilities that it might bring, and then I'll be swept away by the romance of the language, the almost-poetry of its name, and go straight into a philosophical spin.

The Internet of Everything, where everything is connected. Where we'll no longer give our names but introduce ourselves by our IP address. Unique, because the world is full of Daphnes, but there is only one 192.168.1.6, and that'll be me. And I will forge connections over wireless networks and transmit data, more relevant, more valuable than ever before. And my coffee machine will know when I wake up in the morning and start brewing, and if my blood sugar drops, IP 192.168.0.4 (formerly known as my mother) will come along and feed me a cookie, and if IP 220.153.54.1 (a brain activity monitor in a special facility in Reyjavic, Iceland) picks up the signals of an impending stroke, it will notify my local hospital to dispatch an emergency response team, and save my life. And all my friends, my wireless connections, those who have my IP address, will receive my real-time data and process it, and they will know my pulse rate at any given moment, but they will never know what it was that made my heart beat faster. They will never know how I feel.

I know I'm missing the point; I'm missing the point deliberately. I might send myself spinning through sci-fi nightmares, but I can see the possibilities that this technology could bring. I'm not opposed to the Internet of Everything, and I would never stand in the way of something with such an excellent name. And there might come a day when I am part of it, and I'll be grateful, then, when I wake up in the morning and my coffee's already made.

But for now I'm grateful that I've landed back in today, when I can still remember being excited by a tin can telephone, and a time when mobile phones were science fiction and people appearing on your screen only happened in StarTrek. Today, when we still give names to things that fascinate us, and become fascinated by the names of things. When I'm connected to people without wires and my words are still my words when they reach them, at the other end. When I can still stand in a room and make my voice heard across it, and cross it to talk to my lover without the use of strings. And when the strings that hold us together – loosely, invisibly, and mysteriously – make for connections far more relevant and valuable than Cisco can hope to understand.

And there might come a day when I'll become 192.168.1.6 and I will be unique, but in the meantime I'll just be one of many Daphnes, and, in the absence of data, you'll have to use your senses to figure out if I'm the one you want, and your words to convey what you want me to know. I have no address so if you want to find me you'll have to ask around for the house below the church where the strange lady writer lives. And if you bring two paper cups, I know a game we can play. I've got the string. We can make a connection.

# Day 85

I found where Antagonist was hiding: she was in the pages of a novel I have yet to write. In every paragraph I've left unfinished, every sentence that doesn't lead to the next. In every word that needs to be replaced by another, she's there, hiding in the gaps. Like a weed growing among your seeds, driving its roots into the fertile ground, this patch of earth you've cleared to grow some flowers.

I've started writing a novel, but I've been quiet about it. Like a new lover, I'm careful with it still. We're still tentative with each other, we're still testing each other out: it hasn't earned my trust yet and I haven't won its heart. It's very new, this thing between us. I think it might lead to something, but you never can tell. So I'm holding back a little, protecting my lover, protecting myself. You don't want to go making announcements when the thing you're growing might be a stillborn effort, a love affair that fizzled out. Disjointed sentences that you couldn't finish. A patch of weeds.

Weeds grow deeper than you imagine; they know they need to burrow to survive. If you tug at them they'll snap, but they'll continue growing. You have to dig much deeper than you think to pull them out. And that's where Antagonist is hiding: the dark places where I try to plant my seeds. The dark places that are made when you come to the end of a sentence and you can't think of how to start the next. That's where she grows, as sturdy as a weed. She is the doubts you have about your new lover, the questions that you'd like to ask but hesitate. Your fears that this will go the same way as everything before it, when you forget that everything that went before has brought you here.

I'm not growing flowers, I'm growing spinach. Spinach is more substantial than flowers; its dark, fleshy leaves can survive the winter. I cleared a patch to grow it, drew a border around it with stones. I prepared the soil and planted my seeds and waited for the rains, and the weeds seized their opportunity and took over. The rains came and my spinach shot up out of the ground, but it's drowning in clover. Like a new lover wearing the wrong shoes or saying the wrong thing, Antagonist is in the details that you're not sure, yet, you can forgive. The details that might grow into weeds and take over, or might grow into love.

Like a new lover you never thought would come, I've waited for this novel for a long time. The first few days were a whirlwind; we couldn't get enough of each other. I didn't eat, I didn't sleep, I gave up on tasks halfway through to rush back to it, and it would call my name whenever I left the room. It left no room in my head for other thoughts. It was exhilarating. It was exhausting. It couldn't last forever. Now, as the days go by and the first rush fades, Antagonist creates room for doubt, a space for questions that wasn't there before. This is the space, the time for my new lover and I to get to know each other and see how far we can take this thing we've started. It's frightening. It's exciting. It's a possibility, stirring in my belly, but it's too soon to tell.

I waited for this novel for a long time. Like a new lover, I wanted to protect it, to let it grow taller and deeper before I exposed it to the world. Like the spinach in my garden, I spent hours pulling at the weeds. But for every root of clover that I dug out of the ground, I dislodged a fragile spinach shoot. I was killing my spinach, and the weeds kept on spreading. And I think, now, that if I learn to trust it, the spinach will find a way to grow despite the weeds. Some of its tender shoots are taking on the shape of leaves already. It's starting, now, to look like spinach, distinctive dark leaves, differentiating itself from the clover growing wildly all around. And when it's ready to pick, I'll be able to tell the spinach from the weeds.

And I think, now, I could learn to trust this novel, and unlearn the superstition that I thought I'd left behind, disregard the voice that tells me possibilities should be kept quiet until they turn into proof; that's Antagonist, too. 'Don't jinx it,' she says, but the jinx is already on you, if you listen. You can drown a thing in silence as much as you can drown it in words, and possibilities need to be planted and exposed, like seeds, to the rain, so that they have the chance to grow into whatever they were destined to become.

And words, one after another, adding up to sentences, adding up to paragraphs that make chapters complete are the only thing that can drive Antagonist away. Every gap I fill moves her on to the next one and the next one, and once I get to the end and place the final full stop, she'll have nowhere left to hide. But I have no way of knowing how far this thing will take me. You can't prove a novel, you can't prove a love, you can't prove anything against failure, not with silence, not with caution, not by uselessly snapping off the weeds. All you can do is let it out into the world and disregard the bad shoes and trust it to grow into love or into whatever it was destined to become. And when it's ready, you'll be able to tell.

# Day 86

I almost went to a church festival yesterday. Almost. Almost as close as you can get to doing a thing without actually doing it. I put on my thickest socks and I was ready, but I didn't go. I drank hot chocolate and looked at pink and yellow clouds instead.

Yesterday was the 6th of December and the feast day of St. Nicholas. A day that I've been hearing about since September, but it seemed so far away, then. But days have a way of coming around sooner or later, and yesterday was the day of the unmissable festival, the one I'd promised Christina I'd go to. Almost. 'Probably,' I'd said. 'If you go, I'll probably come.' It was to be my exception to the rule of non-attendance, my giving-this-thing-a-chance. Out of all the festivals in the year, Christina said, this was the best: they dance until the morning. My stomach gave a lurch of fear, but I smiled bravely and said maybe. I was almost certain, then, that I'd go, on that faraway day in December that would probably never come. And it came, and it was yesterday.

Today is a day I almost gave up on. I felt like being a shop and closing for Sunday. Shops are closed on Sundays in Greece. Still. It's partly a religious thing that lingers, the day of the Lord, the day of rest. The seventh day, when the world has been made, and we must now sit back and admire it. Our work is done, until tomorrow, when it begins again from day one. The other part is a mad notion put forward by the trade unions and, apparently, supported by 85% of Greek merchants, that allowing the shops to open on Sundays is anti-constitutional, illegal, and a violation of workers' rights. As someone who's lived in London for most of my adult life and worked almost every Sunday in all those years, I don't get it: it's just another day. But today, this Sunday, I felt like closing shop. Pulling the shutters down and sticking a note on my door, polite but firm: Closed for business. I'm tired; I've been making the world all week.

For all my fake-brave smiles and earnest maybes, I'm a coward. Christina is very brave: not only does she attend the festivals, but she dances. I am in awe of this. The most I could aspire to would be to stand quietly in a corner, half-in, half-out of the circle of people that delineates the dance floor, there and not quite there, part terrified and part intrigued and all of me trying to stay inconspicuous, and, if I'd been talked into a shot or two of *raki* and I felt wild and reckless and my cheeks burned red, I might forget myself for a moment and join in the clapping that keeps the rhythm going as the dancers dance.

I would have gone. I wanted to. I was tired, but I wanted to go for the company and the walk. Christina had brought a friend along, Maro, and the three of us would walk there together, to this little church by the sea, a forty-five minute pilgrimage in our zipped-up jackets and our most suitable shoes. It sounded perfect, this trek through winter Sifnos, with those two women who felt like friends, and the weather just bad enough to add an edge of adventure and make us grateful for our scarves. We'd set off at half past four and arrive just after sunset and have a coffee, Christina said, and a shot of *raki* to warm us up. Then there'd be Vespers, and a feast of chickpea stew and fried fish (no meat this time of year, on account of the Christmas fast), and then the dancing would begin.

I wouldn't dance. I probably wouldn't stay that long. I'd go for the company and the walk, and have a coffee there if it was offered, and then I'd set off again and walk back home. I'd use my phone as a torch if I had to. There was a full moon, too, and it would rise and light

340

my way. And this is how it almost happened. I wore my thickest socks and tucked my vest into my jeans and pulled on my warmest jumper and packed a bag with an extra top and my scarf and a roll of tissue, just in case. And then, at four, I called Christina and found out that the romantic winter walk I had imagined would come after we'd driven almost as far as Cheronisos, at the farthest end of the island, where the path to the church of St. Nicholas began. And, subsequently, the forty-five minute return journey would only take me as far as the road – dark, desolate and rarely used, even in summer – where I would stand and hope for the headlights of a car heading into town. Never mind the full moon: this did not sound like fun.

All of a sudden, I was seized by an urge to curl up on my sofa and drink hot chocolate. Just that: warm and quiet and with the heating on. I put my bag down and walked to Christina's house to tell her and Maro in person, as they changed into festival-appropriate clothes, that I wouldn't be joining them after all. They gave me sad looks and possible solutions, but they didn't push too hard, and I almost gave in, but I didn't. I saw them to the car and walked back home slowly, taking pictures of pink and yellow clouds along the way. I stopped by the supermarket and bought milk and cocoa powder for my hot chocolate, and a few things I would need for today, which is Sunday, and the supermarket is closed. I've done that before, forgotten about Sundays, but I have learnt that lesson.

What I'm learning here, mostly, is freedom, and I think freedom is in knowing when to give up, when to give in, and when to stand your ground. When to go to a festival and when to go home and drink hot chocolate. When to look at dancers and when to look at clouds. When to say no to well-meaning people and when to say no to yourself. When to forget yourself, for a moment, and when to remember, and stand up for the coward that you are. And how to tell the difference between missing an unmissable festival and missing a chance. And how to forgive yourself, for both.

I almost went to the festival, and it is almost like I've been. I can imagine it, like I imagined the walk there: the Vespers, the chickpeas, the dancing and the violins. The hubbub of people, cold hands and the heat of the drink. The full moon shining off the white of the freshly-painted church. I would have been there, almost a part of it; I would have seen all this from the sidelines, where I belong. I am a watcher of things, an observer. I don't put myself in the middle of circles for people to clap. I would have been an almost presence, even if I'd gone. I would have enjoyed it, but I had hot chocolate instead.

I've been making the world all week and I am tired. It isn't easy, writing worlds into existence every day. But today is not the seventh day, it's day 86, and I'm glad I didn't give up on it. My work is not done. It will be done, one day, and then I'll take a day of rest, be it a Sunday or a Tuesday, and I will sit back and admire it, with the shutters down and a note on my door. And then I'll start again, from day one. Our work is never done, I hope: There are always more festivals. There are always more chances. There are always more worlds to make. The freedom is in choosing.

# Day 87

This is a day of olives and brine and of how they are not symbolic of anything at all.

I was talking to Laura this morning. We caught up on our news, mine being, mostly, how I'd spent the morning preparing brine to cure my olives, which I've been soaking in water for the past two weeks to draw the bitterness out.

'The water needs to be changed daily', I informed her. 'It's a long process, making your own olives. It's not easy.'

'But you'll have olives to give as presents for Christmas,' she said. 'That's pretty cool.'

'Not Christmas. They'll have to be in brine for about a month.'

After this fascinating exchange, Laura filled me in on her life in London, which did not involve olives or brine, and the latest from the yoga centre where we both used to work. We talked about that for a bit, and then we talked about our feelings, and then we talked about how tired we are of having to talk about our feelings all the time. Laura shared her frustration with the world of yoga and the need to always be connected and aware, and I came back with mine at always looking for the connections between things and making something meaningful out of them.

'It's too much,' we both agreed, and went on to trash the inspirational quotes and self-betterment articles we are being subjected to, daily, on our facebook feeds. We said fuck a lot, and forgot about being positive all the time. It felt good.

'You need some balance,' I suggested. 'You need to go out and drink and dance, with no awareness at all.'

'No awareness? That's hard.'

'It's possible,' I said from experience, remembering how my yoga-trained body has often collided with the furniture when I dance around the living room. 'Try it. And maybe try consciously judging a few people a little.'

Observe; don't judge. Share. Feel. Love. Breathe. Connect. Be present. Be aware. Be at one. Find your true purpose. Embrace your inner beauty. Open your heart. Cultivate your soul. Awaken your divinity. Count your blessings. Express your gratitude. Release your anger. Let go of your fear. Five things happy people do differently. Ten things that make you spiritual. Twenty things you thought were good for you but are not. A hundred things you're doing wrong.

How about, sometimes, I just want to drink coffee and smoke cigarettes and talk to my friend on the phone? How about, sometimes, I slump my shoulders and forget about keeping my pelvis tucked in? How about, sometimes, I just want to do some yoga and not talk about it, and sometimes I don't want to do it at all? How about, sometimes, I don't feel like thinking anything meaningful and have nothing meaningful to say? How about, sometimes, I just want to say fuck it, and call it a day?

This is a day of practical things. Of going to the supermarket to buy salt for the brine. Of working out the correct salt to water ratio for preserving the olives. Looking for jars and tubs and bottles to fill up with olives and brine. Cleaning the kitchen of the mess I made. Collecting the laundry off the drying rack and tidying it away in cupboards and wardrobes. Making pizza dough for dinner, and placing it by the heater to rise. Baking cookies, since I'm putting the oven on. Feeding the cats and picking lemons. Mopping my wet footprints off the floor.

'Seriously,' I said to Laura later. 'What do I write about today? How do I distil some meaning out of these olives?'

'Perhaps there's a brine angle,' she joked. 'Perhaps you could connect to the brine on another level, and let it guide you.'

'Does brine have different levels? I asked.

'Well, there's the fact that it preserves...'

'But that's it. That's the one level brine has. It's the only thing it does.'

'Maybe you could reflect on that,' Laura said desperately, before giving up and leaving me to fend for myself, searching for meaning in my practical, meaningless day.

I'm sure I could work on the brine angle and draw some meaning out of the fact that it preserves. I could say something about the salt to water ratio and striking the right balance. I could talk about the long process of curing olives; I could make something out of that verb, "to cure". I could make it meaningful and symbolic, if I tried. But, actually, all that any of it means is that, provided I did get the water to salt ratio right, I'll have my own olives in a month. And that's pretty cool.

No day is meaningless, and it's good to know that you can always find meanings and connections; you can make something out of anything, if you try. But it's also good to know that some days are not for trying. Some days only have the one level, like brine. Some days you're just gonna drink coffee and eat pizza and put away the laundry, and reflect on nothing and forget about awareness and tending to your soul. And one thing happy people do differently is they know when to say fuck it and call it a day.

Fuck it: this is a day.

# Day 88

There is political drama going on in Sifnos, and Christmas is being cancelled. The Christmas Village will be a refugee camp and the village square a no man's land of empty benches and the ghosts of Christmas lights. The weary travellers will have to find a different Bethlehem and the Three Wise Men another star to follow, and another place to deposit their gifts. Santa will not be visiting, because we've not been good.

This Christmas tale is set in the present, but it began many years ago, in 1958, when the local Mavromatis family donated the thus far privately owned square in Apollonia to the people of Sifnos for the erection of a World War II memorial. Legal reasons meant that the space was signed over to the Sifnos Association rather than the local government, but it was the donors' intention and everyone's understanding that it would belong to the residents of the island. It was soon established as the village square and known to all as Heroes' Square, in remembrance of the fallen. Like village squares everywhere, it became the hub of the community: a place to meet and a place to rest, with small children kicking pine cones and balls around, older children loitering, old men taking strolls with their arms folded behind their backs, and lovers holding hands on the benches. The Municipality of Sifnos kept it clean and lit up and everyone was happy, and for the last three years running, a makeshift barn has welcomed Jesus, Mary and Joseph and a variety of farm animals, and the stars suspended from lampposts and trees have led the faithful, the uncertain and the wise, the people of Sifnos, to the annual Christmas Village.

Not this year. This year the square will not be visited by Three Wise Men bearing gifts, but haunted by the

Three Ghosts of Christmas. This year, the Sifnos Association decided, in the spirit of Christmas and community, to play the role of Ebenezer Scrooge. As preparations for the Christmas Village began, the president of the Sifnos Association sent a letter to the Municipality, stating that the legal documents establishing ownership of the square had been interpreted in bad faith and that the square itself, which is the legal property of the Association, could henceforth not be used by the Municipality (and, by extension, one might surmise, the people themselves) in any way without prior written permission from the former, and threatening legal action if a violation occurred.

The Municipality argued, reasonably, that the property in question is the island's main square and belongs to its residents, as per the donors' express wishes, as it always has. They would not be bullied, and the Village that hosts Christmas would be built in the Heroes' Square, this year like all the years before it.

Picture the scene: a small village square in a small, quiet island. A mellow Thursday afternoon in December, low breeze, thin clouds, a pale and patchy sunshine. A handful of people gathered together, laughing, making jokes, as they work to put together the structures that will turn the square into a Christmas Village, where children will meet the baby Jesus and play games and sing carols, and their parents will drink wine and catch up with their friends, and a few loners, like me, will wander around and look at the lights and think that maybe Christmas is not so bad, after all. And Santa might visit, they say, if we're good.

But we've not been good, because what happens next in this Christmas fable is a lawsuit against the Municipality. The Sifnos Association now casts itself in the role of the Grinch that stole Christmas, and the local police are forced to play the villains and arrest the Mayor at the square, as he oversees the work. He is taken to the station and held for four hours, whereupon he is released by authority of the Assistant District Attorney, remotely, from the island of Syros. The court in Syros issues a temporary injunction against the Municipality of Sifnos, forbidding any use of the square pending a final decision on the matter, on December 12. But the Mayor will not be bullied; he won't give up, he tells the court, he won't back down. Heroically, but I don't think he wants to be a hero. There are no heroes in this story, except the ones remembered in the square.

The Christmas stars still shine but they don't lead to Bethlehem. The square is haunted by the Ghost of Christmas Past, and the Ghost of Christmas Present lingers in the skeletons of the structures of the would-be Christmas Village, left behind. The Heroes are lonely; none of us are allowed to visit them. We come, the faithful and the uncertain, the people of this island; we follow the stars and stand on the perimeter of the square we cannot enter. We don't sing carols. We don't bring gifts. We stand in silence and wait for the Ghost of Christmas Yet To Come, if it comes, if the court in Syros decides to let it through.

The stars still shine but there are no wise men. There are no heroes in this story, yet. And there should be no villains, either, no Grinch, no Ebenezer Scrooge, no ghosts haunting the square. There should be no Municipality and no Association, just people of this island with nothing to divide. And men would be wise to remember what this is all about: not politics, not ownership, not even Christmas, but community, and a good faith that has nothing to do with contracts or which god you believe in. They would be wise to look at the stars and see some sense. There is still time for a Christmas miracle, and if the men stop behaving like fools there might be heroes yet, and the Christmas Yet To Come will not be a ghost but a village square dressed up in lights and tinsel, where the faithful and the uncertain, the families and the loners, the heroes and the wise will all come together and sing carols and remember what this is all about, and what it means to be good.

# Day 89

Today I'm contemplating the meaning of life as exemplified by the profound lyrics of Opus' eighties hit *Life is Life*. Which posits, very succinctly: *life is life, nana-nanana$^x$*. And that's something worth reflecting upon.

It's December and that means, among other things, that it's the month of reflection. It's a time to reflect upon the year that's gone by, our achievements and our failures. It's a time to collect all our latent desires and the dreams that we put aside, once again, so that we can build our expectations high and precarious and dump them in the lap of the year that's about to begin, as a welcome present, along with our resolutions. And then put our party shoes on and go watch the fireworks. Because that's where December really keeps its sting: right at the end. As if Christmas and all that reflecting weren't enough, it then hits you with New Year's Eve. The climactic, ceremonious transition between one year and the next, the old and the new, all that you did wrong and all that you'll do differently. The day that sets the tone for all the days to come, until December comes round again. You've gotta make it count.

This may well be the Dippy Hippie talking, but I'll let her have her say: I believe that there are forces in the world, outside of ourselves but also connected, and that they're conscious, if not exactly sentient. I believe there is such a thing as destiny and that it can be altered, and that all the answers we need exist somewhere, if we take the time to look, if we figure out the right questions to ask. The problem with this theory is that the number of places to look can be overwhelming, and we mostly tend to go no further than our own heads, ask ourselves the same questions and come up against the same walls.

What I like to do sometimes, when I tire of running circles in my head, is ask the universe (or whatever you want to call those forces) for a hint, and I've decided, for the sake of convenience, that the universe can speak to me through my iPod. I don't know why I attribute such powers to an electronic device, but, as the Greek proverb suggests, *the human soul is an abyss,* and if we can make anything out in that darkness, pull any strands of sense out of it, then it's good enough. Some things you just don't question. So my iPod is a modern day oracle, like the famed Pythia of Delphi minus the hallucinogenic drugs. I set it to shuffle, ask the question, skip three songs, and let song number four be my answer.

It doesn't always work. Sometimes the iPod oracle makes as much as sense as Pythia herself, and I have no priests at hand to interpret its gibberish. But there are times when it is scarily accurate, like when I was contemplating a relationship that had demonstrated no signs of life for months, and had taken to lurching around like a zombie, oozing unspeakable substances and groaning horribly every time I looked its way: the answer was a very straightforward *I Know It's Over* (The Smiths), accompanied, I swear, by a very impatient roll of the eyes. The universe is honest, but it isn't your grandma; it isn't known for being kind. On another occasion, the universe amused itself by declaring *The answer is blowing in the wind* (Bob Dylan), proving, conclusively, not only that it is, in fact, sentient, but also that it has a sense of humour. I interpreted this to mean *fuck off with your questions and just get on with it,* which, as it turned out, was the correct course of action.

In this case, what I was struggling with was a general sense of *what's it all about?,* prompted, perhaps, by December – not the end of the year, but the end of one hundred days and the questions that raised about the days that will follow. If I was looking for certainty, some solid footing, some kind of grip, the universe was not going to play along: it gave me *Life is Life.* I looked at the song title on my screen. I heard the opening notes. I thought: *you are fucking kidding me, you arsehole.* The universe winked. I laughed. *Life is life,* said the song. *Nana-nanana.*

It's an interesting fact that there are people in this world – not one, but several – who have taken the time to make videos of "Life is Life, With Lyrics". There are a few of them on youtube. It fascinates me, the motivation behind making them and, even more so, watching them. Who are these viewers? What are they looking for? I imagine them sitting in front of these videos, attentive, focused on the words, and nodding in understanding, at last, as LIFE IS LIFE NANANANANA scrolls across their screens. Perhaps it's because it's hard to believe that this is actually what the song says; I can't think of another explanation. These lyrics might be profound, but they are not complicated.

It might sound stupid, looking for answers in songs. But my electronic oracle is no different to the little superstitions we live by, the *if this happens, then,* the stepping over the pavement cracks and the red top you always wear when your team is playing. It's no different to believing in New Year's Eve, and that what happens on that night and on the first day of the year has any bearing upon the 364 days that follow. I could argue against time as a construct, but our calendar is definitely a made-up thing.

I'm skipping New Year's Eve this year, as well as Christmas. I will resist the urge to stay up until midnight to count the new year in. If I'm up, which is likely, I won't look at the time. I'll pay it no attention; I will reflect on nothing and make no resolutions. I will let one day drift into the next, seamlessly, as if that's all they are: one day, and then another. And I could argue with days as well, as an arbitrary unit for measuring time, but I'm not looking to change the world. We have to make a few things up, create some shapes we recognise, to make some sense of the abyss. I'm not looking to change the world; just my own experience of it, if I can.

And *life is life* might well be the answer, as stupid as it may sound. It's no more stupid than ascribing meaning to a made-up calendar and some fireworks shot up into the sky. Those lyrics aren't complicated, but they may just be profound. The universe can be an arsehole, but it's rarely wrong. *Life is life*: simple. Fuck off with your questions. Get on with it. You'll never make sense of the abyss, but you can learn to live with it, with all your little superstitions, and that'll be enough. And if you spend some time in there, it's like any darkened room, and your eyes will adjust, and you might see some shapes you recognise. And you can get some fireworks and set them off any night of the year, and light the place up. And in those flashes of light, you might get the answers you are looking for, and they might be garbled up gibberish, like Pythia's prophesies, or they might appear like words scrolling across your screen, LIFE IS LIFE NANANANANA. And you will nod in understanding, at last. And get on with it, and make every day count.

# Day 90

There is a girl running up a mountain. I don't know her.
I've never met her before. She has red cheeks and her
face glistens with sweat. She looks vaguely familiar, but
I don't know who she is. She's wearing multicoloured
leggings with some sort of psychedelic butterfly print,
and fancy running shoes. She's got a plastic bag
containing a potted plant in either hand, and she seems
to be trying to swing her arms. The bags keep knocking
into her hips. She looks awkward. She looks like she's
about to have a heart attack. She looks happy. I don't
recognise this girl. I've been here for ninety days, and
I've never seen her before. I've never met her, in thirty-
six years.

It was me: I went running. It wasn't accidental. It
wasn't spontaneous, like dancing on the street. It didn't
take me by surprise. It was deliberate, and planned.

This is how I became a smoker. Deliberately. I was
fifteen and I had never touched a cigarette before. Not a
puff. I had sailed through the peer pressure, turning
away from every cigarette proffered and every jibe. I was
the sort of kid who made anti-smoking pamphlets and
destroyed my dad's cigarettes for his own good, the sort
of teenager who shook her head sadly as others puffed
away and declared it 'such a shame'. Self-righteous and
awkward and really not cool, but an anti-smoker,
through and through. Until one night at my dad's house.
I was having a small party, a few friends sprawled
around the living room, listening to records. A couple of
them smoked, but I didn't ask for a cigarette. I excused
myself, went to the shop down the road and bought a
packet of Marlboro Reds. I took them back to the house,
slipped into the downstairs bathroom, locked the door,
and lit up. I don't remember if I choked or coughed or if

it tasted horrible; all I know is that I went into that bathroom determined to be a smoker, privately and deliberately. That I sat down on the toilet and smoked that cigarette from top to bottom, right down to the filter. I went into that bathroom an anti-smoker and emerged as a smoker, and never looked back. I rejoined my friends in the living room, and didn't say a word. And when my friends saw me smoking the next day, they didn't ask. I have smoked every day of my life since that evening, and nobody's ever asked, and I don't know why. I just decided to be a smoker.

I didn't decide to be a runner, but I ran, and it was premeditated. I put my leggings on, and my running shoes, a yoga vest and a t-shirt on top. Purse and phone and keys in the pockets of my jacket, to keep my hands free. I left the house and walked down to the ring road, and as my feet hit the tarmac, I said goodbye to the person I've been for the past thirty-six years of my life. I left her behind, dumbstruck, frozen on the side of the road, muttering something about picking oregano, and I ran. I didn't look back.

I ran for a hundred metres, then walked, then ran again, setting myself landmarks – that bush, that bin, that tree. I ran down the mountain and then I ran up the hill. It felt odd, but not terrible. Not natural, either: my legs seemed to understand what was expected of them, but I didn't know what to do with my arms. But I ran, nonetheless, in my uncoordinated, experimental way, and it didn't feel terrible. It felt good.

I stopped when I reached the outskirts of town, and walked the rest of the way. My cheeks began to tingle, and my legs felt strange: light and heavy at the same time. But I wasn't sweating. I wasn't even out of breath. I had run and I'd survived and I felt better and better. I got some cash out at the bank and bought cigarettes; I smiled like a maniac at every passer-by (there were

355

three). On the way back, I stopped by the garden centre to ask about chilli pepper plants.

'We only have these two,' said the man, pointing at two pots of yellow and purple chillies, right by where I stood. I took them both and floated back onto the road.

I hadn't planned on running back. Even this crazy stranger who had stolen my leggings understood, through her endorphin haze, that running up a mountain road on a 45 degree incline is not a good idea. Not when you've been a runner for a grand total of 0.4 kilometres, with walking in between. Not when you're a smoker, and carrying two potted plants.

But fate had other plans. 'You want to be a runner?' it said. 'Let's see you run.'

I didn't understand at first, but then I saw him: a man stumbling out of a doorway, and something about the way he moved put me on alert. I don't know if he was drunk or simply dangerous or misunderstood, but he looked straight at me and grunted and made some worrying remarks, and set himself in motion on my trail. I picked up my pace and didn't turn around, but I could hear him shuffling behind me, muttering to himself. I walked faster, staying close to the bends, in and out of sight, and as soon as I reached the bottom of the ring road, I ran. I ran up the mountain, on a 45 degree incline. I ran with potted plants and smoker's lungs. And when I finally turned my head and saw only road and knew that I was out of danger, I carried on running. Just for the sake of it; just because I could.

It lasted a few seconds and then, obviously, I was dying. My heart thrashed against my ribcage, my legs shook, my arms ached and I was drenched in sweat. My face was burning and my hopeless attempts at yogic breathing had no effect. I felt dizzy. I staggered on, panting and wheezing all the way home. It was terrible. It was crazy. But, fuck me, it felt good.

Ninety days: so close. I could have made it. I thought I would. Ninety days and thirty-six years, and I thought I knew who I was: not a runner. And yet, there was a girl wearing my leggings and running up a mountain, and she used to be me. She *was* me: I went running. And though I know this means that I couldn't make it to a hundred days without losing my mind, after all, losing my mind felt really good. And I might never do it again, but I'm glad I got the chance to meet that girl, red-faced and drowning in sweat and gasping for air, running up a mountain with potted chilli plants. She is crazy and awkward and she doesn't know how to run, and she's going to be in a lot of pain tomorrow, but she's happy. She's the kind of girl who'll put on a pair of leggings and go running because she feels like it, and won't let a mere thirty-six years of being one thing stop her from being something else. I'm proud of her for that, even though I don't really know her. And I might never do it again, but she has taught me something; maybe I could try to be a bit more like her, even if I never go running again.

# Day 91

The tap water is coming out brown. There is no denying it, and I tried. I tried to pretend it wasn't happening, because the alternative is brown water and the implications are not good.

'It's a trick of the light,' I reasoned.

'It's not,' Sifnos Chick said stoically. 'It's brown.'

'It's probably just a bit of soil,' I tried. 'Because of the rain.'

'It's not,' Sifnos Chick said again, smiling her maddening I-am-at-one-with-this-island smile.

A bit of soil I could live with, though City Girl calls it unacceptable and insists we call someone. A bit of soil I could overlook; it won't do any harm. But it's not. Manolis disabused me of that notion when I brought it up.

'Yeah,' he said cheerfully, 'that's rust.'

Rust, leaking from the pipes and into my water. Turning the water brown. I am not amused at all. I'm not sure what the effects of ingesting rust daily over a prolonged period of time are, but I am fairly certain it's not recommended as part of any healthy lifestyle plan. I am resisting the temptation to look it up. There was once a part of me, known simply as the Hypochondriac, and she would love to display all the symptoms of heavy metal poisoning. I have banished her from my daily life, neutralised her with coconut oil and herbal teas and positive thinking, but this is the sort of thing that would rouse her from her sleep, and it's too crowded in here already. I don't particularly want her wandering round the house all agitated, and diagnosing us all as terminal.

I first noticed the brown water when I was making the brine for the olives, and tried to blame it on the salt, which is white.

'I've messed up,' I told Manolis. 'I've made brine with rust.'

He shrugged. 'Ah,' he said, 'it's not a problem. You'll just rinse the olives out before you eat them.'

There are quite a few recipes for curing olives, but I've yet to come across one that recommends soaking them in water, salt and rust. I don't know the physics of this process but I'm sure osmosis plays a part and, as original as rust-infused olives might be, they're not a delicacy I'd want on my plate. I was planning to flavour them with more conventional ingredients, like garlic and chilli, rosemary and thyme. So it tipped them all out, all seventeen jars of them, and made a fresh batch of brine with mineral water. Which, lo and behold, wasn't brown.

I am a city girl, and I am not amused. I don't know what to do with brown water. I've come to terms with the London version, tap water laced with antidepressants and contraceptives that no amount of breaching can remove. But rust has me stumped. I can't boil it out of the water, I can't Britta filter it out. I'm powerless against it; I don't know who to call.

'You could tie a piece of cloth over the tap, like in the old days,' my mum suggested, and I could see Sifnos Chick's eyes light up as she contemplated which of our tea towels to rip to shreds. I'm all for being resourceful, but the object is to make water safe for consumption; we're not panning for gold. You can't get the brown out of the water with a scrap of cloth.

'Put the scissors down,' I told Sifnos Chick firmly, once my mum was off the phone. 'We're getting mineral water.'

'Couldn't we get our water from the spring, like we used to?'

'Of course,' I said pleasantly. 'If you have a car I don't know about.'

She doesn't. None of us drive. Mineral water it is.

We used to get our drinking water from the springs. The nearest one was located off the main road on the way to the beach of Platy Yialos, a thirty minute walk from the house, but we did have a car then. It was a natural spring in the grounds of the monastery of Our Lady of the Spring, and people would stop by to fill up their bottles and water their animals. The houses in our village didn't have running water in those days, and we drew water out of the well to have showers, threw a tin bucket on a length of rope into its depths, careful not to lean over, and pulled it back up. It was freezing, even in the height of summer; I remember my sister and I screaming and trying to run away every afternoon, when we came back from the beach and our parents insisted on rinsing the salt off us. Sometimes, if we planned ahead, we could warm the water in the sun. Those were good days, with less screaming. We were grateful for slightly warmer water and bottles filled up from the spring. Now we have forty minute showers and scream at each if they are less than scalding, and fight over who will carry the mineral water from the shop.

We think we're powerful, in our cities. We think we're in control. Problems are unacceptable. When something goes wrong we call someone, some authority, and they fix it for us, and that's what we think of as power. Here, there is no one to call. There might be a number and you might dial it but you don't really expect anyone to answer. Like Vangelia on the day of the powercut, you go through the motions: you place the call to the appropriate number, but there is no frustration when you keep getting their answering machine. You just assume they know about the problem already, and that they're probably out trying to fix it. You trust that it will be fixed, eventually, and, in the meantime, you have another coffee and work around it. You take the problem into your own hands, instead of calling it unacceptable and handing it over to someone else.

'I am not amused,' I tell my friends and family but, actually, I am a little bit. I am amused by my own reaction, my going ahead and making three litres of brine with brown water because I was determined not to accept that it was brown. I am amused by the reactions of those I tell, and the more horrified they sound, the funnier it all seems. Brown water is funny. It's funny, that I'm a city girl pretending to know how to live on an island, with brown water coming out of my taps. I hear myself saying it, stoically, cheerfully, that I've been boiling my pasta in rust. 'I'll just have to use mineral water,' I say. 'All it means is a few extra trips to the shop. I'll just have to be extra frugal, and save the water from the pasta to use it again. I'll just have to work around it, until it's fixed.' I hear the doubt in their voices, their concern, how powerless they feel on my behalf. But I'm more in control here, when I have to do everything myself, with problems that sound funny in the retelling and solutions that are simple, after all, and that thing about accepting what you cannot change. Like brown water coming out of your taps.

And as I hear myself laughing when I tell them, it occurs to me that, by some process of osmosis, I have been infused with a bit of that cheerful stoicism that keeps this place turning around. That somewhere along the way I stopped pretending to know how to do this, and started to learn.

# Day 92

Once is weird. Once is a funny story to tell my friends. Twice is scary: I went running again yesterday. And then again today, making it three. Three is serious. They don't call it the magic number for nothing.

It is a funny story: *Once upon a time, Daphne went running.* I told Alexis and he laughed. 'No!' he said. 'You didn't. You mustn't. You must never run!' I wasn't offended. He's only expressing the general consensus, a truth of which I am the most ardent advocate: I don't run, and I shouldn't. My body just wasn't made for it. The way my limbs flap about when I attempt to run has often reduced people to tears, and all those years of yogic body awareness have done nothing to change this. It's good comedy; it's not good practice. It probably causes untold damage to my joints but it's fine, because I never do it and I've never wanted to. Until now. My body wasn't made for running, but it seems to have forgotten, or no longer care. Something's happened, and it really wants to run. My mind is struggling to catch up.

Once upon a time, but then it was twice, and I did it properly this time. I didn't run on the way into town. I wasn't running away from anyone. I left the house with the express purpose of going for a run. I ran purely for the joy of running. Joy. Pure physical sweaty achey dizzying joy, running uphill through the mountains, against the wind, in the drizzle, in the dim pre-sunset light. What the fuck.

Which is exactly what Mel said when I told her this morning. I only had two runs to confess to at that time, but I knew she'd understand.

'A terrible thing has happened,' I said gravely.

'What?'

I lowered my voice. 'I went for a run.'

Her shock was palpable; it travelled through the phone line. She didn't think I was being melodramatic. She knows me; she knows what this means.

'What the fuck?' she said.

'I know!'

'Who *are* you?'

'I don't know.'

I'm not being melodramatic. I honestly don't know. I don't know who I am when I'm doing this. I don't know what this is about.

Three is the magic number. Significant things always come in threes. Three is symbolic, powerful. From scripture to folklore, from the gods of ancient Babylon and the Egyptians to Christianity, from Homer to Shakespeare to fairytales and nursery rhymes and pop songs, you can't get away from the number three. The Holy Trinity. The Three Wise Men. Three little pigs. Three blind mice. Three witches. Three wishes. Three times a lady. Third time lucky. Third time's the charm.

Three times. I did it again this afternoon. I was on the phone to Susanne when the urge came.

'I'll call you later,' I told her. 'I want to go for a run.'

'You *what?*'

'Yes,' I said, almost as surprised as she was. 'Let's not talk about it. Let's pretend it's not happening.'

Third time's the charm, and it felt a little familiar. Pulling on the leggings, lacing up the shoes, zipping up the jacket. A face cloth in my pocket to mop up the sweat. Headphones in, iPod on shuffle. Play. Run. I know people often make special running playlists, songs to help them power through, but I don't seem to need that. I don't need motivation. I run for joy. Any song will do.

I ran through the stillness of this slow-paced island life. I ran through the silence with music in my ears. I ran through the mountains, past olive groves and fields of clover, past houses and churches and farms, past dogs guarding work sites and a horse and a herd of sheep. I ran as the sun, half-hidden behind the mountains, picked out the village on the hilltop and lit up the clouds and glinted off the sea. I felt like someone had created a perfect little bubble for me, an idyllic scene made up of a thousand beautiful pictures, and sealed me inside, like one of those snow globes without the snow. I felt, conversely, that the world was wide open, boundless, and I could just keep running and never stop. I didn't want to stop. I ran like children do, without agenda, without chasing anything or being chased. I ran wildly, mindlessly, and my mind began to catch up. Mind, body, spirit, another trinity coming together at the count of three. It's the magic number.

I stopped eventually, breathless with more than physical exertion. I sat on a ledge looking westwards and let my iPod decide on a final song before I took the steps back up to the house. It was a Greek song, and I knew as I heard the first few notes what it meant. It's a song named for a Greek hero, and the chorus goes like this: *Who am I, really, and where am I going, with one thousand pictures in my mind?* I smiled as it all came together and my mind caught up and stopped asking, and the sun set and turned the fields dark.

I don't know who I am or where I'm going. But I can do this here, like this. I can run in my snow globe. I can run on my endless mountain road. I won't run in the city, or on a treadmill. I don't know what this is about, but it isn't about that. If I ever tell myself I should go running, then I won't. This much I understand. This isn't about forcing anything, or powering through; it probably isn't even about running. But it might be about breaking through the story, the once upon a time of don't and shouldn't and can't, running for joy until you break through to the other side. Watching yourself change, and letting it happen, even though it's weird and scary and serious. It's probably, again, about freedom and the boundaries we set to stop ourselves from going too far.

Don't shake up my snow globe. Don't tell me the road will end. I don't know who I am or where I'm going. Let me run on, through my one thousand pictures, and the answers will come. Let's not talk about it. Let's pretend it's not happening and just let it happen.

# Day 93

Is it karma when you've been killing weeds and you get stung by nettles? This happened today, and there's more to the tale than that.

I went a little crazy in the garden, but it's time I told the truth: it's not a garden. It's never been a garden at all. I call it that for the sake of calling it something, but it's a field, bare and dry in the summer and overgrown in winter, as I've found out in recent months. It's rectangular, longish and narrow, with three large fig trees at the back that give fruit in August. Close to the front, against the drystone wall that separates it from the neighbour's property, is an elderly almond tree that's been there forever, from before we built the house. It bears almonds sometimes, sparsely, smaller and rounder and slightly tangier than the ones produced by the other almond tree that stands guard over the front door. In the right hand corner, where the field meets the yard, is a giant prickly pear cactus, adding a touch of the Wild West, though it's very common on these islands, and not exotic at all. The rest of the field had been bare, historically, until an olive and two lemon trees appeared, in random places, over the winters of our absence when the field lives a secret life of its own. It must be a few years now because the olive is a medium-sized tree, but nobody remembers exactly when they were planted, or why. Last winter, Maria, the Bad Tenant, attempted to create a small vegetable patch in the space between the two lemon trees, in the middle of the field. There were tomatoes, most of them sad, dried up stalks by the time I arrived in July, aubergines, courgettes and melons. Of those, only the aubergines remain. And that's the field that I inherited, the space I've been calling my garden. A dry patch of land, heavily saturated with stones; three fig trees, one almond, one olive, two lemon trees whose leaves are curly from pests or disease, and a cactus, whose fruit I don't know how to eat.

I worked on it a bit last summer. We all did. We cleared it up so it could host my sister's wedding, look like a garden for one evening, dotted with tables and chairs and hung with fairy lights. We harvested layers upon layers of stones, pulled parasitic plants out of the ground that had grown into trees, cut back the prickly pear that loomed dangerously and threatened to stick us with its pricks, removed the last of Maria's agricultural efforts, and stomped on the soil to make it compact. I went a little further and planted geraniums along the border ledge to Stelios' field; I used some of the stones that we'd dug out of the ground to mark them as flowerbeds, and save them from getting trampled. Not all of them survived. But for a time, towards the end of August, you could stand on our patio and look out towards the fig trees in the back, and almost see a garden. There was a neatness to it, a wilderness held back, in the process of being tamed.

I made more flowerbeds, and vegetable patches, and planted seeds and harvested more stones. I drew neat borders, telling nature where it ended, but it was laughing at me all along. Autumn came, and then winter, and the almost-garden reverted to its true self. The secret life of a Sifnos field in winter: only secret to those of us who see the world tinted brown through our sunglasses and think, unthinkingly, that everything stops when we leave. We press pause and this place becomes a still image that we can carry around with us in the intervening months, and set it back in motion when we're ready to return and step back into it.

But no, of course not. Autumn came, and winter, and the rain, and there's nothing left of that sun-scorched dusty field of brown and gold. It's lush and green and damp and wild and completely out of control. It's beautiful, and foreign, and nobody believes me; I had to take pictures to prove it. 'Switzerland,' said Eleni – a

367

foreign land – when she saw them. But it's not Switzerland: it's winter Sifnos, and we just happen to spend our winters elsewhere. The world carries on without us, whether we're there to see it or not, and yes, if a tree falls in the forest and there's no one around, it still makes a sound. Nature isn't a performance put on for our sake.

I'm here to see it, this time, and I'm lucky because it's beautiful. But it's also dangerous. There are weeds in my garden as tall as my waist; I can no longer see the aubergine plants and I can't find the hose. My neat, pretty borders have disappeared, naïve little lines of stones thinking they could hold back the onslaught of green. It's beautiful to look at, but it's getting more dangerous by the day. This is not an overgrown garden in the city, it's a field on an island, surrounded by more fields, and there are creatures here that don't appreciate being stepped on while they sleep in the grass. And they'll wake up eventually, because after winter will come spring, and they'll slither around like they own the place, which they do. Snakes, like weeds, don't really care that I've called this patch of land my garden.

It's been on my mind, this garden. I've looked at it, over the last few weeks, and felt as helpless as my spinach, drowning in the weeds. I've fantasised about wielding a scythe, swinging it wildly back and forth like the Grim Reaper in jeans, but I don't own such an item, and I doubt that's the way to go about it, anyway. I did it, instead, with my bare hands. I didn't mean to. I didn't go out there today with the intention of pulling weeds, but the sun came out and I wanted to feel it on my face, and that brought me to the garden, standing knee-deep in green, with the cats prancing about and Sifnos Chick tugging on my sleeve and warning about snakes. I bent down, and tugged on a weed experimentally: large fan-shaped leaves on long stems that have overtaken even the clover. It came up easily, along with a clump of soil, and that was it: the next hour of my life. I was cautious at first, methodical, grabbing the stalks as high up as possible and making sure there was nothing lurking underneath, but some of them had roots as thick as trees, and I had to get in deep, close to the ground, to pull them out. Soon enough I was just thrusting my hands in there, into the cool, damp darkness, ripping out roots almost blindly, while Sifnos Chick whimpered in my ear and the cats ran off in alarm. I broke the cardinal rule of island life, *never stick your hands in the grass*, but luck was on my side and it was only worms that I disturbed. And I prevailed. The garden was strewn with piles of pulled-up weeds, and I found the hose, curled up in hibernation amidst the clover, a terrible reminder of what might have been.

But I forgot about nettles. I thought nettles were a thing of childhood, and that's where they'd stay. But then my fingers closed around another patch of weeds and I felt the sharp, searing pain, and I remembered. And I remembered something else: the weeds I'd been attacking so ferociously, those fleshy, fan-shaped leaves, were dock leaves: the antidote to nettle stings. Childhood friends, growing helpfully next to the nettles to take the pain away when you fell over and got stung. When you ignored the rule and stuck your hands where you shouldn't. As my hand began to swell, I snapped off a leaf and rubbed it over my fingers. And it took the pain away, this enemy I'd been attacking all morning.

I don't think it was karma. Nature doesn't punish us deliberately; it's not a performance for our sake. Plants are living things and you can kill them, but I don't think pulling weeds is an evil act avenged by nettles. That's just my mind trying to tidy up the wilderness, to draw definitions with borders of stones. It's calling a field a garden and expecting it to behave accordingly. But nature doesn't care about our definitions, our need to give things names and call one thing a flower and another thing a weed. It doesn't care about our sensitivities or our excuses or whether we feel guilty for pulling out weeds. It won't punish us to quell our need for justice. If you pull up weeds it will grow more, and all falling trees will make a sound, and if you stick your hands where you shouldn't, you might get stung. It's not karma, it's cause and effect. There is no justice and no redemption. No karmic retribution to make you feel righteous again.

But there is kindness, I think. There is a plant that gives you pain and next to it, always, a plant that takes the pain away. There is a plant that doesn't know its name, that doesn't know you call it a weed; it only knows to grow close to the nettles. It doesn't take it personally when you reach right down and rip it out of the soil. When you stick your hands where you shouldn't and you get stung, its leaves will take the pain away.

And the fact that this makes me feel guilty is none of its concern. It's my mind trying to tame the wilderness by calling it a garden. Perhaps it will teach me to remember about nettles and dock leaves and not sticking my hands in the grass, instead of seeking redemption, afterwards, for a kindness I don't feel I deserve.

# Day 94

There is a sense of wrapping up, now. A sense of slowing down, of tumbling towards an inevitable conclusion. Of putting my affairs in order, and pulling down the blinds. The days all start with the number 9 and soon it'll be 100 and there will be an ending. There will be a destination, reached; a journey completed. Because I said one hundred.

It's an odd story I'm writing here. One hundred separate days, each leading on to the next, as days do, but each one ending so the next one can begin. Each day a clean slate, a new chapter, a call to start again; each day an answer to that call, with its own conclusion. One hundred chapters, numbered, ascending towards 100, but not building up to any sort of climax. One hundred chapters, self-contained, adding up to nothing more than that.

One hundred days, but this isn't a mountain I'm climbing, and 100 is not a peak I can stick my flag in and call it a conquest. There will be no volcanic eruption to encase everything in meaning as the flowing lava solidifies into permanence. This isn't an Odyssey; it's not a crossing of the seas. It's one hundred stepping stones, one hundred stations along the railroad, but there is no destination. It looks like a linear journey, but the end of the line is just another station, another day. A number in a series of numbers. 100 makes no promises to keep or to break. It'll come and it'll go, like all the others.

There are some similarities to a conventional story. There have been twists and turns and tangents, crisis and conflict and climactic incidents, suspense and resolution and several journeys, completed or begun. There have been heroes and anti-heroes, villains and passers by, people missed and people found and people invented. There have been trials and tribulations, and monumental revelations, and small quiet moments of understanding that you could easily miss, in real life. There are similarities, but they end at the end of each day.

It's an odd structure for living. When you break up your life into one hundred separate stories, you start to live it that way. Each day must end so the next one can begin. Some things spill over – leftovers from today that I will eat tomorrow, a task postponed – and there's a thread than connects them all, which is me, even though I might be different from one day to the next. But each day is a story that calls for closure, its own conclusion, and each day is wrapped up at its end, wrapped up in words and added to the pile, before the next one begins. It looks like I'm building up to something, but there will be no peak, no revelation, no booming voice to give the answers to my life. I have lived my days in ascending order and they will add up to one hundred, but 100 will bring nothing more than the ninety-nine days before it. It will come and it will go. It has promised nothing. All I'm building is a collection of one hundred days, each wrapped up in its own story.

There are some similarities to conventional living. There have been mornings and afternoons and evenings, waking up and going to bed and the things that happen in between. There have been quiet moments that I might have missed. There are similarities, but they end as each day begins.

There is a sense of wrapping up and it's inevitable. Once you start to count, you start a countdown, even if the numbers are going up. There is a sense of drawing the curtains, tidying up the house after the party, alone, in the quiet, once everyone's gone. There is a sense of anticlimax, or the absence of climax, of walking down a flat country road and just stopping somewhere along the way, a place marked with a sign that says 100 but nothing else, and behind and ahead just road. An arbitrary stop in the middle of nowhere, because I said one hundred.

There is no destination. This isn't the Ithaca of Odysseus, the longed-for homecoming, the reward at the voyage's end. There are some similarities: ships and seas and winds, bustling cities and hidden harbours, mistakes and dilemmas and curses and spells, temptations and transformations, terrible monsters and witches and gods, and helpful Phaeacians, and the single-minded dedication to a purpose. But it's where the similarities end that my story begins, and Sifnos isn't Ithaca, and Ithaca isn't the purpose. The purpose isn't day 100, nor is it the voyage's end.

But there might be something of Cavafy's Ithaca in this. An excuse to start a journey, to see the world before you settle down. To see what other lives are possible, what other choices, before returning to the one you left behind. To see that you can choose not to return, but to keep going, walking past the landmarks and the signs, into one day and then the next, for as long as the journey is still in you.

Because when you start living your days as stories, you find that there's a story in each day and that is what you might have missed, in your real life of waking up and going to bed, with mornings and afternoons and evenings in between. You miss the stories that make the days count, even when you've stopped counting. But you don't have to stop, and you don't have to miss anything.

So when I reach 100 and see the sign on the side of the road, I will keep going. I will keep collecting days and stories, wrapping them up in words, and there will be no meaning to bring them all together, no grand conclusion, except me. I will keep living my days as stories and they might not be numbered, but they will count. I will set off for Ithaca every morning and get there, and search again, for as long as the journey is still in me. Because I've read the poem and found the stories and seen how many lives there are, and they are all just as real when you live them. And there might be something in that, in understanding what signs and purposes and destinations and Ithacas mean, and looking for meaning where it can be found.

# Day 95

I have been impersonating Egyptians all my life, and I wasn't aware of it until last night. I had an inkling a crime was being committed, but I didn't know what it was called.

I am reading a book about the British penal colonies in Australia that mentions, in passing, that capital offences in 16th century England included murder, rape, larceny and "impersonating Egyptians". This immediately conjured an image of the typical depiction of ancient Egyptians, with their ornate headdresses and their arms and legs thrust out at odd angles, to the soundtrack of the Bangles' *Walk Like An Egyptian*. It got me quite excited; I had to find out more.

These Egyptians were, apparently, the people who later came to be known as gypsies, Romany travellers who first appeared in England in the early 16th century and were rumoured to have come from Egypt. They were not popular. They roamed the country in large groups, reading people's fortunes, besides which their faces were unsettlingly dark. Henry VIII was particularly unimpressed by them, these wanderers "who used great, subtil and crafty means to deceive the people" and legislated against them. So terrible was the crime of being an Egyptian that any form of association with them was also declared a felony, and those guilty of keeping company with the wonderers or disguising themselves as one, "causing their faces to be made black as if they were Egyptians", were promptly sentenced to death. Some escaped this fate and were shipped, instead, to Australia, where they could carry on impersonating Egyptians, if they must, in the company of other convicts and away from the good people of England, who didn't need their fortunes told. They didn't want to know.

The laws punishing wanderers by death were repealed in the 18th century, and, since then, "persons pretending to be gypsies, or wandering in the habit or form of Egyptians" were merely deemed rogues and vagabonds. To be avoided, of course, by sensible citizens, but not killed.

What is it about wanderers that we find so unsettling? Is it their freedom that makes us nervous, the fact that they choose a way of life that we don't understand? We perceive any lifestyle different to our own as a threat, an attack on our values, and we punish it, with words and acts of violence, if not with laws.

*Walk Like An Egyptian*, which did, indeed, refer to actual ancient Egyptians as they were painted on the temple walls, was released by the Bangles in the eighties and it was just a pop song. No harm came to those who attempted it. But this changed during the 2011 Egyptian revolution, when the phrase was reappropriated and came to mean rebelling, overthrowing tyranny, making history, walking the walk. And, for a time, impersonating Egyptians became once again a crime, and was punished by death, as hundreds of protesters were killed for standing up for the life they wanted to live. Henry would have been proud.

I was called a gypsy in school, picked on for my darker skin, but I never understood why *gypsy* was an insult. I thought gypsies were cool and exotic and free; they lived in caravans and sat around open fires and they could go anywhere they wanted, and they were beautiful. The older women were rumoured to have powers, to be dangerous; they would curse you, we were warned, if you crossed them, but I only felt awe, not fear. I found them fascinating, and when the mean, fair-skinned kids called me a gypsy I said 'thank you' at first, before I knew they were trying to hurt me, which confused them, and then made them angry. They thought I was being insolent, making a stand, but I was just as confused as they were. I had been impersonating Egyptians without meaning to, and I wasn't popular at all.

No one calls me a gypsy anymore, and we have laws that ostensibly protect us against discrimination these days, though people still fear the gypsies when they come to their doors offering to read their palms. And those mean, fair-skinned kids, who were only repeating their parents words, now call themselves liberal, and spend their time roasting on sunbeds, smothered in expensive lotions, to emulate that skin tone that they once picked on me for, while I sit in the shade, with my face already dark, and smile. But I still make them nervous, with my wandering ways. They are still just as confused. And sometimes I wish adults were as direct as kids and said what they thought to my face, called me a rogue and a vagabond, a wanderer, a gypsy, so I could say thank you, because they can't hurt me anymore. Or I could mutter under my breath and pretend to curse them, impersonating Egyptians once again, deliberately this time. But, actually, these people who still fear the curse of the gypsies can relax: the curse is already on them, in the way they live, in fear instead of awe. The worst has already happened; they might as well hold their hands out and hear their fortune told.

No one calls me a gypsy anymore, and I'm not impersonating anyone except myself. Some people still find it unsettling, that I won't settle, that I insist on walking this walk. I'm not trying to make them angry and I'm not being a rebel, I'm not making history and I'm not making a stand; I'm just sitting by my open fire, reading my own fortune in my hands. But I will walk like an Egyptian, if I must, if it means I get to go where I want.

# Day 96

The weatherman lied about today: he had predicted sunshine and clear skies but there was rain. Thursday was marked with a big yellow sun and the morning delivered. I got up and the sky was wide open and the yellow sun was climbing higher towards the peak of 17 degrees that had been promised, urging me to match it with a promise of my own, made for the next such day of yellow sun. So I got dressed, grabbed a large plastic bag and a pair of secateurs, strapped my rucksack to my back, and set off to pick sage.

Sage loves this island. It grows out of the hard, dry soil; it grows out of the rock faces, alongside oregano and spiky wild thyme. It grows on the edges of the fields and on the side of the road. The air is scented with it, a heavy, heady smell, sweet but earthy, uplifting and calming at the same time, with a hint of the medicinal and the meditative. To snap a branch off a bush and rub the leaves between your fingers is to know why this common herb is considered so powerful, why it's been used for healing and cleansing for thousands of years, at every place in the world where it grows. Celtic druids and Native American shamans have traditionally used it to ward off evil and cleanse the spirit, and new age shops sell sage smudge sticks to hopeful Westerners, to wave about their homes. Its name, *salvia officinalis*, stems from the Latin *salvere*, which means to save, to heal, and a sage is a person of wisdom. And it's all there, between your fingers, as it releases its scent.

*Salvia officinalis,* common sage. There is nothing common about it, but the fact that it grows everywhere makes me smile: according to English folklore, sage grows best where the wife is dominant. It doesn't surprise me, its abundance on this island. There's something feminine about it, in its subtle but consistent presence in this rough, rugged land, how it stands quiet and fragrant, always in the margins, with its soft leaves and its strong scent. How it doesn't advertise its power and yet everybody knows. It reminds me of the women I've met in the last few months, ruling from the sidelines, from where they can watch everyone who goes past.

I had been meaning to pick some sage and then I promised: next sunny day I would walk down to the port, and fill a bag along the way. This is the best time for it, Margarita told me, after the first heavy rains have rinsed it clean. There's something incredibly rewarding in picking herbs growing wild out of the rocks. Just walking along and bending down and picking. Growing your own vegetables is close, but not the same. That takes some planning and some work and it's a good feeling when salad leaves appear in your garden and then on your plate, but you're still the one who put them there. Wild things grow wild regardless of your intentions, and it's almost like they were put there for you. It's like a gift; it's like the way the world was put together making sense, for a moment, when you walk along the road and fill your arms with sage. And you don't even have to rinse it because it's been washed by the rain.

It rained this afternoon, but the day delivered half its promise and the sun shone as I walked towards the port. I came back as the clouds began to gather, with a bagful of sage and my own promise kept. I laid the sage out in the spare bedroom, on towels, to dry, and then I laid myself in bed, in that eerie glow of cloud-filtered light, and listened to the patter of the rain against my window. It didn't patter for long: it soon began to pound, and the shutters rattled as the wind picked up and threw sheets of rain, hard, against the glass. I got up to close the shutters and lay in darkness now, listening to the thunder and the wind, with the lingering smell of sage on my fingers. I lay in darkness and thought about power and wisdom and sages and sage, healing and being saved, and how I would make bundles and give them as gifts, and pass the gift on, once the sage had dried.

I lay in my bed as the unpredicted storm raged outside and washed the herbs and the plants and the roads and houses clean, as the scent of sage, subtle but powerful, drifted through the house and, for a moment, it was like I had wisdom, like I'd been washed clean by the rain. Like the way the world is put together made sense.

# Day 97

I ran into Yiannis in town this afternoon, and he said the most astonishing word to me. The word was: snow.

Another word that has come up is loneliness. Yiannis said it, and so did my dad, and these are both people who, more than many others, understand what I'm doing here. Yiannis doesn't know me that well, but he knows what brings someone to this life; he is a man who chose Sifnos over the city. My dad is a poet, and the words in his head need space, just like mine. If you gave him a desk in a room in a quiet place somewhere, he'd sit down and start writing. I don't think he'd ask any questions. But both these men said loneliness and I listened, this time.

I'm not anti-social. I'm just not overly social, and there's a big difference, which I've learnt in the last few months. Solitude and isolation have taught me how to enjoy other people's company in a way I never had before. I have not become socially inept, so used to my own company that I've forgotten how to relate to others, nor have I gone the other way and become desperate for those rare instances of social contact. There have been days, not few, when I've not spoken to another person at all, and I've not even noticed. But when I spend my time in the company of others, I'm actually there, fully present, ready to offer what I have and open to receiving what they want to give. I am available. I'm not in my head, I'm not chasing thoughts and trying to catch up with myself. A little bit of loneliness is the space to do that in my own time, and leaves me with time to spare, to give to others, to catch up with them.

These are my social interactions over the past week: Last Friday, I spent an hour with Margarita and her sister Evi, chatting and drinking coffee and smoking cigarettes, while Margarita cut my hair. They gave me advice tailored to the holiday season, and I told them tales of my solitude to make them laugh. Yesterday, when I was in Kamares, I stopped by to see Martha in her shop; I met her once before, in the summer, when I went in to buy something, but she got in touch when she read my blog. I only stayed for twenty minutes because I had a bus to catch. Next time, we agreed, I'd come for coffee; she told me she could drive me home. Today, I talked with Yiannis for a few minutes as we walked through town, and with a neighbour who was hanging up her washing on the line. I have smiled at many people, and they've all smiled back. I've said hello to everyone I've met.

I think what makes us become anti-social is the constant demand to engage with other people, to give something of ourselves even when we've nothing left to give. There have been times, in the past, when I've felt so depleted that I couldn't handle even one word exchanged. When I've chosen a shop further away, where nobody knew me, so I wouldn't even have to make eye contact. There have been times when I've walked the streets with my head bent down and a shield raised around me, a cloak of hostility, a force field to protect myself. Don't speak to me. Don't look at me. Don't touch me. And people always do: they speak, they look, they touch. It's this constant exposure that makes us shrink away. A little bit of loneliness is the space to take the shield down, take stock and replenish your reserves. There have been times, too many, when I didn't have that space.

Now, when I walk down the street and hear another person coming, I look up and meet their eyes and say hello as our paths cross. I have smiles and hellos to give, and I replenish them daily. I have the time to do that, now. And I walk away from these exchanges with a feeling of satisfaction and reciprocity. I walk away feeling whole, like a person interacting with another person, both giving something, both receiving, but nothing being taken away.

Yiannis said loneliness before he said snow. I ran into him by the square and we walked together for a while. He asked how I was doing, and I told him how easy it's been. 'I told you you'd make it to Christmas,' he said. 'No problem. It's afterwards that it gets tough.'

Everyone says that. Nikoletta called January and February "the bad winter", as opposed to December, which has been good.

'So what if I stay?' I asked. 'What's gonna happen to me then?'

Yiannis laughed. 'Nothing will happen to you. It's just the loneliness. Whether you can take it.'

'I can take it. I have so far.'

'Yes,' he said, 'but how long for?'

And I thought about it, and I told him what I tell myself, that it's a choice. That's it's temporary, and I can make it stop at any time. It's easy because I'm choosing it, and there's solitude left in me yet, so I'll carry on choosing it until it runs out. That's how long. Yiannis nodded, as if he understood.

'I'm not going to Athens for Christmas,' I added, to back this up perhaps.

'Good plan,' he said. 'The city is a shock. You have to wait to cross the road, and you keep saying hello to people on the street, and they all think you're crazy.'

'I know! I did that, last time I was there!'

We both laughed, united in our crazy island ways.

He stopped outside the doorway to his shop when we reached it. His wife was inside; she gave me a nod and a smile.

'It's only until mid-March,' Yiannis said, in parting, 'and then you'll see a whole new kind of beauty, if you stick around. And,' he added, 'we might get snow in

February.' He grinned, knowing this was a carrot he was dangling.

'Snow? In Sifnos?'

'Snow,' he confirmed. 'In Sifnos. It happens sometimes.'

Nevermind the bad winter; I want to be astonished. I choose the snow. I can take the loneliness for that long.

My dad hesitated before saying it. I was telling him about my sage picking expedition, my walk down to the port. Sitting on the beach and watching the waves roll in, before heading back home.

'It's a nice life,' I said, conscious of how he'd spent his day, behind a large desk stacked high with papers, and phones ringing constantly, and people coming in, with more papers to look at or sign.

'It's a very nice life,' he agreed, 'but.'

'But what?'

'But lonely.'

'I suppose,' I said, resisting the instinct to be defensive. And then I listed the people I'd spent some time with in the last few days, to soothe his worry, and mine. Few people and little time, but all of it good. And I knew, as I told him, that neither of us have anything to worry about. This is a choice I'm making, and it's making me more social, not less. Loneliness isn't the price. It's the space to see other people for what they are, the space to invite them in.

Hell is other people but, also, other people are the reward. But you have to be open to receive it, you have to be available, and you can't do that when your shield is up and you're wearing your cloak. This life of mine, this solitude, is temporary, but the space I've claimed can last for as long as I choose it, and I can carry on choosing it wherever I am. I don't know how to do this in the city; I suppose I'll have to learn. I'll have to learn how to be solitary in a crowd, just like I learned how to be social in isolation. I'll have to learn how to stay open when the crowd closes in around me, and keep a little loneliness aside for when I need it, for myself. And remember these crazy island ways, and the life I had here, for a while, and the astonishing things that sometimes happen, and keep choosing them for as long as I can. And maybe, sometimes, smile at people on the street, even if they don't smile back.

# Day 98

These are some things I've learned.

Always shake your shoe out before putting it on. Never stick your hands in the grass. Don't disturb sleeping creatures. If you break the rules, you will get stung.

If it flies in, get it out.
If it crawls in, assess.
If it doesn't bite, leave it alone.
If you can, trap it and release it outside. Always have a glass and a postcard handy for this task.
If it bites, kill it. Make your peace with karma after.
Death is inevitable. But never kill bees.

There are no boats. There are no buses. Do not rely on boats or buses, seas or winds. These are unpredictable forces, no matter what the internet says. You are at their mercy. Enjoy having no control. Enjoy being stranded sometimes. Be amused. There is always something to be amused about.

When the sun comes out, open the windows. When the sun goes in, close them again.
When the wind blows, secure the shutters. Weigh down all objects that might be blown away. Play loud music to drown out the howls.
When it rains, close everything. Apply towels and rags to all openings. Pray that the water doesn't spill over the windowsill and into your electric heater underneath. If you have no god to pray to, make one up. Find something to trust in, or stand by the window all night, dabbing at the rain as it seeps through the cracks.

Don't break down doors when you can smash a window. Try to install handles in advance. Don't be afraid of rosemary bushes; don't be afraid of closing doors. If you lock yourself out, find a way back in. Don't be afraid of making mistakes.

Ask for help. Ask for advice. Change lightbulbs when you can. When you're frightened, tell someone. There are too many things that require courage; don't be brave all the time. Give people the chance to be heroes. Allow yourself to be saved by unlikely things. Let sage soothe you; let weeds take the pain away. Don't be fooled by the names of things. Don't call yourself names. Don't be a fool. Don't be a martyr. Accept help, whichever way it comes. Say thank you.

When the water is brown, it's brown. Denial is not a good strategy for living. Do not drink the brown water. Do not boil your pasta in it. Do not cure olives in rust. Accept the truth, and buy mineral water. Apply this to all areas of life.

Use coconut oil sparingly. Do not wait until you're almost out of coffee to make panicked phonecalls to Athens. Plan ahead, or drink instant. When fancy goods such as chilli peppers, coconut sugar or Himalayan salt appear in the shop, buy them. Do not take rare things for granted. Do not let chances pass you by.

If you feel like eating, eat.
If you feel like sleeping, sleep.
If you feel like running, run.
If you feel like stopping, stop.
If you feel like dancing, dance.
Unless you can think of a good reason not to, do what you want.

You will always feel like dancing when the song is right. If the song isn't right, change it. Never miss an opportunity to dance. Never listen to a bad song, if you can help it.

Never miss an opportunity to go to the beach. Never walk past a beautiful thing. Stop and look. Pick flowers. Pick herbs. Stare at clouds. Watch the waves rolling in and rolling out. Look at the mountains every day. Look at the horizon. Look for the beauty. Remember where you are.

If you have something to say, say it. If you don't, be quiet and think. Silence won't hurt you; the wrong words can. Choose your words. Choose your stories. There are always good stories to tell. There is something in every day worth keeping. Find it. Look for it until you do.

Love.
As a verb. As a noun.
Subject and object.
Whichever way it comes.
It all comes down to love.
Unless you can think of a good reason not to, do what you love.

Make that your story.

# Day 99

It's very quiet this morning. Slow clouds, and the sun undecided. So still that it feels like the day is encased in stillness, immobilised, rather than just not moving. I went outside and stood still, too; it feels wrong, somehow, almost absurd to move in this landscape. Only a bird cuts through momentarily, small birds in low flight, the fleeting motion emphasising the stillness, not breaking it. Still life, *natura morta*: dead nature, but it is very much alive. It's just that nature knows how to stay still. It's only humans who think they need to be in motion all the time.

Today is the Winter Solstice. The shortest day of the year; the longest night. 'It's officially winter,' Iro told me, but winter is just the earth tilting towards spring. From tomorrow, the days will start stretching, incrementally, a few seconds at a time, pushing against the nights, gaining upon them slowly, until the Spring Equinox, that short moment of balance when night and day are equals, before the balance shifts again towards the longer days of summer.

Perhaps what this day is doing is paying its respects to the night. Standing still, to attention, to mark its moment of supremacy, this once-a-year triumph of dark over light, before the struggle begins again. But the sun made its mind up regardless, threw off the shyness of autumn and chose the solstice to be reborn, blazing, in the winter sky, as the legends said it would. The day exploded in light.

I went outside again and stood still in the stillness, with my arms open wide and my eyes shut and my face turned towards the sun. Me and all the flowers and the plants of this still life, turned towards the sun. It was too strong to look at; it burned orange behind my eyelids, in perfect complement to the blue of the sky.

I saw the world in motion last night. This place that has become my world, my winter version of Sifnos, so quiet and still that it had me fooled: I saw how it moves on a Saturday evening. I owe it to a stranger, that I saw this. I owe him for showing me, another debt of gratitude, of many, that I've accrued in these past ninety-nine days.

There was nothing extraordinary about it, this evening that moved me, gently, from where I stood. I could have spent it on my sofa, as always, in the solitude I've learned. But I went for coffee in a café with a stranger, at 6:30 pm. This happened because he wrote to me and asked and then last night, maybe a month later, I said yes. I don't know why it took that long. My first instinct was no, I'm not meeting strangers for coffee; my second was that I'm not here to make friends. And then suspicion, cynicism. "There are no strangers here; only friends you haven't yet met", but strangers aren't all good people, and staying still is easier and safer than making a move that might turn out wrong.

But then, last night, something shifted. It might have been the fact that I called it one hundred days and named them for solitude, and they are coming to an end, and I am passing into days that are not numbered and not named. It might be that I've learned the solitude, and now it's time to learn new things, like meeting strangers and making friends. Time to make a move and step into this world that I inhabit.

The secret café of winter Sifnos is only secret until you stop walking past and walk in. Perhaps I didn't feel that I had earned it, the right to enter, while I was playing a game of one hundred days. Perhaps that's what moved me from my sofa. I pushed the door open, and a stranger looked up and raised his hand, and we had coffee, in a café, on a Saturday evening, with music low enough to have a conversation, and the air swirling with smoke, and the smell of coffee, and the hum of voices, and people coming and going and waving and saying hello, and winding and unwinding scarves and opening and closing the door. Nothing extraordinary about it, just the ordinary life that I recognise, and easy, like spending an evening with a friend. Which is what makes it extraordinary: there are no strangers here, on this island, but few of them turn out to feel like friends. And I've been lucky that I've met them, despite the game of solitude I've learned to play so well.

Is it significant that Day 99 coincides with the Winter Solstice and I go into Day 100 as the world tips over into winter? Is that the right verb even, coincides? Was it scheduled, like the solstice and the equinox, like the fact that, at opposite ends of the year, light conquers dark and dark conquers light? Is it coincidence that it took me this long to see through the stillness and move into ordinary life? Someone asked me if I timed it on purpose so that my hundred days would end before Christmas, but there was never any plan. But as I stand here, one day short, on the dark end of the year, I wonder.

I saw the world in motion last night, but I'm taking my cues from the solstice today and staying still, against my nature but in keeping with nature, to pay my respects to this day and this night, and all the days and nights that came before them, one short of a hundred, before the world tips over and it begins again. I will observe the stillness and stand in gratitude to all those people, the strangers and the friends, in every part of this world that's always moving, who helped me find light in days that grew darker but never felt dark, that grew shorter but were always long enough, those people who moved me, and stilled my fears, and kept me moving when I became too still, and kept me here, one day short of one hundred. Who showed me things I hadn't seen and have me, always, in their debt.

And as I stand here, still, on the dark end of the year, I can see all the way across it to the Summer Solstice, and between then and now only days, unnumbered and named for nothing, wide open and growing longer as the light pushes against the night; ordinary life, only secret until you stop playing a game and push the door open and walk into a place that you recognise. There are no strangers, and the secret is how easy it's always been.

# Day 100

Should there be a drumroll at this stage, or a quiet slipping, like I said, from one day to another? It could be either, and neither feels quite right, and day 100 is not a summary of days, and you can't bring one hundred days together with words, so that they mean something.

Eleni told me a story that made me laugh. It was about her brother-in-law, John, who, upon tasting his first sugared kumquat, apparently commented: "It is like making love for the first time. You don't really understand what's happening to you." It made me laugh, and then it made me think: about love and making love and the things we don't really understand.

My first time wasn't like a kumquat. It was a strange experience but, looking back, kind of tasteless. The act took place at a house party, an hour out of town, in the early summer of 1994; a bunch of us were staying overnight, unsupervised. This was a couple of weeks past my sixteenth birthday, and my boyfriend and I had just celebrated our three-month anniversary. The stars didn't line up to bring us together in sweet, if awkward, lovemaking on a mild June evening that we would both remember fondly. It was coldly understood that this would be the night. It was about opportunity and the dispatching of a task. So much for the romantic dreams of teenage girls; so much for the endless lines of poetry this teenage girl had written for other, earlier loves. There was no poetry in this, and no romance. I liked the boy well enough and we had called it love. But the truth was a cold one: I just wanted the thing over with and I remember it, if anything, with shame.

And so it was, a task performed, awkwardly and quickly, on one of two twin beds we had been allocated for the night. I knew what was happening to me; I knew the mechanics of the act and what to expect, and my expectations were met by a mechanical act. I was a little disappointed that it didn't hurt, as advertised; I grieved a little for the drama that wasn't there. A trip to the bathroom yielded a single smudge of blood, a private hanging of the wedding sheets. I flushed the tissue down the toilet, returned to the bedroom to get dressed, and went to join my friends, in other rooms, leaving my boyfriend, used up, still and silent on the bed. We both knew what had happened, what we'd done, but neither of us understood. Neither of us said a word.

He was gone when I returned, out in town with the boys, and I was relieved. This was a private thing, and he was no longer part of it. I found my walkman and crawled into a hammock in the garden and swung, back and forth, all night, listening to a song on repeat. The song was called *Thanatos*: death. I had been cold on this warm summer evening; I had gotten rid of my virginity and my boyfriend by a single act, and I felt nothing. But I thought I understood that love hurts, and in the absence of love I chose the hurt, and a song called *Death* with beautiful, heartbreaking lyrics to fill the gaps where poetry should have been.

There has been love since, and poetry, and lovemaking that hurt in the ways that it should and didn't need a soundtrack, and I still don't really understand. I can't speak for kumquats, but I don't think lovemaking is meant to be understood. There have been times when I have stopped, midway, to say "What is this? What is happening?", and those are the times I will remember. Wonder, bafflement, awe: that's how you know something extraordinary is happening to you. It will be a terrible day, a day of mourning, when such a thing as love can be understood.

I think I understand now that I was mourning something on that night in June. The passing, maybe, of the teenage girl whose poetry amounted to nothing, the girl who thought a mechanical act could be transformed into something meaningful just because you call it love. But I think I learned something, too, about the absence of love; I learned it, on that night, as I swung in a hammock with a song called *Death* on repeat, but it took me twenty years to understand.

You might get lucky and throw kumquats and love and poetry and death together and make some kind of sense, but you can't bring one hundred days together with words. And day 100 is not a summary of days, and it isn't the day that love was understood. But I think I understand, finally, about its absence: you can do things without love. But if you live your life mechanically, performing acts and dispatching tasks in cold understanding, you leave no room for poetry or bafflement or awe. You can't transform that into something meaningful just because you call it a life. You've gotta put in the things you love and leave gaps that ache and need to be filled up with some sort of poetry, whatever stands for poetry in your life. You can do things without love, but they'll amount to nothing, and you will remember them with shame, if you remember them at all. That's what I learned in that hammock, and it took twenty years and one hundred days of doing what I love to understand.

And day 100 is not a summary of days. Maybe it's like a kumquat; like I've tasted something I cannot quite describe, but want to taste again. It's like one of those times that I'll remember, and I'm lying here, naked and aching and a little out of breath, and I'm thinking "What just happened?" and I don't really understand. But there is wonder and bafflement and awe and scattered lines of poetry trying to put into words what you cannot, and I know it was something extraordinary. And it's like that first time, too, a thing completed as I expected it would, and my sheets hung up and flapping in the wind for everyone to see, one hundred days of word-stained sheets to prove it, and nothing to show for it in private but a smudge of blood and a sense of mourning. Day 100 is both: it's both a drumroll and a quiet slipping into something else, the day after, whatever comes next.

Or maybe it's a drumroll to distract you, so I can slip away, quietly, out of sight, and mourn it a little, in private, the end of a hundred days, and celebrate it, too, because I did it, for love. And then I'll sit alone, in a solitude no longer shared, and think about love and making love and all the things that I don't understand. All the things that I cannot put into words, and will keep trying, regardless, for all of my days, because this is what I love. This is what comes next. This is what I call a life. It baffles the hell out of me, and it has a weird soundtrack, but it's extraordinary.

# Gratitude

Thank you Peter, Niko Geo, Joslyn, Pia, Vilka, Malik, Jill, Sue, Richard, Vanessa, Ela & Mark, Theodora, Stelios, Katerina & Duncan, Costis, Aram, Polyna, Nassos, Maria, Yvonne, Leslie, Nikhil, Jo, Agnieszka, Bryony & Philip, Periklis, Sophia, Faidra, Melina, Aaron, Arek, Siva, Tomek, Danai, Marie, Emma, Ola, Nicos, Giti, Nikos, Tamzin, Zaneta, Eleni Kotta, Janine, Ryo & Fabio, Eleni Kasimati, Elly and Daniela, for your kindness, support and generosity: this book would not have been written without you.

Thank you Eleni D for being with me, for these 100 days, from start to finish; for dancing, for music, for cayenne pepper and lemon trees and olives; for too much to list.

Thank you to my family: my mum, Fotini, my dad, Dennis, my stepdad, Spyros, and my sisters, Ariadne and Margarita. Thank you to my grandma and granddad, for the frequent and thorough weather reports. And special thanks to Dimitri & Natalia for the Kindle.

Thank you Eileen, Alexi, Aliki, Mel, Susanne, Iro and Eleni A: you are my family, too, and I'm incredibly lucky to have you.

And thank you Marshall for the everything. And everything else, et cetera.

\*\*\*

It wasn't really one hundred days of solitude: thanks to all of you, I was never alone.

# Notes & Quotes

[i] "The Satrapy", C.P. Cavafy, *Collected Poems*. Translated by Edmund Keeley and Philip Sherrard, Princeton University Press (1992)
→ www.cavafy.com/poems/content.asp?id=197&cat=1

[ii] Paraphrased from "The Satrapy", as above.

[iii] This Reluctant Yogi: everyday adventures in the yoga world
→ thisreluctantyogi.blogspot.co.uk

[iv] "The Raven", Edgar Allan Poe (1845)
→ www.poetryfoundation.org/poem/178713

[v] As above.

[vi] As above.

[vii] Yep. Same again.

[viii] Day 52 makes several references to the lyrics of Pink Floyd's *Wish You Were Here* (1975). Look them up.
→ youtu.be/217JOBWTolg

[ix] Check her out.
→ alexandrabelegrati.wordpress.com

[x] Opus, *Life is Life* (1984)
→ youtu.be/EGikhmjTSZI

Made in the USA
Columbia, SC
17 March 2020